AF363291

SUGAR PEOPLE

Oliver Ferrie

Sugar People by Oliver Ferrie

Published by Gallant Publishing
928942457
Tinnsjøstrånde 477, 3656 Atrå, Norway
gallant.no

Copyright © 2023 Oliver Ferrie

Characters, places and incidents in this book are fictitious.
Any resemblance to persons, living or dead, is entirely coincidental.

Cover by Shea Parfait.

ISBN: 978-82-693096-1-4

All rights reserved. No portion of this book may be reproduced in any
form without permission from the publisher. Unauthorised acts in
relation to this publication may incur criminal prosecution or civil
claims for damages. For permissions contact: gallant.no

GALLANT

*This story is for those of you who were never able to speak up at
the time.
Those who were not heard.
Those who were not believed.
Those who were far too scared (and with good reason).
How easy it is to feel as though the whole world is rewriting
your memories into something more easily consumable.
This is not easily consumable. But I hope it helps.*

CONTENTS

Wasn't it funny? Hear it, all people!
Little Tom Thumb has swallowed a steeple!
How did he do it?
I'll tell you, my son:
'Twas made of white sugar—and easily done!

~ Mother Goose

CHAPTER ONE

Refusal

Kestrel stood awkwardly in front of the college administrator, watching her watch him from behind round-rimmed spectacles.

She exhaled, slowly, as if what she had to say was terribly unfortunate, although her eyes did not share the sentiment.

'I want to help you, I really do, but this piece breaks our exhibition rules.' Another critical look at the canvas on the table.

'What—why?'

'It's the...' She trailed off, bracelets jangling as she motioned in the space above the painting. 'It's the hands... Oh, it's just not appropriate.'

'It's art.'

'We can't display it. I am sorry.'

She was not sorry. Kestrel could tell. He stuck his own hands in his pockets, as if hiding them would hide some sin he had not committed. He was starting to feel sick.

'I don't understand how this is any different from Goya's *Saturn*,' he said, speaking all too hastily so she could not stop him. Invoking a famous painting as if art history credentials held any weight, and maybe that was petty at this stage, but he didn't care. He gathered his canvas up, sliding it back into the plastic bag with a crinkle far louder than he wanted it to be. He was rushing, but that was fine. He just wanted to leave.

It was the sound of her sucking in air that gave him pause. He turned. Her eyebrows were doing that thing, the thing that meant she was probably going to ask him if he was okay, if he needed help with anything. But she didn't. She just sighed out the breath, and let him go.

Frost still lined the edges of the sycamore leaves and dead carbon crunched beneath his feet as Kestrel took the narrow path out of campus. He preferred the south entrance; it was always quiet. The pillars that held the gates leading out into the town were made of a soft, light-grey limestone, cut in a traditional, blocky style that seemed somehow too provincial for the college.

His phone buzzed. Bethan, checking in.

—At the café. Where r u?

Just heading down now, he replied.

—Cool. I'll get u a latte while I wait.

At least there was that.

He carried on, past the sycamores, down the street with its low brick wall crusted with lichen and dead moss. The sky seemed too bright and too grey; his bags grew too heavy. By the time he reached the small café his shoulders were crying for a break, and the sickly feeling in his stomach had climbed to the back of his throat. There hadn't even been enough time on the short walk to get through a song, and he couldn't just stop it halfway, so his earphones had stayed in his pocket. He wanted to pack it in, go home, stew in his thoughts and not have to see, talk, be around anyone.

But you know you'll feel better the instant you talk to Bethan. Just keep walking, one foot in front of the other, easy as anything.

The café was popular with the art students; that was why they picked it. Cheap enough and pretty enough, if that stood for anything. The barrier between the sharp outdoor air and the warming rush of the café changed his mind on going home. A cosier embrace than anything else he had felt that day, maybe longer.

Kestrel went through the perfunctory social awkwardness of scanning the café, the making clear to anyone who might be watching him that yes, he was looking for a friend, he wasn't being weird. The fact he was having trouble squeezing his bags past the serving table didn't help. One false move would mean sugar and napkins and stirring sticks everywhere.

He kept looking, seconds away from feeling desperate.

And there, Bethan, with her long curls and her colourful hoodie—neon pink and blue, how had he missed that on first glance?—hunched at the small high table with shoes hooked under the footrest rail. Her olive skin seemed somehow desaturated in the cold day, despite the café's best attempts to create warmth. She hadn't noticed him yet. He spent a moment just watching, because right then it felt like taking a step forward would ruin something, take something away that couldn't be gotten back. Bethan looked tired, but still as carefree as ever, and it almost seemed a crime to intrude. Much as he knew it would make him feel calmer.

Eventually he did move forward.

She broke into a grin, slid his coffee over to him. 'You made it! Oh—rough day?'

His face must have said it all. He shrugged his rucksack off his shoulders, and let his bag of artwork come to rest against the wall.

'They didn't accept my piece for the exhibition.'

'Really? How come?'

'Said it was inappropriate.'

'For real? What the fuck.' Her thick eyebrows creased and she pushed a curl out of her face. Not happy. Felt nice to have some commiseration.

'They're all kind of biased anyway, when it comes to this stuff. It's stupid.'

'Can I see it?'

'I dunno… I'm not really feeling very confident about it right now.'

'S'ok. I feel that.'

He wanted to tell her about the uncomfortable feeling in the pit of his belly, about how much it felt like being drowned. About all the nonsensical stuff whirling around in his brain that had made him paint the picture in the first place. But it was too difficult to elaborate, so he just sipped his coffee. Bethan talked about her classes—graphic design with a side order of psychology— trying to make parallels with his situation, trying to make him feel better. After a while he was starting to regret taking traditional art; hers sounded far more interesting. Late February, halfway through the second term, too far into the school year now to change subjects.

But for all their talk of school and assignments and the injustices of bureaucracy, they were both dancing around the main topic. These were decent enough distractions, but last time they had hung out, they had done the same thing, and it felt awkward.

Bethan broke into it first.

'So. I haven't heard from Tala in ages.'

Kestrel thought about it for a moment, tried to come up with something to say that wasn't stating the obvious. 'Uh, yeah, she's still…'

'You're closest—you should drop by and check on her.'

Easy for you to say.

Tala was ill, which was the simplest way of explaining a tricky situation, and Kestrel severely doubted that he was the best person to go talk to her. He understood Bethan's reasoning; he had known Tala the longest out of all of them. But what help could he possibly provide that someone like Bethan couldn't?

What he ended up telling Bethan, though, was, 'Okay, sure.'

'Good—cos Aaron told me he wants to continue our tabletop campaign. And I figure, if she's depressed, it might help to get the gang back together.'

Kestrel did not correct her on the *if*.

'Yeah, that's a good idea.' He grinned, despite his own low mood. 'You sure you can put up with my rogue's shenanigans, though?'

'Dude, my barbarian is more than equipped for that,' she shot back.

'I'll steal every gem in every dungeon. I'll ruin all your carefully-crafted plans.'

Bethan's eyes sparkled. 'Hah! I'm counting on it.' And then, coffee cup drained, she stood. 'I'd better go—my shift starts soon.'

The aesthetic was not the only reason they chose this place to hang out; she worked at the corner store right next door. And yeah, he could see the garish green name tag poking out from under the lapel of her hoodie. All dressed up and ready to go.

'Ugh, yeah. I should get this stupid thing back home.' He rustled the bag with his canvas inside.

'Well. See you round campus. And—I'm sorry about the exhibit.'

Kestrel shrugged, and went on his way.

When he got home, the canvas found its place against the back wall of his bedroom. Beside it, an easel, and a slab of old wood that served as a palette, because what was the point in wasting money on a proper one? The paint he had used yesterday was half-dried in dollops atop it—probably still wet inside, and if he had the urge to poke at the rubbery skin it had formed, he would expect it to ooze out.

He left the paint well alone. Let his thoughts settle. Didn't have the energy to draw anything more, and couldn't bear the thought of looking at his journal, although he knew he had homework to do.

A ping from his mobile phone.

—You comin out tonight?

Bram. Probably done with his lectures for the day. Wondering if he was going to show face at the student bar. Oh yeah, it was Wednesday, half price Pimm's, Bram loved that.

He usually went. He usually enjoyed it.

—Nah, (and now he needed a good excuse, come on, come on…) I have a headache.

That was a terrible excuse.

—Yeah, drinking's prolly not gonna make that better.

Okay, good, Bram didn't mind.

Then a few seconds later:

—Next time, eh?

He sent an emoji back, and played videogames instead, drinking on his own (the shitty Jamesons that Aaron had brought over for New Years) instead of drinking at the bar. The latest update for *Morningstars* was out, and that should have been fun, there was nothing like an online arena game to distract the senses. He tried to focus on what new skins he was going to equip his character with, what new maps he wanted to tackle first, but his thoughts kept turning back to Tala.

Should I text her now? Is it too late in the evening? Perhaps that would just stress her out.

He decided not to.

Tomorrow, then.

CHAPTER TWO

Suffocate

It's dark, and he's acutely aware he is running. His thighs burn with the effort, his calves strain, but he keeps going. Around him, the darkness shifts into spindly shapes; trees, shrubs, undergrowth. It smells of humus and wet grass.

He doesn't know how far he is from the thing behind him, but he does know that if he turns around, even for an instant, it will fix its baleful eye on him like a tired parent calling home their child. Exhausted with his antics. Care and concern, but such damning power behind it. And oh, when that hammer comes down.

The ground is soft and marshy, and he sinks into it with every lunge forward. It doesn't take long for him to trip, catching his worn-out shoes on some wayward root. Before he knows it, his face is planted in the mud and the cloying material threatens to fill his nostrils.

He snorts. Coughs. Heart pounding, forces himself to his feet and in front of him now is a mirror.

No, not a mirror. Glassy water that casts a perfect

reflection of his dirtied face. And behind him, the burning eye grows closer, purple as a bruise. Tendrils of smoke flare out from its centre. It's shapeshifting, becoming something else as it grows closer.

He is trapped watching it change, because as much as he wants to run, as much as he tries, his legs won't register the command. Heart pounding so hard now he can taste blood in his throat. On his tongue; he's bitten his tongue.

The bruise becomes a swirl of acrylic. Petrol blue and muddy purple collide, and the canvas buckles and strains like it's alive.

He is utterly transfixed.

The hands materialise from his painting, not grabbing but placing themselves oh so softly on his waist. A firm, but commanding touch. It's familiar enough that he stills himself instantly. He knows there's no escaping.

For a moment things are soft, and he feels held like a babe in swaddling. But he knows it is wrong. This thing, this groaning entity, is going to rip into him any second.

He can't be present to let that happen. The dirt, the salt marsh, he forces his mind down into it, imagines himself sinking, decaying, becoming nothing.

One last dying gasp.

Kestrel woke up filled with shame. His cock was semi-hard. The dream lingered and he couldn't focus, he wanted nothing more than to be sick. He curled up on his side, foetal position, because he didn't want to see the embarrassing bump in the covers. Better to wait for it to go down on its own before dealing with getting up. Think about something, *anything* else. And then the bedcovers felt too clingy about his body, so he had to get up anyway.

Coffee would make him feel more real. Class would

make him feel more real. A workshop session today after lectures—good. He drew back the curtains, let the light stream in to his cramped room. Today he would draw and draw, and yeah, it would never be enough but it was better than nothing.

Kestrel's dull thud of a hangover still hadn't shifted by the time he made it outside. Not like he had far to go from his dorm room to the main campus, but even that short distance felt like a slog with his head stuck in the mire that it was. The sun, too bright. The air, too sharp. Everything, too much and too loud.

'You doin' okay?'

'Bram! Hey.' Kestrel had flinched at first when the hand fell across his shoulders, but now he fell into step beside his friend. Classroom wasn't far.

There was something about Bram's face that always made Kestrel smile. He seemed so optimistic, with his wide eyes hiding behind a dark, heavy fringe. That infectious attitude, despite the fact he still dressed like an edgy little scene kid from high school, made him seem adorably innocent. Hard to hate, even for the people who made fun of his name ('Bram as in Stoker, not Abe as in Sapien,' he liked to say). His full name was actually Abrahán, which was the product of having Colombian parents with a strong slant towards Catholicism.

They had met in Sunday School, once upon a time, and Kestrel had been immediately drawn to Bram's chaotic energy. He rebelled against religion every chance he got, something Kestrel had never had the inclination or the willpower to do. Of course, there was a lot of kickback from Bram's parents, from teachers, from the nuns that ran the school, but despite that he had never lost that impish edge.

Kestrel might have even fancied him a little. Had no idea what to do about it, though.

He realised he had not answered the question.

'Yeah, I'm okay. Sorta. Sorry I didn't come out last night.'

'No need for apologies, man.' Bram slowed down a bit, to give them more time to walk together. His thin band hoodie—jet black, emblazoned with a silver grungy logo proclaiming *The Malcontents: Cupid Killed The Future*—was not enough to keep out the cold, so his slower pace made him end up with this shivering sort of walk, pigeonlike, small steps, hands in pockets. 'We got like, a thousand other days to go out drinking.'

'There's uh, way less days than that in a year.'

'Lol fine.'

'Did you just say lol in real life? Jeesus.' Bram's response was simply to laugh aloud. 'I'm not wrong though,' Kestrel continued. 'It's a *foundation year* course for a reason.'

'You arse.' Bram sidled into him, slowly-on-purpose. 'Okay. Next time you come out, and you buy me a Pimm's.'

'Deal.'

'I'll hold you to it, for sure. Hey, what you doing Sunday?'

'Uh… drinking with you?'

'Heh, nah, I was gonna say, Aaron texted me. He said, look—*Forget Mass, come get this bread on Sunday instead.*' Bram flashed his phone at Kestrel. The text was accompanied by a d20 emoji.

'Oh, yeah, Bethan mentioned something about that, too.' Kestrel could feel the pincer movement from the pair of them, and it made the hairs on his arms stand on end. The familiar sensation of a new adventure approaching. The group, assembled; the ethereal call, made. Aaron had plans, and this was good.

He smiled as he huffed out in the crisp winter air. Looked like a dragon breathing out smoke—he'd thought that ever since he was little. A sidelong glance at Bram. 'Well, I'm free on Sunday.'

'Midday?'

'Sure.'

They carried on down the path, and the conversation drifted naturally to other things. *Good night out? Did you do the coursework? The new Malcontents album is pretty good— you heard it yet?* It was enough to cover the silence. And he liked seeing Bram's face light up talking about music. It lifted Kestrel's mood considerably, that was, until Bram turned his attention to the Easter exhibition.

'Aw maaaan, I wonder who got in.' Bram stretched out one arm above his head to ping at a bare overhanging branch, and Kestrel studiously said nothing. He'd already said enough to Bethan last night. For a moment Bram looked like he was going to ask, *didn't you have your assessment last night?* but he didn't.

C Block was getting closer. That familiar off-white square rising up from a backdrop of poplar trees, so spidery in their leafless, wintry state. Kestrel found it hard to suppress a groan.

'Yup. I feel that.' Bram huffed and dug his hands deep into his hoodie pockets. 'Dunno why they're making us learn about Cubism. I mean, yeah, I know, we gotta learn all these different genres and stuff but—why is it just... so much balls? So many balls. All the balls.'

Kestrel snorted.

Bram continued. 'I mean, this is *not* what I expected

when I signed up for art school.'

He was right there. Kestrel had imagined hall upon hall of open workshop space, and countless hours to fill where one could just draw, draw, draw to the heart's content, and then maybe hit upon some stream of artistic genius like a miner might find a vein of ore by chance. Probably every other student had thought the same thing.

'Only two periods, then free workshopping until lunch.' Kestrel let his voice dip into the over-dramatic register he usually reserved for character roleplay. 'We'll survive these dark times. We have to. For the sake of the world!'

'And just like that,'—one hand emerged from the hoodie pocket, punching the air—'the party was filled with… *determination!*'

A reference to a game they had both played many times. Kestrel laughed—so hard he almost tripped on the gravel path. Small blades of grass poking through at the pathway edges, determined to survive the frost, caught his eye. And then a wisp of wind; he pulled his scarf closer about his neck.

There was a natural silence between them, one that gave Kestrel space to think again about the night and the sickly feeling that still settled in the pit of his stomach. Why was it so hard to tell Bram about the exhibition?

What he could have said: *They refused me. And I went home, and thought even harder about being punished for it. And I dreamed…*

'Hey. Hey, you know you can tell me. If anything's up, like.'

God, he was bad at masking his feelings. He might as well offer up some of the truth.

'I, uh. Told Bethan I'd go visit Tala.'

Now, the first quirk of those dark eyebrows.

'So I guess that didn't help how I was feeling last night,' Kestrel added.

'No, man, that makes sense.' Bram sighed, and for a moment neither of them knew what to say. Then Bram nudged his shoulder. 'C'mon, let's get there before the good seats are taken.'

It was later in the day when Kestrel felt the urge to separate from his friends.

The chapel was only marginally warmer than it was outside, and Kestrel still had his woollen hat pulled tight over his head and ears as he sat near the back, gazing up at the cross in silent reflection.

He had intended to stop worshipping since he left his mum's house, but old habits died hard. And so, here he was, back in the arms of his jilted god, finding a quiet space to think before lectures began for the day. It was the end of the week now, but that fact alone brought none of the relief it should have.

Kestrel craned his neck.

The walls, white as powder snow. Clean from lack of use. Up at the ceiling, the arches converged into something that was more of a polygonal space than a perfect half-moon. Modernist, designer influence, which made sense for the college. He still had trouble wrapping his head around the style, accepting it as something church-worthy. Everything he had known in his childhood was so much more grand and so much more Gothic. This place he judged, however subconsciously.

But it did cast the light about beautifully, that he could not deny.

He shuffled, knocked the pew in front. It was a small enough space, but still the sound echoed. He tugged his hat further around his ears, then let his hands fall, clasped together between his knees. Afterwards he lowered his eyes, and let the silence overcome him.

The fabric blocked sound well, so he only realised someone else had joined him when a shadow fell fuzzily across his eyes.

He got up. Bent a knee toward the space where the tabernacle would have been, had it not been a non-denominational space of worship.

'Ah. Catholic?'

'Yeah.' Kestrel pulled his hat off—a bid to hear better which only resulted in his hair falling haphazardly across his face. He hastily brushed the long brown strands out of his eyes and looked up at the newcomer. An older man with barley-blond hair and a disarming smile. Day-old stubble on his sharp jawline, and intense eyes that seemed green from one angle, and golden brown from another. He wasn't quite sure what to make of the man, other than a strange sense of familiarity that pinged around his gut. Before he could stop himself, he blurted out, 'Oh!'

'Oh?'

'I think I've seen you before.'

The man smiled, and adjusted the collar of his jacket—not a plaid or tweed affair like many of the professors had, but a fashionable brown faded leather.

'Around campus, probably. What're you studying?'

'Art.'

Again, that smile. So familiar, so unplaceable. 'That would be why we haven't spoken before. I spend a lot more time around the Theology department.'

'You teach theology?'

'Oh, no. I'm just a religious counsellor. I know—it sounds kind of lame.' He must have caught the dubious expression on Kestrel's face.

'I don't think I'd, uh, call it *lame.*'

'You're too kind. There,' he said, and by way of introduction pointed to the leaflet on the pew before Kestrel. The small print at the bottom.

For more information, see Daran Bailey, Counsellor, Block D-4 Humanities.

'That you? Daran Bailey?'

'Yes. Pronounced D*ah*-ran.' The *ah* was spoken like a sigh of relief. His eyes glittered electric. 'What about you?'

'I'm, uh. I'm Kestrel.'

'Kestrel. It's a beautiful name.'

People always said that. And, because people always said that, Kestrel had not been expecting to really take note of their awe, other than to muster up one of perhaps a dozen phrases learned by rote: "Yeah, my parents were proper hippies," or "It's better than being called Peaches," or maybe "It's very confusing for others when we visit the zoo". But when Daran said it, it was a different flavour of awe. Like the way someone might talk when reading a psalm aloud. It lent a strange sensation to the surface of his skin. By any other standard, a flush. He barely managed a *Hah* in response.

Daran seemed to spot his bashfulness, and interpreted it as a sign to end the conversation. 'Well, I shan't interrupt you any longer.'

'Oh! No, I wasn't—' Kestrel had been about to say *I wasn't praying,* but he stopped short. *Why?* He didn't know.

Wanting to impress? Maybe.

He needed something less self-immolating.

'I mean. I was just gonna get back to class soon anyway,' he said, settling on the most generic sounding thing he could.

Daran waved his excuse away. A battle of politeness.

'I only came in here to check the electrics. Needed to swap out a faulty mic cable.'

'Oh.'

'You don't mind if I…'

'Oh! No, go on ahead. I'll just…'

'I don't mean to rush you.'

Something about the measure of his voice gave Kestrel pause.

'You're not! It's okay. I'm, uh, I'm basically done already.'

Daran smiled at him, and it was so soft, it was the kind of smile that made him want to inhale—and exhale— deeply. 'You're too kind.' It was the second time he had said such a thing. For a moment Kestrel thought Daran was going to rest his hand on his shoulder, but he did not. Strange, how disappointed that made him.

I'm really not, he wanted to reply. *I'm just awkward.* But he said nothing, and he let the silence settle, as he fretted internally about the zip of his jacket and how to pull it up without making a fool of himself.

Daran, luckily, filled the silence.

'Hey, if you're interested, check out the chapel's intranet page. I'm trying to get a lot more stuff started up this half-term. Easter Stations, for one. You're more than welcome if you want to join.'

'Yeah!' Kestrel smiled. 'That'd be super cool, actually.'

'No pressure, though. I just figure it's nice to give people a space where they don't have to think about their daily stresses.'

That did sound nice.

''Kay. See you round.'

Daran nodded. He said something, it could have been a

God bless, but Kestrel was too quick to leave, and was unable to absorb the words properly. It only seemed fair to let the man continue his chaplaincy duties, to stop taking up so much of his time. So, out from the clean-slate walls, white and polished as marble, and into the cold February air, the gravel path back to the main campus, the well-tended shrubs and the Brutalist blocks of the college's sharp exterior.

As he was walking down the frost-lined pavement back to C Block, he finally managed to place the feeling.

It carried *weight*, the whole encounter with Daran carried weight.

His eyes shuttered closed as he passed beneath the hawthorn trees. Thought back to the prayer he'd been partway to forming earlier, before being interrupted—not that he resented that.

Hey, God, I don't know if you're there... probably not, but yeah. If you are. I guess I... I have trouble starting these things. I'm not even sure I want to talk to you. I don't know if I can ever forgive you for how Mum ended up.

Maybe that was a little unfair.

Even if God was real, could he really blame him for letting her go off the deep end? Kind of a tall order, even assuming he was omniscient. *Take care of this one particular person out of a world of billions.* And besides, not like God came up with the Creed, nor the fifty two books of the Bible, nor any of the rules and regulations that followed. People, it was always people.

His mind flew into a spin and he was thinking about her and his father and yeah, even his own weird relationship with the whole thing. Always striving for some kind of ascension, some kind of *connection* beyond the mechanics of the ritual.

Speaking of connection, he hadn't called her in a while. It was usually up to him to do it, a sort of test of love, a test of faith. One he put a lot of energy into trying not to resent.

It didn't matter. Fuck, it didn't matter.

You can start, at the very least, by making good on your promise, and going to visit Tala. Regardless of who is watching above.

That much was true, and at least for now, it gave him something to focus on.

Tala's mother was a small, skittish Filipina woman, with dark skin and even darker eyes. She had let Kestrel in with a worried sort of smile, clearly grateful for his intrusion. Then she had left to go sort things in the kitchen after waving a hand toward the back of the house, where she said Tala was drawing away. He supposed there was not much to sort in the kitchen, because when they had passed it, it had seemed spotlessly clean, but it must have provided a good enough distraction for her.

Before he had knocked on the front door, Kestrel had been proud he had finally worked up the nerve to visit. Art class had been okay, but he had too much time to think about things, and he would have struggled to forgive himself for not doing the right thing and checking in. He thought he had been ready. But when he finally came to it, he did not feel ready at all. If he responded to that primitive part of his brain that was chittering away like a mad thing, he would have up and left already.

The door to the conservatory was open. A wind chime swung gently in the breeze; a small tinkling of tiny plates of metal. Should have been a tonic for the nerves, but instead it was disturbing. The air: almost stiflingly fresh.

Clear, and with a scent so familiar yet unplaceable. Art supplies lay scattered over the table, and a box of what he assumed were more supplies was dragged out to the centre of the room. Inside, Tupperware containers that held things that glinted in the light.

And there, his eyes fell upon Tala. In the middle of the conservatory she perched on a rattan chair, legs drawn up to her chin, head bowed, dark straight hair falling over her face just enough to be a bother to her drawing, but not enough for her to care to push it back. If she had noticed him enter, she made no sign of it.

'Hey, Tala.' He spoke quietly. The pencil scratching stopped. At first she did not move but then, in the time it might take a bird to run a circle round the lawn, she tilted her head towards him. There was something captivating about her eyes—there always had been—but right now it was stronger than ever.

'Don't tell me off for drawing,' she said.

'Uh. Wasn't planning on it.'

'That's good. The doctor said it'd be good physio for my wrists anyway.'

She seemed oblivious to the implications of that settling in around them. Kestrel watched where she gripped the pencil, wondered if it hurt, and tried and failed to think of something to say.

'I've been having terrible dreams,' she said. Her words were all stilted, like she was choosing the shapes of syllables from a voice synthesiser.

'I'm sorry. That really sucks.' He gave her his softest smile, and hoped it would convey what he intended; that there was no need to be so guarded around him.

She opened her mouth, about to speak, then she let the breath go and turned back to her artboard. All her lines were grey, spidery, skittering across the page and making almost no discernible shapes. Although, if he turned his head at one angle, it looked like human bodies, clambering out of concentric spirals that amassed on the page like black holes in the sky. A wave of something grim and terrifying washed over him, and for one crystal-clear moment, Kestrel understood how it was for his teachers to look at his own work.

How to say *everyone is worried about you* without coming across as patronising?

God, this was hard. He really wasn't equipped for it.

'We, uh… We miss you.'

'Already? No,'—she shook her head, studying the pendulum lamp above her—'I don't know how to make you understand.'

I'm right here, Kestrel wanted to say, *so try me*. But that would have sounded too challenging.

'The gang's getting back together soon. You, uh, wanna join?' When Tala looked up at him, so curiously, like he was speaking another language, he clarified. 'We're starting a new tabletop campaign. Aaron's GM'ing. It'd be really good to have you there.'

A faint smile pushed at the corners of her mouth, but found it too hard to break through.

'You…' she began, but then she lost the rest of the sentence. Kestrel did not sigh, did not shuffle about, did not show any sign of impatience. He could tell how hard this was for her, although he had no hope of understanding what it felt like.

If he peered close he could see the medical tape poking out from the underside of her long sleeves. Vertical scars, that's what they had said. Easier to open up the vein that way. Matching on both sides because Tala liked her symmetry.

Some dark and frenzied ball of energy roiled around in his stomach, threatening to upset its meagre contents. He should have eaten lunch. Should be running on something more than empty. This feeling, it was too much like his dreams. And, rising alongside the cloying sense of wrongness, he felt… rage, although he wasn't sure where to direct it. Not at Tala, never at such an easy target.

'We're meeting up on Sunday. I'll swing by here first, 'kay?'

''Kay.'

'Is it okay if I sit down, by the way?'

Her eyes flashed wide, first at him, then at the table. She shuffled some papers away, closed the lid of the box, in the same embarrassed movements he used when he wasn't quite ready to let other people see his work. Then she looked back at him, pushed a strand of hair away from her face, and nodded.

He took a seat, trying to ignore the obnoxious creak of the rattan furniture. Breathe in, breathe out, watch the pendulum lamp, hear the birds outside. He tried to fall into the same rhythm she appeared to be running on in the conservatory, to attune to it somehow, in the vain hope it would make her more comfortable.

There was nothing he wanted, nor needed to say. Maybe a minute passed.

Then she reached out with her left hand, grabbing his wrist with fervent urgency. It was such a rapid movement, her feet slipping from their hold on the edge of the chair, body rolling forward, that at first he thought she was falling, and he tried to brace. But her grip on his wrist was too intense. Must have hurt her—the medical tape was straining at her skin. He fell slack, just so it wouldn't make anything leak through the bandages. It had been a few weeks, but the cuts had been *deep*, and how long did that sort of thing take to heal? Chicken scratches and scoremarks didn't count, so he had no frame of reference.

She was looking at him like she was possessed.

'You, most of all.'

Kestrel could feel his eyebrows twisting, inching upward. Should there have been a first part to that sentence? This made no sense. It was obviously important, but it made no sense.

'You, most of all,' she repeated, eyes hard as diamonds. Then, 'I'm so sorry.'

'Hey. Hey, it's okay.' He controlled his breathing, hoping it would make her do the same.

'But it's not though, is it? It's not, it's not.' Her voice grew tremulous, a few degrees away from a meltdown.

He had to do something.

'Hey, c'mere.' He extended his free arm—she was still gripping the other one—for a hug. But she shied away.

'No, no, I can't, I don't… *deserve*… Augh—'

The cry her words devolved into made Kestrel squirm. *Shit, exactly what I had been hoping to avoid.*

Moments later, the door to the conservatory creaked open. A small, worried face poked through. Tala's mother.

'Is everything all right in here?'

This was finally the point where Tala let go of Kestrel's wrist. He glanced down, didn't doubt she had never intended to grip so hard but yeah, there were fingernail indents in his skin. He let his arm slip to his side, so nobody would worry. The whole room felt like a minefield.

He got up. 'I'm sorry. I—maybe I should go.'

'Okay, yes, yes, that's maybe a good idea. Thank you for coming, though.' Her mother was speaking too fast. Bags under her eyes—she had not been sleeping well, clearly.

Kestrel nodded. He sorted his jacket, and stepped as calmly as he could towards the door, where he turned to look back at his friend one last time.

'Tala, I don't think anything bad about you.'

She gave him a look that was unmistakeable in its intent. *If only you knew.* He didn't try to push it by repeating himself. Just kept his eyes soft, expression soft, everything soft and caring.

'I'll see you on Sunday.'

CHAPTER THREE

Blackwater

Kestrel did not see Tala on Sunday.

It wasn't for lack of trying. He had indeed swung by her place first, but her mother had answered the door, and told him no, not today. Not a good time.

He said he understood. He said he'd be back another day.

Now he was in Aaron's living room, sitting cross-legged at the dining table, fidgeting with his shirt lapel while they prepped for the campaign.

Aaron's house was an oddity. Both his parents were rich —richer than Kestrel's or Bethan's or Bram's, at any rate— and this meant that their dining table was a tabletop RPG player's dream: spacious enough to lay everything out and still have enough room to stretch and put down snacks. His parents worked as news correspondents, the pair of them, and now that Aaron was old enough to take care of himself it was rare they were home, and that just made the house seem bigger. But for all its size, the interior of the house sported very little to signify its status. Sometimes Kestrel thought it looked more like one of those hippie pop-up furniture stores you'd find around town come Christmastime; lots of eclectic furniture, wood carvings, mass-produced porcelain elephants and mandala-patterned candle holders. It made for a strange mix alongside the more usual photo frames, mirrors and modern light fixtures. Perhaps the biggest signs of wealth were the expensive black piano in the corner, and the dark high-backed chairs at the dining table which might have been real mahogany, although he'd never asked.

He wasn't about to now: Aaron was busy laying out the map on the table. Their little character miniatures were bundled off to one side while he spread out the paper, weighing it down with decorative stones, candles, paperweights, whatever he could find.

He enjoyed watching Aaron work. That slightly curled chestnut-brown hair bobbed over the gentle arch of his slim brows—quite a childish face, one that suggested absolute innocence, although with all Kestrel's experience having Aaron as his Game Master, he knew he was anything but. It was an entertaining anachronism, and the illusion only broke when Aaron's mouth quirked upward in a crooked smile that hinted at the plotting and planning that lay beneath.

Bram was fiddling with the sound system. Engrossed in his task, laptop at his feet with the browser tab open on a background music aggregation site. Bethan was knocking about in the kitchen, looking for snacks. She returned with armfuls of canned soft drinks, most of which found their place at the edge of the dining table. One can of coke she scooted over to Kestrel. He didn't really have an opinion on the stuff, but he accepted it because he didn't want to squander her gift.

'Oi, Bethan, isn't there any beer?' Aaron, glancing up, eyeing the array of drinks.

She responded by putting her legs up on the table—angled enough to not disturb the map. 'Get it yourself. I'm not getting up again now.'

A pout from Aaron, and a gesture at his half-finished work.

'I'll get it.' Kestrel exaggerated a sigh and extracted his legs from their comfortable crossed position on the wide chair.

'Good man, good man.'

On into the kitchen.

A stream of music blasted from the sound system, top volume, right as Kestrel opened the fridge. An embarrassing sound left his mouth, the fridge door shook, and God, he hoped nobody heard that over the noise. He recognised the band though. Envy Bridge. Another one of Bram's favourites.

'Jesus Christ, man!' Aaron's yell was followed by something that sounded suspiciously like a handful of plastic miniatures clattering to the floor. Kestrel smiled, glad he wasn't the only one who got a shock.

Bram's reply: 'Sorry! Sound testing!'

His smile grew into a laugh as he brought the beer out. Aaron, still flailing in his bid to reassign order to the table. 'You idiot,' he said as he handed him a bottle.

'Yes, well. Heh. We ready?' Nods from Bethan and Kestrel. '*You* ready?' Directed at Bram this time.

A wry look from behind that long black fringe. 'Haha, yeah.'

Kestrel leaned in, clasping his hands together and focussing intently on Aaron. 'Right, Games Master—what devious dungeon delving delights do you have for our party tonight?'

'Now, if I told you it would ruin the surprise!'

'Aw, c'mon.'

'But like, what *sort* of campaign,' Bethan asked. 'We doing Skullbreaker?'

The rulebooks for Skullbreaker had only just been released, and it would not have surprised anyone if Aaron had already gotten hold of it. But he shook his head.

'Take another guess. It's one we've talked about before.'

Kestrel considered.

'I mean, I've wanted to do a cosmic horror campaign for a while…'

A laugh from Bethan. 'Yeah, Kes, we *all* know that.'

'I mean. Tentacles and mind control. What's not to like?' He grinned, goofily enough to hide the reddening of his cheeks. Then, quietly, 'Please let it be that…'

'It's not. Sorry to disappoint.'

'Aw maaaaan.'

'Come on. I'll give you a clue. Think about where everyone got to in the end of the last adventure.'

Silence.

Kestrel thought about it; the dwarven village on the edge of the swamplands, where, during the last term's quest, they had picked up their reward for defeating the Clay Golem that had terrorised the mines. Any sensible dwarf would have built their home further inland, on more solid ground. He hadn't given it much thought before, but suddenly, Aaron's excuse of 'but the Golem and its kind had forced them further afield' seemed awfully convenient. He felt almost sticky as he considered it. Swamps. A sensation of humus and wet grass. Glowing golden eyes in the dark.

'Blackwater Marsh?'

Aaron smiled.

'I knew it!'

'Blackwater, hm?' Bram's eyes lit up.

'Classic,' said Bethan, cracking open her coke with vigour.

'I've got a homebrew rule kit in mind, if that's okay. So, um, if you've played Blackwater before—okay, nobody has, cool—well in that case nobody needs to worry. It's a little different—'

'Knowing you, always is.'

'—but it should be fun.'

All smiles and agreement there. Kestrel let himself relax a little. The mood was good.

Aaron pulled the campaign book out from its hiding spot. *The Secret of Blackwater Marsh* was emblazoned on the top in that familiar blocky font. The book looked ancient; Kestrel wondered if it had belonged to an older relative, his father, or uncle? He was still fixated on it as Aaron moved on to handing out everyone's miniatures. 'Bethan, there's your barbarian. Bram—necromancer. Kestrel—your rogue.'

Bethan leant in to peer at Kestrel's model. A sprightly young elven man, delicately poised with daggers in hand. His hair was shoulder length, about as long as Kestrel's own and just as straight and flyaway, but that was where the similarity stopped. Instead of lacklustre mid-brown it was green, and not the neon punk kind. It was the soft grey-green of old forests, of moss-covered rocks. When they had painted them last summer, Kestrel had agonised long and hard over the acrylic mix to get that colour. Base coat, lowlights and highlights, it had taken forever. And so, he felt a little proud as he saw the creases of Bethan's smile. 'Aw, I've missed Quinn.'

He nudged the figurine over to her bulky half-orc, simulated a hug. 'He missed you too, Marcus.'

One miniature remained unclaimed at the centre of the table: clad in white and gold, and sporting a long braid of orange hair. Tala's elven druid, Leilani. She held her staff raised in a defiant pose, eyes cast up to the heavens. It was the most intricately painted miniature of the lot; a testament to Tala's stubbornness.

He remembered well how much of a surprise it had been when she had announced she wanted to play the healer. Fighting on the front line had always been more her style.

A cough from Aaron.

'Now. Before we start. Anyone know what the deal with Tala is?'

A silence fell around the table.

'Um,' Kestrel began, but he didn't know what to say next.

'What I mean is, do we keep her character in this campaign or not? Cos I've got some storylines to use if not, I just need to know.'

'Did you talk to her in the end?' Bethan asked. All eyes turned Kestrel's way.

'Yeah.'

'And? She planning on coming?'

'Safe to say no,' Kestrel murmured, then, 'I'm getting a beer too.' His can of coke was barely broken into. He didn't care.

He heard Aaron get up behind him and follow him into the kitchen. Behind the shutters and the hippie-beaded doorway, Aaron cornered him in the still and the quiet. Warm yellow walls caught the late-winter light far too well, and Kestrel suddenly felt incredibly tired. But he couldn't relax, not with Aaron breathing down his neck.

'Dude, c'mon, spill the beans.'

'How d'you mean?'

Aaron looked at him like he was dumb. 'How's she *doing*?'

'She's, uh, not doing well. I think.'

'You think?'

'I dunno, I'm not… I don't know a lot about this stuff.'

Aaron sighed, and leaned against the fridge. It creaked backward under his weight.

'Great. So she's fucking mental, and we don't know what the hell to do about it.'

They had been an unstoppable trio since they were incredibly young, so it was hard to hear him spitting so caustic about it. So Kestrel said, 'Yeah, maybe don't phrase it like that,' and Aaron simply responded, 'You know I don't mean it bad,' and went back to staring at his own bottle.

There was more silence in the air. Enough time to make Kestrel wonder: had his opinion of her really changed so much?

Aaron broke the silence himself. 'We should invite her back to the game, at least.'

'I already did.'

'Ugh… Okay.' He opened the fridge door, but he didn't retrieve anything from it. Another second and his facade cracked. 'Dude, I'm just worried. She scared us all. I don't want…'

Kestrel didn't ask him to finish the sentence. It was what they all were thinking. He didn't want Tala to die either. And *God*—she had been so bright, so active, so full of *life*. She was a little weird, sure, but weren't they all?

They stared at each other awkwardly, and it was just a

second but it felt like so much longer.

'I'll ask her again,' Kestrel said.

Aaron nodded.

Back to the living room.

Bethan and Bram were focussing on their character sheets. If they had overheard anything, they gave no sign of it.

'So,' Aaron said, stretching out his hands and adjusting his chair, 'we left off in Mud—'

'Mud?'

'The village was called Mud, remember?' Kestrel poked Bethan. 'Dwarves aren't the most inventive at naming things.'

'True.'

'Okay, so we'd reached Mud, and the four of you had just gotten your reward for killing the Clay Golem. Now, since Tala isn't here, I'm gonna go out on a limb and say that our druid Leilani has returned to her mentor in the Valley to meditate. She's told you guys she'll be back soon... ish. Whenever her meditation is done. So for now, you're gonna go on ahead without her.'

And, like that, Tala's elven druid was written out of the campaign. It should have been a more portentous moment, and it surprised Kestrel how it just passed like another breath, no pomp or circumstance. It felt almost insulting.

'Okay, so. You're in Mud, and you've collected your prize money from the miners, who've all packed up and left the village to repopulate the mines again. You don't know anyone else here, and it seems to be a smallish village with only the basic necessities—a town hall, a grocer's, an inn. So. What do you want to do?'

Bethan wrung her hands together and crossed her legs up on the chair. 'Well, since we only just got here, we should probably take a rest at the inn.'

'Yeah. I think it would be sensible to find out more about this place while we do it, too.'

'Well, let's ask folks at the inn,' Kestrel suggested. 'If we try and explore too much before we rest,' and he glanced at Aaron accusingly, 'we'll get sucked into trouble before we know it.'

'And ask about stables. My horse needs a rest too,' Bram said.

Bram was the only one with a horse. His character, Thorvald, had won it in a bet against a highway robber early on in their adventures, and, with the bond between them being so strong, Kestrel was beginning to suspect he had plans to make it his familiar.

Aaron motioned to Bram for the laptop, pulled it closer and kicked off the playlist. A low, folksy melody started up.

'Okay. The three of you look around the village square, taking note of the few inhabitants you see. Small, grey-clad dwarves, scurrying here and there. None of them seem keen to talk, in fact, despite you guys having helped the miners out, these villagers are all looking at you rather suspiciously. But the building to the left of the square is clearly the inn, if the sign outside is anything to go by, so you make your way inside. Except for Thorvald — you take your horse to the nearby stable, which you spy at the edge of the inn's ageing stone walls.'

Five silver pieces lighter in pocket and Poe, Thorvald's grey stallion, was fed, watered, and sitting safe. The group went on into the inn.

'Here, you all find yourselves in a sullen, cold room with only a few patrons drinking out of deep tankards. Nobody talks; there's only the occasional clinking as tankards are set back on the tables. At the far side of the room there's a rather rotund looking dwarf, who doesn't seem to be up to much while he potters behind the bar. When he sees you, he does seem to perk up a bit. "Ello there, travellers. Anything I can get you?"'

'"A pint of ale, for starters,"' Bethan said in a deeper register than usual, manoeuvring Marcus into the limelight.

'"And beds for the night,"' Bram added, in Thorvald's calm, more academic voice. '"Marcus, must you always think about ale?"'

'Marcus looks at Thorvald like he's gone mad. "Ale first, sleep second."'

'The innkeeper chuckles, and pours out the ale first. "So," he says, "You folks beat the Golem in them mines, I hear?"'

'Quinn steps forward, all cocky like, and grins. "Yep, we sure did!"'

'"Well, ain't that a blessing. Mebbe a town like this has use for adventurers like you, eh?" The innkeeper's eyes twinkle.'

'Oh, you just *know* he's got detail on some terrible fiend,' Bethan murmured.

'Totally. And we're the only ones who can deal with it.'

'I bet I know what it is, too,' Bram taunted.

'You haven't read the campaign, haven't you?' Aaron's eyes, sharp in mock-condescension.

'I swear I haven't!'

'Well, good thing this is homebrew,' Aaron muttered. 'I changed a few things up, you know.'

Kestrel thought about it. Cold and damp areas tended to attract a particular kind of monster. 'I bet it's a... tentacle monster?'

'More like mud monster,' Bram interjected.

'Ew, hope not.'

'What do you mean, "hope not?" They're practically the same.'

'Mud isn't sexy. That's the difference.'

'Jesus Christ, Kestrel. You should've been a bard.'

'Thief isn't that far off…'

'Not all bards are absolute sluts,' Aaron said.

'Uh, yeah they are,' said Bram, and Bethan slapped him. 'Oi!'

Bethan burst into a fit of laughter. 'That's what you get.'

Aaron had the final word. 'You guys gotta stop assuming you know what's gonna happen.'

There was something odd about that, the way it stuck in Kestrel's mind. It wasn't Aaron's fault, not by a long shot, but all the same, it made him feel small.

'Ominous,' said Bethan, but then the moment passed, and they all continued, oblivious to Kestrel's continuing unease.

'What I mean is, you gotta think outside the box,' Aaron was saying. 'Beyond the realm of classic monsters. Anyway, enough of that. So the innkeeper's looking at you all, a kind of apology in his tired eyes, and he says, "But let's not dwell on work, shall we? Forty for the night, both bed and bread, and… well, speaking of bread, Margaret will have the stew ready in a few hours."'

'"Is it all right if we explore the area until then?" Marcus asks.'

'"Of course it be, son. Jes', be careful of them South Gates. Nothin' but wild country beyond there. The Blackwater Marsh, us folks call it, though, it's been called that longer'n we've settled down roots here."' Aaron continued in his narrator's voice. 'Now, you notice the innkeeper looks flighty as he speaks of the southern gates. His eyes dart over the countertop, and he seems to be attempting to control an inner panic.'

'"What's out there?"' Bethan, positioning Marcus forward slightly.

'The innkeeper seems to realise his flightiness has been noticed, and reins in his worry. "Eh, jes' the usual dangers of the bog an' the mists. Some say there's spirits as what roam the marsh. Folks're superstitious."'

'Quinn says, "You don't need to worry about us. We just want to check out the town, and we'll be back in plenty of time for food."'

They left the inn.

'Well, I'm immediately interested in those gates he mentioned,' Kestrel said.

'Same.' Bethan.

'We should totally go through the gates,' Bram said, mouth quirking up into a sly smile. 'I'm super intrigued about what's out there.'

Aaron eyed them all. 'You really wanna do that?'

Yes, was the unanimous response.

'Well, all right. If you're sure.' That twinkle to his eye again. 'You wander through the village, still curious about the fact that nobody wants to tarry long enough to talk. The clouds are thicker now overhead, and when you reach the South Gates, you see an intimidating stretch of greyish green that lies beyond. You can smell it from here: salt and soil. It seems endless, like an ocean. Now, you all, of course, are already aware that Mud is a curious village perched on the edge of marshland, but, coming in from the western side, with its thickets and harder ground, you never got the chance to see how close this village truly was to the marsh. But it's close, far closer than is comfortable.

It's almost as though the marsh is doing its best to seep in.' He paused for dramatic effect. 'You walk through the gates.'

'Wait. I need my horse,' said Bram.

Bethan snorted. 'You sure you wanna take a *horse* in *there*?'

'He's my emotional support horse! I can't leave him! Plus, he's got all our spare supplies on his back, remember?' Then, to Aaron, 'Are there pathways?'

'There are. They're narrow, and just your basic dirt pathways, but you can all see it's clear that people have attempted to forge routes through the marsh earlier, and, at least, from here they are easy enough to see.'

'Okay, good. I'm going back for my horse, then.'

'That's gonna take too much time.'

'We'll just say you picked up Poe when you left the inn,' Aaron said, plucking the horse miniature up and setting him next to Thorvald. He took a deep breath in and rubbed his hands. 'So, you all head out to the marsh.'

Aaron paused to queue up the next track, and let the music segue slowly into it. An eerie synth swept over the room, with a barely-audible bassline providing a throbbing layer of tension just beneath.

'This first bit, this is just a small stretch of marshland, it's the bit the dwarves have attempted to cultivate, and failed. Here and there you squelch past withered pumpkin stalks, and wooden pikes driven into the ground for vines that failed to take. In the distance, amid the blueish-green haze of grasses and reeds, you can see strange humped shapes—'

'Can I determine what they are?' asked Bram.

'Sure. Roll for arcana.'

Bram cast his die. 'Seventeen.'

'Okay, so, from your previous studies, Thorvald, you know that these strange humps in the landscape are *barrows*, or, places where people were once buried. Now, these might have been folk of import, but it no longer matters. All that matters is right now, the land has become a mixture of hallowed *and* desecrated ground.'

What a way to say it. Kestrel could see it so clearly in his mind's eye, the landscape; its sallow greens and blues become a meeting point for things contradictory, its hummocks and grasses beckoning.

'This means,' Aaron continued, 'that no patch of ground is safe. The wights that one might find in such a marsh could well drag the party down to their deaths. And that — as you know, Thorvald — is just the background activity of such a location. Who knows what else is going on?'

Aaron let that settle in with the group for a moment. He was good at that.

'After a while, you come to a stream, interrupting the path. It's lined on all sides by those tufts of long blue grasses, and it's perhaps one and a half, maybe two metres wide. With the mud and the dull reflections from the overcast sky, it's impossible to tell how deep it is.'

'I get the feeling we shouldn't go in the water,' murmured Kestrel.

Aaron raised his eyebrow. Of course, he wasn't going to say whether this was a good or a bad thing.

'What do you want to do?'

'We should jump, or ford across, as quickly as possible,' said Bethan, and everyone agreed.

'Okay. Dexterity check.'

They all rolled their dice. Kestrel: fine. Bethan: fine.

'Aw, man.' Bram howled at his die.

'Four, huh? Let's see.' Aaron checked his booklet.

Waiting for him to talk was like waiting for a sentencing to be passed. 'You try to make it across in a swift leap, but the bog is deceptive. Your legs sink into the soft mud beneath, and you're sucked in up to your shins. You can feel it caving in beneath you, ready to open up even deeper. You barely manage to pull yourself free, grasping for purchase in the reeds.

'Your horse, however, is not so lucky. As he tries to canter forward and jump across along with you, he is set off balance. Poe flails and whinnies in terror as he sinks down into the bog, leaving only bubbles in his wake.'

'No!'

'"Can I jump in to save him?"' Bethan spoke in Marcus's deeper voice.

'You can try.'

'Damn. Rolled eleven.'

'Okay, that's technically a fail, but it's just south of the border, so... You reach in with a strong arm, with one foot sinking into the mud and the other on the safe path. It's pulling you in, too, and despite your size and strength, Marcus, you find it hard to steady yourself—'

'I steady Marcus as much as I can, on my side,' Kestrel cut in.

'Quinn grabs your belt, which allows you to reach your entire upper torso in and search through the slick mud. But the bubbles stop, and you realise you're too late. You do, however, manage to retrieve the body. And, uh, soon the poor horse is just sort of... lying there on the grass, drowned and sodden and covered in pondweed and grime.'

They all sat in stunned silence.

'Aw man, why? *Poe!*' Bram wailed. Once he had finished dragging his hands down his face, he leaned forth and knocked his character model flat. 'Okay, Thorvald is *not* going to be coping well with this.'

'Awkward flashbacks to The Neverending Story,' Bethan cut in, and this was accompanied by a soft cry of *Artaaaaax* from Bram. Shaking a fist to the sky.

'Sorry, man, that was some bad luck there. To soften the blow, I'll say Marcus managed to get the supplies back as well.'

'I want to raise him from the dead.'

Aaron opened his mouth, but Bram repeated himself, absolutely intent. 'It's a level five spell, don't forget it's been on my sheet since Evenstar.'

'Yes. You can use Raise. It'll cost you a gem, but you've already got a few from the Golem reward. And just to remind you, he'll only have one hit point when he comes back, and a penalty to all saving throws.'

'That's fine.'

'Spell takes an hour to cast, so here we go.' Aaron rubbed his hands together. 'Okay. Time for Thorvald to take centre stage. He brings forth his staff, and, eyes closed, starts to hum an ethereal tune. You all feel an elemental rush like wind across your skin, and it pulls you under its sway; a dark magic that should be unspeakable.'

A hush fell over the table. Bram was enraptured in the moment, but not so enraptured that he didn't take the time to set the music to something that amplified the tension like the ticking of a clock.

'So it takes an hour, in which all you others just sort of… stand around and wait, hah. But eventually, you finish the incantation, and when you do, it feels for a moment like gravity bends around you, tugging at all your souls. It's like there's a thunder rolling all around you, underneath you, and it increases in strength like a bubble ready to burst, until—it stops. Your ears are ringing with the absence of sound.' Aaron waited, held the moment for longer than was comfortable, then he made a horrendous choke of a noise. 'Poe snorts, and spews a gelatinous, sickly mass of bog water out from his nose. He starts to move his hind legs, shaking and shuddering in shock. He's almost frenzied, and—yeah, Thorvald, you can move in to calm him now. It takes him a while before he's able to stand, but when he does, it's strange, it's almost as though he hasn't realised anything is wrong any more.'

'Whew.' Bethan wiped her brow. Kestrel took another swig of beer. So did Aaron.

'You did it.'

Bram glanced around the group. 'This horse has a bond with me it can never know about—*must* never know about.'

'Lord, you got that right.'

A dark thought entered Kestrel's head and he played into it. 'Yep, and on occasion, you'll catch that horse with a sort of faraway look in his eye. Like he's on the verge of remembering something, but he doesn't quite know *what*. But then, the cold memory of death slips away and he's back to normal, with the truth of his horrific experience hidden away deep inside.'

'Aw, don't, man, that's too cruel!'

'Your poor traumatised horse,' Bethan said, patting the little figurine. 'Brought him back, *but at what cost?*'

'Ha ha! I mean, maybe that's what happens to us all when we stare off dumbly into the distance,' Kestrel continued. 'We all do it.' He sidled closer to Bram. Maybe it was the effect of the beer. 'What if you've watched *me* die? I'd never know.'

'Mate.' Bram admonished him, but he was still laughing

like the rest of them were, in mirthful horror.

Aaron clapped his hands together. 'So. You now have a death-amnesic, mildly messed up horse but don't worry, he still loves you. Would you like to continue?'

'Um. Let's stick to the paths. But yes,' Bram said.

'Same.'

'Yup.'

'Okay. You walk on. Poe neighs a couple of times, a throaty sound with the remnants of bog water in it, but otherwise he is enjoying trotting along. Thorvald, you might wanna have your hand firm on his reins as you lead him. But the path seems solid enough, and as long as you stick to it, and steer clear of the gaps in the grasses you're fine.' Aaron moved their miniatures further up the map, up to a spot where the hand-drawn path converged with another, next to a crudely-drawn lump of rock.

'Do we see anything else of note as we're walking?'

'Perception check,' Aaron called, and they rolled, and only Marcus succeeded. 'You do notice that the tracks you follow have started joining up with other ones, and they all seem to converge at a central point in the distance, like rabbit runs winding up at a burrow. There's something big rising up out of the mist, and you, Marcus, are tall enough to see it.'

'What do I see?'

'It's inanimate, and the closer you focus the more you realise, it's a monument of some kind. One big stone edifice, with a smaller stone edifice beside it and a little way off. Combined, they look like a lopsided gate, but very different from the precise, geometric-cut Dwarven gates you went through to get here. No, these seem far more ancient.'

Bram spoke up.

'I'm not sure I want to go too much closer. Poe needs to get back to the stables, ideally.'

'Come on, it's not far.'

'I want to get him back soon, cos of the penalty. If we run into anything else… I don't want him to die *again*. Of course,' Bram said, coming out of character, 'Thorvald whispers this, because he doesn't want Poe to hear.'

'Shouldn't have brought the horse at all,' Bethan said.

'He's my best friend! But fine. Won't bring 'im next time.'

Aaron slapped his palm down on the table. It wasn't violent, but it was sharp enough to get their attention. 'Before your group can argue a second longer, an eerie cry rips through the air, echoing across the marshland like a banshee, but many octaves deeper. Something, somewhere in this wild and watery land, is aware of your presence.'

'Fuck.'

'Told you we shoulda gone back.'

'It was your idea to come here in the first place!'

'Guys, don't argue so much, or that thing's gonna hear us,' Kestrel admonished. Then, to Aaron, 'I leap up on the rock to get a better look across the marsh.'

'Okay. You do that' —and Kestrel positioned Quinn over the rock symbol on the map—'and, does anyone else wanna do anything? No? Okay, Quinn, you've got an advantage on dexterity, so roll—good, that's a seventeen. You—'

'Wait, I wanna draw my sword, just in case,' said Bethan.

'Okay. Marcus arms himself, pulling his hefty, jagged sword up close and at the ready. You wait, bristling in the murk and the grime, ready for a fight. And then, Quinn, you see it.'

He paused.

See what?

They were all thinking it.

Aaron cracked a grin.

'It's tall; much taller than a man. It seems oddly proportioned, bones like rakes, all angular and jagged. Something sharp and twisted rises from its head, maybe horns, maybe bracken, you can't really tell. The aura that exudes from it is menacing, and you get the overwhelming sense that this creature knows no mercy. You're tensing up, and the others follow your gaze. Now, you all fall still as you see it moving in the distance, shadowy as fog and just as silent.'

'I wanna position myself at the front of the group,' Bethan said immediately.

'No—okay, so, when I say you all fall still, what I mean is, this is an involuntary action. There's something hanging heavy in the air that makes you stop moving, like a wild animal in the presence of a predator. It's an immense feeling.'

The music in the background segued masterfully into something even more breathy and atmospheric. A dull, resonant thud of a bass note, worming its way into their guts. Kestrel stole glances at Bethan and Bram, relieved to see they were as enraptured as he was.

'Kestrel, Quinn's currently balanced on that rock, so I'm gonna allow him to steady his feet. But you can't quite find the energy to leap back down and join the others. And now...'

And now, what?

'It catches sight of you.'

'Ah!' Bethan shied away, but in contrast to her real-world actions, she instinctively reached out and placed her berserker in front of the others. Remembered, 'Oh yeah, I can't do that,' and reluctantly placed him back in his original position.

'Oh no,' Bram said quietly.

'Not you guys. Just Quinn.'

'Me?'

'He's closest.'

'Oh,' Kestrel mumbled. 'Lucky me, I guess?'

'It catches sight of you, most of all,' Aaron continued, 'and for a moment it stops. You think you sense something, like it wants to speak. But all you feel is a cold chill in your bones, as if a gust of icy wind has blown through you. Your palms are sweating. But before you can decide what to do, its lamplike eyes flicker, and it dips into the shadows again. The eerie presence that had kept the party transfixed… you all feel it break its hold. Once again, you can move and react like normal. But—you're starting to see why the townspeople are so scared.'

'Oof,' Bethan muttered.

'Kes? Quinn can get off the rock now.'

Kestrel had to kickstart his mind into action. He was thinking about what Tala had said. *You, most of all.* He looked down, where his fingers were still gripped, trembling, around Quinn's little figurine. A mumbled 'Yeah.'

'Was that a mud monster, then?' asked Bethan.

Aaron laughed.

'It was all tall and spiky and shit. You know, the way mud isn't,' Bram said.

'Fine. I guess we'll wait and see.'

'You'll have to.'

Aaron led them back to the town, where they got their rooms for the night. And that wrapped things up for the day.

Bethan stretched.

'Whew! Well, how was *that* for a first session?'

'It was really something.'

They were all feeling the strain, as tired as their weary travellers, and ready for rest. In the lethargic calm that followed, they slowly packed everything away and finished their drinks. Kestrel got up to shake his legs out. His habit of sitting cross-legged was not so compatible with the hard, high-backed dining chairs. He paced, tried to coax life back into them.

'Next Sunday, same time?'

'Yeah. Works for me.'

As Bethan and Bram started discussing the campaign so far, Kestrel looked for a distraction to spirit his mind away from the swamp and the strange encounter. His fingers danced across the bureau until he found a book. Picked it up. 'That Samuel's?'

Aaron nodded. 'I'm surprised he forgot to take that one with him.'

'Is he still living here?'

'Yeah, but… He's spending so much time in the priory. Doing time on behalf of me.'

'Yeah?'

'I'm bloody glad about it too—Mum and Dad care far less about making *me* go to church now.' He looked at Kestrel. 'You still into all that stuff?'

Kestrel avoided the question with a shrug and a weak 'Eh.' It was too difficult to explain. But he angled the book so he could read the blurb.

An interpretive model of the Book of Revelation.

Okay, it had his attention. He flipped the pages.

As for what heralds the coming of the Rapture: in Malachai

4:5, *"Behold, I will send you Elijah the prophet before the great and dreadful Day of the Lord."*

'Anything good?'

'Just shit about Revelation,' he replied.

'Heh. Figured you'd be interested, Quinn *Therion*.' There was a knowing twinkle to Aaron's eye as he spoke Quinn's full name, and Kestrel couldn't help but think, *you and your brother are quite the pair, huh?* One, studying theology, the other studying philosophy, both intelligent enough and hungry enough for knowledge. It was not a hidden fact that Aaron thought he was better than his older brother for choosing the more logical science.

Kestrel would have liked to see Samuel again.

'But Kestrel didn't, that's what I'm saying.'

The use of his name brought him to attention. Bethan had moved to the sofa to finish her coke more comfortably, and was busy telling Bram something. About him.

Bram was sat at the piano, playing a riff from some rock song. But when he heard this, he stopped on a sharp *plink*, and spun around on the stool.

'You're shitting me.'

'Am not.'

'What the fuck? Mate,' and Bram scrutinised *him* now, 'they really didn't let your work in to the exhibition?'

Kestrel breathed out as calmly as he could, and replaced the book on the bureau. He had been hoping she would say nothing on that front. 'It's... fine, really. I mean. It doesn't matter.'

Bram huffed. 'Pisses me off, though. That was the acrylic stuff you were working on, right? Yeah. I saw you start on that background.'

I'd be a bit embarrassed to show you the finished product now, though. Maybe there really is no place for it.

'Dunno what they're thinking. Why'd they do it?'

He just shrugged.

'Pretentious twats,' Aaron muttered.

Kestrel appreciated the concern, and it was nice to have them on his side, but all the same he left Aaron's house with a strange feeling weighing heavy in his chest. Too may spotlights on him in too short a space. Night had already drawn in by the time he was back on campus territory, and as the leaves rustled in the dark, he couldn't help but think this, this was another *You, most of all*, caught atop the rock in full view of everyone, and how nice it would have been to clamber down and hide.

CHAPTER FOUR

Habits

'Tell me why—I don't like Mondays,' Bram sang as they made their way to the classroom.

Kestrel laughed, and it was more of an involuntary bark than a laugh. 'Just, don't shoot up the class, okay?'

Bram's eyes twinkled. 'Boomtown Rats are a classic, right? But yeah, let's not be whats'erface.'

They had Fine Art Techniques all morning, and this was bearable, because it was Mr. Ruiz, and he was all right. Young, for an art teacher, but despite his thick black curls and his barely-there beard, his hairline was already starting to recede—a sharp M shape that was only visible when he pushed his fringe back too far. His accent had a Mediterranean twang, and he was a lot more relatable than most of the other teachers. By the time they reached the room, Ruiz was already talking, waving them on to their seats with a half-joking frown. Then, back to the projector screen.

'What is *chiaroscuro?* A fancy word for shadowing?

Something your pretentious aunt might say to the waiter in an Italian restaurant?' Mr. Ruiz paused for effect. Some students giggled. 'No. It is the interplay of light and dark. Fundamentally,'—and he underscored the word in the air —'funda*mentally* opposing forces, but used in *such* stark contrast that it accentuates the whole.' He flipped to the next slide. 'You see?'

Kestrel saw. The contour lines on the bodies pictured were half in shadow, half in light. A man, half naked and pierced through with arrows, and a curious angel leaning in to inspect the nearest wound. A small footnote said *San Sebastiano curato da un angelo.* It was impossible to look at the picture and not consider it made more terrifying by the dramatic lighting—even as the sharp edges lent it a more cartoonish quality.

Mr. Ruiz tapped at the projector screen, sending the image billowing softly. 'Baglione—whose work you see here—was a proponent of the style, and used it to create strong, intense images that left many feeling uncertain as to whether they were meant to be sacred, or profane. I mean, you can see here, by the submissive stance and the focus on the musculature, why many people consider this to be highly sexualised. But that's part of the point of the chiaroscuro technique—it accentuates the subject matter through the use of lighting, so that it can evoke a much stronger emotion. Now, Baglione was only one of numerous painters from the Baroque period and onwards who used chiaroscuro heavily in their work. There were many others.'

Kestrel thought of Goya's *Saturn.*

The pierced man vanished from the screen and was replaced by a more clinical looking bullet list. The lecture went on. Notes were made. Then it was half past ten, and their time was up.

'Now, for your homework, I need you to practise chiaroscuro technique, but this is how I want you to do it: start with a painting, something simple, say, a profile of a face. Paint it as you would a normal painting, but don't worry too much about the shadowing at this stage. For the purposes of this exercise only, it's *after* you've laid down the groundwork that you will start adding your dramatic lighting.' Mr. Ruiz gestured with his hands. 'Now, you'll be making multiple passes over the painting from here. Start in increments, and make the light bits lighter and the dark bits darker each time. And, uh, take photos of your progress. So we can compare in class next week.'

'How many stages?'

A murmur through the room.

'As many as you feel it needs to get the most drama out of your work. Realistically, this might be six or seven, but don't be too intimidated by that. Think of it as, as building steam with a grain of salt.'

Rei, one of the louder students at the front of the class, held up her hand, but didn't wait for him to nod before she started. 'Hey, I know that phrase. Wait, *you* listen to DJ Shadow?'

Kestrel caught Bram's surprised gaze.

'Well, I mean, it's good stuff. Might be the best thing to happen to hip hop in the past few decades. Anyway.' Mr. Ruiz sounded a little bit chastened, as if he had only just become aware that this wasn't really part of the curriculum. A small moment in which he seemed more like a child caught daydreaming than a teacher.

'Okay, that's pretty cool,' Rei said, and her hand fell slowly. Then it was over, and Mr Ruiz continued where he had left off.

'So, that's your main assignment for this week. Next Monday is when it's due, okay? Oh, and there's one last thing. Is anyone still planning on submitting a piece for the exhibition?'

A murmur through the class. Kestrel diverted his attention away, started doodling in his journal. He was aware that Ruiz was still talking about it—'Good, well, you have four more weeks to make up your minds, the exhibition's taking place just after Easter…'—but he let it go on somewhere just up and to the left of his head.

People had started getting up. Kestrel rose out of his fugue, and began packing up his books along with everyone else.

'Kestrel, could you come here a minute?'

It was strange how so many years could pass since those initial embarrassments of primary school that everyone went through, and yet, being summoned by name by a figure of authority still gave him such a guilty flush. Kestrel stuffed his journal hastily away and went over, a little more promptly than necessary. The class broke apart, flour through a sieve, and nobody was paying much attention to him, more eager to reach the canteen and the fresh air. When the door at last swung to, and the silence hit his ears, it was abrupt.

Mr. Ruiz pushed back his curls and looked at him directly. It was hard to tell if the eyebrow slightly raised was a sign of critique or concern, and that set his heart tripping. Finally, he spoke.

'I think we need to talk about the exhibition.'

'I don't think we need to talk about the exhibition.'

'Kestrel…'

He didn't like the tone. He glowered.

'…just hear me out. I know art is a personal thing, and

it's subjective, but this is a little more complex and it's not why the administration decided to refuse your first submission.'

Kestrel watched warily.

'There's a *tonne* of themes that are, in themselves, perfectly valid to express in art, but not all of them are the right choice for every exhibition. The task of a curator is to ensure every piece is appropriate. Your work is… well, challenging is probably a good way to put it. Right?'

An attempted smile, which he didn't return. His insides were twisting.

'That's what she said. It's "not appropriate".' He couldn't avoid making little quotation signs with his fingers as he said it.

Any second now. You're gonna agree. You're gonna say it's obscene.

Ruiz sighed, and it was deeper, more wistful than he had expected.

'It's not just that. As a teacher, I have a responsibility toward my students.'

Yeah, sure.

'So, when I notice a recurrent theme in the work, I know I shouldn't ignore it entirely. I need to check. That everything's okay. That there's nothing you're not—'

'*God,* how can you—' He cut himself short. Too antagonistic. He huffed, and paced by the desk. Fuck, this was a mess. 'I'm not trying to be difficult.'

'I know. Look…' Mr Ruiz sounded like he wanted to make a point, but ran out of steam on the way there. So much for that grain of salt. He lapsed into silence, struggling internally with what to say. It probably should have made Kestrel feel awkward, but instead, it was something of a relief to hear a teacher struggle with words too.

It's not that I don't want you to understand. It's just hard when… when even I don't understand.

And, more than that… what if he said something, and Ruiz laughed?

That would be too fucking unbearable to handle.

Things he would say: *Something dark moves within me and it's about all I can do to stop it swallowing me whole. So I bleed it out like it's a poison. And all the time, I feel guilty, for daring to be affected by something like this when it's clear that Tala has it so much worse. You're a teacher, don't tell me you haven't heard.*

Tala would have said something back. Not the way she was now, but as before; belligerent and in a mood to refute any of their shit. The times where she had called out teachers who tried to mock her, however subtly, for drawing comic art, who flashed their superiority when a student came in late to class and was clearly struggling. Her voice would take on this sharp, acerbic quality and nothing could match it. But thinking about her all fiery and full of fight was too much right now. The memory of that sharpness just became bitter.

So he pushed her out of his head, and in the space that was left behind, Daran Bailey entered unbidden. That strange, enrapturing meeting in the chapel. The words he had said. *You're too kind.* It stood in direct opposition to the crushing guilt. It didn't feel true, but it was *something*, and he latched on to it.

Then he realised he was standing still, and hadn't said a thing. Mr. Ruiz was watching him with a mixture of concern and curiosity. He huffed again, held up his hands, made as if to go.

'I still think you should submit something, for what it's

worth. Something a bit different, of course. Just—know we have people you can talk to, okay? If you need to?'

Kestrel's feet twitched on the linoleum. Almost out the door, itching to just be permitted to leave. He wasn't even taking in what was being said. He mumbled a quick word of agreement. *Okay, sure.* And—doors open. Breathe.

It was only when Kestrel was out in the fresh air once more that it hit him: perhaps Mr. Ruiz had been attempting a sort of intervention.

Bram nudged his shoulder. They sat on the stone wall in the east courtyard, sipping at energy drinks, legs swinging. 'Why'd he keep you after class?'

How to choose the right words?

'I dunno. I think he wanted me to submit something for the exhibition.'

'Oh. Right. After he told you no the first time?'

'That wasn't Mr. Ruiz. That was, uh...' The name escaped him. 'God...'

'Help me out here.'

'Uh. Round glasses. Lots of jangly bracelets. She's the—'

'Miss Warren. Yeah, the course administrator.'

'Uh huh.'

Bram kicked back against the wall, balancing his near-empty can so precariously it made Kestrel's fingers twitch. 'Well,' he said, 'that figures. But at least you've got Ruiz on your side, then? Or... well, what did he say, exactly?'

'Um. He saw my submission. He thinks I'm acting like I'm some tortured artist.'

'Too gothic for the school's tastes?' A knowing flicker of attention came his way.

'Something like that.'

'Oh God, he wasn't *worried*, was he?'

'Maybe.' Kestrel let out his breath, too sharp and too fast. 'Whatever. It really rubs me up the wrong way.'

Scenes from a movie: teachers calling parents in for a chat when their kids wrote fucked-up stories about death and shit.

This was just… vent art. Nothing worthy of that reaction, surely?

He stopped thinking about it. It was getting too hard to focus.

For a second, Bram locked eyes with him, and there they were, both caught on the inhale, in a moment that lasted too long.

Bram broke it with a smile. Hair falling in his eyes, rapidly pushed back.

'Don't let 'em dictate your creativity, mate.'

'Don't worry. I won't.' And, because the spotlight had gotten too glaring, Kestrel launched into a completely new topic, fast as a change in the weather. 'I started drawing everyone from the new campaign.'

'Oh man. That's rad as hell.'

He had no examples to show him, though—the stuff he'd doodled in the fringes of his journal during class was too embarrassing and sparse to reveal—so he had to settle for animated discussion instead. 'I'm making the innkeeper look kind of like, what was his name, Bombur from The Hobbit. Like, he's jolly enough, but he could probably crack an apple with his bare hands, right? And I'm starting to headcanon that Poe just has pondweed foaming at his mouth now, like, all the time.'

'Aw, mate, no. Too cruel.'

'Hey, he's a happy horse. He's alive.'

Bram nudged his shoulder—not quite a punch, not quite a poke. But he laughed, and Kestrel went on describing.

The drink cans emptied. Things felt more normal again.

'I wonder what's gonna happen in this campaign, though.'

Bram chuckled abruptly in the cold air.

'Oi, are you even listening to me?'

'Sorry.' A small chuckle still forced its way out. 'Bethan literally just sent me this. Cute rat pic.' He tilted his phone at Kestrel.

'I wanna be annoyed at you but yeah, that's cute.'

'Rats are great. I'd get rats if I could.'

'I mean, why not?'

'Dorms, my man.'

Kestrel knew at least one person in his block that had a pet gerbil. 'You could get away with, like, one.'

'Nope. They have to be in pairs, or they get depressed.'

'Oh.'

'Yeah. They're too much like us. That's why people always test antidepressants on rats. So like. I gotta have multiple rats, with enough space for them to play, or I don't get any at all.'

'That's fair. Also, that's such a necromancer thing to say. You're just gunning for a familiar in real life.'

'True.' They settled into a comfortable silence, and after a while, 'Hey, I know I keep bugging you, but, you should come out tonight.'

'Tonight?'

'Yeah, there's no half-price Pimm's but there's gonna be a decent DJ set.'

Kestrel eked out a smile. 'I'll think about it.'

Every spare inch of wall in the student bar was adorned with posters and paraphernalia. Gigs and events, Student Union updates, hobbies and interest groups all vying for space like commuters on an underground train, jostling their A4-paper elbows into each other's way. Everything screamed its importance, so much so that it made nothing feel important at all, but Kestrel was on his third beer and he simply felt ensconced and safe amid the activity.

He had made good on his promise with Bram, and it was fun. Always was, once he was actually there. They had nestled comfortably around one of the tables just off the dancefloor, and were drinking more than they were talking, because the music was too loud to hold a decent conversation. People came and left; the table was broad.

A guy he didn't know all that well crashed into the spare seat to his left. He draped an arm jovially around Kestrel's shoulder, pointing at a girl acting brash on the dancefloor.

'Her friend says she's well up for it. Nice rack, huh?'

Kestrel smiled pleasantly, because he wasn't looking at her tits at all.

'I mean, I guess.'

'You *guess*? What, mate, you gay?'

'Yeah, actually.' Maybe a bit bold but it didn't matter. He took another swig of his beer, and the other student stopped embracing his shoulders.

But he just said, 'Okay. Whatever floats your boat,' and he turned to the guy on the other side of the table, because it was apparent he wasn't going to be able to discuss the lewd pleasures of female anatomy with Kestrel.

Bram smiled and slid another beer over to him, which he took, and they carried on.

When the alcohol had infused into his blood enough, he got tired of staying static. The music shifted into something dark and dangerous—just the sort of seductive groove to get the students grinding on the dancefloor, sweating and panting and, ultimately, buying more drinks. Kestrel was aware of the capitalist endgame, but at the same time, it didn't stop him sinking into the music's sway.

He moved further into the crowd, and somehow, he found himself face to face with an incredibly attractive young man. Dressed in a simple black shirt, unbuttoned just a little bit too low. Hair falling in front of his face, slightly tinged with sweat. The face was familiar in that loose way; he was undoubtedly someone Kestrel had seen around campus before. Looked like he was in foundation year, too, not that that counted for anything. Kestrel kept moving but his swaying started to match his new dance partner's. His gaze fell slack and he was completely entranced, taken in by the cut of that jawline and the wild lightness of his hair. The guy before him smiled, coy and perfectly aware of the effect he was having, and he moved like waves on the ocean, slow and powerful and with a tremendous sense of purpose.

All Kestrel could think was *Shit, he's hot*.

Pulled in by his gravity, Kestrel let himself be led to a darker corner of the room, shielded from the scrutiny of the dancefloor by a pillar.

Things were going really—*really*—fucking well. They moved up against each other, growing more handsy with each passing second until it was just the heat and the noise and the closeness the *closeness* the touch on his hips the hands round his sides the pressure as fingers sought deeper purchase—

How does it feel, to be fenced in like this?

A whisper, borne up from some dark depth in his mind. His leg twitched. He wanted to scream. And he realised, with immediate urgency, that he had had enough to drink.

He was aware he was apologising, pushing the hands

away.

The other student muttered something he could barely hear over the music, but it was clear he was put out. *Cockblock*, the word looked like. *Don't be a.* He was still trying to tease, to coerce him into closeness again.

Kestrel pushed away completely. More excuses. The guy tried to get his attention one last time, then shook off, gave up, sunk back into the heaving throng.

Something bubbled in his stomach. Fuck. Too much alcohol.

He stumbled out of the bar, not thinking to say goodbye to Bram. Air hit his shoulders with the kind of chill that should have made him shiver like crazy. He felt immune.

It wasn't the guy's fault. He just wanted to get off—that was fine, it was relatable enough. But how the hammer had come down; suddenly that guy didn't matter any more, it was just him and his own mind, fighting.

Where did you think it was gonna end up? Why lead him on if you were just gonna bail?

Fuck, he was such an idiot.

It's that thing you always do. You get too open and it's all so innocent but then reality hits and you fucking run. Too terrified of what you want.

His foot snagged on a cracked bit of pavement. He cursed at a bin. The way back to the dorm rooms seemed to take way too long. He felt dumb, and nothing was helping.

In the dark and quiet of the dormitory halls, Kestrel felt his way back to safety. Turning on the light would have alerted the shadows, so this was better; better than fumbling for the switches, anyway. The shapes of things in the darkness were unfamiliar; bigger and closer than he expected, and strange, too strange to explain.

He could barely turn his key in the lock, but once he did, it felt like a dam breaking and he faltered into the room, let his jacket drop, albeit awkwardly, and sank into his chair.

For a moment, he sat there, numb and lifeless, body seemingly giving up on all movement as it allowed his mind time to recalibrate. And, eventually, thought came back. This was fucking stupid. But he had an idea of what to do to calm the noise.

He scooched the chair closer to the desk. Settled in and turned on his computer.

Cheap rum and coke still buzzed in his head, still lingered on his tongue, and he could hardly remember the point at which he had switched from beer to spirits, not that it mattered much now.

He needed *something* to make that numbness comfortable again. Something gently-whispered, something that resounded in high archways on white. An offer. An invitation.

You're more than welcome if you want to join.

His fingers hovered over the keys.

Wait, no, I have the leaflet. Somewhere.

Uncoordinated hands fished in drawers and bags until he found the—slightly crumpled—scrap of paper that Daran Bailey had handed him from the back of the pew. There, in even smaller print than Daran's name and university office, a URL.

There was something akin to excitement rising in his chest. A small sliver of trepidation. It was similar to the feeling he got on starting a new TTRPG campaign, and for a second it was terrifying, as if he couldn't tell whether he was going closer to or further away from the fear that had engulfed him in the student bar.

But he finished the task, punching in the keys on his keyboard and navigating to a very basic page that had clearly been put together in a free version of a content management system. It wasn't the Nineties monstrosity he had been expecting, and, in fact, it didn't look half bad. The header was a modernist shot of the chapel's interior walls, taken at a strange angle that made it look like an art installation. He had been expecting trees and flowers, or some bullshit like that. A title below that, and a short introduction to the chapel, penned and digitally signed by Daran Bailey, Religious Counsellor. Instead of the standard headshots-on-white thumbnails that most college staff seemed to settle for, Daran's photo was taken outdoors, with him leaning against a… gate, it looked like, wearing a different leather jacket and sporting a lanyard with some unreadable symbol on it. People thronged excitedly around him, and yet, his gaze demanded all attention from the viewer, as magnetic as it was in real life. Slowed by the alcohol, Kestrel lingered on his face for longer than was necessary. When he became aware of his actions, he forced his eyes to the corners, refocussed on the photo as a whole. He couldn't tell if it was a music festival or some college-related expo.

When he finally pulled himself away from the webpage's preamble, it took him less than thirty seconds to find what he was looking for. Latest events. Meeting times. Next arrangement: Stations of the Cross. Wednesday lunch.

Again, that thud in his chest. The apprehension of taking that first step.

You know what? I might just go.

It was late. Or early, depending on how you wanted to look at it. He should sleep. But no sooner was he horizontal and trying to relax than he thought about the dream, with the reeds and the mud and—*oh God*—the hands, and he was up again, head throbbing, body begging for rest. He did something he hadn't done in a very long time, fished around in a drawer and found his cross, put it on. A stupid bit of sentimentality, or perhaps superstition. Whatever worked.

It was a drizzly Wednesday, but the frost had at least shifted by the time they all gathered at the arboretum entrance. Kestrel recognised Daran from a long way off, something unmistakeable in the cut of his profile. He seemed simultaneously regal and casual, waiting beneath the largest of the horse chestnut trees. In the spring, that tree would blossom with candelabra-shaped flowers, towering high amid an array of wide saucepan leaves. But at this time of year, it merely painted the space overhead with bare branches, spindly as Tala's strange drawings.

Daran's eyes alighted upon him and, yeah, they really were intense. More so against the cloudy backdrop with its murky natural lighting. A small part of Kestrel was trying to translate it into *chiaroscuro* terms, to imagine how it would look on canvas.

'Kestrel! Ah, so good you came.'

Basking under the attention of another was a rare thing for Kestrel, but here he let it happen, because it felt so real and well-intentioned. Daran seemed genuinely happy to see him, and for once, he felt like he could approach a situation on campus without the pressure of expectation. Here, the only expectation was already fulfilled; he had turned up, and that was all that had ever been asked of him.

He still wanted to run from the spotlight, especially as the others present turned his way, but less so than he had expected. A couple of girls and a guy from another class. 'Kestrel? Hi, I'm—' He forgot their names almost immediately after hands were shaken; social anxiety running the show.

'Here's a sheet to follow along with,' Daran said, and he handed a small A5 printed thing over with his left hand, before proffering his right. 'Also, welcome.'

Oh. Right. His turn.

Kestrel shook his hand, and kept his eyes down after just a flicker up at Daran's radiant face. He noticed the man's jeans were faded and grey, the kind of jeans someone in an indie band might wear. Somehow, the anachronism between that and the fact he was conducting the Stations of the Cross was satisfying.

'I'm very glad to see you here,' Daran said. There was a moment, in which Kestrel thought he might say something else, but he didn't, and turned to the group instead. 'Not bad for a first meeting, I think. Let's begin.' Daran took the part of minister, clearing his throat and holding his own sheet up.

'We adore you, O Christ, and we bless you.'

Then he fell silent, and let the group perform the response. Everyone knew what to do; the notation on the sheets was familiar enough for anyone who had grown up within the church.

'Because by your holy cross you have redeemed the world.'

It felt weird to be speaking such a refrain out loud after so long a time. Out here, in nature, in *public*, and so far removed from the walls of any spiritual place, it really did seem a lot more cultish than he had ever realised before. *Maybe you just don't notice that sort of stuff when you're a kid.*

He wasn't sure how much he actually believed it, either,

because he could think of plenty of people who certainly wouldn't agree that the world had been redeemed.

But he couldn't leave once he had started, so he carried on.

Since there were only five attendees, it meant that when it came to reading out each of the fourteen Stations, they got multiple turns at it. Kestrel had not been prepared for that, accepting the small printed sheet as if it was a mere formality, something to follow along with. Daran led them through the arboretum, stopping by a different tree for each Station to be read aloud.

'I'll take the first one,' said Daran. He took a measured pause, before beginning to read aloud the first Station; Jesus, condemned to death. His voice was rich and resonant, filling the space around them and, as he spoke, small spatters of rain began to fall. Kestrel stood, enraptured.

'Pilate said to the crowd, "Then what should I do with this man you call the Messiah?" They said, "Let him be crucified!" He spoke again, "Why, what evil has he done?" But they shouted all the more, "Let him be crucified!"'

The way he spoke, he would make an excellent GM. Perhaps Aaron could learn a thing or two.

'So, when Pilate saw that he was gaining nothing, he took water and washed his hands before the crowd, saying, "I am innocent of this man's blood; see to it yourselves."'

Kestrel only realised he had been fixated on Daran, watching the way his eyebrow raised (so curiously when he described Pilate's self-absolving actions) when Daran caught his eye.

That might have been why, when they reached the next tree and all stopped to gather in their circle, Daran looked to him first.

'Kestrel. If you wouldn't mind...'

The question, implicit in the trailing sentence and the encouraging look. Kestrel filled in the rest of the request with a fluster of paper and a small and only *slightly* awkward clearing of his throat. 'Oh! Yeah, of course.'

He stood a little straighter. Breathed deep to prepare himself, taking in the scent of wet grass. 'Second Station. Jesus takes up his cross.'

Another encouraging look from Daran. *Go on.*

'The soldiers of the Governor took Jesus into the headquarters. They gathered the whole cohort around him. They... stripped him, and twisted thorns into a crown, and put it on his head...'

The story went on. It was an uncomfortable passage describing the humiliation of a rebel citizen, the degradation that would precede the eventual torture, and it felt indecent to say it aloud in a public space like this.

Some wry and chiding part of his brain seemed very keen to tell him that *wasn't this the whole point of the Stations of the Cross?* and that perhaps he should stop his complaining. After all, he knew the story well, had done since he was young.

But it didn't matter how many times he revisited this same old story; it still made him feel sick. He didn't doubt that some of that emotion made its way out into his tone of voice, and he would have felt embarrassed by it if the group didn't seem so caught up in his telling. As he came to realise when the others took their turns, he surprised himself by having the strongest diction of the group.

Later on, he ended up with the twelfth station: *Jesus dies on the cross*. It held too much importance, and again, the creeping sensation of being under the spotlight came back. But there was some magic in the retelling of such a traumatic story, amid people who seemed truly invested in it, that made it special.

When they parted, Daran said 'Thank you, you read wonderfully,' and he sounded like he meant it. Kestrel finally felt like he was doing a good job in *something*, for once, and he kept the words close to him as he went back to class.

He had gotten as far as the vestibule at the southern entrance when Aaron spotted him. That was always how it was with Kestrel: other people spotted him, other people made the first move to say hi. Could be he was always too wrapped up in his own thoughts, could be that he lacked some key social skill, and honestly, the latter would be worse. The first, at least, seemed fixable.

Aaron seemed undecided over what he was doing with his scarf as he approached, winding it round his neck, tying it loosely so it hung in front of his checkered shirt, then giving up altogether and wrapping it around his hand like a wedding favour. It was only mildly damp from the rain, so Kestrel guessed he hadn't been outside as long as he just had. He would have asked where he'd been for lunch, but Aaron got in there first, a big, wry smile on his face. He pointed over Kestrel's shoulder, and the loose end of the scarf danced in the air.

'Was that you out in the gardens? With that group of people?'

Kestrel laughed it off. 'I didn't expect you to say gardens when a word like arboretum exists.'

'Sure, sure. But you're deflecting. What were you doing?'

Aaron had the unique capacity to say things that, on any other person, would make them sound like an asshole. On him, it just came across as pushy, but interested, a bit like an anime protagonist.

'We were, uh, doing the Stations of the Cross.'

'Oh, Easter.' A curt nod. 'That's good. Thought you'd taken up LARPing without me.'

'If I was going to take up LARPing, I'd call you and make you take my place. You know I'm no good with that social stuff.'

'You did *that* pretty well—what I saw of it, anyway. Like, I only saw the last bit.'

'That's different, though,' Kestrel said, and Aaron gave him a teasing smile. 'It is. It's—oh, you probably know the guy who set it up, actually. He works in D Block, he's the religious counsellor.'

'Oh, what, the tall guy? Uh…' Aaron paused, stroking back the hair from his face, and holding on to some of the curls as he tried to remember. It was a few seconds too long. When he became aware the moment had fully pushed into awkwardness, he simply gave up, shrugged. 'Dunno. Probably. Anyway, that's kind of mental, doing the Stations out in public. You guys are like, one step away from black hoods and weird initiation rites. Like, I don't mean that in a bad way—it looked sort of cool.'

'Sort of.'

'Well, about as cool as religious shit can be. Hey, if I'm gonna give Sam grief for this sort of thing, then you're getting it too.'

'Fair.' He knew Aaron didn't mean ill by it. Aaron never did. His was a mutual hate-and-let-love for the church, the kind that could only come from growing up with open-minded but still deeply religious parents. It was probably why they got on so well together.

'Doesn't it make you feel self-conscious?'

'Well… *sort of.'*

They both looked at each other, smiles slowly spreading over their faces. Those smiles grew into snorts, half-laughs that seemed hard to recover from in the short while it took them to get to the courtyard that divided up the Arts and the Humanities blocks.

Aaron clapped him on the shoulder. 'Well, Descartes calls.' And he disappeared into D Block, leaving Kestrel alone to think and think and think about what had been said, until he found his way back to Daran's intent face as he read aloud under the trees. Daran just seemed so… unashamed, that was it. Unashamed of his actions. His mouth a tight, grim line as he spoke the words that condemned Jesus Christ, like this was something that needed to happen. It was so outside the scrutiny of others that Kestrel felt jealous. Now, if only he could emulate that —on campus, in the classroom, on the buses and trains, around the sorts of people who might say what Aaron said but mean it as an insult.

CHAPTER FIVE

Belial

Tala was in the conservatory again. Her mother, like before, was content enough to let Kestrel make his own way there, and the fact that he wasn't seen as a threat was a comforting one.

'I want to show you my project,' Tala said. She was standing up near the edge of the room, fiddling with the bamboo-roll shutters. The rain hadn't stopped outside. Her eyes flickered his way when he entered the room, but not for more than a second.

Kestrel followed her line of sight. A hot plate had been dragged in to the conservatory—the kind that never got hot enough to burn skin, but which would do the trick for heating simple liquids. It was small enough that it could sit comfortably on the rattan coffee table and still leave plenty of space for other things; in this case, a marble chopping board, a rolling pin, a jug of water and an open bag of regular granulated sugar. The box from last time was standing open by the table, once again, its contents disturbed. What Tala was doing, or so it looked, was melting sugar into a small crucible atop the plate.

'It takes ages,' she murmured, not looking entirely happy with this. Kestrel didn't need to guess why she hadn't been given anything that would do the job faster.

'What are you—'

'I'm making sugar people.' She glanced at the box for a split-second, then looked guiltily away. Again he caught a crystalline glint of the things she had wanted to hide from view before. He wanted desperately to get a closer look, but contented himself with the tease of shapes through Tupperware.

'What are they?'

For a long time, she said nothing. Just waited by the bamboo shutters. Eventually, she grew impatient with herself, and went over to the table. She stirred the crucible with a chopstick, pulling up long, wispy sugar strands in her wake. 'Better,' she said softly, but she looked stern. Then, she looked over at Kestrel, and the critical expression faded. 'It was the only way I could think of,' she said.

'The only way of... of what?' He could feel himself tiptoeing around asking the question more directly, and he hated himself for it. Such a lack of confidence in his voice: it must be clear as day that he was way too awkward over this.

'Of fixing this. I needed to... I didn't mean for it to be like that at first, I just wanted to feel better, but... now I think it's the only way.'

'I'm sorry,' he said at length. 'I, uh, don't really understand.' He had expected this revelation to be met with disappointment, but instead, she looked relieved.

'That's good,' she said. 'That's really good.'

He got the feeling that questioning this would only lead

to more awkwardness. So he tried a different tack.

'We still miss you. I mean, if you still wanted to join us for the campaign… there's a place waiting, Aaron's ready to write Leilani back in at any point—'

'I'm not coming,' she said. 'They won't—they won't *like* me any more, how can they stand to…'

She broke off. Fussed and fretted at the edges of the table until he was about ready to intervene. Then, turned to him, eyes bright. 'It's bad enough with *you*.'

Blood rushed to the surface of his skin and he felt as if he was burning. All that attention, all that focus, as if he had done something wrong, only, he didn't know what it was.

'I'm sorry,' he said, almost on reflex, and she gave him such a strange look.

'Why do you…'

But she never finished the sentence. The distant look was back, and wherever she was, it was decidedly not *here*. He tried again to call her back.

'I don't know how else to tell you, but we *do* want to see you again. All of us. I get it might be hard to believe…'

She had moved her hands to her ears. A rogue strand of sugar filament clung to her hair.

'I don't wanna talk to you any more.'

He barely stopped himself from saying his first gut reaction, which was, 'What, ever?' And he was glad he held back, because God, that was a bit of a reach. Shouldn't deal in absolutes, and other life lessons learned from space operas.

'Okay,' he said, carefully. 'If you need some time…'

'I need to focus.'

Her eyes were dull again, her expression flat. This wasn't a point of contention. Not wanting to outstay his welcome—however little of a welcome it had been—Kestrel said his goodbyes, and, like last time, said he would be back the following week.

He left the conservatory, humbled and disappointed. Back into the warm kitchen, with the smell of oyster sauce and melted butter. Tala's mother was hunched over the oven, peering in through the translucent glass. When she heard him, she cleared her throat as though it was an apology, and gave him her full attention.

'How's she doing?'

'She—' And he paused, because it probably wasn't worth worrying her with the awkward way the conversation had ended. 'She's making these, uh, sugar sculptures.'

'Oh, yes.' Tala's mother had a misty look to her eyes now. 'She asked me for the hot plate again this morning. Did she… ever tell you why?'

Kestrel thought about the strange things Tala had said. But it looked like Tala's mother was ready to tell a story, so he just shook his head. 'No, tell me.'

'One year, when she was very small, we went to mainland China to visit her father's side of the family. A street artist in Tianjin made her a little dancer out of blown sugar. My heart, how captivated she was.' She smiled, and patted down her dress for lack of anything else to do. 'I guess she never forgot. Anyway, it's nice to see her doing something creative.'

Kestrel supposed she didn't count the spindly scribbles as creative. And, with all that had happened, he could probably grant her that. He thought about her dad, about all the pain there that hadn't really left. And he wondered, briefly, if her mother was okay. Perhaps nobody ever thought to ask her that any more.

Something surged in his chest and he looked up at Tala's mother, feeling his brow crease. There were so many things he wanted to say, but in the end he just settled for putting the focus back on her daughter again.

'I wanted her to come hang out round Aaron's house again. I don't think she's ready.'

'Oh—for that dragon game you kids play? Thank you for inviting her. I think… I think she has good friends.'

Kestrel brushed off the compliment awkwardly. Spotlights, again. 'I, uh… I'll keep coming back, if that's okay?'

She nodded. 'We'll both be here.'

Before he left, she offered him an empanada, fresh from the oven. He took it gratefully, letting the warmth seep in to the palm of his hand as he went back out into the gentle rain.

This Sunday was just like the last: Aaron was the only one home. Kestrel didn't bother asking where his parents—or his older brother Samuel—were, and Aaron didn't ask where Tala was. The clouds had not cleared, and the air breezing in through the French windows felt just as wet and moody as the scene Aaron was describing. He sat poised on his chair at the head of the table, opening their next gaming session with his usual aplomb.

'A new day dawns on the small village of Mud, and you all wake up after a cramped and uncomfortable night at the inn. You stumble down the stairs, trying to find your bearings after the eerie events of last night. The innkeeper's already behind the bar, jolly as ever. "So, you folks have fun exploring the village last night?"'

'Do we mention the marsh?' Bethan asked, leaning in

towards Bram and Kestrel.

'Best not,' Bram said.

'Isn't Poe going to raise some eyebrows in the stables, though?'

'Uhhh…'

'You can cast a glamour over him, Thorvald,' Aaron offered. 'But I'm going to say that, for now, nobody really noticed anything wrong. Mostly cos it was too dark and too wet last night and the stablehands don't really get paid enough to care.'

Kestrel stifled a laugh. Trying to imagine the horse frothing at the mouth with pondweed and the stablehands just… ignoring it was too hilarious. But Aaron was giving them some lenience, so they took it.

'Um, okay,' Bethan began, manoeuvring her miniature towards the bar. 'Marcus nods to the innkeeper. "Yeah, we had a look round last night. Nice, quiet town, like."'

'"Ah, so ye noticed the town's a bit… solemn at the minute."'

'Just a bit,' whispered Bram. Aaron ignored him.

'"Truth be told," the innkeeper says, "we've 'ad some strange disappearances of late. We need someone to investigate, but we don't 'ave much of a police force, and… well, it's a sensitive issue. Dwarves are missing their loved ones, an' it's just… it's just not right."'

Aaron's acting was on point for the small-country innkeep. There was a perfect balance of emotion and gruffness, peppered with just enough reticence to make them feel that he was really holding something back.

'We should do something,' Kestrel said, motioning Quinn forward.

'"Yeah, we can find your missing people!"' Bram piped up, pushing Thorvald over to join him.

'Hold up,' said Bethan, and she turned Marcus towards the innkeeper. '"What's in it for us?"'

'The innkeeper looks mildly disgruntled at his cold response, but he just sighs and waves a hand idly. "'Course, ye'll be wantin' compensation for yer efforts, and I'm offering a full bag of gold each, for sorting out our li'l problem. So, will you 'elp us?"'

The answer was a unanimous yes.

'"Marvellous, marvellous." So you notice the innkeeper looks noticeably relieved. Then he turns his head back, towards the kitchen. "Bloots! Get in here!" he shouts, and a while later you hear a crashing of pots and pans from the kitchen… then, seconds later a young, clumsy dwarf emerges. He's got this… this kind of wry, bashful grin, and you get the impression he's a sort of a, a kind-hearted troublemaker.

'"Aye, sir? Whaddya want?"

'"Well, these fair adventurers, they says they wants to investigate our missing persons case."'

'"Oh!" Bloots turns his eyes to you, and you detect a tinge of hopefulness, which is the first expression of its kind you have seen in this dismal town. "Well, I'd be happy to help you out, be your, um, whassit called, escort. Bodyguard. Thing."'

'"Thank you, Bloots, that's very kind of you." Thorvald does a short bow.'

'"No problem, no problem at all. Now. Latest lead was over at the baker's place," Bloots says, and he starts motioning for you to follow him out of the inn.'

'"Is your name *really* Bloots?"' Bethan couldn't help but ask.

'"Yer, 's'right. Me pa, and me pa's pa were both proud Bloots of the Rosycheeks family. Gotta keep traditions alive, an' all that."'

Bethan laughed. 'Bloots! I love him. I really love him.'

'So Bloots leads you happily down the street to the baker's house. Now, are you all keen to follow him?'

Another unanimous yes.

'Right. You go down a little cobbled side-road to a small, tall house with a thick chimney that looks like it ought to be producing lots of smoke, but isn't. The sign outside says "Baker Dobbs" in simple block letters. Now, Bloots comes to a slow stop just in front of the door.'

'"Hey, Bloots? Shall we go in?"' Bram asked, pushing Thorvald towards the door on the map.

'Bloots looks at you. "So, um, the baker, like... 'E ain't 'ere at the minute..." And he trails off and just shuffles his feet.'

'"Why not?"' Kestrel moved Quinn to join Thorvald.

'"Is he one of the missing people?"' Bethan did the same with Marcus.

'"Well, no, not exactly..." And now Bloots looks a bit bashful, like he's ashamed to say something. "It's, er, difficult to explain, like. 'E's not 'avin a great time, fair's to say. Spends a lot of time drinking at the, uh... slightly cheaper inn over the other end of town."' That last part was rushed, and Aaron enunciated it like Bloots was embarrassed.

'"Drinking? What, at this time of day?"' Bram feigned shock in Thorvald's voice.

Bethan spoke up, and Marcus did not sound impressed, but for a very different reason. '"You mean we've been paying a premium for bed and booze this whole time?"'

'Bloots shuffles about awkwardly, reluctant to answer.'

'"Ah, well, such is the curse of the adventurer," Thorvald says sadly. "Never a good deal in a new town.

But don't worry, Bloots: you're a good sort. We won't hold it against you."'

'The young dwarf visibly relaxes as he watches the—slightly intimidating—necromancer say this. "Right, er, thanks. I mean… shall I show yous inside?"'

Bethan held up her hand.

'"Wait, first—what's the deal with this place? Like, I want to know what the lead they found here is."'

'Bloots considers. "Not much, actually. Baker said 'e 'eard weird noises coming from the walls. Like something was breathing through 'em."'

'Well, that's disturbing,' said Kestrel, 'I guess, Quinn wants to know, "What kind of a something?"'

'Bloots shrugs. "Dunno. But when folks started to go missing, 'e couldn't stand being here any more, so 'e jes' stays at the alehouse all the time. Hmm. 'Aven't 'ad a decent loaf of bread in a while, mind." And with that, he creaks open the old wooden door and ushers you inside.'

'"Wait, it wasn't locked?"'

'So, Bloots explains to you, "Naw, 'e never bothers to lock it these days. No idea why. Prob'ly scared, or summink. At this point I don't think 'e cares if anyone steals the flour."'

'Suspicious,' Bram muttered to the others.

'Yeah, maybe,' said Kestrel.

'What do we see around the house?' Bethan asked.

Aaron readjusted in his seat, and checked over his notes again. 'You step inside, and there's a layer of flour and dust so thick over the floor that even the slightest movement kicks it up. It swirls up around you, catching in what little light comes in from the door and scintillating slightly, making the corners of the room seem extra shadowy, as though overrun with ghosts. It's enough to set anyone on edge, and sure enough, you see Bloots shiver as he holds the door open for you all with a scrawny arm. Through the dust, you start to make out shapes, mostly shelves and baskets with decaying loaves of bread upon them. At the back of the room are some worktops and bread-making ovens, and to the left is a till, and a couple of doors.'

'Where do the doors lead?'

'The closest one leads to the upstairs of the house, where the baker sleeps. The furthest leads down to the cellar.'

'I think we should explore downstairs,' said Kestrel.

'Yeah, that's a good idea.' Bram nodded to him. 'Thorvald's in.'

'Sure,' said Bethan. 'We can always check upstairs later if nothing turns up.'

'I have a feeling the cellar's gonna turn up something,' Kestrel murmured.

Aaron merely smiled.

'You head on downstairs, and here you find a dark, dusty cellar filled with old sacks of flour and whatnot. There's a couple of grain stills, a water tank, and a bunch of crates bundled up against one wall, although it's a bit hard to see.'

'I'm going to check the crates,' said Bram.

'Just the crates?'

'Yeah.'

'You notice nothing. They're just regular crates filled with flour.'

As Bram groaned, Kestrel took up the slack. 'My turn— I'd like to check for irregularities along the wall.'

At this, Aaron's brow raised incrementally. 'Ah, a shrewd investigator in our midst. Perception check, please.'

Kestrel rolled. 'That's a… thirteen.'

Aaron sucked in his breath.

'Also I have Night Vision, does that count for anything?'

'Yes, that'd do it. So, you notice that at the far side of the cellar, behind the water tank, that the bricks look kind of cracked in comparison to the rest of the room. The water tank is affixed to the wall with rusty attachments, and it appears to be empty.'

'I could probably tear it away from the wall, with a bit of effort,' Bethan said.

'Yeah, that works. You'll need to roll for strength.'

Bethan moved her barbarian into position. 'Marcus stands there, and squats down a little, he grasps the sides of the water tank with his large brawny arms and holds firm, then…' She rolled. 'Hah! Perfect twenty.'

Aaron paused, letting them sit in silence for a few seconds longer than necessary. Then:

'Bam! The tank comes apart from the wall with a loud wrenching noise and Marcus staggers back, steadying the tank before it can fall on the group. Behind the tank, you can clearly see that the bricks have come apart and fallen into a heap of crumbly rubble, exposing a hidden passageway beyond.'

'Holy shit,' Kestrel whispered.

'Marcus the beefcake,' Bram said, his thick eyebrows raised impossibly high. Meanwhile, Bethan looked incredibly pleased with herself.

Aaron shuffled through his notebook, retrieving a folded piece of paper. He laid it out next to the cellar—the next part of the map.

'You enter a hidden corridor. It doesn't look like it's part of the baker's house at all; it's made of a different shape and size of brick altogether. At the end of the corridor is a stone archway that leads into a small chamber. Some old tallow candles flicker low, sending long shadows up the chamber walls to a concave ceiling.

'What the hell?'

'"I didn't know there was a room back here," says Bloots, and he's breathing out real slow, like in shock.'

'So Quinn says, "Seems this town has a lot of secrets. You think the baker knew?"'

'Bloots just shrugs, but you all recognise the look on his face; you've seen it on countless villagers in other places before. It's the look of someone who's just started to doubt his fellow man. You can see the confusion and fear starting to seep in.'

'I feel kind of bad for him,' said Bram, and Bethan agreed.

'Well, nothing for it,' said Kestrel. 'We should carry on. "Come on!"' He moved Quinn further into the room.

'Ah—' Aaron held up a hand.

'Oh no, what did I do?' Kestrel regretted moving so fast almost immediately.

'You barely take a step into the secret underground chamber when you stumble across something strewn on the ground. It's not big enough to make you fall over, but when you look down, you see it's a bone. Do you want to pick it up?'

'I, uh… I should probably investigate it for poison first.'

'Okay, good. Wise. You discern a sticky residue clinging to the bone. It appears to be… mildly acidic, but otherwise, it's safe.'

'Yeah, I'm not keen on touching that.'

'So you stoop down to examine it, and you notice that it's a femur, but it's incredibly small, even for a dwarf. It has some strange shapes etched into it, but most importantly, you realise it belongs to a child, or at the very least, a youth.'

'Oh, ew.'

'Oh no...'

'I'm afraid so.'

Kestrel could hear the serious tone in Aaron's voice, and he could hear Bram muttering into his beer. He was aware of Bethan's chair creaking back as she pushed herself away from the table in disgust. But he saw none of this, because he was studying the imperfections in the mahogany table with an interest he had not had mere seconds ago.

Something was happening, and it was important to think—

To think about what, exactly?

Come on, pay attention.

'I should probably keep hold of that bone,' said Bram. 'You said there were markings on it?'

'Yeah.'

'Right. Might be useful, later.' Bram fished for a pencil, and scribbled down an entry in his inventory.

'What else is in this room?' asked Bethan.

'Well, there's an altar—more of a table, really—at the centre of the room, and more bones piled in clusters in the corners. Aside from that, and the candles, there isn't much else here. Although, the piles of bones seem to shift their shape eerily as the candle light flickers, and you can't shake the feeling that you're not alone in here.'

'Quinn,' Bethan wailed, 'why did you have to rush in?'

'You hear a thick squelching sound off to the right. You turn, and see a figure hunched in the darkness.'

'Oh, crap.'

'Who's there?'

'The figure steps into the light. It moves in creaky, muddled steps, as if half-possessed, and you see that it's an old dwarf, dressed in black, tattered robes. His teeth catch

93

the glint of the candlelight as he half-smiles, half-snarls at you, and for a second it looks like he's going to rush you. He doesn't appear to be armed, from what you can see, although there's no way of telling what's under the folds of his robes.'

Bram suppressed a snigger at that, which made Kestrel unable to control his own laugh.

'I grab him,' Bethan said, and Aaron responded almost instantly in a high, hissing voice.

'"Mercy! Mercy! Ow, not so hard!"' Then he dropped the voice, and looked Bethan directly in the eyes. 'Make a dexterity check.'

'Nine. Damn.'

'The dwarf twists around, reaching for something beneath his robe. In a flash, he's struck out with a short blade, catching you, Marcus, on the outside of your thigh. Now, since your roll wasn't a total failure, you do still manage to keep hold of him, and his blade clatters to the ground, but you lose two health points.'

'Am I bleeding much?'

'A little, but he didn't get a major artery.'

'Aight. So, Marcus looks around at the others, and sort of shrugs while he's still holding the little guy, and says, "Nothing a potion won't fix." Then he rounds on the dwarf and says "You little bastard."'

'The dwarf fidgets under Marcus's iron grip, and he says "I didn't mean nothing by it! I swear!" but it's clear that he's trying to hide a chuckle. It's curious; it's almost like two things are happening at once in his mind.'

'Is he being possessed?'

'You'd have to ask him.'

'Wait, I wanna try something else first,' said Kestrel. 'Quinn gestures around at the piles of bones. "Are they all kids?"'

'"Yer."'

'"Why?"'

'"Simple," says the dwarf. "Says the younger they are, the better sacrifices they make."'

'"Who says?"'

'The dwarf makes no reply.'

'Must be his master,' Bethan murmured. 'He has to have a master—this is totally some creepy cult.'

'Yeah, I'm with you there,' said Bram. 'We should ask him.'

'I'm busy pinning him down. You ask him!'

'Okay. Um. Thorvald goes up and says, in his most intimidating voice, "Whom do you serve, Dwarf?"'

'The dwarf's mouth twists up into a wry grin. "Ain't telling you nothing."'

'Yeah, we're not gonna give up that easily,' Bram said. '"I'm a necromancer, you know what that means, don't you? I can make you regret not answering us properly. Death is a walk in the park next to me."'

Aaron grinned. 'Very edgy, Bram, very nice. But I don't think our little evil underling here is particularly swayed by your words, cos the next thing he says is, "A necromancer, is that all? Hah—you're not even in the same league as my Lord."'

'Lord, huh?'

'It's a demon, isn't it?'

'Either that or an Elder God.' Bethan made some notes on her character sheet, and leaned back in for a drink.

Kestrel's mind raced. He couldn't think of anything from the lore book that matched the profile here.

'"Tell us,"' said Bethan, '"or we break your arms. Your legs are next."'

'"You think your puny threats frighten me? They are *nothing* compared to Him."'

'Yeah, he just needs a stronger show of force,' Bethan said. Then, bluntly, 'Marcus twists his arm to breaking point, until you can hear the gristle as the bone starts to pop from its socket.'

'Wow, Beth.'

'"Ow, ow, ow, ow, agh, fine! Okay!" The dwarf screeches as the pain takes hold, and fear enters his eyes.'

They were all on the edge of their seats at this point, curious to see if Bethan would actually go so far as to break his bones.

'Um, let's see if you have enough charisma to make him talk,' Aaron said, and even he had a tinge of genuine surprise in his voice. 'Otherwise, we'll have to do an attack roll and see just how many bones you break.'

Bethan primed her roll.

'Nineteen.'

'Nice.'

'What do you mean, "Nice"? I don't even get to so much as dislocate his shoulder, it's a terrible letdown for a barbarian.'

'Yeah, but at least you've proved you're intimidating enough.'

'"Tell us, Dwarf,"' Bethan said, in Marcus's gruff voice.

'You wait with bated breath. For a tense moment, a series of troubled expressions cross his face. Then, eventually, he relents. "Belial," the dwarf says, and then his neck tilts back. A shower of dark magic whips through the room, whisking around his head, burning blackish-blue light into his eyes until they melt. His insides seem to burn from within, and there's a horrendous screech in the air as the poor dwarf is buoyed up like a puppet, until eventually, he collapses, nothing more than an empty shell, on the ground.'

'Jesus.'

Bram swore long and low, then took a deep drink.

'He's dead, right?'

'Afraid so.'

Bethan breathed out. 'I didn't want to kill him.'

Meanwhile, Kestrel was thinking. Belial, Belial, such a familiar name. There was some place he had heard it before, some event that seemed like it had happened only yesterday. But it was like trying to remember a dream—it remained translucent, hanging just out of reach, and attached to it was the vague threat that he might not want to remember at all, as if the dream had actually been a nightmare.

It didn't feel good.

It took some time, but he snapped back to the room. Covered his zoning-out with a sigh. 'Damn, I really thought we were gonna meet the main Big Bad today.'

'So soon?' Aaron smiled coyly. 'You should know better than that.'

'I feel like I've heard the name Belial before,' Bethan said, in a tone that made Kestrel's heart race.

'Well, if you're thinking of the Fire Lord from that other system, forget it. This is something else, something older,' Aaron said stoutly. 'I told you this was homebrew. I've been mixing it up a bit with the names, and this one... yeah, it means something else.'

Bram was checking over his spell list. 'Can I resurrect him? The dwarf, I mean. I still wanna ask him some questions.'

'See, the problem with that,' said Aaron, 'is there's a very good reason why he wasn't scared of your necromancy. You bend over his husk of a corpse, and notice that, in the grisly process of his death, everything has burned away except for his bones. You poke at his robes, because something falls out—a small glass vial, and it's shattered.'

'A soul box,' Bram murmurs.

'Exactly.'

'So he was a lich already.'

'That's strange,' said Kestrel. 'It didn't seem like he was the kind of character who was seeking immortality.'

'Yeah, it feels more like he became a lich as a side effect of serving his master. Pretty sure he was possessed.'

'I'd almost feel bad for him, if it wasn't for the, y'know. Horrific crimes.'

'Well, in that case, I'm definitely not gonna try reanimating him,' said Bram. 'There's been enough terrible in this room already.'

'I don't think you *can* anyway, if his vial's been broken.'

'So what do we know?' Bethan seemed keen to get back on track. 'We found a bunch of bones down here, and that possessed dwarf said they were all kids. So I wanna ask Bloots: Who exactly has gone missing?'

'Bloots is looking ready to cry. He turns away; he seems reluctant to look any of you in the eyes. "Th-the baker's sons, the stablemaster's youngest, even the mayor's daughter."'

'Damn.'

'"Hey, Bloots, do you know who that guy we just fought was?"'

'The dwarf edges forward and peers at the contorted face of the dead guy on the floor. "Uh, 'e looks sort of familiar. Mebbe from the north end of town, but I can't be sure. Think I've seen 'im hanging around the merchant's carts before. Prob'ly a grifter."'

Bram cracked his fingers. 'We should ask around up there, see if anyone noticed anything suspicious.'

'Do we tell them this guy's dead?'

'Of course not. Not just yet, anyway. What if he has accomplices who overhear?'

'There's also the baker,' Kestrel reminded them. 'We could check out that cheaper pub.'

'Can we… can we go back to the inn, first?' asked Bethan. 'I have some strong words for the innkeeper.'

Bram and Kestrel nodded, so Aaron launched into narrative. 'You leave the damp, putrid cellar and clamber back into the pale light of day. You march back to the inn, Marcus leading the way, Bloots following along solemnly behind. Now, the innkeeper is a bit surprised to see the lot of you barging in, not least the angry barbarian at the head of the group. He puts down the empty beer steins he was handling as you approach the counter.'

Bethan began. '"You should have told us from the start it was *kids* that had gone missing!" And yeah, no, Aaron, I'm moving Marcus right here, right in front of him.'

'The innkeeper looks at the party with a mixture of pity and remorse. "It's a delicate matter."'

'"Yes, but if you're going to keep secrets, why enlist the help of adventurers at all?"'

'"You have to understand, us dwarves are a tight-knit lot. Getting one of our own to investigate another is as good as laying down the finger of blame."'

'"So it's better as a public secret, then?"'

'"Like I said, it's a delicate matter," says the innkeeper, and he doesn't seem keen to justify himself any further. But he does kind of wink, and add, "Lest ye forget, there's plenty of coin in it for you."'

'Quinn says, "We haven't forgotten. We still intend to investigate," and he sort of, tries to calm the situation down.'

'"I'm leaving,"' Bethan said, in Marcus's gruff register. '"Need some fresh air."'

'"It's about as fresh as it's going to get in this 'ere marshland," the innkeeper calls after Marcus.'

'Is he taunting me?'

'Sort of. Yeah.'

'Ugh, I'm starting to get really irritated by this guy.'

'I'm guessing they've probably had adventurers walk out on them before,' Kestrel offered.

'It's still a dick move.'

Kestrel didn't argue on that. He got Quinn to make some embarrassed excuses to the innkeeper, and went after Marcus.

'Bloots follows you, by the way.'

'Do we wanna trust him? Wasn't he kind of in on it as well?'

'Not really,' said Kestrel.

'I still think he's culpable. They shouldn't be so hush-hush about this kind of stuff; they're not doing themselves any favours, and they certainly aren't getting their own problem solved any quicker.' It was admirable, and kind of cute, to see Bethan being so hardline about this, but at the same time Kestrel didn't want to condemn Bloots so quickly. The whole situation made him feel queasy.

'I'm going to trust him,' Kestrel said in the end. 'Quinn goes over to Bloots and pats him on the shoulder. "Don't worry, mate. We'll get the demon who did this."'

'Aaron smiled at him. 'Well, Bloots looks up at you with relief on his face. "Thanks. 'Preciate it, I really do."'

'Oh yeah, we'll get 'im all right,' said Bethan.

'You can count on it,' Bram added.

'While you stand there, in the gathering mist of the quiet town square, I think this is a good place to wrap up for the day,' Aaron said. 'You've uncovered the grisly secret of the village of Mud, and now all that remains is finding the culprit.'

'You make it sound so simple,' said Bethan.

'It's what I'm best at. There's lots of clues to mull over for next time,' Aaron said, with a twinkle in his eye. 'I'm intrigued to see where you're gonna go next.'

Kestrel and Bram made their way back to campus together, and the remainder of the evening descended into a mad rush to finish their chiaroscuro assignment for Mr. Ruiz. They had exhausted themselves discussing the possible theories behind the Blackwater Marsh sacrifices, and now it was finally time to play catch-up.

'What have you got so far?'

Kestrel showed him. 'I've only really mocked up the background.'

'Lotta moody blues. Sadly, not like the band.'

'Heh. What about yours?'

Bram proudly held up a portrait of a radiant young woman in a rather dated blouse. 'I found this old photo of my gran, from like, when she was younger. Thought I'd try and replicate it. I mean, she looks almost Victorian. I think I can get a sort of atmospheric gothic thing going.'

'Wow, that's really good.'

'Yeah, we'll see… Might change when the shadows hit.'

Kestrel smiled, because Bram was cute when he was batting away compliments, and then he shifted in his chair, fishing for a hair tie to pull those stray locks back to the nape of his neck. 'All right, wanna put some music on? We should get to it.'

The album of choice that night was My, What A View, by a small punk ensemble called Frum. The music was generally upbeat, although it frequently took a dive into more moody territory, which worked for Kestrel. He soon became immersed in his work, putting down layer after layer until the foggy blue background had been accented with trees and hedgerows, and the figure that he had decided would form his centrepiece. Every so often, he would glance at Bram's work, and Bram would glance at his, and they would take a photo of their progress and carry on. They worked in that way until the album was over. Bram reached for his phone, presumably going to start the album again from the beginning, then stopped.

'Hey. The exhibition piece you made... Is it okay if I take a look?'

The question caught Kestrel off-guard.

'I... I guess?'

Silence settled between them, and just as Bram was about to ask where, Kestrel pointed to the corner, the narrow space between his desk and his wardrobe. Tucked out of the way was the canvas, discernible only by the taut white fabric and spatters of paint that haphazardly decorated the edges.

Bram lifted the canvas.

'So, this is... Whoa.'

Kestrel fell still. *What else might he say?* The waiting was agonising. He felt laid bare, and God, there was something so familiar about that, something that made his blood burn hot beneath his skin.

Best not to think too hard. It's just vulnerability. Everyone gets it with art, especially when it's personal.

Eventually Bram spoke.

'You show this to Aaron?'

'No.'

'Huh.' Bram fell to studying it again, eyes travelling over the contours and the lines of action. 'It looks really similar.'

'To?'

'To the Blackwater Marsh.'

Oh.

'But you painted this before the campaign started, right?'

He nodded.

'Yeah,' Bram said, clicking his tongue. 'That just makes the whole thing weirder.' He inhaled, deeply, and towards the end of the moment Kestrel recognised the quality of the sound, and he really should have figured, he really should have known that Bram was about to cut too close and *fuck*, he was an idiot for not seeing it coming soon enough.

'The fact it's a kid is, uh, kinda dark.'

Kestrel would have agreed, but even the smallest *Yeah* would have come out too weak, too mumbling, and that would have been worse than saying nothing. He didn't need to look at the canvas to see the numerous hands rising out of the mire, grabbing at the subject's body. Thighs— neck—navel; which one was Bram focussing on now? He could have been contrary and said *it's not a kid, it's more like, a teenager. Maybe even our own age.* As if that made it any better. So he picked at his fingernails and focussed on the paint stains on his easel. The room was too stuffy—was it acceptable to open the window at this juncture or would that seem too much of an obvious deflection on his part?

Bram's breathing came more softly now, and there was something melancholy there. 'It's really powerful,' he said at length. 'I don't think I'd have the skill—or the guts—to pull off something like this.'

'I don't really know what I was thinking,' Kestrel began, aware that Bram probably needed no justification but too eager to supply it anyway. 'It just … felt better to have it on there than in *here*.' He motioned at his head.

And then he looked away, because if Bram was about to shoot him a pitiful look, however well-intentioned, he didn't want to see it.

'Way better on there than stuck in your head. So, uh, if you don't mind me asking, why did you come up with it?'

Kestrel could feel his mouth twist into a grimace. Still wasn't looking Bram's way.

'You totally don't have to answer.'

'No, it's… I don't know. There's not really a reason. I just… felt a lot of things.' A tonne of those nebulous feelings washed up to coat his thoughts again, and there, in a flash, he was in front of Miss Warren and her stupid bracelets were jangling and she was telling him how *inappropriate* it all was, feelings be damned. 'They made me feel so gross about it. Like… like just because I had drawn it, that I somehow was responsible for it. The subject matter.'

'Ugh. I mean, with the teacher thing, I guess people don't like being made uncomfortable. But they sure do seem keen to tell us how art should show us the things that real life neuters.' When Bram said this, Kestrel felt brave enough to look up at him once more, and he could feel the hopeful raising of his own eyebrows, the silent plea to continue. And Bram did. 'It's like Picasso and Guernica. Not everything's happy. But pretending like it is is worse. And besides, didn't the exhibition tour for Guernica raise like a ton of money for the anti-war effort?'

Kestrel couldn't hide a snort. 'I'm just surprised *you*

paid attention in Art History.'

'I'm not a complete mess.'

'Just most of the time.'

'Only around you.'

The laughter was sharp, and cleared the air of the horrendous sticky feeling that had settled in. Kestrel found himself beaming at Bram, feeling so incredibly grateful, but still a bit overwhelmed, and Bram, who had known him long enough to understand the latter, decided to leave it at that and head out.

'We're gonna fucking rock tomorrow, okay? There's no way Ruiz is gonna say shit about your work *this* time. It's too awesome.' He jerked a thumb to the almost-dried chiaroscuro piece sitting on the easel.

'So is yours.'

'Heh. Buy me a drink if he says mine's better.'

'You're on.'

Back in the marsh. This time the hands belong to a body —a man, a demon, he can't tell, but it's solid and it materialises out of the slick, oily mud like a lump of toffee. There's a smile cracking in the dark, a crescent moon lighting up the half-sunken plains, tapping for his attention.

He doesn't want to look, because somehow, looking feels like sacrilege.

Peat is soft beneath his feet; it sucks at his shoes, threatens to steal them with every step he takes. Hard lumps of bone, white in the moonlight, stick out of the mud, knock against his ankles. But he keeps moving. The hands reach out. The smile falters, and the figure speaks.

I am so disappointed you showed him.

CHAPTER SIX

Intercession

Monday started afresh. Art class: take two. They were gathered at the front of the room, where Mr. Ruiz had laid out space for everyone's homework to sit. He was going from person to person, bidding them show him the progress pictures on laptops or phones or digital cameras, whatever anyone had brought with them. Kestrel was feeling less than enthusiastic, and kind of ill—he'd had too much coffee on an empty stomach—and he would not have been there at all if it was not for Bram's little bet. He didn't want to hear what Ruiz, or anyone, had to say about his work.

'So what's this picture you chose to do?'

'It's uh. A man. Under a tree. In the rain.'

Mr. Ruiz surveyed the painting, sucking in breath. 'Remember, we said to keep it simple…'

Kestrel's eyes fell.

'But despite the complexity—and I appreciate, everyone, it's a hard thing to do—you did pull it off well.

There's—' Ruiz leant closer to the canvas, studying it like he was looking through a telescope at a distant landmark, '—something about this one. Emotion. Melancholy. The shadows are perfect.'

Kestrel caught Bram's gaze from a few metres away, and it was clear that he had won the bet. Bram seemed happy about it; conceding, but happy.

One small side note before Ruiz moved on. 'Maybe you should put this one in for the exhibition.'

Kestrel paled.

'It's just something to think about, okay?'

When class was over, he left the room, head whirling. Put that piece in for the exhibition? No way. Absolutely no way. If Daran, or anyone from the group, was to see it, they would recognise the scene, and the mere thought of that made him cringe. He didn't even know what had possessed him to paint that moment—it had just seemed to make sense. Some feeling he couldn't possibly hope to convey in words swept through him, making him feel nauseous in the kind of way that he knew lunch wasn't going to solve.

The next time he saw Daran was on Wednesday, at the arboretum near the southern entrance once again. The sky was as overcast as it had been the week before, but there was no gentle rain pitter-pattering on the leaves as Daran waited for the group to arrive beneath the horse chestnut's widespread boughs. Kestrel couldn't help but go back to thinking *why did I paint this? Why is this image so strong in my mind?* But he made no mention of anything, and just let the feeling wash over him, letting Daran make small talk with the others until everyone had arrived.

They progressed through the Stations of the Cross with

the same ritualistic precision as before, with Kestrel taking the readings immediately following Daran's, and the other members following on with slightly-less-impassioned attempts. Kestrel thought everything was going fine, until the end of the procession, where Daran met his eye and beckoned him over.

His very first thought was crap, did Ruiz show him the painting?

'Kestrel, are you okay?' Daran's voice was so measured, with a quality to it that made Kestrel want to fall still beneath it.

'Huh? Yeah, why?'

'Well, it's just the readings. You looked rather upset at some parts.'

Kestrel's stomach turned, awash with embarrassment. What a way to be called out. It felt like his insides were being flushed with hot liquid, like a first gulp of coffee. He couldn't tell whether this was better or worse than if it had been about the chiaroscuro homework.

'Oh, um. Yeah. I just… feel a bit strongly about it, I guess. Why he had to suffer.'

Something passed over Daran's face then, an indescribable emotion that made Kestrel feel as though maybe, just maybe, he understood. 'That's only natural,' he said at length. 'It's a barbaric thing.'

It really was. Kestrel could have said so aloud, but he merely nodded.

'It's good to understand the gravity of the situation.' Daran's voice was soft. He seemed impressed, and Kestrel felt his cheeks burning. 'Well, enough about such things. It was nice to see you here again.' Daran stuck his hands in his pockets and looked out across the campus grounds. 'I'm, ah, not sure if you saw on the website, but I'm starting up the youth group again tonight.'

'Oh, cool.'

'Yeah, there's not really going to be Mass on campus or anything, although I won't rule that out for the future. Tonight's just a general hang-out. Drinks and snacks, nothing fancy. Marisa—she was reading just after you today—she's bringing cakes. Uh… feel free to tell me it's lame.'

'No—no, it's a great idea!'

Daran's eyes searched his, and a smile started to tug at the corners of his mouth. He seemed, in that moment, hopeful, and Kestrel found himself saying the next bit hardly being aware of it.

'I'll be there, yeah.'

Kestrel was still thinking about it, the *gravity of the situation*, when he entered the café after class, and Bram loudly proclaimed, 'I feel like I'm having the weirdest bout of déjà vu.'

The whole gang was here—the whole gang minus Tala —occupying the corner table with the comfy cushions. A tall latte with ridiculous amounts of sugar and cream was waiting in the one empty space, presumably for him.

'Could it perhaps be because we were in here just the other day?' Aaron teased.

'No, like this specific situation. My card was full so I got a free one, and I used it to get Kestrel's before he got here. And like, the flowers had just started blooming but it was still chilly as fuck out.'

Kestrel followed Bram's line of sight. The café was sporting daffodils in the windows: the first sign of spring.

'Iunno. Just a weird feeling.'

'I get what you mean, though,' said Aaron. 'I feel it a

little bit too.'

Kestrel sank into the free chair and took a long sip of his coffee. 'Thanks, by the way.' Bram smiled, a soft 'Any time, mate,' and returned to his own drink—a hot chocolate loaded with marshmallows, probably the only thing on the menu that was even sweeter than Kestrel's.

The cold had only grown in strength as the day had moved on. Even indoors, the chill was palpable. Bethan had zipped up her electric blue/candy pink hoodie and fluffed her curls around her neck in an attempt to keep in the heat. Bram was wearing tight-knit fingerless gloves with a band logo sewn on, and he clutched his mug like an orphan in a Dickensian novel. Aaron persisted in wearing his fashionable urban jacket, which offered little insulation even compared to something as simple as a hoodie, but it looked like a sacrifice he was willing to make. He was clearly still thinking about Bram's déjà vu moment, because the next thing he said was 'What if it was a way of, like, telling the future?'

Bethan snorted. 'What do you mean?'

'Like, I don't think déjà vu is sensing something that was happening before. I think it's warning you about something that's about to happen, like a kind of mental alarm clock.'

'I think it's more like remembering things we've forgotten,' said Kestrel. 'Pushed out of our minds for whatever reason. Like, uh... psychological repression, that's it.'

'I think it's just the circuits in your brain processing the event a split second before your consciousness is aware of it,' said Bethan.

Aaron rolled his eyes. 'Yer I know but c'mon, don't be a killjoy. Now, if you could choose between, say, having déjà vu to tell the future, or having visions, you know, like the Oracle of Delphi or some shit, which one would you pick?'

'Déjà vu would be sooner to the event,' said Bram. 'I'm shit at remembering my dreams. Shit at remembering appointments, too...'

'And classes.'

'Hah—yeah. Déjà vu sounds like more of a handy reminder kind of prophecy, I think that'd work well for me.'

'I'd choose the visions,' said Bethan.

'How very Greek of you,' said Aaron, and she laughed.

'My yaya would just call that sensible. And it's true: I don't think déjà vu would give me enough time to react. If it was a crisis or something, I need more warning time. More time to prep.'

'You just don't like things being kept a secret from you 'til the last minute, huh?' Aaron grinned.

'Are you referring to your bloody innkeeper?'

'Yeah.'

'Fuck's sake. Look, I mean fair enough, but also, if all we got was déjà vu of a tsunami, it'd be on us before we had time to run inland.'

'Fair.'

Kestrel's turn. 'I'd choose visions too. You know the Oracle at Delphi basically just got high off incense and fumes from the mountain, right?'

'Seriously?'

'Yeah, it was radon gas, coming out the rocks.'

'So her visions were just one big trip?'

'Yeah.'

'Sounds great.'

'Long as it doesn't kill you. Also, if I had visions of the end of the world or something, I'd totally want it to be turned into some neat mural or epic poetry before we all snuff it.'

Aaron grinned. 'Ah, the meat of the issue. So you want fame.'

'Eh. When you put it like that, I guess.'

'I don't think you're that kind of guy,' said Bethan. 'You'd want your work to survive, but not because it's yours.' It was a sweet thing to say, sweeter still how she refused to let him put himself down.

Bram rested his head on the crook of his elbow, sliding further across the table. 'Man, I get so sleepy after hot chocolate.'

Kestrel poked him but he made no attempt to move.

'Wanna come out tonight?' Bethan asked abruptly. 'My shift ends at nine.'

She definitely meant the student bar, and the thought of it had the heat and the crushing atmosphere all around him in an instant. The problem with that feeling: it was as attractive as it was suffocating.

'I'm probably just gonna head back to dorms.'

'You sure?'

'I feel like I wanna paint.'

She nodded—this was fair enough—and she turned her attentions to Bram, pulling at the cord of his hoodie. 'Oi, how about you?'

'Hm?'

'Half price cocktails, Bram.'

'Oh, yeah, sure! I'm in.'

'Aaron?'

'Course. But count me out of the cocktails.'

'You still on that Johnnie Walker shit?'

'It's not shit.'

Bram raised his head, mouth pulled into a joker's grin.

'I'm gonna pour whisky into a coke glass just to annoy you.'

'Fucking no you won't.'

'Hah—watch me.'

They arranged to meet a little after nine, to give Bethan time to change out of her garish green work uniform. Kestrel left them to it.

When put side-by-side with getting shit-faced at the student bar 'til two a.m., going along to a youth group meeting did seem kind of lame, as Daran put it. Kestrel wasn't really sure why he was going. A bit of calm, maybe. Something different, away from the clustering of over-excited bodies. His friends still thought he was going back to his dorm to paint. It was an embarrassing conundrum: he was old enough to know that caring about what other people thought was a child's game, but still young enough to feel deeply affected by it. Being the uncool kid in an art school was, in a way, a badge of honour, but being the uncool kid who also went to church without being forced to was, well, potentially embarrassing.

Potentially being the operative phrase. He was well aware that most of this was just his own over-analysis. He stopped outside the door. Brushed back his hair, tried not to agonise about it being too lanky and unkempt. This was fine, he wouldn't stick out.

When he opened the door to the chapel hall, he was greeted by the sight of no more than a dozen students milling around, all seemingly trying to decide where to go while some obscure indie rock played in the background. The first few minutes were the exact sort of tepid, awkward social situation Kestrel had been actively trying to avoid since the first time he had ever had a parent-teacher meeting in junior school.

Just as he was starting to feel a bit too spare, he noticed.

Daran was here, oh *thank God* Daran was here.

The only downside was, he was way off over the other side of the room, avidly in conversation with a couple of students. Kestrel had to navigate the route to him alone.

He stopped by the snack table first. Trying to play it cool, trying not to seem awkward. Too late: he was hyperfocussing on the biscuits, the array of thermos flasks, the little sachets of tea.

'Wait a second, Kestrel? Is that you?'

The sound of his own name made him flinch. He tried not to grip too hard the biscuit he had just picked up, and he turned to face the owner of the voice.

Samuel. Aaron's older brother. There were two years between them; two years and a lifetime of study. Samuel was softer and more elegant than his brother. Taller, too. It was fitting he was studying to become a priest, because Kestrel completely and unironically thought he looked like an angel.

But now he was staring, and he had already taken too long to reply. Time to catch up.

'Oh, hey, Samuel!'

He was rewarded with a gentle smile.

'I didn't expect to see you here.'

'Same! Well, I mean, it makes more sense for you —'

'Because of the vocation?'

'Yeah. I mean, I figured they might have expected you to come.'

'Well, you're not wrong. My tutors want me to get as involved as possible with the community. It's not mandatory, but… it helps.'

'Gotta get those brownie points.'

'Something like that.'

Kestrel was feeling good—really good—talking to him, and as a natural lull came in the conversation, he started to panic, eager to fill it before Samuel lost interest.

'How's the vocation going, anyway? You're in your third year now, right?'

Samuel laughed bright and clear. 'Yeah—third year out of five.'

'Oh God, is it really going to take so long?'

'Poor word choice for a chapel,' Samuel reprimanded, but there was a smile in his eyes. 'But yeah, I guess they want to make sure we don't regret our decision. I'm enjoying it, though. It means a lot to me.'

Kestrel smiled. He didn't know what to say, although he wanted, somehow, to show his approval. But what to say in front of a guy like Samuel—the closest he was ever going to get to a literal angel? It was intimidating.

'So how come you're here?' Samuel asked, but Kestrel never had to worry about the answer: Daran had joined them, all focus on Samuel, reaching out with his hand in a bid to grab his attention.

'Samuel, sorry to interrupt, I was wondering if—oh, Kestrel, you came!' Daran's businesslike expression was instantly replaced with a wide smile, and for the second time that night, the warm flush of being recognised crept across Kestrel's skin. He smiled back.

'You boys know each other?'

'Yeah, we... Well, I play this tabletop RPG with his brother, and—'

'Oh, Dungeons and Dragons?'

'Not quite... it's a different system but... yeah.'

'I see,' said Daran, and at first Kestrel worried that he had somehow punctured his pride. But Daran merely

116

smiled warmly, casting his eyes from one boy to the other. 'That kind of thing was all the rage when I was at school, too.'

Kestrel laughed, a little self-consciously. Daran patted him on the shoulder—'No need to feel embarrassed'—and motioned for Samuel to join him up by the end of the hall, next to the stereo. A couple of minutes later, and it became apparent why. The stereo volume was tweaked down, and Samuel took centre stage to say a few words. He began with the priory, and its ties to the college, how *since we don't have a dedicated seminary in this diocese, the union of these two institutions plays such an important role in the training of young priests*. Kestrel hung on to every word, until he realised he was listening to the quality of Samuel's voice and not what was actually being said. His brain stumbled over itself trying to pick up the meaning that had been left by the wayside, but ultimately, it failed. Something about community, the importance of. He felt like a fool.

After a while, Daran stood up, and ushered him aside with a reverent 'Thank you, Samuel.' Then he turned to the small gathering, and although they were not in the chapel itself, merely the hall alongside it, Kestrel was overcome by the notion that he was about to launch into a sermon, and understood in that moment why he had been appointed counsellor. It was a subtle thing, contained in nothing more than the turn of his shoulder and the timbre of his voice, but it held such command. 'Now don't worry, this is all the official talking we're going to be doing today. The point of us being here is not to be a bunch of stiffs—I'm sure you get enough of that in class—no, it's to relax, and chat with people who may come from all walks of life, but with whom we share common ground, in Christ if nothing else.

Having said that, ah—there is one last thing I would ask. I need someone to help clear up at the end.'

Kestrel raised his hand. He wasn't sure what prompted him to do it, maybe some desire to prove himself. Samuel had already stepped up, after all.

Others started raising their hands too, a little hesitantly and mostly out of guilt, and Daran shooed them back down. 'That's great, thank you Kestrel.'

There was some small satisfaction in that.

Many cups of tea and handfuls of biscuits later, Kestrel was knee-deep in conversation with Samuel and a history student named Michael about the potential historical accuracy of Noah's Flood. Michael was incredibly enthusiastic about the possibility, after finding out about sediments from a flash flood in the Black Sea, dated to something within a few centuries of what scholars assumed to be Noah's time. 'If it lines up,' he said, 'then the story might be less of a myth than people treat it. Imagine that—allegory becoming reality.'

He was so passionate about the subject that Kestrel was starting to get a new appreciation for history and geology, although there was something portentous about the idea of such weighty, spiritual topics being grounded in reality. It felt like different time streams crossing over, and somehow that felt more sacrilegious than thinking of parts of the Bible as fantasy. Things being where they were not supposed to be. He felt queasy in the way that one might before a storm was coming. Run for cover and batten down the hatches, and hope that reality doesn't hit you too hard.

'I would stay,' Samuel said, as though privy to his thoughts, 'but I have to get back to the priory.'

Kestrel called up a mental map of the town in his mind. The priory was a good thirty minutes from the college—

ten, if Samuel still had his bike. That was something he remembered from when they were younger.

He wasn't sure if he should shake Samuel's hand or hug him goodbye (surely a hug would not be out of place?) and internally debated it for a few seconds too long, after which he was pretty sure a hug would be weird. So he proffered his hand instead. There was the slightest quirk of Samuel's lip, no doubt amused at his awkwardness. Samuel took his hand, and used it to pull him in for a short, tight hug. It was the sort a friend would give another after years apart, and, well, that made sense because it had been years, and it made Kestrel feel a little dumb for doubting. A few seconds passed in which they were close enough for Samuel's soft brown hair to tickle his brow, close enough for him to smell the linen of his shirt infused with something herby like rosemary, and then it was over.

After that it was like any party: people made their excuses quickly enough once the activity had died down, because nobody was keen to be the last hanger-on.

Since Kestrel had already promised to help clear up, there was no point in him going anywhere. Soon it was down to just him and Daran, occupying the corner of one of the rickety fold-out tables, as the songs on the stereo wound down to the final track.

The tea was rapidly cooling.

Kestrel pressed along the Styrofoam with a fingertip, feeling it yield in an oddly satisfactory way. Daran noticed.

'We, ah, need to invest in some better cups.'

'Heh. This is fine,' Kestrel said, but he continued to worry at the edges of the cup.

It came as a shock, Daran's hands on his own, prising his fingers away from the roughened foam.

'You'll get it in your tea.'

Kestrel wanted to think about how, yeah, that was correct, and no, he didn't want that, but something more primitive overrode his mind at that moment.

It's… warm.

He started to say something, but broke off with the breath still hitched up in his throat. For the briefest of seconds, everything felt exceedingly strange and he was compelled to think about something else, anything, some sort of reasoning as a distraction. *It's just one of those things that happens when people make physical contact. It doesn't really mean anything.*

Between one beat of his heart and the next, the rationalisations came and went. He finished the exhale he'd been caught up on. Looked up, almost cautiously.

Daran's hazel eyes were dancing on the greener edge today; they looked verdant as leaves after the rain.

'You've made quite the pattern on that thing.'

Having attention drawn to the evidence of his anxiety made him want to recoil. It almost didn't matter that the words were spoken kindly, if in amusement. Concern meant being exposed, meant having to explain himself, meant having to *give* them something just so they would leave him alone.

Rising in tandem with that urge to escape was an almost belligerent attitude.

'Yeah,' he replied, and he could have added *and so what about it?* but he stopped just short.

'Usually, people fidget when they're trying to avoid thinking about something. Is that what you're doing right now?'

Kestrel's breath caught in his throat. It felt… almost shameful, being noticed like that. Daran's words cut right through, but it would be rude to get up and just leave. So he paused a while, trapped in limbo, trying to get the measure of the situation. Had it been one of his teachers, he would have gotten defensive, and he knew this because the first thing that came to mind was a ready-made excuse about coursework and homework and typical student stress. Ready-made, but incredibly poor, and completely see-through. But he would have used it in a heartbeat, if only he had been getting a different signal. With Daran, his reaction was unusual. Somehow, he felt like he could trust him.

So when Daran said 'So what's the matter'—like he meant it, like he was absolutely one hundred per cent going to listen and take it in—Kestrel found himself giving up his secrets.

'My friend—Tala—she won't talk to me. I've been trying, but, I don't know, I think I keep saying the wrong thing.'

'Is there any reason why she might not want to talk?'

'Well. You know. She's still not feeling okay since the whole… *thing*.'

'I'm afraid you're going to have to enlighten me a little more than that.'

This caught Kestrel off guard.

'You don't know?'

Daran shook his head.

'I thought they told all the teachers this sort of thing.'

'I'm not exactly a teacher, remember?' A vaguely conspiring smile. 'But more than that. Much of our students' information is confidential. If this—whatever it is—is as big as you're making it sound, then I doubt anyone would be told unless your friend Tala had special lesson requirements as a result.'

'Oh.'

'That not good?'

'No, it is! I…' He trailed off. There was no good way to describe the sudden and fierce loyalty that had swooned over him—anger at the idea that Tala's pain wasn't important enough to warrant a staff-wide memo.

'So what happened?'

It was put so bluntly it came as a shock. For a fraction of a second, he understood why Tala had reacted so aggressively to him doing almost the exact same thing.

But Daran had this commanding aspect about him that Kestrel felt he lacked, and he struggled to put his finger on it. When he said 'What happened?' with little pomp or circumstance, it felt as though that was how a mature person *should* say it, and it warranted an equally mature response. He yielded to the question, and wondered if, in doing so, he was also proving his worth.

'She was… struggling, with, uh, mental health… issues.' Something about phrasing it that way rankled him, but Daran was nodding his head slightly like this made sense, so he carried on. 'Anyway. It got bad. She tried to kill herself during the half term holidays. She—' He could feel the words racing around his head before he even said them, teasing as if he wouldn't dare let them out in the open. Distressing, even to just think about. And then he found himself spilling it out, making the words real in a way he hadn't done since he had first heard the news. 'She took an artist's scalpel to her forearms. Tried to… cut the veins vertically. It didn't work, but she lost a lot of blood.' Shit, he was tearing up. His voice was threatening to pitch upward in an embarrassing way he usually associated with puberty, and it took a lot of jaw clenching to get it under control. 'She thought that—she thought she didn't deserve to be alive. And—and I've been trying to talk to her, I've been trying to get her to come back to us and play games with us, 'cos we miss her, but she won't. She even said we must hate her. Like, I really think she believes she deserves it.'

Daran was silent.

At first, Kestrel was compelled to fill that silence with something. But he got the distinct notion that this was not the time. This was a silence that was meant to be wallowed in, his own need-to-please be damned.

'She must have been feeling that way for a while,' Daran said at length.

He didn't want to think about that. It was awkward. It *hurt*.

'I want to help her. I want to… get her out of this shell before she makes the walls any thicker and blocks us out forever.'

'I think she probably needs more time,' Daran said. 'Sometimes, we build walls not to keep ourselves separated from others, but to give ourselves the space to get ready. It's more like a cocoon.'

I'm not so sure that's what's happening here.

It was as though Daran could anticipate his response, because he changed tack, leaning back in his chair slightly and offering a kind smile.

'Well, she's always welcome at the chapel, if she needs some peace of mind.'

'Thanks,' Kestrel mumbled, and then he repeated himself, because he didn't want to seem ungrateful.

'I'm sorry, this sounds like a difficult situation. But, ah— what's worrying me is how much it's affecting *you*. I hope you aren't beating yourself up over it.'

Kestrel made the smallest noise; derisive, at himself, and

dismissive of Daran's concern. Then he felt something shift before him, and he looked up once more to find Daran had leant forward again and was fixing him with that deep, curious look.

'Would you accept a blessing?'

It was not what he had expected. Not that he had known *what* to expect. So, exhausted and in desperate need of comfort, he nodded.

Daran raised his right hand, and brought it to rest softly on Kestrel's forehead. Again, the warmth.

'Lord, hear your servant's plea, and grant him reconciliation.' When he spoke, the words held their own gravity, demanding his full attention. And he gave it. For a few quiet moments, with Daran's palm braced against his head and the weight of the words echoing in his ears, it felt like a pact was being sealed.

When Daran moved away, Kestrel became disturbingly aware of his own breathing—*too loud? too embarrassing?*—and he cleared his throat, feeling incredibly vulnerable.

'That should cover your anxiety,' Daran said. 'You're going to have to do the rest yourself, though.' He smiled, and the smile shone through in his eyes. 'But you already know that, don't you?'

CHAPTER SEVEN

Bardic Instigation

The next session picked up in the town square, where they had left off after fighting the possessed dwarf.

'No Tala today?'

'No.' Kestrel didn't elaborate. There wasn't much to elaborate on: she had refused to talk to him last night when he had turned up to visit, and he had been left at the door awkwardly, with her mother making apologies.

I know what to do, but it's not enough.

Daran was right. She needed more time.

He sighed, and it was a sigh he felt from his shoulders to the base of his spine. The tall-backed dining chair held his body upright with a sturdiness he lacked, and he braced against it and looked at his friends. 'We should start.'

There was an awkward air that impregnated the room. They nodded, shuffled awkwardly in their chairs, rearranged their miniatures on the board and pushed through that fog. Because what else was there to do with such a moment than try and get through it?

Aaron cleared his throat. 'As you stand in the town square, the mist slowly clears, revealing a pale yellow light from above. The sun is still shrouded in high sheets of cloud, but this seems as light as it's going to get in this place. Judging by the strongest glare of the light, it must be about midday, and the town is more active than it was when you first departed for the baker's house. You have a number of leads at this point, so: what do you want to do?'

'Right,' said Bethan, easing herself into her chair just so that she could lean in across the table and study the map, 'what do we know? What can we do?'

'Well, we know the baker's probably drinking at that other pub,' Kestrel offered.

Bram looked at his notes. 'Or we could go check out the markets. That's where Bloots said he'd seen that dwarf before; I bet we can find out more information there.'

'We could also just confront the mayor about all this,' said Bethan. 'I assume this town does have a mayor?'

'You'd have to ask Bloots.'

'Ugh.'

'Wait. I have that bone I picked up from the cellar, with the strange markings on it. Maybe we should try and determine what that says before we go any further.'

Everyone looked at Bram.

'That's not a bad idea.'

'Yeah, that's pretty solid.'

Bram nodded, and turned to Aaron. 'You said the bones had some strange shapes etched into them?'

'Yeah.'

'I'd like to examine them.'

'Okay, Thorvald, if you look closer at the bone you kept, you can discern that it is written in Demonic script.'

Bram checked his character sheet. 'Neat, I have a basic understanding of Demonic. Can I read what the bone says?'

'Yes. First, there is this sort of symbol, and it looks like this—' Aaron shuffled through a bunch of papers, eventually fishing out a printout of dubious quality '—a series of spindly lines with strange geometries.'

Kestrel squinted. If he looked at it a certain way, the symbol looked like a bizarrely-altered skull, with lazy eyes staring back at him amid a flurry of crosses.

What was even stranger, though, was that it reminded him of some of the spindly lines he had seen Tala drawing in her conservatory.

'This part isn't written in Demonic, but it's clearly the sigil of a demon,' Aaron said.

'It's gotta be Belial. That's what the dwarf said before he died, right?'

Aaron smiled. 'Moving on to the script. You translate the first word to Matanbuchus. The second word is shrine.'

'So the Shrine of Matanbuchus, huh. Wait, it's not the cellar with the altar we were in last time, was it?'

'No. With your powers, you would have been able to tell, Thorvald. That was just a cellar shrine—a makeshift place of worship and, uh, in that dwarf's case, murder.'

'Matanbuchus... I bet that's another name for Belial. Demons always seem to have multiple names, right?' Bethan tried to shoot Kestrel a sidelong glance, but Kestrel was too busy feeling anxious. This revelation felt too on-point, and in a way that was too vague for him to express properly. But it felt like it was dancing too close to something he had seen before.

Aaron continued. 'The third word is pledge.'

'Huh. What does that mean, like, an agreement or

something?' Bram asked.

'I think a pledge can be, like, an item to be delivered as well as an agreement,' said Bethan. 'So in this case, the child's bone is probably the item being delivered.'

Bram slapped his palm to his forehead. 'Oh, that makes sense! And it's telling whoever to take the item to the Shrine of Matanbuchus. It's a delivery note.'

'Maybe a stamp of ownership too.'

'What do you think, Kes?'

Kestrel was thinking about what it would be like to have something so damning so deeply imprinted on your bones.

What he said was, 'Oh. Sure.'

Bethan pushed his can of coke a little closer. 'Wake up.'

He grinned sheepishly—hopefully that would be enough to cover his weird moment—and took a deep swig.

'We still have a problem, though,' said Bethan. 'We still don't know how to get to this shrine.'

'Maybe we should explore the town further.'

'Yeah—let's go back to what we said before. Markets or pub?'

'Markets then pub?'

'Sure.'

Aaron smiled. 'Bloots is shuffling about, eyes flitting between the three of you and the decorated bone as if it's a dangerous animal, alive and ready to strike. After a moment, he pipes up, hesitantly. "Um, I can take you to the market, if you like."'

Bethan rolled her eyes. 'Okay, why not.'

'Hey, be nice to him, he didn't mean to do anything wrong.'

'Bloots mutters some additional apologies, and takes you up the street to the marketplace. It's a morose display of capitalism: the stalls are covered in dull canvas, and while there are enough people for the place to qualify as bustling, nobody seems in high enough spirits to actually bustle.'

Bethan moved Marcus forward into the street. '"Has anyone gone missing from here recently?"' Aaron raised his eyebrow. 'I mean, like, an adult,' Bethan added.

'Roll for charisma.'

She did so, and the dice rewarded her with an eighteen.

'"I knew 'im! The one what went missing!" You all turn around, and see that the voice comes from an old, decrepit woman hovering behind some of the stalls. She smells rather unwholesome, and the other merchants nearby are keeping a wide berth of her. She stands before a basket of strange, twisted roots, but seems to make no attempt to sell them to anyone. "Reskin Fleetfoot was 'is name. But why should I tell yous any more?" She folds her arms and settles in, clearly waiting for you to offer up something in return.'

Kestrel considered trying to show her the bone, but the roots at her feet seemed infinitely more interesting.

'Quinn peers in the basket. "What are these?"'

'The woman looks up at you incredulously. "Can't tell a marsh mallow when you see one, lad? This 'ere is the fruit of the marshes. Uses? Oh, it has many. From sugary treats, to tinctures for those young and old, oh yes." Her eyes shift toward the other merchants as she speaks, and there is a hint of disdain there.'

'"It doesn't seem like you like the other merchants all that much,"' Bethan says in Marcus's heavy voice.

'At this, she shoots Marcus a glance sharp enough to cut. "They try to cultivate the land," she mutters. "Fools! Bleedin' fools. We ought ter only take what the land has to give, not shape it to our own desires." She mutters away angrily. "Our own desires are ugly. Ugly things."'

'Well, she's a strange one,' said Bram.

Bethan wasn't done. '"Why stay here, if you don't approve?"'

'"Oh, I don't live here. I live out in the marsh."'

'"Can you tell us more about Reskin Fleetfoot?"'

'The old woman stares at you as though you have just insulted her.'

Kestrel thought about it for a minute. 'Could I... could I buy a marsh mallow?'

Aaron grinned.

'Okay. Quinn decides to buy a marsh mallow root from the woman. You'll lose two silver in the process, but judging by the expression on her face, your interest could not be more appreciated. Once the trade is complete, she sighs and turns her face to the sky. "The ugliest of desires lived in old Fleetfoot. 'E was a grifter, scrabbling for money to a degree what would put the rest of these charlatans to shame. I started to have hopes for 'im once 'e took an interest in the black water though. I'd see 'im out there while I was gathering me mallows, following the marshlights."'

'"Isn't that dangerous,"' Bethan asked.

'The woman wrinkles her nose at Marcus. "Ain't nothin' untoward about opening your soul up to the land. That corrupted man, seemed as though 'e was finally on a path toward being redeemed. But I only see what I see when I'm gathering." She shuffles forward, her stench becoming ever more noticeable, and she fixes you all with a piercing, intense gaze. "Go to the South Gate. The barrows that lie beyond there hold the answers. But all gods above and below be damned if I'm going to help you figure out which one." She grabs Quinn's arm, for no other reason than because he is there, and he is closest. "And remember this: do not approach the shrine if you are not prepared to serve."'

'Well that's not disturbing at all,' said Bram. 'I, uh, guess we should go to the South Gate then?'

'Are there any other leads you want to follow up before you do that?'

'Wait, I still want to check out the other pub Bloots talked about. Baker should be there. Also: cheap drinks.' Bethan started to manoeuvre Marcus away from the stalls, and the others followed. As they made their way south, Kestrel scrawled a note on the inventory box of his character sheet. Marsh mallow root. Quantity: One. It was curious, how attached he felt to that tiny item already. A strange sort of comfort, neither good nor bad, only his.

So they hit the pub on the other side of town, and the instant they entered the place, Aaron rubbed his hands together. 'I'm so glad we got this far today. I've been waiting to debut this part to you. Okay. Okay, so. As you walk inside, you are greeted by a far shabbier atmosphere than the other inn. It's noisier and busier in here too, and probably on account of the cheaper drinks. You see people huddled in groups, lounging about, drinking deep. And, as you walk towards the bar, you pass this one guy—a lot taller and cheerier than the rest—who tips his hat to you.'

Aaron's eyes were gleaming and Kestrel just knew that, whoever this character was, oh, Aaron had plans for them.

'He's clearly not a dwarf, because he's taller than the lot of you, although, uh… when it comes to Marcus only barely so, I guess,'—Bethan grunted—'Sorry Marcus. Anyway! You all can't help but gravitate your attention towards him. He's taking a huge tankard back from the bar to his table, and his stride is really confident, not like the weary warriors and unimpressed townspeople who usually frequent this place. His hair falls in soft umber waves to his shoulders, untamed but not unattractive. He's not dressed like he's showing off—yeah, it's bard's clothing and it's a little bit extra but it's not over the top.'

'So basically he's fashionable?'

'Yeah. Fashionable. Anyway, his eyes gleam golden—'

'Are they actually golden?'

'No. They're not *actually* golden, they're more like, rich toffee brown.'

'Mhm.'

'But in *this* light, they look golden.' And Aaron fished out a new miniature from his box of tricks. This was a big deal: he usually only bothered to paint miniatures of NPCs when they had a considerable impact on the party.

'Who *is* this guy?' Bethan was intrigued.

'Well, it's no spoiler to tell you he's a level twelve bard from Myrinth.'

'What, is he joining our party or something?'

'That's like, three levels above us. Isn't that a bit high?'

'We get a sugar daddy.'

'No!' Aaron's protest went entirely ignored as Bram started chanting *Oh yeah, sugar daddy.*

'Hey, he's a bard—that should be right up your street, Kestrel.'

'Still think Quinn shoulda been a bard,' Bram grumbled.

Kestrel investigated the little figurine. There was something to the wave of his hair and the casual yet commanding stance. The cut of the cheekbones. The amused expression.

'Did you use the model for Azeran the Betrayer?'

'Uh. Maybe. Don't expect anything so edgy from him,

though.' Azeran was an NPC from another campaign, and one of the models that was most easily available from their local tabletop store. It made sense that Aaron would pick up that model, but it was hard not to read anything extra into his choice.

'Now why don't I trust you?' Bethan apparently agreed.

All this got her was a laugh from Aaron. Kestrel wasn't watching them, he was still focussed on the figurine.

'You okay, Kes?'

'Yeah. I...' He put down his drink. 'He really looks familiar.'

'It's because it's the model for Azeran the Betrayer. Like I said.'

'No,' he said, maybe too defensively, as Bethan started to laugh. 'No, it's not that. I just... I don't know.' He let the moment pass.

Aaron did not wait for the laughter to die down. He launched into the narrative, a dangerous lilt to his eyebrows, daring anyone to interrupt him again. He adopted a deeper, seasoned voice for the newcomer, one that resonated in the high ceilings of the living room.

'"Good afternoon,"—and then he stops, and inspects you more intensely, Quinn. "Oh, now, don't I know you?"'

Kestrel laughed off the sense of familiarity he felt and responded instantly. '"Well, we just saved the village recently."'

'"Ah, yes, that business with the mines." The stranger takes a swig from his ale, and his eyes practically sparkle as he looks at you. He sets the ale down, and it's now that you notice he has an instrument leaning against the table: a small lute. He pats it like it's a beloved pet, and says, "Perhaps I ought to write a song about your brave Golem fight."'

Kestrel laughed awkwardly. 'I don't know,' he began to say, but then Bethan had Marcus interrupting with a 'Oh, yeh, absolutely, sing about our heroic deeds!'

'The bard strums effortlessly on the lute, and sings a soft melody, with a bright smile on his face. "And lo, the adventurers, youthful and brave... Plucked the gem from the monster and showed it its grave."'

'It's at this point that Bloots recognises he has been outclassed, and, still feeling anxious and a little guilty, he makes his excuses and leaves.'

'Aw, no, Bloots, don't go!'

'"I'll check on yous lot later," he calls after himself, and he sort of, trips on a few tables and chairs as he makes his way haphazardly out of the inn.'

'Damn, I actually feel a bit bad for him now,' said Bethan.

'Well,' said Aaron, 'what do you want to do now?'

Bram cleared his throat. 'I'm going to ask this bard guy, "We're, uh, actually looking for the baker. Have you seen him?"'

'"Well, in all honesty, I'm from just out of town, but I believe the chap you might be looking for is," and he points to a dark corner, "over there." And with that, he leaves you to go about your business.'

Bethan: 'I want to go right on up to the baker, and, hmm... buy him a drink.'

'Trying to sweet-talk him?'

'Maybe.'

'Okay. So, you order a pint of ale from the innkeeper and—only two bronze pieces lighter in pocket—you walk on over to the dingy corner where the depressed baker sits. As you walk, you hear the bard strum up a soft melody that seems far too jolly for how the baker is currently looking: you can see as you approach that he's openly weeping into the remnants of his current tankard, and he barely notices your presence.'

'I slap the new tankard down and I say, "Oi, mate, figured you could do with this."'

'The baker turns to look at you, Marcus, and he doesn't even look suspicious, he's just, sort of looking past you, really. His nose is all red and ruddy, and his beard seems misted with… you're not sure whether it's tears or ale. "Thanks," he says, in a voice like gravel.'

'"I was wondering if we could ask you a few questions,"' Bethan said.

'"Bout what?"'

'"We're investigating the, uh, *missing persons* case, and we were wondering—"'

'At this, the baker lets out a loud wail of grief, and it's obviously not the first time because hardly anyone in this pub bats an eyelid.'

'"Just drink up, buddy,"' Bram cut in.

'The baker does so, and he finishes nearly the whole tankard in a couple of deep gulps. "I swears I don't know anything 'sides from… there were these funny noises in the walls, like, late at night. Down in the cellar. Then my kids, both my sons, gone missing…"'

'"Steady on. We found a hideout in the sewers."'

'He asks, "Did you find anything? Did you find my boys?" and an edge of hope creeps into his voice.'

'"We… no, but we did get some information. Apparently there's a shrine out in the marsh… do you know how to get there?"'

'The baker seems to consider it for a moment, then wails "No… Nobody goes out that way." And he falls into solipsism again.'

'I buy him another ale.'

'You sure?'

'Yeah.'

'Okay. Well, you order another ale for the sorry fellow, and all that happens is you end up another two bronze lighter in pocket, because he goes back to nursing the drink and wallowing in his own grief.'

'Damn.'

'However, since you mentioned the shrine, you hear the lute music behind you winding down to a stop. The charismatic bard is waving you over.'

And so they turned their attention away from the poor grieving baker.

'The bard surveys your party with an enthusiastic smile. "I couldn't help but overhear, and, well, I figure you could use some help if you're going out into the marsh."'

There was something about that voice that instantly brought Kestrel to attention. Calm and level and commanding, it pulled him in one hundred percent, all apprehensions shoved aside. If he had been thinking clearly, he would have considered how curious it was, how quickly the tempo had switched. But he wasn't.

Kestrel took the initiative.

'I walk up to him, and I say, "What makes you think we'd need your help?"'

'Oi… you're not gonna ask why he's so interested in escorting us?' Bram raised his brow.

'Yeah… I mean. You shouldn't be so trusting.'

'Eh. We *are* in a pub, and he did overhear us. I reckon he's probably just after an easy wage.'

'I guess.'

'Besides, I'm interested to see how he'd actually plan to get us there.'

Aaron cleared his throat. 'All right. So you're gonna *not* look the gift horse in the mouth and get straight to recruitment?'

Kestrel nodded.

'Okay. So, Quinn says, "What makes you think we need help from you?" And the stranger: "Well now, aren't you a bold one." He looks you up and down, with a sort of magnetic intensity, then looks to the side in a sudden shift of attention that's enough to make even the most self-confident person wonder what they could have done wrong. "I may be a traveller from out of town, but I am no stranger to eager young fools seeking to prove their worth in the wilds." He pauses for a few seconds too long, holding the moment in the air like you would hold an apple in your hand, so firm you can almost feel it start to burst at the edges. "It would be remiss of me to let you wander to your deaths. These parts are inhospitable and I happen to know a thing or two about survival. Please, allow me to accompany you."'

'I'm not so sure about this,' Bethan muttered.

'Yeah, but... what choice do we have?' said Bram. 'I don't want a repeat of what happened to Poe.'

The group exchanged nods.

'Let's do it then.'

Kestrel stepped up to deliver their verdict. '"We accept. It's very gracious of you."'

'The stranger looks down warmly at the young green-haired elf and offers up a pleasant smile. "A deal's a deal. Elijah Grass, at your service."'

'Sam said he saw you the other day.' Aaron mentioned it absent-mindedly, picking at the remnants of the snack bowl. They had not ventured any further that session, stopping in favour of sharing a last drink together before they headed home to perform the ritual last-minute homework rush before Monday.

Kestrel stopped what he was doing—which, incidentally, was making a crude copy of the demonic sigil Aaron had printed out.

'He did?'

''Course.'

'Is he around right now?'

'Dude, it's a Sunday afternoon. You know where he is.'

Fair point. Kestrel shrugged and picked up his pencil again, only to put it down moments later. 'What did he say about me?'

Please don't let that be too obvious.

'Only that it was nice to see you at that club, thing, whatever it is.'

'Youth group.'

'Yeah.'

A smile tugged at the edges of Kestrel's mouth. Even just the fact that Samuel had been talking about him was comforting. Made him feel noticed, but in a good way. He finished jotting down the last few crosses and lines of the symbol, then leaned back against the mahogany. 'Didn't realise just how much I missed him until I saw him again. Remember back in junior school? The forest game, in the summer.'

It had been a thing with them—the usual trio of him, Aaron and Tala, venturing out into the forest on the edge of town, treating it as one big video game, and, as he thought about it, the memory came back with startling sharpness. Tala, leading the party. Aaron, arguing close behind. Tree stumps became save points, and the logging trucks that trundled by, making their way to the copses, became enemy bosses that they were still too low level to fight. Samuel was always there with bottles of juice and a keen sense of direction that led them home.

Aaron sighed, a rare hint of nostalgia leaking out. 'He really did look out for us, huh.'

'He seems to be enjoying his studies.'

'Yeah. Everything changes so fast.'

For a brief moment, Kestrel was not sure if they were talking about the same thing any more. He suddenly did not feel ready to deal with whatever came next, and it was a big feeling, one that seemed to stretch wider than the years he had been given.

But as it happened, the only thing that came next was a comfortable seat on the sofa and a can of beer, and that was enough to make that feeling seem utterly ridiculous.

'Kestrel, it's been a while since you've let me dye your hair.' Bethan carded her fingers through his hair, from scalp to shoulder, so light and gentle that it made the back of his neck buzz. He leaned in to it.

'Heh, you're right.'

'Like, here, I can see the bit we lightened before.' She tugged softly at a lock of hair near the front, slightly more blond than the rest. Last year, while they were both a little bit drunk, he had let her dye it pink, but that had long since faded. It had not made his mother happy, but that had been part of the thrill.

'Okay. Do me like Quinn.'

'I don't wanna dye the whole thing though. I like your natural colour. It's like… like praline chocolate.'

'That's very specific.'

'You know what I mean, though?'

Kestrel thought his hair was more mousy than that, but he'd take it. He closed his eyes, enjoyed the fuss for a moment longer. 'Sure. Okay, just put a green streak in the front, then.'

Bethan nodded. 'I think that'll look good with the brown. Very wood-elfy.'

'It's a deal then.'

The mood of the week. Deals, blessings, promises. There was something to be said there about his willingness to agree with others, but he wasn't quite sure what significance that had.

CHAPTER EIGHT

Cryptomnesia

One nondescript lunch period the following week, Kestrel was eating with Bram in the student canteen, while "God's Gonna Cut You Down" was playing on the tinny speakers; the Johnny Cash version, low, rhythmic drums, a perfect accompaniment to the gathering storm outside. And really, eating lunch was too strong a word to describe what they were doing: they had no more than a chocolate bar and some pretzels between them. Add a can of instant coffee on Kestrel's side, and a tropical energy drink on Bram's, and they had themselves the perfect student combo.

Kestrel had half his attention on the music, and the other half on the sickly-sweet aroma of the taurine in Bram's drink, which overpowered the other smells on the table by an imperial mile. He cocked his head, gazing up at the speakers.

'You think that ever actually happens?'

'What, God cutting folk down?'

'Yeah. Never seems to happen in real life to the sort of

folks he's singing about.'

'Huh. True.'

Long-tongue liars, midnight riders. Kestrel felt his mind skip over those lyrics like stones hopping over water; lightly, to avoid a deep splash. Something about it gave him a knot in his stomach, so he focussed on the next sentence.

'Don't even know what a backbiter is anyway,' Bram said.

'I was thinking about the lines before that.'

Bram's expression turned serious, his large eyes with their dark irises growing more intense than they had been mere moments ago, and the sides of Kestrel's head felt too warm and too fuzzy

—there's a flash of light like lightning in a storm, and his face is streaked wet with rain. There's something cold, hard, at his back. Concrete, maybe, he can't tell. He's looking up at Bram, who's looking back at him with horror on his face. It's dark, it's got to be the middle of the night, and God, his arm hurts like hell
—

Something filled his nose, thick smoke from an incense burner: sandalwood, cedar, pine. Then the dark lifted, as simple and clean as a curtain being drawn.

He was back at the table—he touched it, it felt solid enough beneath his fingers—and even as he understood this, his other senses were so deeply stuck in the mire of whatever that other place was, that it was hard to fully accept being here, now, in the crummy canteen with its pale washed walls. He was overwhelmed by the sense that he had lost something.

'Whoa, that was weird.'

Bram was looking at him, eyes wide. 'You… you too?'

Must have been clear as day on his face, because Bram

said, 'Huh. Fuck. What the fuck.' Bram looked about as ill as Kestrel felt. They stared at each other for a moment too long, and they did not agree on anything verbally, but the conclusion seemed implicit.

Let's just pretend like that never happened.

Back to class. Focus.

The youth group convened again, but this time with less people. The storm had whipped up to a frenzy, so their original plan of crossing campus to watch The Book of Eli in the lecture halls was shelved, and they holed up in the chapel instead, pulling fold-out chairs in a circle for an impromptu Rosary devotion. This was much more intimate than sitting at the pews, and was probably why some space had been left at the back of the nave. Daran shepherded them into the circle, peeling off his storm-stained jacket and draping it casually over the back of a chair. The wry smile he wore was something that could not only be seen, but heard in the tone of his voice; effortlessly jovial amidst the crashing down of the heavens.

'Now, I know it's hardly as entertaining as a movie, but it's Wednesday, so we at least get the benefit of the Glorious Mystery.'

Nobody baulked.

As they settled in, Daran looked up at Kestrel, and, caught in his gaze, Kestrel sat down in the free chair next to him. It was an automatic response to being under the spotlight, and he barely noticed himself doing it.

'Is everything all right? We missed your presence at the Stations today.' The low light and the dark skies outside gave Daran's hair a curious uplit tone, more golden than sandy today. Kestrel was reminded of the glow of marshlights, of will'o'wisps, of—how did that line go in the

Creed? All things seen and unseen.

'Oh. Um, yeah, I...' Kestrel searched for something that sounded less sheepish than *I forgot*, but all that filled his head was lunch in the canteen and whatever weird moment he had shared with Bram. The cold, the rain, the fucking ache in his limbs. 'Lunch was a bit busy today.'

Daran smiled at him, a forgiving smile, and said, 'As long as you're okay.'

Marisa sneezed.

'Oh, Kestrel—would you mind eking open the windows for me, before we begin? Not by much, just enough to get some air moving.'

Kestrel did as he was told, letting some fresh air into the dry, dusty room. And once that connection to the outside world was made, it felt suddenly cosy, being cocooned in this protective space while the bad weather clustered in on all sides. All the allusions to a greater power around him made him feel small and vulnerable, and not in an entirely bad way. He found some solace in the feeling, let his muscles relax into it as though it was a tonic for the strange ache that had permeated his body since the canteen. He returned to his chair, and took a rosary from the little plastic box Daran passed around.

'All seated comfortably? Okay, good. Let's begin. In the name of the Father, and of the Son, and of the Holy Spirit.'

They all joined voices in the *Amen*. Daran's resonant voice carried the Apostles Creed, the Our Father, and the first set of Hail Marys for faith, hope and charity. Kestrel's own mumbling didn't hold a candle to that voice, but somehow that seemed correct; it felt necessary he speak more quietly. A spell was moving in the room.

He had a rosary of his own, somewhere. Probably back at his mum's place. It was a dark wooden one, a lot like this, but with red beads separating the decades. It belonged in a drawer, more often than not, because when he had been small he had reckoned the red beads were eyes, watching him. Child logic had also meant he had never done the conventional thing and rubbed the beads between finger and thumb as he recited the prayer, because that would hurt the eyes. Even now, he found it strange how he held the rosary in the palm of his hand so gingerly, hesitant to impress his touch upon it.

As Daran worked through the script, Kestrel realised he had never really done the full Rosary before. At least, not with all the pauses between sets of beads for reciting the Mysteries. It caught him off-guard at first, but it did not take long for him to settle in. Daran's voice was commanding like that.

'The risen Jesus has proved that man, together with Him, can have power over sin and therefore death. Jesus, you have not deserted your apostles in anguish. You granted to all those who seek you the gift of receiving you in the Eucharist. Through Mary we trust in you.'

And thus began the next decade. Our Father, ten Hail Marys, the Glory Be. Moving into the second Mystery and on through the recitations to the third, the Descent of the Holy Ghost. The wind whistled in the high ceiling as Daran took up this reading.

'And when the day of Pentecost was fully come, they were all with one accord in one place.' The small gathering of students looked sidelong at each other, expectant, enraptured. 'And suddenly there came a sound from heaven as of a rushing, mighty wind, and it filled all the house where they were sitting. And there appeared unto them cloven tongues like as of fire, which sat upon each of them. And they were all filled with the Holy Ghost.'

The moment felt sacred, being with others next to such tangible majesty as the storm gently lowered itself around them. The back of Kestrel's neck was prickling.

It lasted as long as it took Daran to get to the next paragraph, where he said 'Jesus, infuse us with the Comforter,' and Kestrel tried hard to not think of a blanket, and failed. Childhood memories of Mass, of uncontrollable giggling fits at the least opportune times, bubbled up and made his lips twist into an awkward smile. He hid it by moving his clasped hands up to his mouth and leaning forward on his chair, elbows on knees, acting pensive. For the rest of the session, he toed the line between that meditative communal high and his distractable brain trying to find ways to interject with its own thoughts and memories and questions.

When they were done, Daran put the stereo on and set the kettle going. Tea and snacks. Casual conversation. Gentle indie rock in the background. It felt important, in an understated sort of way. All the questions and idle thoughts from the rosary reading bubbled back up, and now seemed like the perfect time to ask.

'Why is there so much focus on Mary in Catholicism?'

'That's very perceptive, Kestrel,' said Daran, and Kestrel got the idea that sometimes he said his name just because he liked saying it. 'It's an old practice, venerating Mary. Something the first Christians did in the catacombs of Rome. And it makes sense, her being the literal Mother of God. But yes, it's a lot more pronounced in Catholicism, and I'd hazard a guess that's because we keep a lot of the traditions from those formative centuries. A lot of modern denominations don't venerate her as much because it wasn't explicitly outlined in the Bible.' He shrugged. 'There's a lot to be said for reading between the lines.'

'Yeah, otherwise none of us would be wearing polyester,' Marisa joked, tugging at her own sweater. That got an easy chuckle from the group—referencing Leviticus usually had that effect. Kestrel did not really find the answer satisfactory, and he wasn't sure if it was because of the conflicting feelings it brought up in him. There was an allusion to progressiveness and he wasn't sure what direction the arrow was meant to be pushing.

People left. Conversation continued. Eventually, Daran finished what was left of his coffee and leaned forward in his chair. 'So, next week, I've got a meeting at lunchtime, so remember we've got Stations on Thursday instead of Wednesday. But also, we won't have as much time for the group in the evening. I'll have to leave a bit earlier.'

The few others who remained said it was no problem. Kestrel asked why. He could have kicked himself afterwards for how nosy that sounded, but Daran seemed not to mind. In fact, quite the opposite.

'Well, there's a band I like playing at the Boiler Room. Kind of a, ah, space rock ensemble.'

'The Boiler Room? Yeah, I know that place.'

It was only one town over from them. Bram never shut up about it.

He was barely aware he was speaking so eagerly until Daran smiled at him, all charm and amusement. 'They're called The Caudal Lure, and they start at seven, if anyone wants to come with.'

'What exactly *is* space rock?' Michael, the history student, looked interested, but in the way a non-nerd might about Star Trek.

'Don't quote me on this, but I'd say it's the musical version of getting high. Lots of drones and reverb.' Daran paused to consider. 'A lot of it would probably be quite good for devotional meditation, actually. Mm, for instance, during Vigil.'

Michael laughed. 'I'll see if it's my sort of thing before I join you.'

'It's probably my sort of thing,' Kestrel offered.

'Is that so?'

'I mean, I like Pink Floyd. I guess their early stuff is pretty space rock.'

Daran's eyes widened. 'You,' he said, punctuating the word with grandeur, 'are the first student at this college to say such a thing to me. Colour me impressed.'

'It's really not me you should be impressed by. I just… have friends that are pretty into this stuff.' He thought of Bram, and wondered if he should mention the gig to him. It probably wasn't his place to crash Daran's party with his own friends, though.

What if Bram went anyway, and they met there, and it got awkward?

He pushed the thought aside.

'So if a few of us were to go,' said Michael, 'how would we get there?'

'Let's see.' Daran crossed his legs, leaned back to think. 'I only have space in the car for three of you, so we'd have to—Kestrel, did you put the latch on the windows?' The rain was buffeting harder against the building, and it sounded like something was swinging to.

'Uh, yeah… I thought so.' He glanced behind him. 'Maybe I… maybe I should check.'

He got up. Daran continued talking. Something about trains, timetables. The narrow windows up near the altar, angled in such a way that it was hard to see how open they were, were in fact open, and far too much. Spatters of rain had dressed the windowpanes and part of the floor near the speaker cables. Kestrel forgot where he was and swore under his breath.

'Is it okay, Kestrel?' Daran's voice was coming from the other end of the room but it seemed so very close.

'Um…'

'It's a simple question.'

Simple, maybe, but the sudden stern quality of it came as a surprise. Kestrel breathed out sharply, and pulled the windows to, fumbling with the latches and fuck, it was too loud. He started to say something on the way back to his seat, but never got further than 'Yeah, I didn't…'

'Please just make sure you do it properly next time. The water gets on the floor if you don't, and it—'

'I'm sorry…'

'—might not seem like a big deal to you, but if it gets on the electrics, it'll short them out. I really don't want to have to fix the sound system again.'

'Right. Sorry.'

The hard edge came off Daran's voice. 'Well, then. No harm done.'

It was a subtle moment, and it left him feeling flustered, all hot and cold at once under the sudden spotlight.

Didn't this happen before?

It seemed familiar. He must have been told off by his parents before, they must have had similar windows once. In which case, he really should have remembered.

But, as he tried to brush aside that strange sense of familiarity, it grew in strength, tugging at his mind for him to notice it, to try to think, to *remember*. And so he turned toward it, searching for its origin. Was it some incident that had happened when a visitor had come to the house? Had the windows been left open and the rain

—*the rain hits the windows, thudding rhythmically.*

Everything feels cold and damp, even indoors. There's a breeze coming from somewhere, and the noise just won't stop. He wants to move but something feels like it's crushing him. So he focusses on the rafters, high and empty—

Kestrel's heart lurched and he thumbed the edge of the fold-out table in a weak attempt to console himself.

It was just a weird day, that was all. Between this, and that moment in the canteen, the only rationalisation he could come up with was that he needed some more sleep. He stuck it out for a bit more, but barely took part in any of the ensuing conversations until eventually, his desire to squirrel himself away overtook the nagging feeling that he had to stay to appease some hidden social quota.

'I gotta get going.'

This was followed by a flurry of goodbyes, some mumbled, some a little louder. Daran merely sat there, and it wasn't until he was nearly at the door that he got up, went after him. 'I almost forgot.' His hand came to rest on Kestrel's shoulder. 'How's that friend of yours? Forgive me —I forget the name.' The words were spoken quietly enough that the others, still perched on their chairs and talking amongst themselves, could not overhear. It was such a shift of pace, it was as though his earlier frustration had been completely swept under the rug.

'Oh—uh, Tala—she's, well, she's talking to me again. Sort of. I think it's good.'

'So she's okay?'

'Yeah. I think so.'

'Are *you* okay?'

Huh. A question he never usually considered. And one that he couldn't possibly answer right now. He stalled too long in his reply, and Daran filled the space by saying 'If you need to talk to anyone—'

'Um, maybe.'

'Okay. You know where to find me when that happens.'

When that happens, not if that happens. Such a decisive word choice. It almost made this belligerent part of him not want to go seek Daran's help when he needed it. Fuck, *if* he needed it.

Back in his dorm room, firmly grounded in the smell of paint and white spirit and all the feelings that came with it, Kestrel's mind broke free of its meditative prison and returned triumphant to the hollows and dark waters where it made its bed. Shaping something new, already. He could see it in the corner of his eye, a painted landscape with dead bracken lying half-in half-out of the water, spindly branches that slowly morphed into the shapes of bones.

He set up his easel. Fished in a messy drawer for brushes. A fresh sheet of hard-backed canvas would have to do for this one; he had none of the good, framed stuff left. There was probably some coursework he should have been doing, but it was less important than following the feeling he was on. So he painted. He didn't care enough today to brush his hair out of the way; if he got paint in it then so be it, a bit of colour would probably do it some good anyway. It would disappoint Bethan if he got there before her, but maybe he should just dye it already, and add some volume like Bram, who always seemed to have the right idea about these things.

Bram also had the right idea about the new Malcontents album.

Kestrel had found it online — same excuse as ever, if he liked it enough he'd seek out a physical copy. This time it checked out; he was not even through the first playthrough, and he had already decided he'd be heading down to the music store that weekend.

One song in particular, *Indelible*, caught his attention—and not least because he recognised the riff that Bram had been playing on the piano at Aaron's. Now, in the late hours of the evening, he spiralled slowly towards playing it on loop while he mocked up the bone-branches.

Write it in black, on the palm of my hand, just in case I forget, just in case you command.

I own you, I own you, I own you.

Songs like this felt like wisps of tree moss snatching at his hair. Almost enough to make him think there was a purpose behind it. Almost enough for it to seem alive. He thought of the etchings on the bone and the Shrine of Matanbuchus.

All these missed opportunities.

Don't let it get the best of me, it's getting the best of me…

He was finishing the outline up, and he was thinking about the lyrics of the song, and about how much it made him want to take the paintbrush to his own skin instead of the canvas. It was a passing moment, but strong in its intensity. An urge to just tear into the flesh, to cease to care about the consequences because fuck, the need to feel a connection to something more than just that particular brand of darkness was too great and too all-encompassing.

But it was okay if it was just a paintbrush, right?

He wondered, idly, if that would help Tala. As an idea, as an alternative. Or would that be too on the nose to say to her?

He stopped painting the arm halfway out of the water, paintbrush sagging and threatening to ruin the detail on the splayed-out fingers reaching for the sky. He stopped, and he found himself thinking of that strange phrase that had come into his head when he looked at Daran today in the chapel.

All things seen and unseen.

There was such comfort in having an invisible, unknowable god. When the connection was inscrutable enough, you didn't need to fret over whether it was there or not. It would be nigh impossible to prove. He needed that connection so badly; a link in to something majestic, something beautiful, something numinous and strong and loving. He could bathe in that forever.

It was a thousand times better than wanting to die.

I keep yearning towards these things. I don't know why. I'm just drowning and reaching and I want those small mercies.

Maybe it was a way of bringing that mercy closer to your heart, so you don't suffer the failure of having it denied by people in reality. This way you always win, this way you don't need to hurt yourself, this way you don't need to die.

Not that he wanted to die. Not like Tala did.

He felt sick thinking about that, so he aligned his thoughts more tightly toward the majestic. Another familiar phrase came into his mind.

O, res mirabilis.

Oh, miraculous thing.

He had first heard it at an Easter Mass, many years ago, back when his mother and he had lived together. The feeling that utterance had given him, when the priest and then the choir had echoed it in that grand high hall, that had stuck with him like a waking dream, sending shivers down his spine as his childish mind's eye somehow connected it to a vast adventurous space inside him. He now knew that feeling as the *numinous*, although, at the time, he had lacked the language to call it by name.

His mother was there, sitting next to him in the pew,

concentrating like a graduate student, her focus a sign of her piety. He had slipped in the lull in praise, and he had spoken aloud. The smallest utterance of 'Oh, God,' promptly admonished by his mother for profanity.

He tried to understand. He had been genuine. But by her stern expression, she had not registered it as such.

Humbled and enfeebled, he had merely nodded. *Yes. Sorry.*

After that the priest had moved on to the Eucharist. *Hoc est enim corpus meum.* This is my body.

Today, at the youth group, Michael had said that those words of consecration were the origin of the phrase *hocus pocus.* His mother had always been more about the focus. Perhaps she had missed a trick.

Kestrel stretched his stiffening wrists out where he sat next to his easel. The music was still thrumming away in the background, the instrumental part of the song winding down into a sad repeat to coda.

He would have remained trapped in his own thoughts for the rest of the night had his phone not pinged.

—Hey, you around?

Bram.

—Yeah, I'm here. What's up?

—Are you free tonight? I wanna get really, really drunk.

He thought about it for a bit. Then, slowly, typed his response.

—I don't really want to hang out. Sorry.

—S'ok. Just don't leave me hanging if you change yr mind, ok?

He put the phone down, all urge to respond neutered. Was it really so different from how Tala was acting towards all of them?

I understand you, Tala. Not completely, of course, but... a lot more than you think, maybe.

That urge to isolate. To get some fucking distance from people, because things were too loud and he needed some time alone just to stop the strain building up.

He looked once more at the message.

Look at you, such a hypocrite.

The voice that spoke came from far back in his mind, to the point where it felt like it was behind him in the room itself. A chill quenched his bones like water.

It sounded familiar, but he had no idea why.

After a while he gave up trying to place it, and just nestled in to its familiarity.

There now.

He put his phone down. Started painting again. The album finished, and he reset the playlist, starting from the first drum-heavy atmospheric track again. He made a cup of tea and kept working, playing through the entire album again, resisting the urge to put Indelible on loop when it came on.

Another ping from his phone. He really should turn the damn thing off. With a resigned sigh, Kestrel rolled over on the bed, reached out for it, ready to tell Bram for the second time that no, he didn't want to go to the bar.

It was Bethan.

—You free?

Huh. Strange way for her to start a conversation. She wasn't usually so blunt. Perhaps she was poking him about the dye job, and he hoped she wasn't, because even for that he did not want to leave his room.

—Uh, sort of. What's up?

—I need to talk to someone. It's about, I, uh

The message ended there. Nothing for another minute. Then,

—Oh god I'm sorry

Kestrel scrabbled upright, sought out his rapidly-cooling cup of tea. Curled up on the end of the bed and sipped it like it would ward off the words that came next. Not that he was stressed she might start begging him to socialise again—this message gave him a different feeling, and it wasn't a good one.

—Well, you're the one who's talked to Tala most recently…

—Yeah

—She say anything about those dreams she was having before?

—I dunno, man. It's not something she talked about

—Ok. Sorry.

Wasn't like Bethan to apologise so much. Kestrel put down his tea. Time for a more direct approach.

—What got u thinking about it?

Bethan didn't say anything back for a while. The silence settled in so long that his phone screen turned off again, and when the next message came through, it buzzed into life.

—I had a bad dream too.

Kestrel's heart thumped. He thought of his own dreams, of the strange vision he and Bram had shared. Why was this happening now? Were they all just feeling some kind of communal guilt thing? Like mass hysteria.

It wouldn't be that weird. He remembered years back, watching scary movies with a bunch of friends; everyone had nightmares that night, everyone shared the fear. A bad feeling could spread like the common cold, that's all there was to it.

—What kind of bad dream?

And then, because that might have been too quick and

too pushy,

—You don't have to talk about it.

For a while, she didn't.

Then,

—I was being dragged into this oily pit. It was so dark… God, I thought it was gonna kill me, and I think it was my own fault, because I didn't…

Kestrel thought of his own dreams, the dark water, the hands grabbing and pulling. He didn't know what to say. Then Bethan added,

—You were there.

She didn't say anything more after that. The familiar nausea returned to Kestrel's stomach, an old friend twisting and turning at his guts. He felt too exposed, through her revelation, and when he thought about it that seemed absurd. But there it was.

Making it all about yourself again, are we?

He breathed out too sharply. Swore to the empty room. He so desperately wanted to ask why he was there in her dream, what he had been doing there, what had happened to him, but every time he tried to force his mind to go there, it swerved away like it was avoiding oncoming traffic.

It was probably better that he say something positive to her, even if he didn't believe it himself. Absolutely no way was he mentioning his own nightmares; why make a bad thing worse?

—Hey, it'll be okay. It's just a dream.

—I don't know…

—Look, you care about Tala, right? That's probably why you're getting these dreams. It's just… your worries surfacing in your subconscious.

He felt so disingenuous as he said it. It felt like he was

merely emulating what a responsible person would say. But it seemed to have the desired effect.

—I guess. Ugh I'm sorry for bothering you

—Seriously, it's okay

—Kay

No more texts came after that. Kestrel tried to ignore the squirming in his gut, the growing uncertainty about what was happening to all of his friends. Some dark cloud was bearing down on them all, like Tolkien's damned shadow in the east. The album ended, and the shadow grew, and Kestrel went to bed with the unease still festering away inside him.

CHAPTER NINE

The Shrine of Matanbuchus

The rain has turned his clothes damp and soggy, that's the first thing he's aware of. It feels uncomfortable, but as he looks around himself for some comfort he sees no solutions, only hillocks of long grass and the stumps of dead trees. His pulse rises. He's in the marsh.

There is somebody there with him, and he is aware of this fact long before he has any proof of it from his senses. His neck prickles and he turns around. A shadow behind him, a moment of solid panic, but hey, it's okay, it's only—

Elijah Grass looks down at him, smiling pleasantly like a fellow hiker might when met upon the road. But something is off, something is wrong. There is more to the darkness, there is a shape in the distance, and he needs no gift of sight to tell that whatever it is does not wear a friendly face. Any moment it is going to see him, and then there will be no refuge: he imagines its bracken-thick limbs ready to snap and twist his bones into submission, he feels it drag him down into the mud and really, it's only a matter of time. The fear roots him to the spot. Elijah sighs behind him, as though he understands this too. Lips all but brush his ear as Elijah indicates to the shape in the mist, and says, in a voice thick as treacle toffee, 'How would it feel… if he opened you up?'

He draws a finger smoothly across his chest, still leaning in by his ear. His touch is as soft and as warm as his breath.

'What—what do you mean?' His stuttering is an embarrassment in the cold air. He can feel Elijah's breath quicken as he chuckles into his neck.

'I think you know what I mean.'

Kestrel woke with a spasm that lanced through his calf, making it cramp up, making him yell. He grabbed the muscle, as if squeezing it so desperately would stop the pain. *Hold it there, grit your teeth, wait for the wave to subside.* Eventually it let up, his calf turned from petrified rock back to soft and pliant flesh once more, and he was able to release his grip, a shuddering sigh escaping his lips.

Why had Elijah been so menacing in his dream? And why did he seem so familiar? Fuck, it didn't matter, it didn't matter, because the more important thing was that coiled, warm feeling in his chest. It took him a while to place the feeling, he had to wait until his heart rate had come down to a more normal level.

Just like Bethan had described last night, it was guilt.

He had to go and talk to Tala again. To try harder. If he could kill every bird with one stone—help Tala, get Mr Ruiz off his back, stop Bethan from worrying—he would.

The painting by his desk had fully dried by now. Hands reaching out to the skies for absolution.

The door to the small bungalow opened, and it was Tala

behind it, something Kestrel had not been anticipating. The day was brighter than the one before, and Tala fitted in with it well, sporting a smile as wide as the daffodils lining the garden path. He had barely said hello when she ducked her head back into the house, all attention elsewhere. 'Yeah, it's just Kestrel, Ma!'

This time he heard it—her mother's reedy reply coming from another part of the house. Then Tala was back, all focus on him as she held the door open.

'Come on, don't stand around outside!'

He smiled and stepped inside, slipping his shoes off and following Tala into the kitchen.

'Want a drink?'

'Uh, yeah… coke?'

He still didn't care for coke but hell, it was something to say.

'Gotcha covered.' She took a massive bottle out of the fridge, poured him a cold glass. He studied her face as covertly as he could, trying to gauge the sudden change in her demeanour. Aaron had told him, some time ago, that sometimes people became immensely positive just after deciding to commit suicide. Something about the relief giving them euphoria.

It didn't feel like that was happening here. It still gave him pause.

'Thanks,' he said, drinking deep. The walk had tired him out more than he had expected.

Tala didn't drink anything herself; she seemed content just to watch him.

He didn't know how else to ask so he opted for bluntness. 'You doing okay?'

She pouted, straightening a tea towel where it hung on the oven door. Then, facing him, her chestnut eyes soft and deep, she said, 'I feel like I'm awake for the first time in ages. I hope it lasts.'

In that moment she had returned to the way she was before. A shimmer in the air around them, a memory of a forest lush and deep. She looked now like she did then, they were twelve, Aaron was fighting to lead the way but she could run faster. Shrieking when she startled an honest-to-God deer among the ferns. And the laugh of relief that came after, it was so infectious. *I thought it was going to be a monster.*

'I hope it lasts too,' he said.

'Heh, why are you smiling like that?'

'I was, uh, just thinking about the time you jump-scared that deer. That was a good day.'

She smiled back at him, fondly. 'It was.' Then the memory of leaves whirled away and she turned to the kitchen countertop. 'You know what the most annoying thing is?'

'No?'

'It's this...' Tala tapped on the wooden knife block, which Kestrel only just realised was empty. 'She's locked them away somewhere. It's stupid. If I wanted to, I'd...' The words died in her throat. 'Never mind.'

'It'd probably piss me off too,' Kestrel offered. 'Like, how can it *not* remind you of it? I dunno, I... I hate being put into focus like that. It makes it so obvious they're tiptoeing around you.' He huffed and leaned against the tabletop. 'Like negative space in art—you remember those lessons. The absence of something says just as much as the presence of something.'

'Yeah,' Tala murmured. 'That's exactly it.' She dragged her hand away from the knife block and turned her deep brown eyes to him. 'I knew you'd know what to say.'

Kestrel rarely felt like he knew the right thing to say, so he just returned her smile. Tala seemed not to notice his awkwardness; she was already looking back at the block, the cutlery drawer, the cupboards.

'Had a hard time putting things into words recently.'

He nodded.

'Come on,' she said, 'let me show you something.'

She took him into the conservatory.

'These are my sugar people.'

The little totems—fruits of her melting spoon, work of human hands—lined the windowsill, catching the shafts of light that made it through the blinds and glittering like gemstones. Their translucence reminded Kestrel of stained-glass windows in a church, only without the rainbow colours, all of them relegated to that burnished white-gold shade that half-caramelised sugar took on.

'There's so many.'

He wished he hadn't said it, because she withdrew just a tiny bit. 'Yeah, I... At first I just needed to make something, work out some feelings a bit. I, uh, never expected it to grow so much.' She looked oddly troubled by that last part.

'That's okay. I understand the need to vent with art, it's not a bad thing.' Then he turned back to the sculptures, caught up again in their light. 'It's impressive,' he said, and he meant it.

She seemed to find this encouraging enough.

So he continued to look. Not all of them were people, like the name implied. Some seemed to be buildings, vehicles, objects. Kestrel breathed out softly in awe, and wandered over, a little hesitantly at first, as though he was approaching an altar, wanting to venerate but unsure how.

'Are you meant to eat them?'

'What? No, you're definitely not meant to eat them. The… the moulding process makes it a bit, uh, unsanitary to eat.' She paused to consider. 'Not like it'd kill us though. I mean, I remember us sharing lollipops in primary school.'

It was good, hearing her talk like this. Some of that pep coming back into her voice, making her more recognisable as herself, Tala, the girl he'd grown up with.

He reached out. 'Can I—'

'No! No, don't!'

He froze, his hand inches away from the nearest sculpture, a little thing that looked almost like a Hot Wheels car. For a moment he was in limbo, too afraid to move forward or back, but then the sound of Tala's panicked breaths brought him back into action and he mumbled a quick sorry and withdrew his hand.

It felt like a barrier had come close to breaking.

Then the moment was gone. He wasn't going to press the issue any further and risk ruining what rapport he had built up, so he shifted his attention away from the sculptures entirely, studying the bird bath in the garden.

'I probably sound like a stuck record at this point, but we'd still love you to come take part in the campaign.'

'Oh,' she said, 'you're not a stuck record. The needle keeps jumping, that's all, but it's not stuck.'

'I…' And he trailed off, because that one had him stumped.

Tala did not attempt to salvage the conversation from her strange tangent, so Kestrel tried again.

'Um, yeah, so. We all still want to see you there. On Sunday. At Aaron's place.'

This time it seemed as though Tala heard his words properly. She replied with a 'Yeah! Maybe,' and she appeared genuinely excited about it.

'I can text you beforehand, to remind you?'

Tala paused for thought, brushing a strand of dark hair from her face. 'Yeah. Yeah, that's fine.' And then, more excitedly, like the sun emerging from behind a veil of cloud, 'I'll be there, I'll be there for sure. This'll be fun!'

Sunday afternoon had Kestrel dawdling outside Aaron's house, anxiously checking his phone for a reply from Tala. He had texted her hours ago.

It was stupid to worry. Could be that she was inside already. Could also be that she had changed her mind, and that was okay too.

'Everything okay?' Bethan, coming up the driveway, calling out to him with a cheery smile on her face.

'Oh! Uh…' He slipped his phone into his pocket. 'I thought Tala might be coming, I was just checking my phone.'

The pained expression on Bethan's face didn't last more than an instant. She smiled, although it was a little reaching. 'Any luck?'

It would have been tempting to say 'What do you think?' but he didn't. Little point in being so caustic when the afternoon had only just begun. He shook his head. She pouted in commiseration and patted his shoulder. 'Ah well. Come on, then.'

In they went under the high ceilings, where light spilled in like broad paint strokes. The air conditioning was on; the hanging beads that led into the kitchen swayed and clattered together gently. Outside, it felt like spring. Inside, it was more like summer. Aaron was already set up, and so was Bram, perched by his laptop with a gentle guitar melody playing.

Aaron spread wide his hands over his tabletop empire.

'We ready to begin?'

Kestrel looked to Aaron. 'No Tala. She seemed keen to come though, so I'll keep checking my phone.'

A brief nod. 'Let's keep hoping. I prepared a hook to bring her back in if she does.'

It was such a summery day that Kestrel had completely forgotten the mood under which they had ended the previous session. But no sooner had Aaron opened than he was transported back to the dismal village with its waterlogged borders, feeling that slow creep of apprehension as they stood at that old South Gate, with the weight of a murder behind them, and the evening foray into the swamps about to begin.

The knock on the door made them all jump.

'Jesus Christ.'

'Well that's weird. Mum and Dad aren't meant to be back until Wednesday.'

'So who the hell?'

Barely a second after his heart rate peaked, Kestrel had a thought.

'What if it's Tala?'

He got up from the table before any of the others, making a beeline for the door, and he was rewarded by being absolutely correct. Tala looked just as uncannily fresh-faced as before; this was a repeat of the other day, only their positions were reversed. Her smile was infectious and he found himself beaming right back as he welcomed her in. He almost didn't notice the slight guarded quality to the way she held herself as she stepped over the threshold. It was there, though, an afterthought that he might never have noticed, had he not visited her so many times these past weeks.

He couldn't fault that. If it were him, he'd be anxious as

hell, panicking over what kind of reception he would get. 'We're just set up in the living room,' he said, pointing down the hall (was it insulting to point? She knew the house as well as any of them). And, it might have been dumb, but as he followed her into the living room he felt as protective of her as Marcus was of his fellow party members. There was the urge to suddenly place himself in harm's way instead of her, as if something terrifying was headed straight for them.

What actually happened when Tala entered the room was an eruption of cheers and exclamations. *Tala! Nice to see you! So awesome you came, oh my God!* Gratitude all around.

'Gosh, it's been ages since I've been round here,' she said, her voice all soft and dreamlike. She moved to the dining table like some fae creature trying to learn what it was to be human.

'We were just about to get to a really cool bit,' Aaron said. 'You wanna get Leilani back in on the adventure? Or you just wanna watch? I've, uh, prepared for both, so don't worry either way.'

'I... would like to join in.' She smiled lopsidedly and sank down into the chair next to Bethan, who immediately passed her the unopened can of coke she had been about to drink.

Aaron grinned and fished about in his bag of tricks for the Leilani miniature, placing the lithe elven druid on the table amid the others. With orange hair and clothes that shone like rays of light, she was like the sun at the centre of the group.

'Okay, let's get you up to speed.' Aaron outlined the journey so far, but quickly enough that it didn't drag on, conscious of the clock ticking away. 'And for ease of storytelling, let's just say you were already in the party when Elijah showed up, having come back from your meditation, uh, sabbatical thing.'

'Who's Elijah?'

'Some NPC who offered to show us the way to the shrine.'

Tala nodded. 'Well, good for him. Right, I'm ready, guys. Let's do this!'

It was so unbelievably nice to hear her excitable voice, to see her energy bubble up once again. Kestrel could feel the glow, spreading across the table, through each of them, and Aaron somehow infused it into his tone as he began the adventure.

'It's barely mid-afternoon but already the sun has begun to sink, lighting up the clouds in a dusky glow, and it's under this waning afternoon light that you prepare to set off. Your ebullient new acquaintance Elijah Grass leans against one of the pillars, basking in the attention he's getting from the lot of you, waiting for one of you to make the next move. He seems in no rush, but still his eyes sparkle, and you get the sense that he quite enjoys this adventuring business.'

He may have been weaving a tale in an ordinary house on an ordinary Sunday afternoon, and the prose may have been Aaron's own shade of purple, but Kestrel was right there in the little dwarven town, watching Elijah watch him with those bright, intense eyes.

'I guess I'll speak up first,' said Bram. '"Right, er, shall we get going, then?"'

'Elijah pushes himself forward so he's no longer leaning, but standing in front of you. He's only just taller than Marcus, but with his sheer presence and charisma, he seems to tower over even him. "It won't do to start off without first knowing where and why you are headed."'

'Should we show him the symbol?'

'Hmm. Dunno.'

'I mean, we're trusting him so far, right? I say we just do it,' said Kestrel.

Bram looked to Aaron. 'Okay, I take the bone from my satchel and show Elijah. Oh yeah, and I tell him, it's got some acid residue on it but not enough to burn you. Actually, I've kept it wrapped in velvet so, it's probably all gone now. Probably.'

'He takes the bone from you, gently as can be, and turns it over with nimble fingers, exploring every facet of it. His eyebrows perk up in a curious way when he sees the sigil etched into it.' Here Aaron leaned in, putting on his best character voice once again, somehow making Elijah sound incredibly rich and storied. It was a voice that made Kestrel want to both run away from it and edge closer at the same time. '"Well now, that is something I never expected to see. I do know the symbol, yes. As do many from these parts, although they would be rather reluctant to talk about it."'

'"Why is that?"' Kestrel couldn't help himself.

'Elijah looks at you directly. "What was your name? I don't think you ever said."'

For a moment, Kestrel almost blanked and said his own name. He stammered in response, a stream of not-quite-syllables that eventually became '"Oh, uh… Quinn Therion."'

'"Well, Quinn, now we have been formally introduced." Elijah holds out his hand, expecting you to take it.'

'I, uh… I shake his hand, I guess.'

'You reach out to shake his hand and he takes it gently, and it's somewhere between a handshake and just him, like, lifting it towards his face slightly with a small, gentlemanly inclination of his head.'

'I feel like I'm in a Jane Austen novel,' Kestrel murmured.

'How romantic,' Bethan said in a teasing tone that Kestrel sometimes thought she reserved only for him.

'"And your friends are?"'

'Thorvald—'

'I'm a necromancer.'

'Leilani—'

'Hi, pleased to meet you! I'm a druid.'

'—and Marcus the Barbarian."'

Bethan put on her deepest, most orcish voice. '"I'm not shaking his hand."'

'"Suit yourself," Elijah says, with a smirk. "Pleasure to meet you, nonetheless. Now, the pattern on the bones, my dear friends, is the sigil of an ancient demon. Old magic, the kind one really shouldn't tamper with. They say his lair is south of here, deep in the swamp."'

'"And let me guess,"' said Bethan, '"you just happen to know where that lair is?"'

'"I know of some ruins, and I have seen that sigil there. Now, I am far from the only one who does, but I am probably the only one who would be willing to lead you there." He gesticulates at the town around them with a flourish.'

'Elijah's so over the top,' said Tala. 'I'm not sure if I like him or not, yet, though.'

'I like him,' said Bethan.

'I don't. Well, Thorvald doesn't.'

'Marcus totally doesn't either. But c'mon—he's so mysterious!' Bethan looked to Kestrel, expecting corroboration.

Kestrel didn't really know what to say, so he settled on a

vague 'Hm', and hoped that would be enough to move the topic on.

Aaron took this as his cue to continue.

'So Elijah leads you through the marsh. "Footing is tricky—do watch your step."'

'Don't need to tell me twice. I still haven't forgotten about my horse,' Bram said.

'Wait, did something happen to Poe?' Tala looked at the group with wide eyes.

'Uh…'

'Yeah, Bram rolled bad last time, so Poe kind of drowned in the river.'

'What? Oh man, that's so messed up.'

'It's okay, though. We rezzed him.'

'Yeah, he's a little traumatised, but he's okay,' said Aaron, and he started to position their miniatures in incremental steps beyond the gates. 'Elijah beckons, and you follow. You pass the same scenery as before, trodding on through the slick, thick mud. Blue grasses grow in bunches, making hummocky knee-high hills all around you, each blade thin and spindly on its own. They almost look like sea urchins, and they rustle with the activity of tiny marsh creatures as you walk between them—frogs, gnats, water voles, things like that.'

Bethan kept Marcus close to Elijah's figurine as they travelled, and not for the first time in their adventures, Kestrel found it endearing how ready she was to protect, to watch out for them.

On to the next map spread.

'The air grows colder, and by now Elijah has led you back up to the stream you had attempted—poorly—to cross the other day.'

'I hate this stream.'

'Oh, is this where…'

'The Poe thing, yeah.'

'Do we have to, uh, do the same as before?'

'You'll have to roll for dexterity. But you get a plus four modifier, since Elijah's with you.'

'Okay, fine.' Bethan rolled a d20. 'Hah. Nineteen.'

Bram: 'Sixteen.'

Tala: 'Hell yeah, twenty-one!'

Kestrel: 'Uh, shit, that's an eight.'

Bethan laughed. 'Oh my God, even with the modifier?'

'Yep.'

'Ha ha, are we gonna get Zombie Quinn now to go with our horse?'

'Oh God.'

'Hopefully not,' said Aaron. 'But still, Quinn… you didn't roll so hot, so here's what happens. You try and ford the stream like the others, but you miscalculate the distance and land smack in the centre of the muddy water. The mud sucks at your shoes, and you're in up to your waist. Roll a d4 for damage.'

'Two. Crap.'

'You can feel pondweeds and tendrils of strange plant-like things grab at your legs. The urge to struggle is strong, and after a few short seconds of panic, it overtakes you and you move about, trying to free yourself. You just wind up injuring yourself, becoming entwined deeper in the weeds.'

It was so real he could almost feel it.

Next to him, he saw Tala twitch. 'Shit, we need to save him!' she said, and she started scanning frenetically through her spell sheet.

'"Stop struggling!"' Bethan called out, as Marcus. '"I 'eard struggling just makes you sink faster."'

'Uh… what should I do? Agh, help, guys. I'm gonna ask

for help.'

Tala spoke up: 'I'm going to cast Water Warp!'

'Yep, that works. You'll need a strength saving throw.'

Tala seemed oddly determined, and there was a strange moment of tension as she shook the d20 and let it fly, a little too hard, across the table.

'Shit.'

'Ah, yeah, sorry. Nine isn't going to cut it.'

Tala bit her lip, clearly still agitated. Then she said, 'Hey, Elijah's a bard, maybe he could give me Inspiration or something? Let me roll again?'

Aaron considered for a moment, eyes travelling over the positions of the miniatures, flitting back to check something on the character sheets.

'He can't do it retroactively, but… I've got something a little better. Also, I don't really want to punish you guys like I did with Poe, so… Elijah saves Quinn.'

'Elijah saves me?'

'Elijah saves you, yeah. So, he's closest, and before anyone else can do anything, Elijah steps forward, planting one leg firmly in the water. He doesn't seem particularly scared about doing this, in fact, the way he moves is more solemn than anything, like this is commonplace, like this is nothing new. He extends a hand towards you. "Hold on for me," Elijah says, and his gaze is warm and trusting.'

'I… I take it.'

'Elijah smiles as you place your hand in his, and his eyes sort of dance golden again in the fading light of day. He grips your hand firmly—he's far stronger than you imagined, for a bard—and with a pivotal, decisive movement, he pulls you from the mud. His other hand finds purchase further up your arm, then around your torso as you come closer to freedom. The slurping sound as the mud gives you up is… pretty gross. Elijah pulls you clean out, and holds you securely as you find your footing once again.'

'Fine, Elijah, flex on me, why don't you,' Tala grumbled.

Kestrel had a very particular mental image right then. Falling into Elijah's arms, shrouded by those waves of umber hair, that ostentatious coat. The awkwardness of disentangling himself from that caring hold as he was set upon firm ground again. It made his belly burn.

'You don't have to roll for anything there, because Elijah has marshland knowledge. Now, he turns to the group. "Like I said, do watch your step."'

Bram sighed. 'Now if only he had been there for Poe…'

'This is why you don't go out into the marsh alone when your GM is really, strongly suggesting you shouldn't.' Aaron chided them, but his eyes were gleaming. He clearly relished the unpredictability. 'Let's continue. Again, in the distance, you see the self-same gates you saw last time, the ancient stone edifices that mark the border into a deeper, more intimidating part of the marsh.'

'Wait. Is that creature from before here?'

'What creature?' Tala asked.

And they explained, how last time, they had seen the shadow in the mist, how it had seemed much taller than a man, and Tala listened in awe—and a small amount of fear that Kestrel probably should have been paying attention to.

'You could make a perception check for anything hostile,' said Aaron, 'but Elijah doesn't seem concerned.'

It was probably fine. They walked on.

'You go through the archway. Immediately the atmosphere becomes more oppressive, and the sky grows two shades darker. Soon, you come to a wide stretch of water, much wider than the stream that drowned Poe. It's like a lake, but not quite. Tufts of long grasses protrude out of the water here and there, and tiny islands of silt and mud pop up at intervals. Your party comes to a standstill at the water's edge, and the mere fact that Elijah has stopped indicates that this probably is too deep and dangerous to ford.'

'Uh, okay. How are we gonna cross?'

'"Elijah, any ideas?"' Kestrel moved Quinn closer to their enigmatic companion, putting plenty of eagerness into his voice.

'Elijah turns to the young rogue, eyes bright, and says "Oh, plenty." He sort of cocks his head in this charming manner and continues. "But for you, I think we can settle for the simplest approach."'

'He turns to the party. "Please stand back. I wouldn't want you getting any more soaked than you need to be." Then he faces the water again and takes out the small lute and starts to play. The water shifts in response to the gentle, eerie notes, and it's like it has become alive.' Bram chose this moment to play some background music that Kestrel was sure he recognised as Pink Floyd. *Their early stuff is pretty space rock. Colour me impressed.*

'The air around you falls still, until Elijah's playing becomes the only sound borne on it. Then the water rustles louder, and in a magnificent moment, it parts, swelling up on either side of Elijah and holding itself there, trapped in time. A passageway through the lakebed opens up to you, and Elijah slings his instrument over one shoulder, casual as anything, and beckons for you to follow, taking a step into the rapidly-setting mud.'

Aaron looked at the group expectantly.

'I, uh, I guess we follow,' said Kestrel.

The others nodded.

'So you take your first steps out onto the lakebed. The mud has almost fully hardened now—all the water has been leeched out to join the shimmering walls either side of you—and it's perfectly solid to walk on. Despite this, the floor is far from even, and all the pondweed and bracken that had been suspended in the water falls in clumps all over the place, pathetic as dried flowers that have long since been discarded. You walk on for perhaps another hundred metres, maybe more, while the walls of water either side of you seem to hum with the effort of maintaining stasis. It's an impressive sight.'

'Hah, like crossing the Red Sea.'

'See, I thought for ages it was the Red Sea,' Aaron says. 'But what it really translates to, is the Reed Sea.'

'Another thing you learned from your brother?' Kestrel cut in.

'Yeah.'

'Also, shouldn't it be Moses who parts the sea, not Elijah?'

'Shut up.'

'I'm glad we brought Elijah with us,' Bethan conceded.

'Yeah, if you'd gotten this far the other day you just wouldn't have been able to find a way across. But anyway.' Aaron plucked up the miniatures and set them on the other side of the crudely drawn lake. 'You're now deep in bog country. Deeper than anything you've experienced thus far. It feels like not only a physical but a supernatural barrier has been crossed, and your surroundings feel more malicious than before. You all feel a primal sort of tingling down your spines, an alertness of the sort that a grazing animal might feel when it's spent too long in the open. Elijah doesn't expend any more energy parting the waters for the lesser streams and puddles, so you're back to the long slog of splashing through stagnant water that only seems to get darker the further you go.'

'Guess that's why they call it the Blackwater Marsh,' Tala murmured.

'Eventually Elijah slows to a stop before a small copse of half-dead trees. Pushing cracked branches out the way, he makes a gap for you to pass through. And you do, trudging on to the centre through the blankety mist until a tower rises up in front of you. A maw-like opening, an arch like a devil's back, and thick stone slabs that make you feel like you have entered the realm of giants. He takes you up to it, and then faces you with a flourish. "And here, I must bid you farewell."'

'"You're not staying for the rest?"'

'"I said I would help you find the shrine you seek. And that, I have done."'

'Damn. I was starting to get used to him showing us around,' said Bram.

'He's not scared, is he? Elijah, are you scared?'

'He looks amused at Marcus's question. "Heavens, no, I merely have a modicum of self-preservation."'

'Fair.'

'"I shall await you at the edge of the lake, so you can return safely."'

'Aw, that's kind of him,' said Tala, although there was an enigmatic look on her face that was at odds with her words.

'With a jaunty wave, and a tip of his hat, Elijah is off, strolling back the way you came as if he were doing no more than taking a walk on the beach. Now it's just you and the shrine.'

'Great.'

'So, with Elijah out of the party, you'll have to decide

how best to proceed.'

'We should probably go in.'

'We should look around the area first.'

'Okay, as you argue among yourselves, you are interrupted by a mournful howl, a fell voice borne on the wind. Your ears prick up, looking for the source of the noise, as you eye the cavernous entrance cautiously. Then, it dies down, and for a few minutes nothing happens.'

'Can I check for traps?' asked Kestrel.

'Go ahead. Roll for perception.'

He rolled high, and Aaron said, 'You scour the entrance, and find nothing hidden that might harm you. It is, for all intents and purposes, safe to walk through, and whatever was making that mournful noise seems to be much further away.'

'Let's go in.'

'Right. Now, as you walk through the entrance, brushing away cobwebs and slick hanging moss, you come to a sort of vestibule, where you see an esoteric pentagram on the ground, pulsing with arcane energy. In front of it are three platforms, and behind it is a tall and heavy door that is very much closed.'

'Okay. Can we go up to the pentagram?'

'Uh, I'm not so sure we should walk over it,' Kestrel said. Bram hesitated.

'Maybe you're right.'

'I don't like this place,' Tala said. Something about the quality of her voice gave Kestrel pause. It seemed so childlike, so regressive, and, like with Bram in the canteen, something tugged at his heart, deep around his solar plexus like it was threatening to take him out of the here-and-now and into... he wasn't sure where.

'Is there anything I can read in here?' Bram asked.

'Well, in the dim light you can almost make out markings on the stone archway that leads into the main hall. Roll for perception.'

'Oh wow, yeah, I rolled pretty high.'

Aaron peered at the die, then passed Bram a slip of paper.

'"Speak not the name of Matanbuchus, lest ye be driven to pay deference."' Bram rolled up the small slip when he was done reading, pretending it was a scroll. Then, 'Wait, shit, does that count? I just said the name.'

'Bram, no!'

Aaron smiled. 'Now, no sooner have you spoken than you hear a voice booming out from all around you, echoing on the stone. "Who treads so softly as a mouse within my halls?"'

Aaron always was good at doing character voices. But here, he really excelled. He had the resonance and the pitch down so perfectly that it made Kestrel's blood ran cold, and he felt frozen in place at the dining table just as much as Quinn must have been in the shrine.

Meanwhile, Aaron continued. 'For a moment you think you see a shape on the walls, but it's as inconsistent as shadows from a candle flame: it looks like some kind of demonic creature, it's all angles and distended limbs, and it's impossible to tell how large it really is.'

'Is it the same creature we saw in the marsh?'

'Perhaps. But it's only visible for a second, and then it's back to the echoes on the stone, and the sounds of deep, pleasurable breaths.'

Bram stepped up to the occasion.

'"Are you… Belial?"'

'The demon screeches: a high, banshee-like sound that mellows down into a guttural growl. "The footprints, do they frighten you?" he says, and it's at this point that you notice there are old imprints pressed into the dirt-encrusted floor.' Aaron jabbed a finger at the tiny details he had put on the map.

'They're all going in… but none are coming out,' said Bethan.

'"Do they frighten you," says the voice once again, and there's a whoosh of wind at your sides; it's like he's toying with you.'

'We should probably be honest,' said Bram. '"Yes. They do."'

Aaron put on an enigmatic cackle. '"You answered my question, now I shall answer yours. I am Belial."'

Kestrel was enraptured, full engrossed in listening to the demon until Bethan cut in.

'Dude, you really need to stop biting your nails.'

He retracted his hand. Bethan shrugged.

Still at the forefront of the group, Bram took the lead again. '"We've come here at the request of the townspeople. From the, uh, village of Mud."'

Aaron launched into Belial's speech again. '"The townspeople, ahhh, the townspeople. They all live there at my mercy, and so, the blood fee must be paid. You didn't seriously think they could settle so close to the marsh without some due deference?"'

'"Is that why your followers were killing the children?"'

'Now, straight in front of you all, the stone starts to hum. An eerie blackish-blue light glows from some of the markings, and it grows until it almost makes the room look like it's underwater. There is a sound deeper in the rock like something is opening up, or like some energy is being charged up.'

Kestrel felt ill. Something was gnawing away at him,

something wanted to make itself known. He cleared his throat, and he wasn't quite sure what he was going for, or why he had to say it, but he did. He didn't even think about how he was making Quinn a target by speaking up. '"What's this all for? Why are you doing this?"'

The words came out more strained than he had wanted.

Aaron raised his brow. 'There's this creaking sound, like the whole world is groaning, and then Belial manifests in front of you. His limbs strain into unnatural shapes and he gathers himself up, tall and terrifying. His smile is wide and thin as a crescent moon and his joints crackle as the air flickers with petrol-coloured flashes of light. He turns to you, Quinn, and stares in challenge.'

For a moment, Kestrel thought Belial was going to pin him down. What was the distance between them? What skills did he have, what stuff from his inventory could he use to defend himself? He was drawing a blank as Aaron continued.

'And he says, in a voice as thick and terrifying as the deepest forest path: "I can't wait for you to find out." Then Belial vanishes into the darkness.'

It took Kestrel a moment to notice what was happening with Tala, so caught up in his own imagination as he was. But when he looked, he saw a frenzied expression that made her face seem alien, like the way friends' faces looked in dreams sometimes. She spoke and her voice was like wire wool.

'He's real! No, you don't get it! He really is!'

'What do you—'

'You don't get it!'

'I—I'm just—'

'Tala—'

'No! Goddamnit!' Tala wrung her hands together, then

rubbed them on her jeans as if to get rid of sweat.

He felt like he was back in her conservatory, watching her unravel in front of him, and it set him bristling. He had no power here.

So he stood up. He didn't need to speak at first, the sound of the chair legs moving so abruptly was enough to bring silence.

'I don't understand,' he said.

'You most of all,' she replied, and she bowed her head, looked at her hands again. Kestrel sat back down. Stared straight ahead of himself. It shouldn't have frightened him, but it did.

Bethan was sat next to Tala, trying to comfort her while Tala shrugged off every attempt at contact.

'It's okay, it's just—'

'Stop it, I don't need to calm down.'

'Sorry, look, maybe we can—'

'Aaron, did you know about this before?'

'What?'

'You wrote this, right? Why would you do this?'

'I literally have no idea what you mean.'

'How can you—Why?'

Aaron suppressed an aggravated huff and got up from his chair. It screeched on the parquet floor louder than it should have, far louder than Kestrel's had, and he could not prevent goosebumps from rising.

This was all going so wrong. Humours too strained, everyone starting to spiral off into their own little pockets of confusion. He followed Aaron into the kitchen.

What he got when he entered was a very weary look from his friend, who was busy slumped against the refrigerator, running a hand through his curls and tugging at his scalp as if it needed reprimanding.

'What the hell happened to her over the half term? I have no fucking idea how to deal with this.'

'Me either,' said Kestrel.

'I don't think she's ready for this.'

Aaron was right. It just hurt to hear. He had tried so hard to encourage her to come along, and to have it turn out so badly made him feel so horribly responsible.

'I'll write her character out of this campaign,' Aaron said, in a voice hushed enough that she couldn't hear—not that that would be a problem, as far out as the kitchen. 'She can join for the next one. But not this.'

CHAPTER TEN

Prosopagnosia

Nobody spoke about it the next day. It was not strictly avoidance, it was just that none of them made the opportunity to hang out and chat, and it was probably better that way. Kestrel had art history with Bram towards the end of the day, and there was the question that wasn't really a question but an expectation. *See you at the student bar later.*

Which of course ended up being another exercise in 'Let's just drink excessively and forget.' They started to talk, but Bram just seemed distracted, so Kestrel settled for working his way through the Happy Hour menu while some other people they knew filtered in and started a conversation about superheroes around them.

The evening didn't feel like much—until suddenly it was. Music kicked up a notch. Drinks changed hands. Conversations shifted but that didn't matter any more because it was getting too hard to hear. Bram, kissing some girl with big hair in the corner.

Well, that's one possibility out of the window.

It was stupid, it annoyed him more than it should have.

He left the table.

The bass was thumping louder, it was getting to that time of evening where the open spaces were filling up with a throng of bodies, and hey, maybe that hot blond guy from the other week would be there again. Scanning the dancefloor, looking for a meal. He had missed out there, too, hadn't he? Too weighed down by his own indecisiveness, his own... whatever the fuck it was that had stopped him.

I think I know what I want but I don't want to go there.

It would take a little more alcohol, probably. Scratch that, make it a lot. He'd go to the bathroom, then see about that. Fuck the whole it-being-a-Monday thing.

He bumped into someone in the hallway coming back from the bathroom. It was dark and narrow and the beer was making his head buzz just lightly enough that he couldn't tell who it was until they said 'Oh! I'm sorry,' in a high and cheery voice, and moved back into relative light.

'Bethan! Hey, wait, you okay?' Because now that he saw her more clearly, he could see her face was flushed and her eyeshadow was smudging at the sides.

'Ah, shit, is it that noticeable?' She dabbed at the corners of her eyes.

'Only a little.'

'Damn. I'm—'

'Are you—'

'—I'm okay.'

He paused, studied a poster on the wall without really reading it. 'Why don't we get out of here? I think this is the perfect time for you to dye my hair.'

Her eyes lit up.

'Lemme just grab my kit. I'll come to your dorm in a bit.'

Bethan didn't take long. She dumped the tote bag full of dye by his desk and stretched out, as comfortable as ever.

'Your room's always so fascinating.'

She was looking at the artwork dotted around. Kestrel got the sense she wanted a distraction from whatever had been upsetting her earlier, but he didn't want the conversation to veer in that direction, so he waved a hand toward the desk. 'Yeah, I'm surprised I was even able to clear a space on that thing.'

There were still a few acrylic paint tubes scattered on it, notebooks pushed into the corners, some stray letters. But it was cleaner than it had been in weeks. Bethan smiled at his mediocre attempt and clapped her hands together with enthusiasm.

'Well! Let's get started, shall we?'

She got to work unloading the contents of her bag, while Kestrel idled for something constructive to do. 'You want a drink? I only really have tea.'

'Tea's fine. Make it herbal though.'

A quick rifle through his collection of miscellaneous sachets and he found some fennel and peppermint. That seemed like something she might like, and a couple of minutes later, once the water had boiled, he was proven correct.

'So I'mma start by just mixing the pre-lightener up — wow, this tastes good — and yeah, you can just… just sit at your desk there, yeah. I'll sort the rest. You got a towel you don't mind getting dirty?'

He pointed toward the bathroom. 'Yeah, take your pick.'

She fetched a plain blue towel, draped it over his shoulders, and arranged her tools around the desk, picking up a comb and an applicator brush with a flourish of her hand.

Kestrel studied her, looking for a crack in the armour.

'How are you feeling?'

She cocked her head. 'After Sunday, you mean?'

'I mean like, with that dream you had.'

'Oh. I… yeah, I'm okay. I had another one but it wasn't as bad.'

There it was; that uneasy thing swimming just beneath her surface. She chose not to elaborate, and somehow that made her seem sadder. Kestrel wanted to hug her, but something made him hold back.

'It's real cute of you.'

'What?'

'When you hesitate like that, when you use those puppy dog eyes, like you're searching for permission.'

'Oh.' Kestrel exhaled, tried to crack a smile, but in truth he wasn't sure how he felt about that particular spotlight. Was that really how other people saw him?

Bethan spoke again, easing him out of that moment.

'I know there's been that weird stuff with Tala and so on, but… that's not all I was sad about tonight. You know Rei, right?'

'Yeah, she's in my art history class.'

'So, uh, you gotta be sworn to secrecy, okay?'

'Sure.'

'Well, she's—she's seeing this new guy. She was being super cagey about it, like she never told any of us about it in class. But… I ran into the both of them during my shift this afternoon and I was working tills so I couldn't exactly excuse myself and… *God*, he was *all over* her and like, fine, whatever, not really my thing in public, but then he was like "Oh, you're her friend, right? *Do you know how to have a good time, too?*"'

'Um. That's a bit—'

'Inappropriate? Yeah. He blew me a kiss, too.'

Kestrel made another face at the mirror. Then, something struck him. 'Wasn't she dating Stuart though?'

'Yeah. At least, she's still meant to be. And it's like, polyamory is a legit thing, but this feels wrong. As far as I know, Stu isn't polyamorous and when I talked to him, he really didn't seem cool with it. It's...' She paused to find the right way to express it. 'It's like this guy is grooming her.' She shivered. 'God, I don't know why that's making me feel so weird. It's not like I have enough information to know.'

'I mean, it *is* a disturbing situation,' Kestrel offered.

'I know, but it's more than that. It's like it's... a tale as old as time,' she said, singing it to a familiar tune. 'Only, time keeps on going and so does that tale. It makes me feel so powerless.'

'Have you talked to her much about it?'

'That's just it—I tried, like, just now, and things got... messy.' She paused to breathe deep. 'He won't let her talk to me alone now. 'Cos I'm toxic.' Her hands fell to the table and she barely cared about the sound it made. 'I mean, I didn't even *say* anything awful! I was just trying to look out for her, but he's made it out like I'm a bad influence and—ugh—it's all to get more control over her and it feels gross.' She stepped back and surveyed his hair. 'We're done with the lightening, by the way. Just gotta wait a half hour now.'

Kestrel got up to stretch, and Bethan took his place at the desk, immediately busying herself with sorting out the next round of dyes, mixing a petrol green and a yellow to get the particular mossy tone he wanted. But she was clearly still thinking about Rei, because after a while spent mixing, she pushed the dyes aside and looked at Kestrel intently. 'How's she doing in art class?'

'She, uh… she's a little quieter than usual, but otherwise okay. I think.'

'Okay.' Bethan breathed. 'I don't like friend drama. I'm sorry for dumping this all on you.' She lay her head on the crook of her elbow, flush against the table. 'I just want everyone to hang out together and have a good time! I know that sounds… fucking cliché, but it's true. I want us all to be happy.'

Kestrel reached out to stroke back her curls before they got too close to the mixing tray.

She looked up at him, eyes glistening. 'Why does it have to be like this?'

'I don't know. It's stupid.'

'So stupid.' She buried her face from view again for a while, and Kestrel just perched on the edge of the bed, sitting next to her quietly.

'Well,' she said at length, 'enough of that. Let's get that dye activating.'

A couple of episodes of some inane anime later, Bethan had completed Kestrel's transformation into forest elf. The streak of green fell down to the right like a hanging vine. With a pleased grin as she assessed her handiwork, she pushed back from the table. Lids went on the dye bottles, and the mixing tray was pushed towards Kestrel. 'Wash these out for me. Make sure you get all the dye out of the brush.'

He took the tray and its contents—little wooden mixing stick, applicator brush—to the bathroom, working wordlessly, immediately.

She giggled.

'What?'

'I, uh, I just became aware I was using my mum tone there. You cleaned that up super quickly. Kind of like someone had lit a fire under your butt.'

'Heh, guess it was effective.'

'You always did respond particularly positively to authority. Just make sure it's what you want, okay?'

The serious inflection at the end there caught him off guard. It made him stop, focussing on nothing in particular in the space between him and the wall. He mumbled a quick 'Sure,' but it stuck with him for a long time after.

Eventually the full gang met up for lunch, and this was a relief, because it wasn't good to keep avoiding things all the time. The mood was as overcast inside as it was outside, and just as predictably, the conversation turned to the one shadow that hung over them all.

'I feel really bad about the weekend,' Aaron said.

'Oh, about...'

'About her freaking out like that.'

'Yeah, same.'

They were all talking save for Kestrel, who was just studying his plate, listening in, wondering why the day felt so expectant. It was the kind of pre-storm feeling that seemed to override everything else, to the point where Bethan's hair dye job on him got barely any attention from his friends—and that suited him fine, but all the same it was unusual, it set everything off on a weird note.

Aaron continued. 'It was just so unexpected. Like, out of all the things she could have freaked about, I did not expect *that*.'

'Belial, why Belial?'

'That something you guys talked about before?' Bram peered at Aaron expectantly.

'No.'

'Maybe it means something different to her.'

Bethan pushed her hands under her thighs and rocked forward on her chair, staring down her drink like she was a base jumper preparing to leap off into it. 'God, I'm so worried about her.'

'Kestrel.' Aaron spoke and it wasn't so much a question as a statement.

'Yeah?' Feeling all eyes turn to him.

'How was she doing? When you saw her last? Like, before the session. I don't think I ever asked.'

'She was…' He paused for breath. How best to describe this? 'Well, she was making these little sculptures out of sugar. At first I thought it was something to do with her homework, cos, you know, she's taking Sculptures and Materials as her main. But, she was getting pretty insistent about it—they were all lined up on the windowsill, and so many different shapes: people, buildings and so on.' He thought about reaching out for the little car, and how stricken she had become. 'She was a bit funny about letting me near them.'

'She's being creative, that's good.' Bethan sounded cheery enough, but her heart was not in it. 'The sculpture thing sounds constructive.'

'It sounds obsessive,' Aaron countered.

'Hey, we've all had our moments like that. Remember last term, Kestrel, even you got quite into the little modelling clay things.'

'Oh. Yeah—I made you that ocarina.'

Bethan laughed, perhaps a little too loudly. 'Yeah, I

could actually play the songs from the game on it. Sort of.'

'Modelling clay's a bit different than sugar,' Aaron mumbled into his coffee. 'So yeah, this is just really fucking depressing.'

Kestrel felt sorry for Aaron. All he wanted to do was run a fun campaign to get their minds off things, and it was a lot of effort, being a GM; he did not envy the having to rewrite bits of the plot to work around Leilani's presence or lack thereof, and he did not envy the struggle of spinning an interesting tale while you were feeling sad yourself. Aaron was the one who usually managed to stay the most positive out of them all, and Kestrel didn't know how any of them would cope if he got close to breaking point.

'There's a song by Thursday about sugar,' said Bram, but he did not elaborate. He was looking at nothing in the air when he said this, and he seemed so forlorn.

The girl from last night walked in, winked at Bram before sitting way over the other side with her friends. Kestrel looked down at his own lunch, picking for a distraction. Suddenly he didn't want to talk about either Tala, the sculptures, or the fallout from the student bar last night.

Luckily, there was a place he could escape to. An offer, freely given. *You know where to find me.* Because he still needed to talk about things, but not here, not now.

'I have to go.'

'Everything okay?'

'Yeah, I just need to go to the Humanities block for something.'

It wasn't out of place to be doing this. It was fine, this was fine. Asking for help didn't mean he was crazy.

Kestrel controlled his breathing and looked up at the

sandy wooden door in front of him, the name tag small and unassuming, in clinical black on white. Knocking was a simple act. He should just do it.

The office to the side had a young woman hunched over a desk, idly eating pretzel sticks while she slogged through a spreadsheet. She wasn't paying attention to him, so his deliberating went unchallenged.

He thought. He picked at his fingernails. And eventually, he knocked.

When Daran opened the door to his office, his face was one of surprise.

'Kestrel! What can I do for you?'

'Um, last time we met, you said,' — *goddamn* he really had to stop mumbling — 'you said if I needed to talk to anyone…'

He trailed off. He was too awkward, and too horribly, painfully aware of it.

Daran filled the space by opening the door to its fullest extent. 'Of course. I said you would always be welcome to do so, didn't I?'

'You did, yeah…'

'So how about now?'

'If that's not too… I haven't interrupted anything, have I?' He could see an office phone placed hastily and ineffectually back in its holder, and it was only then that he remembered Daran had said something about a meeting during lunch.

But Daran seemed unaffected by this.

'I wouldn't have offered if you were.'

Of course. He was right. Kestrel felt his confidence shrink under Daran's gaze. He had to do something, to make it clear he hadn't intended to offend him. *Had he* offended him?

Stop. You're overthinking it.

'I… I'm sorry.'

'Why are you apologising? You don't need to.' Fringes of a smile danced at the corners of Daran's mouth.

'Sorry,' Kestrel said again, then, realising his mistake, 'I mean, okay. S—yeah.'

He entered the room.

So this was Daran's office. It was lighter than he had expected. There was nothing out of the ordinary about it: a couple of bookshelves neatly and perfectly filled with what looked like various religious tomes, a coffee table with some ornaments, a desk and a computer that was standard office issue. The calendar on the wall featured some ageing rocker—he wanted to say Tom Waits but he didn't know enough—and there were no plants anywhere in the room.

There was a bunch of paperwork on the desk, and a biro rolling gently on its side. Kestrel got the distinct impression that he had, in fact, interrupted whatever Daran had made time for in lieu of doing the Stations march that lunchtime, and that only served to reinforce his guilt. No backing out now, though.

Daran sat in one of the two chairs by the coffee table, leaving Kestrel to take the more comfortable one.

'You've done something with your hair.'

'Oh! Yeah.' Kestrel tugged offhandedly at the green streak. 'My friend Bethan did it for me.'

'It looks pretty cool.'

'Heh, thanks.'

Daran did not talk again until Kestrel was seated, until he had his hands in his lap, until he looked up and smiled shyly and indicated he was probably as ready as he would ever be to begin.

'So. How are things?'

What he wanted to say came easily in his mind. *Hey, so I managed to get through to Tala but then I fucked it all up by triggering her during our gaming session at the weekend, and how on earth do I fix something like that? You're much older and you probably know a lot about how to handle this sort of stuff and I'd really appreciate that right now.* Bit of a mouthful, but it didn't sound all that complicated. It wasn't all that complicated.

And yet, the thought of having those words actually, physically, come out of his mouth made him feel irrationally terrified.

'I, uh...'

He suddenly felt too awkward sitting down, and he shifted about, started to extricate himself from his jacket, considered standing up but didn't know how to make that seem natural. He was the wrong shape for his jacket, for the chair, for everything.

'It's kind of hard.'

'That's all right. Take your time.'

Kestrel breathed. He was finally free of his jacket, and he rolled it up, bunching it beneath one arm. He heard what he wanted to say in his head again but it didn't make it out.

'I'll get us some coffee.' Daran extricated his legs from their loosely crossed position and stood up, limber and energetic, not giving Kestrel the chance to decide.

In his absence, Kestrel cautiously stood up too. He was intrigued by the bookshelves. He didn't know how long Daran would be with the coffee, so he decided to risk being incredibly rude and went over to check out the titles.

A Bible Commentary for English Readers. Handbook of Communion Ministry. The Imitation of Christ.

That last one caught his attention and, as carefully as if

he was pulling a chocolate bar from the shelf at his mother's house, he slid the book out of its spot on the bookcase and into his eager hands. The bindings were leather, the title embossed, and the interior pages crinkled with that thin vellum quality that religious books tended to have, at once so fragile and so intimidating. He traced a finger over the page the book had fallen open on, appreciating its texture beneath his skin.

The door creaked behind him and he tensed.

'Ah, did I frighten you?'

'No. Yes, I mean, a little.' He turned around to see Daran watching him, a ceramic mug in either hand. Daran smiled apologetically, and pushed the door to a close ever so gently with his foot.

'I see you've found my bookshelf.'

'Yeah. Is that okay?'

'Of course.' There was something to the tilt of Daran's eyebrows, a curiosity, no, an approval of Kestrel's curiosity.

Kestrel smiled, feeling a little flushed.

'I like these books,' he said, thumbing the pages. He half expected Daran to tell him off, to pull his hands away from the gilt inlay, but he didn't. He just looked at him, smiling back.

'You can definitely borrow them whenever you like.'

Yeah, Daran's all right.

'But for now, let's sit back down. We can have a drink, and you can tell me anything you need to.'

Such a calming voice. He was right, as well. Kestrel nodded, and replaced the book on the shelf.

Voices in the corridor outside. That office woman next door, and a younger, sharper voice. One he recognised.

There was a brief rap on the door, but Daran was not

given any time to open it. It was pushed from the other side with no small amount of urgency, and the person who did it was Tala: dishevelled and out of breath.

'Kestrel! You're here! Thank God—'

'Oh!' Kestrel moved away from the bookshelf. 'How come you're on campus?'

'I had to tell you something, and I just saw the others in the canteen and they said you'd probably be in the Humanities block and then the receptionist out there said the room at the end so I…' Tala started to take in her new surroundings properly, and slowed down her movements in such a way that it made Kestrel look around to assure himself that the whole world had not suddenly hit slow-motion. She fixed her eyes on Daran, hard and wary as an animal, and her face turned pale. Then she cast back to the door, muttering the room name, reading the small name tag beneath it, cursing as if annoyed she had overlooked it in her haste. She took a harsh breath in. 'What are you doing?'

'I was just talking to Daran.' He did not elaborate, because how in the hell would he possibly begin to explain that she was the reason why he was here?

But she seemed not to care about Kestrel's motivation at all.

'You were… just talking?'

Daran looked between them in confusion. An uncomfortable moment passed between the three of them, and Kestrel imagined casting Invisibility, disappearing from the moment in a puff of smoke.

Something was wrong, clearly, and Tala was not going to say what it was. More than likely, she had mistaken Daran for somebody else. It wasn't a surprise, really, considering how she had been acting recently.

He felt immediately awash with guilt. She wasn't well—Daran must understand that, surely?

'Tala… this is just Daran, he's the—'

'No,' she said. 'No, no, no, no…' She edged backward, until she was grasping at the doorframe. Then, she fled.

Kestrel turned back to Daran, aware he must look so, so stricken. He didn't need to say anything—not that he would have known what to say anyway—because Daran inclined his head. 'Don't worry,' he said, and he seemed unnaturally calm. 'Go after her. And be well. I'll see you tonight.'

Kestrel nodded, too caught up in all that was happening to say goodbye properly. He ran out after Tala. She was already down the stairs and he had to jump multiple steps at a time to catch up.

'Wait up! Tala!'

She didn't listen.

'Tala, please! What did you come here to tell me?'

She slowed down outside, but didn't stop completely.

'I was going to tell you sorry. For the other day. But I can't—I need to sort this out, because it's already happening.'

'Wait! Where are you going?'

This time she ran to the end of the path before she turned around, throwing her hands wildly at her sides. 'I'm going home.'

Once it was over he felt nauseous. Something bitter and tightly coiled was busy clawing away at his insides, trying to birth itself from his bile. His stomach felt unnaturally distended, fit to burst. His mind, repeating over and over *What did I do wrong?*

In one crushing moment, he wanted to die. But it wasn't

really death he was after, just a way to gouge out the black spot he was leaving on everything he touched. What he wanted: punishment and redress, in one fell swoop. He did not want to think about the consequences.

How stupid. You're mad that she was overreacting, but right now you're the one doing so. You're feeling all that frustration and anger of being backed into a corner here and you just can't fucking take it—

It surrounded him, that teasing, sickly-sweet voice. *Just take it, just take it. Whatever they choose to give.*

There were more important things than him, here. But it would be a real bonus if he could just stop fucking things up.

The staff car park was larger than Kestrel remembered. It was cold out, and he was pacing awkwardly, because he had no idea which car was Daran's. The wind was whipping up against his coat lapels, and the clouds were rolling thick and fast across the sky. It felt like rain was coming. Another storm perhaps, just like last Wednesday. He knew that the early spring weather was fickle and changeable and by tomorrow, would be drastically different again, but whilst he was under this sky, it felt like it was never going to end.

He tried to pace as though he knew what he was doing and where he was meant to be waiting. A few teachers passed by, drove off in their own cars, paid him no mind.

Eventually Daran came out of D Block—Kestrel could tell straight away that familiar casual stride. Daran had no coat, just the same well-worn leather jacket, left unzipped against the elements. Either he didn't feel the chill or he didn't care. As he approached, he twirled the car keys in his hand, almost carelessly, and gave a winning smile.

'Sorry that took a while. Had some admin stuff to sort out.' He pointed to an unassuming black sedan. 'That's me.' For a second he was so close that Kestrel wondered if he was going to put an arm round his shoulder, the way a gym buddy might. Not that he ever went to the gym enough to know. But the moment passed, and they walked side by side against the oncoming wind.

'Is your friend okay?'

'Oh. I don't know.'

'That was Tala, wasn't it?'

'Yeah.'

Daran sighed. 'I feel for her. She seems like she's having a rough time. But, ah, just remember not to take her behaviour too personally. People sometimes act irrationally when they've had a hard time like that.'

Kestrel nodded, and hoped it was convincing enough.

Daran seemed to sense the moment was not a good one to linger on, so he segued into: 'So, nobody else coming?'

'Uh, I think it's just me,' Kestrel said.

'Well,' said Daran, with a glint in his eye, 'their loss.' He leaned past Kestrel to unlock the passenger's side—manual keys, Kestrel noted—before walking leisurely round to his own side.

Kestrel traced his hand along the seam of the door. Spatters of dirt flecked the windows, not enough to warrant a wash, but enough to leave a film on his skin. A strange sense of nostalgia hit him in a rolling wave, and the cold metal made him feel sad, though he couldn't place why.

The rush of that hermetic seal being opened hit his ears with a pop and for a second it felt like the floor had bottomed out beneath him into a vast, empty space. It was going to drag him down... until it wasn't and he was just an ordinary boy standing by an ordinary car, about to go and see a band that would make his best friend deliciously jealous. Apprehension and excitement were basically the same thing, anyway.

He got in. Sank into the soft leatherette seat. Struggled with the buckle: the car was old enough that it stuck when he tugged. He could feel Daran's smirk without even looking.

'Shut up—I'm just not used to a car this old.'

'Oh, don't call her that!' Daran stroked the thin steering wheel. 'She's merely a lady of a certain age.'

Kestrel laughed. 'Okay, I'm sorry.'

Daran reached over to press the stereo on—an honest-to-God tape player—and it was a tonic for the damp mood outside. Soft twanging guitar, chords moving from minor to major, and it was almost enough to imagine there was a break in the clouds and a small sliver of sun greeting them. Again, the gentle sadness, and he didn't know why.

A rev of the engine and they were off. The ancient air conditioning unit kicked into gear, and there was something unique about the smell of petrol, cloying but addictive, as though once it entered his senses it would settle in his veins and never leave.

The venue was clustered and small, in the kind of way that, although he could see every corner, it felt as though he could get lost just wading his way through the crowd. Kestrel found himself sticking close to Daran as they wove their way through to a free standing table. A promotional leaflet for the gig was tacked to the wall beside them: The Caudal Lure proudly proclaimed in a font evocative of the Seventies.

They settled in, Daran lounging casually with one elbow

on the tabletop, and Kestrel unconsciously mirroring his behaviour.

'I'm not going to buy you alcohol, but you're welcome to spend your own money.'

Kestrel caught his gaze. Normally he would order a beer, at the very least, but something about this situation made that feel a little odd.

'Oh, I'll just, uh, have what you're having.'

Two orders of cola later, and the band had come out on stage to begin their warm-up. Crowd murmur dropped away against the spacey reverb of the guitar and keyboards. Daran let out a soft sigh, closing his eyes as the noise filled up the small nest of a room. The frontman started to vocalise, half-words and emotional crooning that Kestrel could barely make sense of.

So this was space rock.

The musical version of getting high, Daran had called it. And he could see how that made sense.

The surging melodies wove themselves around him so completely that he began to fall into a meditative state. It would have been comforting, had it not been so surreal. It gave him space to drift, space to think, and he found himself confronting that strange feeling he had had earlier on opening the car door. The yawning chasm. As familiar as some of his dreams, and as thick as the paints he worked with. It felt like that shadow had followed him here, and it was a feeling that he found increasingly hard to shake as the evening went on. There it lay, waiting in the bathroom stalls, clinging in the corners of the small venue like an old friend trying to catch his attention.

Why did it have to ruin something good? He was actually enjoying himself for once, even if it was a little unexpected. He resisted the temptation to switch over to beer, and tried to separate the comfort from the discomfort. Enjoy the fucking evening. Daran was looking at him. Checking he was okay. *He went out of his way to bring you here. Don't squander your gifts.*

The ethereal bassline persisted out in the damp chill of the night air. From the smallness of the venue, and the strength of the amps, Kestrel's chest was still pounding with the aftereffects. He slid into the passenger's seat, happy and jelly-legged, as though he was drunk, despite not having had more than a few pints of coke. Daran was clearly euphoric too, and in every glance and grin as he got sorted and settled, Kestrel saw the echo of those blissful instants from back in the venue—head tilted back, eyes shuttered closed as sound washed over him. It didn't seem to matter where or when; Daran was so acutely present in the moment, to the point of intimidation.

As the car groaned into gear, as the wipers started their battle against the rising rain, Kestrel decided he wanted to be more like that.

The music that came through on the car's tinny stereo was already such a quiet contrast to the gig, but it was made even more so by the increasing volume of rain outside.

'Look, I'll just drive you right back to campus. This weather's atrocious to walk in.'

Kestrel had a faint recollection of the original plan—get dropped off at the nearest station—but that was when more people said they'd be coming, and besides, he had been so distracted at the last youth group meeting. Didn't help that the rain on the car windows reminded him of the feeling he had in the chapel that day. For a short moment, it was too intense, and a warm blush of complicated feelings swelled in his chest, not entirely good, not entirely bad. Most of it was the fear of disappointing Daran, stupid as that seemed right now. He ended up accepting Daran's offer, and it earned him a smile.

The music segued into a softer, sweeter track. *Time everlasting, time to play b-sides.*

Daran noticed him paying attention. 'Blue Öyster Cult,' he said.

'It's good.'

'Yeah. God, I had the LP's of this when I was younger.'

'Heh, cool.'

'Shame those things went out of fashion. Sure, they were a pain to play, but I do think they sounded better.'

Kestrel nodded. Not that he could relate to that, but he didn't know what else to do, and he just hoped the commiseration didn't come off as too false.

It was when they reached the small rise leading up to the college dorms that the sky poured out all its fury. The driving rain was bolstered by a peal of thunder, a crack of lightning that lit up the velvet blue darkness.

Daran noticed Kestrel's sudden rapt attention and slowed the car. As it came to a gentle stop, he kept the windscreen wipers and the stereo going, and just sat there in silence. It was clear enough why, and with unspoken permission Kestrel watched the storm unfold.

'Hah! Wow.'

The excitement as he held his breath, balanced on the edge of the moment. Waiting for another lightning flash to come.

'You are easily pleased by the weather, aren't you?'

Kestrel stared at him.

'It's not a bad thing, don't misunderstand.'

'Okay, good.' And he returned to watching the sky.

Daran was still watching him, and he could feel it, the attention at the back of his neck.

'Sometimes I think you're very much like your namesake. Flying free on the breeze, subject to the whim of the clouds.'

Kestrel felt his cheeks redden. Flattery seemed so ridiculous that it was almost frustrating how effective it was. But at the same time, he got the most intense feeling that Daran absolutely meant it.

'I just really like lightning strikes,' he said, and because Daran made no attempt to fill the silence, he continued. 'Some people think that when you've seen one, you've seen them all. But it's different every time. And when each one comes, you never know if it's going to be the last one or not. You just have to wait and find out.'

'So you like the uncertainty?'

'I don't know if I *like* it, I just… get too caught up in it.'

'I can relate.'

They sat in silent awe for precious moments more, then Daran sighed like the world was ending and cranked the handbrake down. 'I suppose I should get you back to your dorm.' The engine groaned into life and the car moved off, leaving Kestrel feeling as though something had just been narrowly avoided.

Because lightening the mood was his habit, he said, 'So, uh, thanks. For today, I mean.'

'Any time. And Kestrel, I really do mean it.'

Kestrel didn't know what to say after that. In a few more seconds, they would be at the driveway and it would all be over. So he gestured to the stereo.

'This is a good song.'

'Veteran of the Psychic Wars.'

'It's almost a shame to leave it halfway through.'

Daran smiled with a sudden infectious glee, and with a flick of his wrist he swung the car back around. 'Once more around the block then, just until the song's finished.'

Kestrel was content with that.

For one hundred excellent seconds, up and down the hill and round the corner, they played out the rest of the song against the force of the driving wind, and by the time they once more returned to the dormitory driveway, the track had wound down to the final resonating riff. Daran let the car roll until it felt like it had stopped of its own accord, and he kept the engine running but turned the stereo off, leaving an abrupt analogue kiss upon their ears. Kestrel wasn't quite sure how else to explain it, but there was a missing moment in the air. Like a gramophone needle skipping over a track. The moon had broken out from behind a cloud but it was still raining hard. In the time it took him to unbuckle his seatbelt, Daran had fished an umbrella off the back seat and had offered it to him.

'Take it. You can give it back whenever.'

He accepted it gingerly, trying not to make it awkward by letting his fingers brush Daran's. A fucking miracle that he succeeded. He dipped his head, said thanks and goodbye and probably overdid it on both but whatever, just ignore that, time to walk out into the night.

He had barely been home for five minutes when a knock came on the door.

Bram peeked out at him from the narrow gap, eyes wide and hopeful behind a flurry of black hair. It was telling that Kestrel's first thought was *thank God he hadn't come to the gig as well.*

'Where were you? I been trying to get hold of you all evening.'

For the first time in hours, Kestrel thought to check his phone. A couple missed calls. 'Um, I was at a, uh… church thing.'

Bram gave pause for a moment, but in the end this seemed to satisfy. 'Oh yeah, isn't it Easter soon?'

'Yup.'

Bram nodded. 'Better you than me, hah. So, I wanna run some playlists by you. For our campaign. Mind if I come in?'

'Sure.'

He hopped inside, laptop tucked under his arm, and made himself at home.

'You split pretty quickly the other night at the bar, too, so I was just—oh, I meant to say earlier, nice hair!'

'Yeah, that's actually why I left. Bethan wanted to dye it.'

Never mind that I just ghosted on you yet again without saying a word.

Bram didn't seem to be all that bothered about the ghosting. 'She did a good job,' he said, and Kestrel started to think *yeah, okay, good, maybe I don't need to worry about anything.* Then, 'I swear I would've mentioned it at lunch but then—oh my God, the whole Tala thing! Did you manage to meet her? I mean, did she meet you? She was looking for you.'

Kestrel paused. Word Tetris. What was the perfect combination to make that whole fucking line of conversation vanish off the bottom of the screen?

'She's still upset.'

It was the right combination. Elicited a soft-spoken *Damn* and nothing more than an uneasy question of 'Uh, lemme know if she feels any better, okay? I'm not very good at this stuff.'

You and me both.

'Sure,' he said, and that was that.

'Oi, what d'you think of this? For the next session.' Bram rotated his laptop, offering Kestrel the driving seat. 'You think it's too much?'

'I dunno. Give me a chance.'

Playlist ID 148—Bram had a lot of them. The massive play button pulsed gently at the top of the page. Kestrel started it up.

'Mm, very atmospheric.' He let it run on a bit. 'Seems fine. Flows nicely.'

'That second track is mine. They got a new MIDI sequencer on the site. Lets you put together some of your own stuff.'

'Oh! Nice.'

The second track started out as a jaunty little melody that segued into something darker. Heavy percussion interrupting the arpeggios like gunshots. Sustained notes, slight pitch bends. It made him feel sour. And then it made him think. The music at the start, that jaunty tune, was something a bard might play. A bard like Elijah, perhaps. He was instantly transported back to the inn, to where they had left off at the end of last session. And like ice melting into water, the scene shifted into the cave. The Shrine of Matanbuchus.

Belial, Belial, inside his head and out, groaning with the weight of the world on his shoulders as he lurched closer to Quinn. Belial, *that name*, and a frightened expression paired with it that was neither his nor Quinn's.

It was Tala's.

Today, with Daran, was the second time she had reacted to meeting a newcomer with such shock. Well, it was more than shock. She had been frightened, but not for herself.

Did it mean anything?

He thought about it some more, but it just made him feel ill, so he shook it off. It was stupid to let her problems work their way under his skin like this. He was getting too close, he knew that, winding in to her vicinity like he was a dwarf star orbiting around another. He never could seem to avoid doing that.

Fucking stop it. Don't let it get to you, it's making you paranoid.

'That's a really good track,' he said to Bram.

'Yeah?'

'Of course. Dude, you've got a knack for this stuff.'

It was worth it to see Bram's eyes light up like that. The big, goofy grin that accompanied it, the ecstatic little bounce to his movements as he pulled the laptop back his way. 'Thanks, mate. I hope Aaron likes it too. Yeah—next session's gonna be awesome, right?'

'Definitely,' Kestrel lied.

CHAPTER ELEVEN

Damsel in Distress

A bright night, somewhere.

He's walking on a hard surface that glints under moonlight. Asphalt, spattered with a sheen of light rain that has long since stopped falling.

To his right, a gentle whistle. He turns, and sees his dear friend and travelling companion, Elijah Grass. The man is sitting on a plastic chair, the type one might bring on a camping trip. He is at the edge of a dwindling campfire, and the night sky is stained purple behind him. The asphalt surface is so expansive in the clearing, bordered by trash bins and road lights that have long since lost power. It looks like it once was a car park.

'I am sorry, Quinn, but I know what you want, and I have to admit, it is quite salacious of you.'

He stares at Elijah. His lips part, his mouth falls open, but he doesn't know what to say. The question of how much truth may lie behind that insinuation—why *am* I here and what *is* this thing that he says I want?—is something

211

he has no desire to confront.

'I don't know what you're talking about,' he says, cursing himself for stuttering. 'I should… I should go.'

But when he turns, when he tries to go back the way he came, something grabs his hand. The sensation only lasts an instant, and when he turns it makes no sense, because Elijah is still a metre away and sitting down comfortably. His hand is empty, grasping at nothing. The night feels dangerous.

'No,' Elijah says. 'You don't want to run. You've been running for so long.'

He bites.

'What do I want, then?'

'Well, you want to come with me, and I'm going to let you. Although, I doubt I would give you much choice in the matter.'

The threat goes straight to his belly. It's the exact same feeling as having one too many drinks and realising that it was a horrible mistake, that he has been too friendly and gone too far and maybe, just maybe, given the wrong impression. Now he wants nothing more than to run on home and throw up and forget that other people exist.

But he is rooted to the spot, and Elijah still wears that shit-eating grin like this was all to be expected.

A sound from the pine trees makes him glance around warily. Elijah laughs, but softly.

'No need to fear. The demon won't kill you if I'm here. But either way, it won't be pleasant.'

The night feels so still. The rustling has stopped. The moon continues its solitary vigil, and the stars shimmer, little acolytes to the larger flame.

Elijah Grass stands up and stops time still with the wave of a hand. For a moment it feels as though his intestines are being pulled out from beneath him, twisting and turning as the world around him does the same. A dark miasma coils around the little bubble of spacetime they are trapped within, and Quinn cannot move at all.

Elijah, however, can.

'What are you... wait, no...'

He tells his body to start running, but it does not. It is locked to a new centre of gravity, focussed right around the campfire. Elijah comes closer, slowly, taking his time because he knows he can. He moves behind Quinn, enjoying his whimpers and protestations, and gently as a mother cat tending to her young, he rubs the scruff of Quinn's neck. It's warm, so warm, and almost would have been comforting if it had not been so unwanted. It gets worse: his hands move down, threading around Quinn's waist where they hold firm.

There's a sound in the distance like violins tuning up for an orchestra.

He's about to cry because he's already said no, stop, and his plea has gone unanswered. He's thinking about puking —if only he could move, if only he could have some control—and that's when Elijah's hands start moving, kneading his flesh as they feel him up and down. The heat increases at his back as Elijah presses closer, buries his face in the crook of his shoulder. Stubble scratches at his skin. And Elijah sways softly, as though the orchestra has begun, but only for his ears.

'Oh, Quinn, I could do this all night.'

He finds his own voice once more. 'Why—why are you doing this?'

Elijah mimics him, evidently finding this delightful. Then his voice dips back to its regular register. 'My dear boy, I will do this as many times as it takes... for you to understand.'

He doesn't know what it is he's meant to understand. He starts to ask, and Elijah clamps a hand over his mouth. He yelps into the action, and tastes salt on his tongue.

'Shh, don't make a fuss. I only want you to watch.' Elijah's free hand spreads out, as if painting the skies.

Again, his stomach lurches, and the heavens start to shift. Beyond their little sacrosanct bubble, it looks as though the trees are splitting apart and the stars are separating to come kiss the asphalt.

'I can control everything, from inside here. I'm surprised you haven't figured it out by now, honestly.'

He casts a sidelong glance at Elijah—for lack of moving his head, that is all he can do. He can feel the fear he's telegraphing but he can do little to stop it. He is firmly at the man's mercy, and in a perverse way, perhaps if he lets him see his fear, it might please him enough to...

To what? Treat him more kindly?

His skin is vibrating as if the air is cold, but he's pretty sure it's just the position he is in. As Elijah glides a hand around his midriff, his fingers thrum with that energy, feeding off it, taking more, until it stops just short of his groin, abruptly and with little ceremony. Elijah is sitting down, back on the camping chair, and the heavens are ordinary once more.

He backs away with a jolt, but Elijah seems not to notice. All he does is look up, and he seems so genuinely friendly that it's hard to imagine that anything untoward just happened. Quinn continues to back away, and thankfully, the cue is taken.

'Well,' says Elijah, 'I'll be seeing you again soon.'

Kestrel woke up. He felt shaky, dehydrated, as if he was hung over—although nothing of the sort could have occurred. Last night had been unbearably alcohol-free. His chest was slick with beads of sweat, and his back was drenched where he had pressed into the bedsheets. Peeling his shirt off was an uncomfortable affair, and even the cold air did little to purge the sticky heat festering beneath his skin.

His efforts to get clean in the shower merely ended up exacerbating the problem, because the instant the hot water hit his skin, that delicious and terrifying energy rose once again. The dream still surrounded him, too thick to slough away from his skin, and it was making him aroused, it was making him hard, and that was something he didn't want to be.

The trouble with such a thing was, once you started feeling it, there was only really one satisfying way of making it stop.

He closed his eyes, focussed as hard as he could on the water running down his face, tried not to see Elijah or the trees or the car park or the fucking rain on asphalt despite the shower's best attempts to remind him of that.

I think I'm gonna go insane. I need to do something about this.

Then he reached down and finished the job.

Stopping by the café on the way to class meant a short detour from dorms down to the south street, and it meant walking a little way into the town centre proper, but it was a brisk, sunny morning that deserved some attention, and so Kestrel was happy to go the extra distance.

Feeling the leaves squish underfoot as he walked alongside the low stone walls served as a tonic for his nerves after the unsettling night. Spring bulbs were busy pushing their way through the sodden soil, and finches chittered away in the hedgerows. The sun was hardly strong, shining out behind a veil of high cloud, but still it was an order of magnitude brighter than the landscapes in his mind, to the point where it seemed hyper-real.

He happened to enter the café at the same time as Aaron.

The chance encounter put an involuntary smile on his face. Same for Aaron, who fixed him with a cheeky grin.

'I was really hoping to run into you, actually.'

'Oh, yeah?' He got the feeling a question was coming, and he wasn't wrong.

'So, uh, Kes, I need to talk to you about something.' Aaron ducked out of the café's main thoroughfare, beckoning Kestrel in around the condiment table. There was barely any rush of customers that morning, so it was hardly necessary, but despite his blasé demeanour, Aaron was a conscientious sort and this small detail made Kestrel smile. He scooched in alongside him.

'Sure, what is it?'

'Just like, a plotline thing, for the campaign. See—I was planning on having Belial capture somebody, when you guys reach the Shrine.'

'You want it to be Quinn.' There was a twisting in his gut even as he said it.

Aaron gave a guilty half-smile. 'It seemed like the only thing that would make sense for the plotline. Because he's the only rogue in the group, and uh, that sort of gives you an advantage. Like, as for what you can do when you get captured. If you're okay with getting captured.'

'Right, um...'

'Are you okay with it? I mean, I ought to ask before

putting your character in a situation like that.'

'Yeah,' Kestrel said, all too quickly. 'Yeah, do it. I don't mind.'

Aaron grinned. 'Cool.'

The sun continued its struggle towards spring as the day wore on, with all the enthusiasm of an underpaid retail worker tasked with opening shop. Kestrel couldn't fault it for that; he barely had the energy to slog through the day, and the only thing he was looking forward to was the lunchtime ritual, the walking and talking with the right words at the right times by the right trees in the arboretum.

There they were, all waiting with Daran by the horse chestnuts. Now, those candelabra-shaped flowers were growing thick and fast, blossoming in white stacks upon stacks, thriving in the aftermath of yesterday's storm.

It was interesting, he thought, how the countdown to Easter was the opposite of Advent: there, the candles started strong and got whittled down the closer it got to the time of celebration, but here the candles only grew and grew, albeit on trees. There, everything cosy and warm and indoors; here, everything out in the wild, in the cold air. He felt a pang of nostalgia for the smell of cinnamon and mince pies, made all the more forbidden from the thought that Easter was the more important festival and this, this was what he should be celebrating. Out here, in the chill of spring, was where he should be placing his faith.

He joined the group.

The first thing Daran said: 'It's so good to see you, Kestrel.' The second: 'Slightly less interesting weather today, hm?' He gave him this knowing look, and something about that made Kestrel feel self-conscious. Was that what blushing was? Either way, he felt noticed. He felt part of something that the others were not.

It did not surprise Kestrel that he was chosen for the second reading. It did not surprise him that he was chosen for the twelfth, either.

'Darkness came over the land, and Jesus cried with a loud voice, "Eli, Eli, lema sabachthani?" that is, "My God, my God, why have you forsaken me?" When bystanders heard it, they said, "This man is calling for Elijah." At once one of them ran and got a sponge, filled it with sour wine, put it on a stick, and gave it to him to drink, But the others said, "Wait, let us see whether Elijah will come to save him."'

The twelfth had made him feel uncomfortable before, but now doubly so. Too oddly specific, and way too surreal, to the extent that he started wondering if he had ever woken up today at all. He could turn his head just slightly to the side and maybe see a little clearing in the trees, a small campfire, a vacant plastic chair. The ground was, after all, still glistening with yesterday's rain.

'Kestrel?'

He snapped out of it. He had barely noticed the readings were finished. People were already saying their goodbyes, and Daran was locked on to him in that familiar intense way, proffering something from his hands. The Stations printouts, collected from the group. All of them, save for Kestrel's, which he still gripped too tight in his own hands.

He took what Daran gave him without even thinking. Such a reflex action, and it amused the more detached part of his mind as he did so.

'Would you mind taking these back to the chapel for me? I have a meeting to run to. It'll really take the load off for me.'

'Uh, sure.'

'Fantastic. Just run the keys back to me when you're done.' A hard, irregular shape pressed down on his palm atop the sheaves of paper. Keys on a trashy green keyring. A pat on his shoulder, light but firm. 'I appreciate this, Kestrel.'

And then Daran was off, not towards the north end of the campus, but to the east, where the hulking shape of the Humanities block sat. It was curious how he could move with such purpose, but not seem rushed, despite clearly being short on time.

He thumbed the keyring charm. It was a squat little frog, shaped in modelling clay. Some rough scratches on the bottom—initials? Probably handmade. Kind of nostalgic. Somehow this was amusing to him, and he awkwardly squashed the smile as he looked up to say goodbye to the others.

They were already too far off for him to bother waving, so to avoid the weird feeling that was settling in his stomach, he just headed north, to the chapel, alone.

He was interrupted en route by a call from his mother. It wasn't one he could ignore, and he instantly felt a crushing guilt because it meant he had failed that little test of faith.

'Hi, Mum.'

'Kestrel! My dear, how are you? Is everything all right?'

'Yes, everything's fine. Just, uh, college things.'

'I suppose you've been busy.' The tone was charged.

'Yeah. I mean, it's going well, though.'

'Oh good. Good. I'm glad to hear one of us is having fun.'

Here we go. How the hell was he meant to respond to that?

'Mum, I—'

'Are you coming back for Easter? Please tell me you are. Your father's being an ass about it and—ugh, I just don't understand why he's so intent on making this holiday insufferable for me.'

Kestrel had been so close to apologising for not calling her, but now he held back on that. His parents were not together any more, but she still sometimes talked about his dad like they were, and that usually was the frontloading for a rant.

'Why are you being so quiet? Can you hear me?'

'Yes. Sorry.'

'Good, that's okay. Well, as I was saying, he's only thinking about his own feelings, as per usual, and he's got it into his head that *you* are going to go see *him* instead of *me*. Which, of course, is ridiculous. I think he's started to move away from the church altogether, and I'm pretty sure it's his new girlfriend's fault.'

No, Dad just has his own autonomy, and maybe he doesn't want to be wrapped up in that stuff any more, Kestrel thought. *And honestly, I'm glad he is, because it wasn't helping him when he was ill, and you do seem to forget that fact a lot, huh?*

If he had had more time, if he had been a bit stronger, he might have even said those thoughts aloud. But he had no desire to turn this into a marathon, so he let her sprint towards her own finish line.

'Oh, honey, it would be *so* good to see you over Easter. My new parish is excellent, they've been holding all these extra classes for things, like the Laying of Hands, and you know, it really is very interesting.'

'Oh, right?' Feigning interest, hoping it wouldn't come off as too fake.

'It's a way to cleanse negative energies from your body,'

his mother said, and she sounded like she was almost singing as she spoke. 'So,' and the sharp tone edged back in, 'what's your plan?'

Kestrel took a deep breath.

'I'm not coming to see either of you. I'm sorry, I really am—there's just too much work to do over the holidays.'

'So… you're going to spend it on campus, like a loner?'

He resented the stress on the word. Fuck, she sounded more like a teenager than he did sometimes.

'You do realise I'm paying for this, don't you?'

Yeah, you and Dad both, he thought. But he didn't say so. 'It costs the same either way,' is what he actually said, and then, because he had reached the doors to the chapel, 'I'm sorry, I have to go.'

'Your lunch break is over so soon? I thought it didn't end until the hour.'

'I'm, uh, helping out at the chapel on campus.'

'Oh, you are? Well, that's excellent, I'd expect no less of you. You must tell me all about it.'

'I'm really sorry, I'll tell you more later. They're waiting on me.'

He could hear her petulance in the way she was breathing. It was frustrating how little it mattered—he could be a servant for the damn Pope and she would still complain that he wasn't giving that attention to her instead. There was no way to win.

'Love you, Mum,' he said, and once she had retorted with the clipped *Love you* back, he hung up, and hastily stuffed the phone back into his pocket. Fuck all of that.

The chapel was a lonely friend, when he was the only one that filled its halls. He hung around under that high, white ceiling longer than he needed to. Part of it was destructive, chasing an urge to find the source of that hammering rain from before, to tread the hall in the hope of activating that strange vision again. Part of it was just desperately seeking a way to distract from the call.

He almost ran out of time. The chapel wasn't going to give up its secrets, and class was about to start. He moved fast enough that it was a wonder he didn't trip over his own feet: filing away the printouts in one of the small cubbyholes at the chapel's vestibule. He had not needed extra instruction on where to put them. Some muscle memory from church never really left, and he guessed Daran had also assumed as much, implicitly trusting him with the job. He would do it justice—and what a glow that gave him, even amid the pressure. The sensation mingled with the smell of the dusty chapel: the ageing scent of resinous incense, the particular type of shampoo used on the carpets, and it made him feel like a young child, keen to please his parents (even more keen with the fact that, right now, he was not able to please his mother). He locked up the smooth doors that formed the chapel's entrance, double checked it, then ran off to the Humanities block, the keys and their ridiculous keyring stuffed hastily into his jeans pocket, edges digging into his thigh but it didn't matter, there was no time to adjust.

One last thing to do before class began.

It would have been easier to wrap up the job he had been given if Daran had actually been back at his office. But the door was closed, and nobody answered when he knocked. Fidgeting about for fear of time, he poked his head into the adjacent office.

'Isabel—yeah, hi, do you know where Daran is?'

The intern watched him with a cheery smile that was

clearly plastered over some deeper ennui. 'I don't know, he had some meeting to go to. He'll probably be busy for a few more hours. Try coming back later?'

'He told me to take the keys to the chapel back for him, Uh, maybe I can leave them in his office?'

'No can do. It's locked.'

'Uh…' He racked his brain. He had already missed the roll call.

'Hey, don't stress. Come back between your next periods maybe. I'm around for a few more hours so if he still isn't back I can just hold on to them for you.'

'Thanks.'

After his next class, Daran still wasn't in his office. That meeting, whatever it was about, was sure taking a long time. Kestrel spent five minutes walking around—between the Art block and the Humanities block, the narrow walkway between C and D, the main courtyard, the path back up near the chapel. Nothing.

He resigned himself back into Isabel's good graces.

She didn't seem too bothered to see him again, and it went a long way to quelling his anxiety. 'No luck, then, huh?'

He held the keys out.

'Maybe you could take them?'

Isabel kept the smile, held out her hand, patted the table non-committally. 'Sure.'

He got the impression this kind of thing happened all the time, and honestly, it was a relief. He left them with her and didn't think much more on it.

The next day, Kestrel was ambushed by a meeting of his own. And honestly, Friday morning, just before lunch hour, was a terrible time to set a year group assembly. Everyone was hungry, and nobody had the motivation, so close to the weekend. To Kestrel's right, Bram was attempting to listen to music, shielding his earphones surreptitiously with his hair. To his left, a girl from his figure study class was busy doodling in the margins of her journal. A few rows in front, Rei sat hunched over, typing furiously on her phone. Kestrel thought of everything Bethan had said, and wondered who she was texting.

Miss Warren stood at the front of the hall, on the small, raised platform that passed for a stage.

'Here are some choices you will have to make. At the end of this term, you will have to start thinking about your next steps, about where you're going to be going come Autumn. Some of you may wish to continue your studies here; others may wish to cash in that Foundation degree and progress on someplace else.' Miss Warren raised a hand. The bangles clinked. 'Either way, you will have to take the initiative.'

'Wish I could roll for the initiative to skip this assembly,' he muttered, before realising that Bram was plugged in and couldn't hear him. So much for trying to be witty. Feeling rather foolish, he did as the girl to his left did, and started making his own doodles in the margins.

Minutes later, though, Bram came out of his musical reverie, removing one earbud as he peered down at Kestrel's page.

'Is that Quinn?'

Kestrel nodded.

'And—oho! I know who that other one is!'

The weird horned, bracken-limbed creature sprung out

from the page, starker for it being drawn in black biro. Kestrel immediately became self-conscious of the heavy pressure he had used to draw it—biro made that so much more noticeable.

'Yeah, I've been trying to draw Belial but, it never really comes out quite right.'

Bram peered closer.

'Huh. He looks—or, well, it looks? You can't really tell with a demon, can you?—anyway, he looks exactly how I imagined he would.'

A loud cough from the centre stage made them look up sharply. Miss Warren was watching them with piercing eyes. 'Pay attention, please. You can fill the room with idle chatter later.'

They separated, Kestrel a little guiltily, Bram more belligerently.

'As I was saying, you have until the end of this term to submit your preferences for the next year, but I recommend you don't wait that long.' She sniffed. 'Now is the time to take responsibility for yourself.'

Kestrel already knew what he wanted to do next year. He was not usually so well-prepared for anything, but this was what he considered an easy choice. Illustration and concept art, either the continuation course here, or at the bigger university in the city. Maybe one day he would be painting images for a tabletop gaming handbook, or concept art for some videogame. So he went to the admin offices at lunchtime, mere minutes after Miss Warren's irritating assembly had ended, and decided to put in his preferences.

He wasn't sure what spurred him on. More of that desire to please, perhaps.

The admin offices were at the front of the campus, just

off to the side of the entrance hall. The light from outside did weird things in here, casting the eggshell walls with golden yellow, making the whole facility seem like it was under a photo filter. For whatever reason, the man at the reception booth he ended up being summoned to was a little out of it—overworked, or just tired, maybe—and he ended up having to repeat himself multiple times just to get a tiny stamp on his form.

It turned out that all he *actually* had to do was file the preferences form through a hole in the wall just past the leaflet stand, he hadn't needed anything stamped by the administrator at all, as long as he had his student number on there. He didn't usually get irritated by incompetence, but this felt like a taste of what he often heard older folk refer to as a bureaucratic nightmare. Seemed like the future was going to be a whole lot of fun.

As he slipped past the by-now moderate crowd, he heard a voice so familiar carry itself over the throng. He paused, letter in hand, and looked around. Was that... Daran?

Yeah—over by the other end of the room, talking to someone in overalls who looked like they were probably the groundskeeper. He wondered why. Either way, it was interesting to note how well-projected Daran's voice was compared to anyone else in the reception area. It was a voice that asked for attention.

So that it didn't seem like he was staring, he set back to business, excusing himself around an idling fellow student and posting the form through the small letterbox opening. There was a disturbance in the light around him, things moving just over his shoulder. Then, Daran, calling him from across the hall.

'Kestrel! Perfect, you're just who I wanted to run into.'

Oh God, was he coming to talk to him?

Yeah, he was separating from the man in overalls. He was definitely headed his way.

Kestrel shuffled his bag to a more comfortable position on his shoulder and hooked a lock of hair behind his ear. Daran walked over to him, hair like wild grass burning under the sun in that fantastical reception hall light. The way he moved was too precise, too definite—it telegraphed trouble. He ushered him to the side, just out of the reception hall, stopping by a fire exit that never saw any attention.

Kestrel thought again of Bethan—*you respond so positively to authority*—and that just made him feel belligerent, which was never a good way to start a conversation.

'Where did you put the keys?'

'I, uh… You weren't in, so I left them in the office with Isabel, in the end.'

'With Isabel?' His eyes grew piercing hard.

'Y-yeah.'

'She's an intern. She doesn't have authorisation to take care of the keys.'

I don't either, I'm a student, was what he wanted to say. But Daran was in too much of a challenging mood, that was clear enough to anyone with a brain, so what he said instead was, 'Should I have… uh… kept hold of them?'

He could hear the upward lilt of his own voice: the peacekeeping tone. He fucking hated it.

'You should have waited for me to come back. Or asked her where I was. Either way, she's not in today and I can't get in to the damn place. I'm having to get the skeleton key from the groundskeeper.'

He was shocked by the thinly veiled rage making it out

in his direction. It felt unwarranted, for such a little thing, and it made him just as angry in return, wanting to defend himself. He couldn't avoid a short huff escaping his mouth.

'You look like you want to say something.'

'I... no.'

'Please stop being so difficult, Kestrel.'

That was too much. Finally, he hit back.

'I did ask her where you were! She said you'd be stuck in meetings for another few hours. I had class to get to, and I even came back between lectures and you still weren't there, so... I... you know what, I didn't think this would be such a big problem. It's just a bunch of keys.'

For a moment he thought Daran might grab his arm, pull him closer. But all he did instead was lean his hand against the fire escape—bracing against the door, bracing against his only way out—and breathe out sharply.

'I don't know why you're being like this.'

'It's gonna be fine!'

'You think it's fine? Come now, you have to stop taking this sort of thing so lightly!'

He could feel himself shaking, he could feel his cheeks growing redder. It was just like being a little kid, being told off for something you didn't even realise you were doing wrong. It wasn't what he had intended, and so this felt unfair. A real slap in the face. He didn't reply, biting his lip and averting his gaze until he got a handle on his own emotions.

Unfortunately, avoidance wasn't a tactic that was going to help here.

'Kestrel, look at me. Look.' Reluctantly, he did, and Daran continued. 'I don't understand what I said to make you react like that.'

That made him feel small, like he was complaining over

nothing.

It was so fucking stupid, the fact that he could feel tears gathering in his eyes. But he had little choice: it was either that or anger, and it was already obvious that getting angry wouldn't work.

He felt his eyes widen as he continued to look up at Daran, and it seemed that something in his fraught expression broke through to him.

'Well, whatever it was that I did, I'm sorry.'

Kestrel stared back numbly. How would he even explain that to anyone? *He made me feel weird and then apologised for it?* Sounded like a totally considerate thing to do. Even thinking about complaining over that… yeah, that just made him sound like the asshole. Bottom line was, he had been trusted, and he had ruined that trust.

There was another part of him, a questioning part, that tried to imagine how anyone else might have acted in the same situation. He doubted they would have gone chasing all over campus for him. He doubted they would have kept coming back between lessons. And… did that apology even count as an apology anyway?

It was probably a waste of time to think of all the arguments for or against. All that mattered was that Daran was disappointed in him. He probably wouldn't have enough faith to entrust the same task to him next week, and somehow that was more crushing than the damn painting being banned from the exhibition.

'I'm—I'm sorry.'

Daran's expression softened almost immediately. 'It's okay. I know you didn't mean it.'

In that instant, he felt like he wanted to do anything to make it up to him.

'I'll, uh, I'll do better next time.'

'Right. I… okay. I believe you.' Despite his softening up, Daran still spoke more brusquely than he would have liked, and quite against his will it made Kestrel long for more clemency from him.

CHAPTER TWELVE

Plenary Indulgences

'That assembly sucked!' said Bram, and he could not have sounded more petulant if he had tried.

They were doing some sketching exercises in Mr Ruiz's class. Last period of the day, but it was a pairs activity and it was relatively fun, and at least Mr Ruiz let them choose their own partners. Kestrel, of course, had gone with Bram. Now they sat at the same desk, opposite each other, sketching each other's faces sequentially in little grids: one in charcoal, then in pencil, one taking five minutes, the next taking ten, one with the non-dominant hand, and so on.

'Have you put in your preferences yet?'

'No. I'm not sure whether to focus on animation or not. Also, why is it that every time Miss Warren tells us to do something, I feel like a fucking pre-schooler?'

Kestrel didn't have an answer for that.

'Makes me feel like doing the exact opposite,' Bram mumbled, bowing his head and scrawling away a rough approximation of Kestrel's hair on paper.

'Oi, look up a sec. I need to see your nose.'

They were halfway through the exercise when an interruption came.

'Hey, Kestrel, would you mind...' Mr Ruiz beckoned from the front of the class.

Kestrel sighed, and pushed up from his desk. His pencils scattered to the side, coming to rest in small wobbles at the edge of his drawing pad.

'What is it?'

'Well, it's about your friend, Tala.' Mr Ruiz spoke quietly enough that the rest of the class couldn't hear clearly, and besides, he ran too much of a casual, talkative classroom that the others were too wrapped up in their own chatter to pay attention. 'I'm also teaching Sculptures and Materials this term, and we've been doing distance teaching via email assignments. She was meant to have a meeting with me the other day, but she never showed up.'

The familiar burning settled in around Kestrel's gut. It was unwelcome, but there she was again, Tala running off down the narrow path between C and D block, her stricken expression clear as day. In his legs, the sensation of adrenaline gathering, as if he could just start running after her.

'I don't know what's happened in the last week, but she's stopped responding.' Mr Ruiz patted the table before him; the sound brought Kestrel back into the room. 'It would be great if you could take these to her. It's just homework notes and, uh, those preference forms Miss Warren was talking about.'

More sheaves of paper, proffered before him. More opportunity to fuck up. Kestrel could feel himself chewing away at his tongue—a habit he hated, a habit that made his face look lopsided—and he really did not want to be in this position again.

'I'm not sure I'm the best person to do this…'

In fact, I'm pretty sure I'm the reason she didn't come to meet you.

'I called her mother, and she's too busy with work to come and collect them herself. But she did mention your name.'

'Her mother did?'

Mr Ruiz nodded. 'Apparently you've been a great friend to her recently.'

Again, he wanted so badly to contest that fact. The evidence, after all, pointed to something quite different.

Kestrel swore in his head. This whole situation was ridiculous, and he was caught in the swell. He heard himself saying 'Okay, sure', he watched as the papers exchanged hands.

Mr Ruiz looked sad for a moment, then turned his deep brown eyes up to him and said, 'My door's open. If you need to talk about anything.'

He couldn't fucking believe what he was hearing.

'Like the exhibition?'

'Like the exhibition. Or whatever else. I'm not here to make you more stressed out—this is a school, we're meant to offer support. Anyway. That's all.'

Kestrel nodded but it came off all stilted, and he went back to his seat with a sinking feeling. Did he not look well? Was it so easy to tell he was unravelling? Maybe Ruiz was just being too overbearing. He came off at times like a well-meaning but fumbling dad. Part of him longed for the more genuine, intense way Daran had offered him the same thing, but after what happened over lunch hour, that brought with it a bad taste in his mouth.

'What's that?' Bram poked at the papers as Kestrel sank

back down into his seat.

'Uhh… homework, for Tala.'

'Oh. Lol. You're not his errand boy.'

'Please stop saying lol in real life.'

Bram grinned defiantly. 'I'll stop when they come up with a better word that doesn't involve actually laughing out loud.' His grin mellowed out into something more sombre. 'Seriously, though. The teachers here gotta stop singling you out.'

Kestrel shrugged. 'It is what it is, I guess.'

He thought about what he had now been tasked with, and that crushing hopelessness came over him again. The potential to fuck things up was too real, it had too much precedent. He could feel Daran's disappointment like oil on his skin; it seeped into his pores, sowing shame, sowing rage. Which emotion deserved to win, he had no idea. Both seemed justified.

Bram shifted from poking the papers to poking Kestrel's arm with his pencil.

'You look like you need to rant a little.'

'Yeah, maybe I do.'

Could never hide these things from him. He knows me too well.

'It's Daran,' he said at length.

'Who?'

'Uh, the religious counsellor. On campus. There was this whole thing with me messing up the keys to the chapel and it just… made me feel kind of crap. Like, sometimes he says things that make me feel like a complete idiot and I just remember that he still sees me as some immature kid or something.'

'He's still a teacher,' Bram said. 'That's probably why. They can be nice but there's still this power divide. At the end of the day he's going to talk over you, no matter how nice he is.'

Kestrel wanted to contend that point. Defend Daran.

'Adults suck,' Bram added.

'We're adults.'

'We're nineteen.'

'You know what I mean.'

'And you know what I mean! Sorry. I'm not making you feel better, am I? I just don't like people making you feel small.'

'Thanks. It's okay. I appreciate it.'

'What kind of things did he say to you?'

'He just… Agh, he was stressed out, I think. He'd probably had a lot going on that day…' He watched Bram watch him, and realised he was making excuses. He could either backtrack now, or go harder, justify the excuse.

He went harder.

'What's worst of all is that I think some of what he said was right. Like, we *should* be responsible for our actions. People in general could really do with thinking a little more about their neighbour, and maybe take some initiative or go the extra mile, instead of just performing duties by rote. I agree that a lot of people *do* lack discipline. And being humble is totally an underrated trait. But at the same time, having him direct all this at *me* makes me feel awful, like I'm being punished for trying. Like I'm being punished more than the people around me who are trying *less*.'

'Well, that's heavy.' Bram's eyebrows were quirking up, not in judgement but in commiseration.

'Sorry. I just… it stings more when everything's been going so well—' He stopped short of saying 'especially after we went to the gig together'. Curious, how he still felt guilty about that.

Bram would have really liked to go too.

Fuck, it would be nice if this week could just be scrubbed from the timeline altogether.

'I don't know why he had to pick on you, most of all.'

The words caught Kestrel off-guard, and his cheeks burned with the attention of it.

'Maybe it's just because I was there,' he said, and in that instant he didn't know if that made it better or worse.

It scared me.

'Come to anime club with me when we're done here. It'll get your mind off it for a bit.'

The first thing Kestrel did before anime club was go back to the dorms and hunt for that bottle of Jameson's. The second thing he did was text Tala.

—Hey, I really need to talk to you.

There must have been something at work in the air that night because she responded almost instantly.

—If this is about last week, I'm sorry. I really am.

—It's okay.

It felt like that was all he was saying to his friends these days.

—You're not gonna… ask me to come again this week, are you?

—No, don't worry. Seriously, you didn't mess up or anything.

This got him no response, so after a few minutes he sent another message.

— I did get some notes to give you, from Fine Art.

—shit. I meant to let him know, but

The pause between that and the next message was so natural, he could almost hear her sigh as she typed.

—I guess I forgot. He's probably worried now.

—Could I come over?

Another long wait before her reply, and when that came, it only confused him.

—I keep telling myself that this time it'll be different. But you keep proving me wrong.

—I'm sorry, I… don't understand what that means.

—I know, I know, I'm sorry… Look, I need more time, okay? Not this week, not this week.

He sagged back in his chair, took a swig from the bottle like he was splashing tonic on a wound. There was a shivering quality to the air. Felt like a splinter not quite ready to come out; everything swelling up around it.

Going to the lecture halls after hours always felt clandestine. There was the delicious thrill of feeling like you were doing something you really were not meant to be, despite the fact that the anime club had already been given permission through the student union to be here. The lights were dimmed in the halls—not off entirely, just enough to keep the power bill down—and the absence of students rushing to their next lecture made the place feel haunted.

They had booked out one of the smaller lecture halls at the end of the block, which only added to the childish feeling of excitement.

The girl with big hair was there—made sense she was an anime fan—and again, Bram was acting very touchy-feely with her, but in that awkward young-love way that indicated they were not quite confident enough to call each other boyfriend and girlfriend. It was surprising to think that he could feel both jealous and happy at the same time about this.

Either way, Bram had invited him out to get his mind off other things. He shouldn't be souring that with such a petty thing.

He stuck it out until the end of the fourth episode, which was about all the club had time for anyway, then made his excuses and left.

The outdoor air: fraught with silence. The sky, split open wide, not a single cloud in sight. Another bright night, somewhere in the world. He did not want to be alone in it.

He texted Samuel.

'You around?'

Half an hour later, the pair of them were sat on the floor in Kestrel's dorm room. They were drinking directly from the bottle, passing it between them. Trappist wine. Super strong. Sweet and heady. Samuel had brought it from his stash at the priory, because of course that was the kind of thing he would have plenty of there.

'How strong actually is this stuff?'

'Uhh. Twenty percent.'

'Fuuuuck.'

Samuel laughed, stole it back, took another swig. It was hard not to hyperfixate on his jawline, his gorgeous sandy brown hair. Most of all, the way he just seemed to relish being there, with Kestrel, drinking indoors on a Friday night.

Just bros being bros. Bit of a wistful thought. He tried to curb it.

'I take it school's been kicking your ass?' Samuel turned those bright eyes his way.

'Yeah. Nothing new. What about you?'

'We've been stuck on eschatology for a while now.'

'Uh… refresh my memory.'

'Study of the end times.'

Of course. He remembered the textbook lying in Aaron's living room.

'Ah, the sexiest part of the Bible.'

'Hah—yeah, sure is that. I'm kind of tired of it now though. Like, at this point I'd probably take psalms over this.'

Kestrel sighed, resting his head back against the bed. 'Sometimes I just… look through the Bible and see what cool stories I can find. Like, the really weird stuff. There's just… so much in there, it's like…'

Samuel nodded, an approval that Kestrel fed off like crazy.

'It's not as stuffy as people say. It's—there's a lot of stuff that's just super surreal.' He paused. Felt a smile spread across his face as he remembered something. 'I think God has a thing against figs.'

Samuel laughed and took another swig of wine from the bottle.

'Seriously! It's in the—what book was it? Ezekiel? And the Gospels. Look, I'll show you…' He fished for his phone, navigated to an online Bible reader, searched. 'Here! Mark 11:4. And Jesus cursed the fig tree, and said "You shall never bear fruit again!" And his disciples heard him say it.'

'People really lose their temper when they're hangry.'

'Hah, right?'

'Seems the Son of God is no exception.'

He re-read the passage and laughed.

'It's just… that's so what your mates would write, isn't it? *And his disciples heard him say it.* They haven't even attempted to sugarcoat it. That's how you know the story's true.'

'I mean, you're not wrong.'

Kestrel kept scrolling.

'Oh, the other reference I was thinking of was Jeremiah, not Ezekiel. He sort of, goes off on one about God judging people, and again, yep, there it is: "there are no figs on the fig tree; even the leaves are withered."'

Samuel brought his hand up to his face, rested a finger in the divot in his chin. 'Maybe all this anti-fig propaganda is because fig leaves were what Adam and Eve used to cover themselves up when they left the Garden of Eden?'

'Heh. Probably.'

'Speaking of Ezekiel, though—I know that wasn't the book you were thinking of, but there's some really neat stuff in that, like, prophecy-wise.'

'I thought you were getting bored of eschatology?'

'I mean, yeah, but that's because everyone focuses on the Book of Revelation. Ezekiel came about six hundred years earlier, and there is just so much weird stuff going on in his visions. You should read it sometime. Or re-read it. You know.'

'I'll add it to the list.'

Samuel hit a change of pace when he said, rather abruptly, 'I'm glad I saw you at the youth group those few weeks ago.'

'Yeah, same,' said Kestrel, and inside he thought *really, you have no fucking idea how happy I am.*

'It's great that Daran started this up. You know, there used to be a youth group a few years back, but it ended when the previous guy left.' Samuel sighed. 'I think Daran's a bit better. It's like he understands us more.'

'He's… definitely not what I expected.' There was nothing more Kestrel could offer up on that front. He didn't want to think about the argument—if it could even be called that.

'I wish he would put on some different music though. Something heavier.'

Kestrel remembered all those times visiting Aaron's house, growing up. Saturday cartoons. The thump of hardcore rock coming from Samuel's room. He really had not changed much. And, because Kestrel wanted to impress, he put himself on the spot and called up all the heavier Christian rock knowledge he had.

'Something like Thrice. Or Virgin Black. You know the singer for Thrice is a pastor?'

Of course Samuel would know that. But he asked anyway.

'Yeah, he had this great thing he said in an interview once about why they make the sort of music they make. What was it…' He searched internally for a moment. '"Making subpar cheesy art for Christians to consume comfortably is a tragedy for everyone."'

This got a good laugh out of Kestrel.

'There's something else, though,' said Samuel. 'Something else, and I can't quite put my finger on it. I don't know. But it's this whole term. It just feels like awfully good timing, the youth group being set up right about now.'

'What do you mean?'

'I don't know. Well. I've been… not feeling so great, and it's the same for some of the others in the group, I know that for sure.' He looked up at Kestrel, searching for something with those soft blue eyes. 'I assume you've also needed something like this?'

'Shit, one second.' Kestrel stood up to draw the window closed; flies were getting in, attracted by the sweet wine.

He could have done what his mother always did and poured out the angel's share in a tiny cup for the flies to get stuck in and die slowly, but the thought of that made him feel sick. Bastards as the flies were.

His legs were stiff from sitting on the floor, so he sat on the bed instead, legs dangling over the side, swinging gently but not so much as to shake Samuel where he leaned back.

'Well, Tala told me something…'

'Tala… oh. I heard about what happened with her. I'm so sorry.' He remembered: of course he remembered. How they had gravitated around each other as kids. How seemingly inseparable they had been.

'It's—' Kestrel stopped short of saying 'It's okay,' because it really wasn't. He played with the loose edge of the bedsheet, he took a few deep breaths, and then he told the truth. 'It's been really shit, recently. Like you say, it's this term. I've been having these, well, kind of disturbing dreams. I feel like I've been drifting so far apart from everything, and it all hurts, and you're right, I've needed… something. A higher power. A sense of connection. Whatever it is, something like that.'

Samuel caught his eye and fuck, that went deep. So easy to fall into that feeling, enjoying not being alone. The urge to slide back down to the floor and rest his head on Samuel's shoulder was overwhelming. He resisted.

Then Samuel unwittingly broke the spell by saying 'What did she tell you?'

The words danced on the edge of his tongue but he couldn't force them out. It was running through treacle in dreams, it was pulling your hand back from the flame before the heat set in, it was involuntary and it felt strange to be inhabiting his body while some other force was driving it, but there it was. He couldn't bring himself to say.

'Ugh, no, I can't.'

'That's okay,' Samuel said. His eyebrows were a gentle arch, his forehead un-creased. No condescension, no questioning.

It went a long way to quelling the anxiety in his chest.

'I know what you mean. About the dreams, actually.'

So much for the anxiety being quelled. Such a simple sentence, but it lit that dying ember and again Kestrel was on edge, hardly believing what he was hearing. Too many people, this was too many people recently.

So, very carefully, he said, 'In what way?'

'I... Heh, this will probably sound stupid, but, you remember those fairytales? About the brook horses? It always starts out that way. Something dragging me down into the shallows. It makes me... okay, it's a little embarrassing, but it sort of, *tempts* me. Like, sexually. I feel out of control and it's fucking awful. Then, next thing I know, I'm at somebody's funeral. Sometimes I wonder if it's mine. I wake up barely breathing. I think something's touching me, but I'm alone.'

Listening to Samuel describe this in such a soft, scared voice made him want to cry. It fast became overwhelming, and for a moment he thought he really was going to. But then Samuel turned his head at a particular angle, still resting on the mattress in part, but tilted just enough to look at him. It was enough of a distraction. Samuel was incredibly gorgeous, when the light hit the side of his face like that.

Those eyes held such weariness, though, and it hurt Kestrel's chest to see.

'Are *you* okay?'

'Well, I'm a bit… conflicted.'

He didn't elaborate.

Kestrel was content to sit there in silence with him, and that may have been what did it, encouraging Samuel to open up. He turned away from Kestrel, took to staring very intently at the wood grain on the desk, elbows propped up on his knees, leaning against the bed in an almost despairing way as he traced the wood grain patterns with his forefinger.

'Recently I've had… things that make me wonder if this path is right for me. But then I… I'm too scared to follow up on them because of *other* things, and it just—it all forms one big mess in my head.'

They had reached the end of the bottle.

Now Samuel looked as though he was about to cry. He extricated himself from where he sat, and rearranged until he was on his knees, in front of Kestrel. When he looked up at him, for a second Kestrel could not bear it, being in such an elevated position over another. Especially over Samuel.

'Kestrel, can you… can you give me your hand?'

Dumbfounded, Kestrel obliged.

Samuel took his hand—the touch of his skin was so soft —and slowly, carefully, he held Kestrel's hand to his own forehead. Closing his eyes as though through this he was being blessed.

As time slowed to a gentle stop, Samuel whispered in the most subdued voice, 'Please, forgive me.' And he started to cry.

Kestrel hadn't expected such a keening, fragile sound, and it nearly broke his heart. He slipped to the floor, and broke off contact with their hands only to hug him close. It was such a relief to feel Samuel melt into him, sobbing and shuddering and clinging on. For what felt like minutes, they hugged, and Kestrel stroked his hair, and told him it would be all right. The smell of rosemary and fresh linen all around him, the tickling of light brown hair in his eyes, strands that seemed gold in the refracted light of his bedside lamp.

When they started kissing, neither of them really expected it. It just happened, as naturally as the hug did; it felt desperate and needy and necessary. He pressed in to Samuel more, felt his lips yield, felt him yield. Such a fucking intoxicating feeling. The way they grabbed on to each other's arms, their hips, gripping and reaching out for purchase, it was like they were both trying to simulate some darker need for pain, for possession, for the sake of just feeling out of control like the way the dreams made them feel.

Something dark unfurled deep in his belly. This time, perhaps because Samuel was just the same as him (how did he know that? He had no idea, just something he felt so keenly), he let it take over.

They ended up on the bed: more accurately, Samuel ended up on the bed and Kestrel stood over him, still fussing at him, kissing his neckline, tugging at his clothes while Samuel did the same back.

He had to do something more. He pushed Samuel gently back on the bed, then clambered up at his feet.

Something about putting himself in this position, now, felt correct. As if this was how it should play out, how it had always played out before. As if it was where he belonged.

'I forgive you,' he said to Samuel, looking up at him full of longing. He watched Samuel's eyebrows knit upward, he watched those troubled emotions dance at their edges, ready to melt on out. He gave him opportunity to say stop, he waited and prolonged the plunge on the cliff's edge until he couldn't fucking bear it any more and he pulled at Samuel's pants, thought of fig leaves, thought of dark waters, of drowning and dying and hurting and wanting to be hurt.

Then he took him in his mouth.

Birdsong woke him, for the first time in ages. Maybe spring was properly beginning at long last. Kestrel shifted in his bed, came up against an unfamiliar obstacle.

In the half light of morning, Samuel beside him, his face golden and perfect in the refracted daylight. Kestrel wanted to paint him, capture that moment forever.

Fuck, they really had, hadn't they?

A blush rose as he recalled it. How Samuel had reciprocated the favour. How they had collapsed into bed together, exhausted and glowing.

How glorious and triumphant he felt, only that wasn't quite the right word, was it?

He grunted, shifted the sleep from his eyes. Untangled the words from his brain like the branches of a thicket blocking a forest path.

Cathartic. That was it.

The only problem now was what came next. The blush intensified as he thought about the vocation, the priory, what this could mean for Samuel. Was catharsis worth the price of the guilt?

He didn't want to wake Samuel up just yet. Better to let him have those few more minutes of peace.

CHAPTER THIRTEEN

At the Altar

When they met up for the campaign that Sunday, Kestrel already knew that Samuel was going to be home. Their parting words on that soft morning, before Samuel had left for the priory once again, had told him as much. It gave Kestrel time to prepare; how he would look, what he would say, how he would react to every little thing. It was impossible to prepare for every little thing. But it felt better for the trying.

Even if he hadn't known, he would have been able to tell that something was different when he entered the house. The air seemed to move a little more than when Aaron was there alone, and the subtle smells were new—a hint of something fresh and herb-like, the scent of grass trodden into shoes lying in the hallway. The kitchen held the warmth of recent extra activity, and, if he listened carefully, there was the gentle thump of music coming from another room further up in the house.

He peeked into the kitchen as he passed. Crumbs and a

discarded breadknife on the cutting board. In the living room, only bags of snacks to be seen. Samuel must have taken his lunch up to his room, then. Giving them space, or getting his work done—bit of both, probably.

'What took you so long?' asked Aaron.

'I just had to sort some stuff.' He jerked his head subtly toward the kitchen. 'Who's making sandwiches?'

'Oh, Sam's around. Apparently his Sunday duties are few and far between today.'

'Cool.'

'You would say that. He wouldn't shut up about how great that whole youth group thing is, especially since you're there.'

'It's been nice hanging out with him.'

'Exactly what he said.' Aaron smiled, and Kestrel tried not to read into it. If he blushed now it would be so fucking obvious. Whether Aaron knew anything or not, he just had to settle for imagining. Less awkward that way.

Bethan and Bram welcomed him into his spot, both of them cheery and excited and evidently, keen to lift the mood after last time. Kestrel accepted it, sinking in beside them and fishing for his character sheet.

'Ready? Yeah, good,'—Aaron stretched across to Bram's laptop, hit play—'So we're gonna say, for convenience, that you all returned back to the town, and got Leilani a room at the inn to recuperate. The rest of the adventure will be just the three of you.'

They already knew that, so why had Aaron bothered in pointing it out? To reassure himself?

Kestrel didn't bring it up.

'Are there any other leads you want to follow up on in town?'

'Nah. Let's just go for it,' said Bram. 'Back to the Shrine!'

Kestrel remembered what Aaron had planned for him, felt that now-familiar dread in his belly, and, unable to stop that wheel now in motion, he slowly nodded. Bethan agreed too. The vote was unanimous.

'Very well,' said Aaron. 'Once your party has dropped Leilani off at the inn, you stand once more in the town square. It's just as dismal as it ever is, as if time simply ceases to function here. At least, it makes one thing easier: nobody really changes their routine much.'

Bram considered. 'That means everyone's probably where we found them last. Hm. Elijah's the only one that can get us there.'

'Unless we can find someone with a boat,' said Kestrel. As soon as he said it he knew it was a stupid idea, as Bram was about to prove.

'And somehow lug the boat through the marsh until we get to that one lake? Assuming anyone even has a boat or is willing to lend it to us. I think we'd be wasting our time.'

'Okay. Elijah, it is.' Kestrel spoke boldly, and he didn't know why he was so keen to take control. Maybe it felt better if he did. Not safer—nothing about this felt safe—but what did that matter if he felt a little less helpless? The illusion would be nice. He placed Quinn at the South gate. Aaron cleared his throat.

'All right, then. Your party heads back on out to the gates, and none are surprised to see the familiar silhouette of Elijah Grass standing there, idling by the pillar, strumming gently on his lute.'

Bram's expertly curated soundtrack crept in as he walked on up to greet them.

'"Ah, my three favourite adventurers!"'

Elijah was always performative, but today it felt different from usual. It felt like a wall more than ever, like a barrier shielding some starker reality behind it.

Kestrel wondered what Elijah would be like if he ever let down that barrier. He wondered where Elijah came from, what reasons he had to help adventurers like them through the marsh. If that intense front was hiding vulnerability, was there a sob story there? A previous loss, perhaps? The tragedy of an old party member drowned in the marsh and the lonely, aching soul it left behind.

That was where he would be tempted to take the story. That was probably not where Aaron intended to take it.

All a sudden, something felt wrong.

'I trust you've come to me to ask for my help, once again?' Elijah said, and Quinn stepped forward. He did it boldly.

—Aaron was talking somewhere, but it was far off and away. Right now, everything was so close he could smell the humus in the soil, he could feel the cloying condensation from the drizzle in the air—

'We have,' said Quinn. 'Please take us back to the Shrine. You're the only one who knows the way.'

A dramatic bow from Elijah. 'It would be my pleasure.' For a moment it seemed as though he might take Quinn's hand again, but he didn't.

He led them through the marsh, same as before, hardly a deviation in the route. This kept it simple enough, but with every step, the mire sucked at Quinn's boots, threatened to steal them out from under him, and he felt unsteady, as if he was about to take one big tumble into the dark.

'Once upon a time, this land was home to myriad strange creatures. But that was long before the empires of man- and dwarf- and elfkind expanded their reach across this world. Oh, to imagine what such archaic times must have looked like, how free those creatures must have been.' Elijah was keen to wax lyrical as they walked, needing no prompting to do so. He did not seem to care if they were listening; Quinn got the impression he was more invested in his own words than in whether or not they wanted to hear them.

As if on cue, Elijah turned around at the head of the group, and winked at him.

—It hadn't been this strong before, the immersion in the tale—

As they approached the shrine, that feeling of wrongness increased, and kept doing so, until he felt dizzy. Again the quote from Malachai entered his head. *Behold, I will send you Elijah the prophet before the great and dreadful Day of the Lord.*

The wind blew stronger, whipping around them as they stood at the unholy entrance, the mist rising in cauliflower billows from the murky waters that lapped up to the shrine's edges. Nothing for it but to go forward, and this time, Elijah did not hang back.

Inside, nothing but an eerie silence. At first Quinn expected to hear Belial's booming voice, but when that didn't happen, he relaxed a little. Then he realised it was because this time, Thorvald had not spoken out the writing on the arches.

He mused aloud. 'How do we get further into the shrine without waking the demon up?'

'We'll have to wake him up eventually.' Thorvald shrugged.

'Yer, but it might 'elp to check around for stuff what we can use against him,' said Marcus.

Again, Quinn took the initiative, walked up to the door. He saw Elijah smile from the corner of his eye, heard the soft, almost teasing 'Do be careful.'

Of course I'm going to be careful, I'm not an idiot. But also, he remembered the way that creature—even so much as thinking his name made him anxious, as if thought alone would summon him—had focussed on him so intently, both in the marsh and the last time they were at the shrine. He might not be an idiot, but he got the feeling that somehow, he was marked.

For what, he didn't know.

So when he touched the door, he touched it carefully, testing it to see if it would give, and when it did not, he moved to searching for any weak points or irregularities in its structure. But all it yielded to him was that it was big, and made of stone, and shut very, very firmly.

'There's not even a keyhole,' he said to the others. Thorvald nodded, began studying what else was in the room.

'These three platforms here. I think we need to open the door somehow by standing on them.'

'I ain't so keen on that idea, Thorvald.'

'Well,'—Thorvald paused, checked the aether—'it's definitely something to do with these platforms, and it would make sense that we all have to stand on them at the same time.' He looked at Elijah. 'Care to help?'

'Oh, no, go ahead. I'm fine watching.'

So, with Elijah standing quietly in the background, they took their positions on the platforms. The blackish-blue light flickered up, as before, and the platforms began to glow and crackle with energy. It felt... stronger than last time. The pentagram on the floor started to glow too, and a chill washed over them all.

'I think it's time I told you what's really happening,' said Elijah, as the stones thrummed with power, as the crackling intensified. 'You see, Matanbuchus is one of just many names that Belial deigns to use. There is another, for the form in which he likes to visit the realm of man. I think you'll find it quite familiar.' He looked from Marcus, to Thorvald, to Quinn, each trapped on their little platform behind that hazy magicked barrier. When he got to Quinn, his eyes lowered, and his smile widened. He took great relish when he said, 'Elijah Grass.'

The unholy roaring reached fever pitch, and then died down altogether. When the haze cleared, Quinn saw that he was not in the hall any more.

'What?' Bethan's shrill voice brought him out of the narrative. '*Elijah* is Belial? Agh, I didn't even expect for an instant! God damn it, Aaron!'

The tension in the room was high, but it sat together with the pure, unbridled joy of the revelation. Aaron had this self-conscious, happy smirk on his face. Bram just stared, mouth agape, one millimetre away from breaking into the relief of laughter, but lacking the drop in suspense that would require.

'I told you things were going to get interesting.'

'You said he wasn't gonna be a betrayer.'

'Technically, he hasn't betrayed anyone, just lured you in.'

'He betrayed our trust.'

'Heh, I suppose you're right.'

Bethan roared again with mock frustration.

Kestrel knew what was going to happen now. He chewed at his fingernails, picked at the edge of his character sheet, because this was where he needed the extra contact, this was his vain attempt to keep himself rooted in reality.

Why do you need to fiddle so? You're like a panicked child.

That devious voice in his head, asking him questions he had no answer for. He couldn't say why. It just seemed incredibly important to stay grounded.

But then Aaron was in storyteller mode and it was so easy to slip back in.

Quinn peered into darkness. He could see only the faint outline of stone walls. Feeling in front of him, the stone revealed no curves of arches, no outlines of doors. He tried to take the initiative, tried to search for anything hidden in the room, but his rogue senses failed him. Resigned to huffing and fretting alone in the darkness, he waited, tried to gather his thoughts.

'Well, well. Look at you. All on your lonesome.'

The voice cut straight through to the bone as if it would take up residence there. The deep, resonant timbre seemed to make the whole room shake.

A shiver ran down Quinn's spine. Arcane energy whirled through the room, brightening it by a few degrees. At first he thought strands of his own hair were in his eyes, but they were shifting too much, growing thicker, more frenetic. He blinked, and started to panic. Those were ribbons of darkness rising up from the aether around him, coalescing into a much more solid shape. He yelped, and backed up straight into the demon Belial himself. Firm hands—claws, whatever they were—gripped his shoulders. Hot breath on his neck.

'No! Wait, don't attack! We just—'

The demon brought a long, bony finger to Quinn's lips. 'Shh. Your pleas do you no favours, little one.'

Quinn bit back his complaints and stilled himself like a mouse in the grip of a lion. Maybe, if he was obedient enough, those claws would not find their way through his throat.

For a moment there was the fear, and Belial dragged it out longer than he needed to. But eventually Quinn was rewarded for his good behaviour: the demon gradually let go, finger by spindly finger, and receded from his back. He heard him shift, slinking off casually into a corner with an almost feline petulance.

He responded by moving to the opposite corner, and found the room was small, far smaller than he had at first thought. A cell.

'Where are the others?'

'I wouldn't worry about them.'

Quinn started to protest, but when the demon shifted, he stopped instantly.

'Okay,' Quinn said instead. 'Why did you separate me from them?'

'Well, see, with *you* here, your friends will have to do just about *anything* I say to get you back.' Belial paused to click his tongue. 'They will have no choice but to entertain me.'

'So I'm a hostage.'

'My, you're a sharp one.'

He ignored the desultory tone and tried to think. Belial was Elijah. Elijah *knew* him. He could talk to him, engage with him like a regular person. Maybe he could still appeal to that.

'Um. Well, okay, let's assume they do what you say while I'm your'—he struggled to get the word *hostage* out of his mouth again—'Will you let me go then? Safe and unharmed?'

'Nobody said I wasn't going to harm you.'

Kestrel pushed back from the table. Something dark and sickly-sweet was clawing its way up his throat. He felt drunk, he felt intoxicated, in the sort of way that meant if he didn't get to a bathroom now, he was going to make a hell of a mess.

'You okay, dude?'

'Yeah, I—I had too much coffee this morning. Guts are all—' He groaned, effectively ending that sentence as he sped out of the room. He didn't glance behind to see what expressions his friends wore; he could deal with that later.

Once he was in the bathroom at the end of the hall, door locked, chest heaving, ears roaring—he let himself sink down onto the toilet seat. He could feel Belial-Elijah's hands on his body, slick and possessive and holding him in place and there was no—God—damn—way to turn the sensation off.

It shouldn't have to hurt like this.

Nobody said it wasn't going to hurt.

Fuck that. He had to focus, he had to stop this whatever-the-hell-it-was eating him from the inside out and—when had his head hit the sink? A dull throb covered the bridge of his nose. He moved his arm to give his forehead something softer to rest on, but it was too meagre an offering. As if it could make the beast loosen its hold.

He keened out his despair as quietly as he could against the ceramic, all the while listening to Elijah in his ear telling him to *Shh.*

It was just a damn game. Should have been easy to just stop it, to think straight, think *straight*—but how could he think straight when the demon had him held like that? He didn't want to look because he knew already that the tendrils were coming up through the floorboards, winding around his body, and—there it was in one horrifying moment of clarity: the picture he had painted during the half term break. The boy in the marsh. He stared back at himself with unbelieving eyes, shocked he hadn't seen it all sooner.

Come to think of it, when *had* he painted that? Was it the same night Tala had attempted to kill herself? He thought of her words, *You, most of all*, and her strange behaviour, and everything that he had seen since then and it became so fucking obvious that she knew something he didn't. Suddenly, magic didn't matter, games didn't matter, depression and demons didn't matter; all that mattered was this feeling and how to purge it.

He had to talk to her. Properly, this time. Break through whatever barrier she had set up around this thing because this had to stop.

When the wave had subsided, Kestrel pushed back from the sink. It still took effort, and he felt sluggish, as if waking up from a nap that had been far too short.

He'd been in here long enough. Time to rejoin the others, before they started asking awkward questions.

It was a cruel example of awful timing that had him bumping into Samuel as he came out of the bathroom. A rush of that familiar fresh smell and the glint of light brown hair filling his face. He flinched on instinct, apologised in a flash.

Samuel's momentary shock melted into enthusiasm as he realised who it was, and then concern as he took in Kestrel's expression.

'Is everything okay?'

His breath caught in his throat, hitched up like clothing on a barbed wire fence. He became incredibly self conscious of the fact that his eyes must still be puffy, that his cheeks were probably red, probably still a bit wet too. They both stood there awkwardly for a moment, waiting around the unspoken fact he had been crying like it was a piece of litter that neither of them wanted to pick up.

'Yeah. Sort of.'

'You sure?'

'It was just… that stuff we were talking about before,' he said, and in his eyes he saw that Samuel understood. He nodded. He didn't press the issue. The sounds of their friends in the living room made it through, and the opposite was probably true as well.

God, though, even just making a passing reference to the thing made that wave threaten to swell up again.

'Anyway, I was just, uh, I should get back to the game.'

'Sure. Hey—we should catch up again next week. Like, not at the youth group.'

'That'd be cool. Hey, do my eyes look okay?'

'A bit red—'

'Crap.'

'—Just say you got allergies or something.'

Samuel leaned in, glancing to the side in a surreptitious way, as if he was about to come in for a kiss. And— something about that terrified Kestrel. It came completely out of the blue, and it made no sense, because he *liked* Samuel, and he wanted nothing more than to press his lips to his and cover him in kisses, worship him again… But all of that repressed desire didn't gel well with the roiling sickness in his belly. It was too easy to imprint the shape of Belial over anything good he tried to put in its way.

'Sorry,' he said. He put some distance between them, and Samuel pulled back, looking guiltier than ever.

'No, I'm sorry. I still want to see you later, though.'

'Same.' Before he headed back to the living room,

Kestrel squeezed Samuel's hand, just a quick and light touch, discreet but enough to reassure. Or so he hoped.

Samuel darted back into the kitchen (clearly that was where he had been headed when he'd crashed into him) and Kestrel took his cue to return to the living room—

shrine

—where his friends waited.

'Wow, you look like shit.' Aaron, direct as ever.

Kestrel grinned sheepishly, holding his stomach.

'Hah, yeah, I don't… I don't know what came over me. Something I ate disagreed with me.'

'Were you… crying?'

Damn, Bethan was too perceptive.

'No! I was just being a bit sick. Like, that makes you tear up a bit, sometimes.'

'Ew, I hope it's not contagious.'

'Yeah, thanks Bram.'

He was going to take his seat back at the table again, and honestly, he was dreading it, but it never happened.

'Let's call it for today.' Aaron looked troubled.

'You sure?' said Bram, and he was struggling to hide the disappointment in his voice. 'We just got to a cool bit.'

'If Kestrel's feeling ill, we'd just be punishing him by making him stay. And we're already punishing his character enough.'

'True.'

Nobody seemed genuinely upset with him, if anything the strange sadness in the air felt more like pity, but even recognising that did little to stop Kestrel feeling guilty. How very Catholic of him.

Whatever. He helped clear the table, then left before anyone else could offer to head home with him.

This time, when he opens the door to Tala's conservatory, he's surprised to find that nobody is there. It's just him, the dappled sunlight refracting through the tall glass panes, and the sugar sculptures, all neatly lined up on the table.

In the quiet seclusion, he is overcome with the urge to get closer, to pick them up. It feels just so enticing, and in that moment he wants nothing more.

But something is nagging at him—where *is* everyone? Much as he usually enjoys being alone, it's too eerie to settle with this silence in someone else's house. He checks right and left, back at the door, out through the glass panes and into the garden, but sees no sign of life. One of the windows has been eked open; a gentle breeze wafts through from outside. Someone must have been here recently, but there's not much he can do to search for anyone without leaving the room.

And the sculptures beckon, twinkling in the sun.

So he moves closer.

When he gets the chance to study them up close, he sees that the sugar sculptures are no longer what they were before. Instead of the mixture of figures, buildings, and vehicles, they are now all in the shape of people, each with a level of detail to rival his tabletop miniatures—and there's something disturbingly familiar about them.

Once again, he moves closer.

The one nearest to him has long, curly hair and wears an oversized hoodie. That dimpled smile: it's unmistakeably, undeniably Bethan. Next to her, with a messy fringe, is Bram, and next to him, Aaron, Samuel, and at the very end, Tala herself. Perfect replicas of his friends, cast in crystal white, barely bigger than a handspan. So perfect in expression and pose that they seem alive, frozen in time.

How the fuck did Tala get this good? is his first thought.

His second is not so wholesome, because *what if they really are his friends?* Once it enters his mind, the idea is hard to evict. It's ridiculous, of course it is, but… what if?

Nobody would believe him if he told them. Nobody would believe him, and what a desperate, lonely feeling that is. He's on his own here.

What happens next is too fast and at first, makes no sense. He's shaken off his feet by some strong force — something glints sharply in the sunlight and all at once he's overcome with cold. Roaring fills his ears and amid it, he hears something shatter.

It's a sudden change in the weather, and when he realises that everything makes sense. The window that had been left open a crack now hangs on its hinges, thumping against its neighbouring pane and catching the light with every swing. He shields his eyes. Somehow the skies are filled with both sun and rain outside. That familiar, rhythmic drumming on the roof starts up as the rain comes down harder, as the wind invades the sacred space of the conservatory gust by gust.

Something shattered with that first gust, but at least the window isn't broken. Relief floods him, until he looks down, and sees the sculptures lying in splinters and shards on the floor.

'No!' Such an ineffectual plea, but he repeats it, growing more frenetic by the second as he stares at the mess on the floor. His heart rate, already shot up in fright from the wind, keeps on its upward trend, but somehow his body is frozen, stunned as he gazes down. His friends are dashed to pieces, and he doesn't have the first thought on how to fix it. For a while longer, he says *no* like it's the only word in the world, and then he starts to apologise to his friends, dropping to his knees and reaching forward. He desperately tries to pick them all up, but the sugar's going sticky in his hands, it's dissolving, their bodies are dissolving…

Fuck. It's not going to work. His eyes start to sting and before he knows it, he's crying.

'Why are you so upset?' asks a voice behind him, and he sniffs, looks up in a flash.

Elijah Grass is there, leaning casually against the door, watching him with curious amusement. He can't make out what's beyond the doorframe, but he doesn't want to, just in case it's the gateway back out to the marsh.

It's strange—he should be more scared. There is plenty of fear, of course, but the grief over what has happened to his friends is so strong that it renders him soft and pliant before the smiling avatar of hell. He doesn't run—where would he run, anyway? Would he just leave his friends dashed to the ground at the mercy of that demon? He doesn't run because, in a way, he has no choice.

'They're broken,' he replies, and his voice is pitiful, childish, needy. He wants to scrub it out almost as much as he wants Elijah to be gone, but he's too painfully aware that he needs help, God, he needs help, and right now, only Elijah can give it.

However, all that Elijah offers him is nonchalance and a low-effort shrug.

'It's not a big deal, you can just make more.'

He can hardly believe what he's hearing. That teasing grin Elijah is wearing—he's messing with him, isn't he?

'What?' he says, feeling more tears make fresh channels down his face.

'You heard me. Just make some more friends. It's not hard, you've seen Tala do it.'

Elijah seems to oscillate between enjoying his plight and

offering—by his standards—down-to-earth advice. The way that expression shifts, it makes it hard to tell if he's joking or not.

Either way, it is not okay.

He tries not to look so helpless. He doesn't know how to achieve that exactly, but he's terribly aware of how he must look to the man. He would stand up a little straighter, if he had any more bravery.

'I don't know how!'

This earns him an even wider grin.

'Should I show you?'

He doesn't want to say yes. Somehow, that seems awfully important.

In the time it takes him to fail to decide, Elijah sighs melodramatically and pushes off from the doorframe.

'Such a shame. I suppose you'll have to learn the hard way.'

As Elijah comes closer, he tries to scramble upright. The sweet sugary mixture coating his hands slicks its way down his fingers uncomfortably, flooding the floor. In no time at all, the liquid is rising, sticking him fast like a pig in the mud, and he is reminded of the physics of Wonderland. He braces himself for whatever is to come. And still, the rain hammers down.

CHAPTER FOURTEEN

Festuca Glauca

The morning brought with it strange weather, and an even stranger message in his inbox.

Kestrel. I hope you don't mind that I found your email through the school system. I wanted to ask you for your help with something. Don't worry—I won't leave you on your own like last time. Mea culpa, and all that. Come to the chapel tomorrow lunchtime if you can, we'll talk then. Daran.

So he came.

It was hailing down pretty hard outside—an odd combination with the strong sunshine—and he used the opportunity to bring Daran's umbrella with him, aiming to return it. He was glad for its presence as he crossed the campus, because the last thing he wanted to do was look up at that bright, beautiful sun amid the rhythmic patter, for fear it would make the dream more real.

He was anxious about meeting Daran again, just in case it would be like the last time, just in case he was still mad at him. Which, of course, was ridiculous. He didn't seem mad at him in the email. He didn't even seem disappointed. And, when Kestrel entered the chapel and came face to face with him again, it was clear that all trace of frustration was gone. Rather, he looked pleased, in an almost relieved sort of way, and that made Kestrel feel that perhaps, it had been the other way round, and Daran had been worried that *he* would have been mad.

Maybe he came across as more of a capricious youth than he thought. Or maybe he was thinking too much.

So here they were, again; just him, Daran, and the high, white walls. The hail had stopped by the time he arrived, so it was just the bitter chill outside, and the pale, otherworldly glow inside. Just like when they first had met.

Daran moved away from the shelf where he had been reorganising hymn books.

'I'm so glad you came.'

Saying 'Of course,' or 'No problem' sounded too trite, so Kestrel just nodded and hummed his agreement. When he did find something worth saying, it was in proffering the umbrella.

'Thanks for letting me borrow this, by the way.'

'Any time. And I really do mean that.' Daran took the umbrella, and his fingers lightly brushed his. The moment after felt like it needed some punctuation.

'So…'

'So.'

'What did you need my help with?'

'Ah, yes. Well, we've had a lot of trouble trying to organise Mass on campus. But even still, I'd like to do something to celebrate Holy Week, if you… do you think people would be interested?'

'I… yeah, I think so.'

He wondered for a moment if Daran was about to ask if it was lame again, but he didn't—he just smiled, and continued his spiel. 'Great. I wondered if it was a bit much to ask, since it's during the holidays, but, well…'

Oh, yeah. It was nearly the end of term already.

'…you've all been so enthusiastic, I figured you might appreciate it.' Daran rested a hand idly on the bookcase, looked around the room. 'So here I am, asking for your help.'

Kestrel was not convinced he was the right person for the job. If it wasn't for the confidence Daran spoke with, if it wasn't for that keen look in his eye, he might have suggested it was purely because he had been present, he had volunteered to help before, he had been in the right place at the right time. *I fucked up, and you're still trusting me. Why is that?*

Well, whatever it was that Daran saw in him… maybe he could start seeing that in himself too.

'Okay. I'll, uh… I'll do my best.'

Daran smiled warmly. 'That's what I was hoping to hear.' He moved away from the bookshelf and strolled down the aisle. Kestrel joined him. 'So, whatever form this takes, it wouldn't be a proper Mass. Canonically, it can't be, not without a priest. I'm only a Eucharistic minister,' — Of course he was, the book from his office made perfect sense now — 'so I have limited authority.'

'So what do we do? Like, order-of-Mass wise.'

'The readings. Responsorial psalms. Anything that's not sacramental. And, ah—handing out the Eucharist, if it's already been transubstantiated.'

'Oh, yeah. You can do that, right?'

'Not the transubstantiation part.'

'Yeah, that's what—yeah, I just meant the handing out

part.' He spoke too quickly, eager to prove his worth.

'Mm. Yes, it's generally something I only have authority to do if the recipient can't come to a proper Mass. Which—for a lot of students, especially those staying on campus over the holidays—probably holds up just fine. Still requires a priest to perform the rite beforehand, and preferably on the same day.' Daran sighed softly, made the smallest genuflection up ahead, and sank down onto a pew. It was a casual perch he made, knees angled out into the aisle more like he was sitting in a pub than a chapel. Kestrel mirrored his behaviour, subconsciously at first, sitting on the pew across the aisle and becoming very conscious not to let their knees knock against each other.

Daran tilted his head towards Kestrel, eyebrow angling upward, and again Kestrel was reminded of heart-to-hearts over a pub table. 'Are you staying on campus over the holidays? I completely forgot to ask.'

Kestrel thought of his mother.

'I am, actually.'

'You look troubled. It's all right: I won't inquire.'

Was he really so transparent?

He deflected.

'Maybe we could get someone in from the priory. Like, if we wanted to do the Eucharist thing. Or—just do it at the priory itself?'

'It's possible, but it's not necessarily the best idea,' Daran said, folding his hands together and tracing a thumb across his own wrist. Thinking, musing. Kestrel held his breath. That fear that he would disappoint him again was absolutely crushing, and he was sure it should have no reason to be. Such a ridiculous need for approval, persistent to the point where it felt insidious. He could try to understand it, but it made little sense. Unless—*no, just be honest with yourself, this is a selfish motive. You just don't want to disappoint because you don't want to be hurt.*

While his thoughts slowly spun out like candy floss on a stick, Daran went on.

'It's a bit of a logistical nightmare, getting them to come here. You might recall the other week, when I changed our lunchtime arrangement because of a meeting? That was me talking to them, trying to figure something out. They do run full masses regularly there, but they *are* a monastic order—'

He listened, patiently. Tried to focus on the words.

'—and it's a bit of an overstep to get so many layfolk encroaching upon their walls. And besides, we really should make use of the space we've got on campus, don't you think?'

'Yeah. Yeah, that makes sense.' But he couldn't just leave it there. He had been brought here for a reason, and it wasn't to be an echo. *Be constructive. Be useful.* 'Well… if we did the Friday Mass, we wouldn't have to worry about Eucharist at all.'

He regretted it even as he said it. The Passion Mass, with its long-drawn-out re-enactment of Jesus' final hours, was a far worse ordeal to weather than the Stations. And it was for that reason alone that he was relieved when Daran also thought this was a bad suggestion.

'The Thursday Mass would be preferable. The Last Supper. The closer to the weekend, the busier people are going to be.' Another sigh, another folding and stretching out of his hands. 'The question remains, though. We'll need to sort out who's doing what.'

'Yeah! So—'

'What would you think if I—'

'—maybe we could… oh, sorry.'

'No, go ahead.'

'Okay. I was just thinking… if it happens, we could get Samuel to lead Communion.'

'Oh.' Daran turned away, eyebrows creasing. He looked —fuck, was he upset?

'I, uh…'

'That's good, though,' Daran said. 'He needs the practise.'

Kestrel hummed his agreement. He felt too awkward to say anything else. The rush of the past week flooded him like rain.

I kissed Samuel. We did things. Does he know?

Is he disappointed in us?

Is he jealous?

Why that last thought bubbled up, he had no idea. It brought a blush to his cheeks. Not something he even remotely wanted to think about, for all that it made his belly burn. But—and this was not a deflection—there was something else that made him suggest Samuel in the first place. It was hard to put into words, it was intangible and far away, but in a potentially dangerous sort of way, like weather moving on the horizon.

I just get the feeling that… it's a bad move if it's not Samuel.

'Thank you. For helping me out. I actually hadn't considered asking him before.'

'Are you sure that's okay?'

'I wouldn't say it if it wasn't.'

Daran started scribbling notes on a small pad retrieved from his jacket; it was somewhere between a pocket notebook and a block of post-its, the sort of thing someone might lift from a hotel or a conference. To the soundtrack of biro scratching away, Kestrel tried to relax, to convince himself that he had contributed something worthwhile.

He cast his eyes to the cross above the altar. The divine intersection his gaze always returned to when everything else was exhausted. It was a plain affair, cut in dark brown wood and showing little embellishment save for the somewhat blocky shape of Jesus strung up on it. Even with the lack of detail it was stark enough and—he got up to look more closely—expressive enough to tug at his gut.

He wondered idly if the kissing of the feet was something that had ever been done on that statue, in however many years it had stood in this chapel. And, the longer he looked, the more that familiar bristling sensation hit him, rising up like a rash. He felt—in the way he did when he was drunk, when his inhibitions were lowered— like opening up, sharing his thoughts. The kind of mood where surrendering some vulnerability might just be worth it.

He found his breath in the chapel's white silence.

'Sometimes I look at the statues of Jesus on the cross and I... I want to take him down and run away. With him. Like, I'm rescuing him.'

He was so caught up in the feeling that he didn't notice Daran watching him with interest until a fair few seconds had passed. Lounging on the pew, notepad cast to the side, he had found the channel he wanted and seemed loath to change it.

'It just...' Kestrel paused to think, feeling self-conscious. 'It's too cruel.'

Now Daran stood up, and came to join him at the foot of the chancel.

'You know, the cruelty is the point. I told you that before, in the arboretum.'

'I know. But it... it doesn't make me feel any different about it.'

Daran smiled. 'You really are too good.'

Kestrel frowned. He didn't consider his feelings on the whole torture thing to be an indicator of *good*, it was just… it should just be the standard human reaction. The bare minimum. Nobody should be comfortable with it. He certainly shouldn't have been praised for it.

Evidently, Daran took his frown as a sort of self-doubt, because the next thing he said, in a voice all levelled and sincere, as if trying to convince him of some immutable fact, was, 'You're special, Kestrel.'

This ripped him right out of his ecliptic spiral on the nature of humankind.

'Me? But I haven't done anything.'

Daran sighed. 'You really don't get it, do you?'

He didn't reach out to him. He just watched him softly, and Kestrel felt rooted to the spot.

'Well, I shan't keep you. Go, sort things out with Samuel.'

Later, as he walked to the priory, it struck him that this wasn't the first time being made to feel special like that felt a little unwarranted. He couldn't place why this was a bad thing, exactly. Perhaps it was just something about the nature of growing up. It felt like a lot of things about the adult world were harsher than they needed to be, and maybe he was just naïve for thinking it could be otherwise. In that instant, everything that came after college seemed incredibly intimidating, and he wasn't sure he was ready for it. He wasn't sure he wanted to be.

The old monk at the gateway eyed Kestrel with kindly suspicion.

'Is, uh, is Samuel here? I need to ask him about a college

thing.'

'Of course, lad. I'll just get him for you.' The monk let him in and turned to go, rearranging his robes about the collar. 'Feel free to wander the courtyard while you wait. Just—don't step on the herbs.'

Kestrel nodded his thanks. When the man had left, he did as suggested and meandered along the garden path, pausing to look at the flowers, study the aforementioned herbs. He didn't know much about plants, but he could at least tell that this one was basil, that was rosemary. Something thin and spiky too, that he wanted to say was chive. They were all young sproutlings, doing their best in the stop-start spring weather, clearly suffering a little with the erratic hail from earlier.

How long was Samuel going to be? He hoped he hadn't interrupted something. What were the canonical hours of the day, again? No—if it had been an important hour, the old monk would have said something. Probably wouldn't have been at the gate himself, either.

He walked on to occupy the time.

Behind the herbs, on a small path winding up to some taller bushes, was a strip of long grasses that were a familiar shade of blue-green. It struck a chord somewhere deep inside, as persistent yet as obscured as a phone alarm ringing in another room.

Then, the creaking of a door, a patter of footsteps, and Samuel was walking out to greet him. The old monk who had fetched him smiled and returned to his post in the quaint little gate-house, immediately taking up the cup of tea and the dog-eared paperback he had abandoned.

'Come on, let's talk inside. It's a bit damp out.'

Into the vestibule, with its wood-panelled walls and its gentle yellow light, they went. It was cosier in here than in most other holy spaces he visited; perhaps it was the fact that the monks lived here too that lent it that softer, homely quality. He traced a finger along the wood panelling, as though it would tell him something, and he came to a slow stop beside Samuel. A small bookshelf, a mantelpiece with intricate designs that caught his attention, and a bench pushed flush against the wall that neither of them sat down upon.

'What did you want to ask?'

'Oh! Um…' He fiddled with his coat buttons.

'You can take it off if you're too warm.'

Kestrel nodded. He wasn't too warm, but he had given that impression now, and so he stuck to it.

As he shrugged the coat off, easing one shoulder out then the other, he could feel Samuel's eyes upon him. But, respectful as Samuel was to the time and the place, he made no outward sign of his attraction.

'So I was wondering if you wanted to, uh—lead the Holy Thursday Mass. At the chapel on campus.'

Something began to glow in Samuel's eyes. A rush of warmth to Kestrel's breast. *I think I just made him happy.*

'It's not a proper Mass, obviously, we were just gonna do the readings, and maybe Eucharist if we can get someone here to consecrate it beforehand—'

'—I'd be honoured.'

'Really?'

'Absolutely. I should ask some of the brothers here if they can help out, though. I'm a bit anxious doing it on my own.'

'Oh,'—he was suddenly struck by the fear of treading on territory Daran had already walked—'I'm not sure you need to, honestly. Daran, uh, already asked.'

Samuel smiled, bright and optimistic. 'Oh yeah, I saw

him round here the other day. Maybe he just spoke to the wrong person. Well, I'm sure I can sort something out — then we might not even have to worry about the Eucharist, they could just do it there and then.'

Kestrel felt buffeted between two forces. The last thing he wanted to do was make either of them feel bad. But maybe this should be less about feelings and more about making the celebration happen.

He nodded. 'That sounds great.'

'So… did you have any idea of when, next Thursday?'

'I dunno. Probably in the evening. I'll, uh, let you know after I talk to Daran again.'

'Did you want to… talk about anything else?'

Kestrel was not very good at subtlety. He did not know if this was a leading question or not, if Samuel was just being coy about the two of them — and whatever-the-fuck they had going on — or if it was merely meant to be taken at face value.

He chose the latter, for simplicity's sake.

'Nah, I'm okay. I wish I could stay longer but, I should get back.'

'Wait, what time is it?' Samuel glanced at his watch. Of course he wore a watch. 'Oh, I'm sorry I took so long coming out, I thought it was still lunch. Will you be okay getting back in time? I'm sorry I don't drive.'

It was in moments like these that he recognised in Samuel that same need-to-please that he himself had. And, how strange, it seemed like the most important thing in the world when he did it, but seeing Samuel do the same, it felt so unnecessary, like there was no real reason for him to worry so much.

'Yeah, it's no problem. I have a free period right now anyway.'

It would take half an hour to walk back to campus and that would put him well over the start time of the final lesson period of the day, but he didn't say this out loud. Better for Samuel to not worry.

That nagging feeling was still present at the back of his head. The alarm, still going off in another room. He saw himself retracing the steps out to the garden and back to campus.

Then, clear as day, he heard Aaron's voice. 'You come to a stream, interrupting the path. It's lined on all sides by those tufts of long blue grasses.'

Something glitched in his brain. The marsh and the ruins and the shrine. It smashed sidelong into the priory's gentle garden, became one and the same for an awful moment.

'Hey, does Aaron come here much?'

'He's visited once or twice, yeah.'

'Huh.'

'Why, what's up?'

Kestrel shrugged, tried to pass it off as nothing, and this only prompted Samuel to ask further.

'Seriously, what's up?'

'Eh, it's just… What's the name of that grass you've got growing outside? It looks really similar to something he put in our campaign.'

Samuel asked which one he meant, and he took him back out to the herb garden to check. 'Oh, that's called Elijah grass.'

Time slowed down.

I know what you want, and I have to admit, it is quite salacious of you.

There Elijah was, clear as day, standing just behind Samuel as he bent over and reached down to inspect the herb tag. Kestrel paled, he could feel the blood draining from his skin as Elijah gave him a winning smile, a curious Cheshire grin, and for an instant that face was superimposed with something other, something distorted but familiar, and he felt like gravity was coming apart, threatening to upset the contents of his stomach.

Samuel was hyperfocussed on reading the small print. It would have been comforting to think he didn't notice, but there was something in the way he rubbed at his neck, the way he cleared his throat, as though he knew someone was behind him. 'Festuca Glauca,' he said at last. 'That's the scientific name, anyway.' And he straightened up, turned around quicker than he perhaps needed to. Elijah flickered out of existence. 'It's strange,' said Samuel, 'but that plant always makes me feel sad, somehow.'

Kestrel felt too numb to respond, but that was okay, because after a moment, Samuel asked about Aaron again.

'Is he doing all right? It's... well, the last few times I've been home he's been kind of off.'

He stepped away from the grass before replying, aiming as if to inspect the cherry tree.

'Yeah, he seems to be fine. I mean, we're all still a bit shook up, after Tala...'

'Yeah. Makes sense.' Samuel's breath fogged in the cold air. 'I guess I'm just worried he's not coping well. Our parents have been away from home a lot recently. And — Aaron always seems to pride himself on handling that sort of thing well. But yeah, that... doesn't mean that's necessarily the case.'

'True. And it's not exactly easy to bring up emotional stuff around him.'

'It's always been hard to avoid hurting his pride,' said Samuel, and the pair of them fell into a hushed commiseration, watching the wet leaves sway in the breeze. 'Well, I appreciate you looking out for him, anyway.'

It felt like the pair of them were standing on a precipice, waiting for the next well-placed gust of wind to come. Kestrel knew he had to leave, and he didn't want to. It was as though the instant he moved forward, the rest of time would start moving again too. Right now, in the corner of the little garden, shielded from view by the cherry tree, things felt halted. Things felt safe.

He wanted to kiss him.

'Before I go...'

His intention was clear; Samuel, reading the longing in his eyes, tensing his shoulder forward, ready to reach out and respond. But his breath caught, and he looked away.

'I'm sorry—I can't. Not here.'

'No, it's fine. I, uh, don't wanna stress you out.'

What am I doing to Samuel? Am I just fucking things up for him?

As if he was aware of his thoughts, Samuel fixed him with a direct stare.

'About last week. Don't think I did anything I didn't want to.'

'Okay.'

'We're both very good at beating ourselves up, that much I know.'

'Ouch, well... that's true.' Kestrel steadied a hand against the bark of the cherry tree. 'What the fuck do we do?'

'I don't know. But I want to come and see you again.'

Kestrel nodded, feeling the tension in his chest as he resisted the urge to kiss, to hug him before leaving. Just a light touch of the hand—and inside, he was screaming at that small, tantalising concession—as he bade Samuel farewell.

The walk back took longer than expected. Kestrel entered the classroom when Art History was coming to a close. Mr. Ruiz was flourishing a hand at the projector, in the middle of saying something poignant about neoclassical and academic art styles.

He started to say sorry, but Ruiz flagged him down. 'I don't want to hear excuses, just take a worksheet and catch up.'

The worksheets, where were they?

Mr. Ruiz patted the table next to him and Kestrel awkwardly went up to collect one. After that he scanned the class for Bram, hoping to find a free space next to him to slide down into.

Bram wasn't there.

Quite a few people weren't there, actually. Rei included. Last thing on a Friday, and this would make sense, but on a Monday it was incredibly irregular. It seemed as though the malaise that was permeating his mind was seeping through into his surroundings.

He sank down into the closest seat.

'Back to Academicism. Now, it's easy to confuse with something a bit more romantic, because while the art style is meant to emulate the prescriptive styles of the great European academies, the themes are often mythological, Orphean—'

'What's Orphean?' The kid next to him, a usually quiet boy named Cyril, asked.

'It's a reference to the Greek story of Orpheus in the Underworld. It's a way to describe things to do with escaping Hades, loss of innocence, making mistakes.'

Something about that settled weirdly with Kestrel. He looked at the projector instead.

He only understood half of the context, but his eyes were drawn to the image on the projector screen. The woman, fully naked, climbing out of the pit with fury on her face, mouth open as if screaming. An intimidating level of righteous retribution shone through despite her state of undress, despite her humiliation. The text above it read: *Truth Coming Out of Her Well to Shame Mankind, Jean-Léon Gérôme, 1896.*

When Mr. Ruiz told them to choose an example of Academicism and write about its cultural context for homework, he took note of the well painting's title and left class quickly, trying not to feel condemned by her piercing gaze.

Bethan had asked them to meet for coffee. After class, sequestered away in the comfortable café, finding something to warm them up against the biting weather that was supposed to be spring. It should have been the same old routine, but as Kestrel left campus he spotted Aaron, in those short moments after the sixth period was over, and it looked very much like Aaron was headed off somewhere alone. In the opposite direction to the café.

It was unusual: Aaron was always chatty, extroverted, keen to butt in to whatever conversation was happening around him. Seeing him separate from the crowd with such a hunch in his step was so out of character it gave Kestrel whiplash.

He called out.

Aaron paused mid-walk. It looked like he was about to continue walking until he realised it was Kestrel calling him. Another moment's deliberation—whatever depressive force he was fighting seemed strong—then he headed on over.

The first thing Aaron said: 'You feeling any better after yesterday?'

Oh, right, I was pretending to be ill.

'Yeah, mostly,' Kestrel replied, and that was not technically a lie. 'Are you… are you not coming to the café?'

'Is that… aw, shit, I forgot. Nah, I got stuff to do.'

Kestrel got the sense he was not going to convince him otherwise, so he said, 'Fair enough.' For a moment, he thought that was all he wanted to say, but then he found himself thinking about the priory's little herb garden, and that sickly sensation returned. Aaron looked like he was fully intending to disappear for the rest of the evening, and this might be his only chance to ask.

He launched straight into it; there was little point in dancing about. 'I was at the priory earlier.'

A wry smile from Aaron. He probably expected to hear something about Samuel next, because he seemed surprised when Kestrel said, 'The blue grasses you described, in the marsh. They're growing all over the priory. Samuel told me they're called Elijah grass.' He let that sink in for a moment. 'Is that where you got it from?'

'Huh. Must've been.' Aaron considered this for a moment, then cast it aside, attempting to plaster a smile on his face. 'So, what were you hanging out with my dear brother for?'

'Just organising some Easter stuff.' He took a decisive breath. 'Sam was worried about you.'

He didn't want to say it. Ever since the start of the term he had been acting as the middle man for someone else. And here he was again, doing the exact same thing. He had grown so used to that cringing feeling of being the messenger, of waiting for frustration to be levelled his way, that it surprised him when Aaron didn't round on him for asking.

'He is, huh?' The smile left Aaron's face and he fell to thinking. 'Damn.'

'*Are* you okay?'

It took Aaron a while to reply. His breaths in and out were gentle and even enough, but they held back a weight that Kestrel recognised. The feeling of having something important to say but not wanting to actually say it.

'I feel like something awful's happened and I feel like it's partially my fault. Only, I'm not sure how. But I feel guilty anyway.'

Kestrel ordinarily would have said *Are you sure you're not just overthinking the campaign*, or something along those lines, but this was not an ordinary situation. Honestly, he was surprised that the break in Aaron's defences had come so easily.

'You have no reason to feel guilty about *anything* that's happened this term,' he said, and he considered reaching out, patting Aaron's shoulder, but the fear of Aaron growing self-conscious and shrugging away from the contact stayed his hand. Would've been fine if it was Bram, but Aaron ran the risk of interpreting it as belittling. Saccharine. Unnecessary.

'It's hard to believe that when everything feels that way.'

'Do you wanna talk about it?'

'I don't know. Maybe.' Aaron glanced to the side, like he was afraid of being so weak. 'I'm not having the best dreams.'

Not you, too.

Kestrel steeled himself, then asked.

'Like what?'

'I'll see really fucked up shit, like, Samuel dies, or sometimes you die. Or… worse.'

Kestrel raised his eyebrow, and when he asked, he was hesitant, like he didn't really want to know the answer. 'Worse like how?'

'Dude, there is no fucking way I am telling you. Anyway. I always lose someone.'

'Fuck. I'm sorry.'

'Don't be. I don't know what the fuck this is, but it's freaking dumb.'

'Have you…' He had to phrase this correctly, 'thought about talking to someone?'

'I dunno, man. I don't want to go to some therapist and have them tell me I've got some repressed-memory shit going on. There's a word for that. Iaterogenic.'

'Uh. That's when a therapist *gives* you a fake repressed memory.'

'Same difference. Anyway, it's not for me. This… stupid thing, whatever it is, it's not worth that sort of trouble.' Aaron waved his hand, derisive, desultory, and Kestrel got a hint of a notion that the whole reason he might be reacting this way was because he was angry at the idea of feeling so powerless.

That was a feeling he could relate to.

'Needing therapy isn't a weakness.'

'Never said it was, dude. I'm not trying to make out like it is. It's just not me, it's not for me, okay?'

'I only said that to convince myself.' Kestrel all but whispered it.

This took the wind out of Aaron's sails.

When he next spoke, he was more vulnerable than

Kestrel had ever heard him before. Quiet as a church mouse and just as weak; everything he had been denouncing mere minutes ago.

'I don't want anyone to get the wrong idea. I don't *have* mental problems. I haven't had some tragic sob story happen that I'm not strong enough to bloody confront. Nothing like that's happened to me. Everything's fine. I'm just having a weird patch.'

Kestrel thought about pointing out the fact that yes, in fact, something tragic had happened, but that would be unfair. It was probable that Tala's suicide attempt had had *some* effect on Aaron's stress levels recently—after all, it was no small thing—but Aaron wasn't looking for scapegoats, and it would just cheapen both Tala's experience and his to suggest so.

So he kept his silence. *Weird patch* it was, then.

The café was quieter than usual.

Maybe it was because of being in the herb garden earlier, but Kestrel ordered a cup of herbal tea. Lemon and ginger. He didn't think he could stomach the sugar of one of those ridiculous lattes. With the atmosphere as it was, both outside and in, it felt like it would curdle in his mouth, turn so sweet it would become sickly-sour.

Bethan was already squirrelled away in their familiar corner.

'Bram's not coming either,' she said, pushing some cushions aside so he could join her. 'Said he was feeling weird.'

'So it's just us, huh?'

'Yep.' She over-pronounced the word, leaving an empty kiss in the air.

'But we always get coffee after class.'

Bethan sighed. 'Come on, more often than not lately, it's just been you and me. I mean, in my case, it's easier, 'cos I work next door. So I guess, what I mean is—thank you. For showing up.'

The herbal tea was too bitter.

'Fuck, I do need sugar, after all.'

'Hey, hey, no—lemme get it for you.' Bethan jumped up, retrieved a bowl filled with sugar cubes from the condiments table.

'Thanks,' he murmured, and he sweetened the tea, listened to the wind rattling against the windowpanes of the cosy café, felt his toes curl inside his shoes as if looking for more stability against the floor.

'You okay?' She was watching him curiously and he realised he was holding the spoon on the very brim of the hot liquid, watching the sugar cube dissolve slowly. He looked to her for explanation, and she said, 'You look kinda burnt out.'

'Wow, thanks.' He fiddled with his hair. 'That bad, huh?'

'Sorry. You're not, like, panda-eyed or anything. It's just… you seem… troubled, I guess. In an exhausted sort of way.'

'I don't know. It's just a feeling I get sometimes.' He thought about the dreams. It was too difficult for him to elaborate. It was too embarrassing to say Elijah's name. So instead, he thought about all the things he would say if he had the courage.

He beckons me forth and I walk with him. I am not willing. I go anyway, because something greater than me is overriding this and I feel like the smallest of waves subsumed by a swell. Like I'm being suffocated, like I'm being drowned.

I feel a tug at my belly. A knot unfurls deep inside of me. It's warm; so warm.

By the time I find the will to run, I cannot move.

He was done thinking, and he realised Bethan has been talking all the while. Something comforting, or so was the impression. The tea had cooled; it was now far too sweet and he was frustrated at not being able to find the right balance there, but she had gone to the trouble of getting the sugar for him so he sipped at the now-tepid liquid, trying to be grateful. An aroma of earthy ginger hit his senses. Wintry. Perfect heartwarming spices, or so the impression was. Didn't work a jot.

Bethan seemed to echo his melancholy. She had trailed off from telling him that burnout sucked and was now sitting there with her chin resting on an open palm. 'I've been thinking, since the other day. Like, since Tala freaked out.'

'Yeah?'

Her eyes met his and they were hard and serious. 'We're undergoing some kind of shared trauma.'

'It's because Tala tried to kill herself, isn't it?'

Saying it aloud was a physical hit, one the pair of them felt.

'I think she knows something,' said Bethan. 'I think she knows something we don't, and… God, I'm sick of feeling like this. I'm still not sleeping well, and neither are you, and neither are the others, I'm pretty goddamn sure of it.' She stroked the side of her coffee cup, an uncharacteristic display of angst, and she took a few steady breaths. When she looked up, her eyes were glistening. 'Talk to her, Kes. You're the only one.'

He stared back, aware he must look as wide-eyed as a rabbit. 'Why me?'

'You've built up the most trust with her since it

happened. I honestly believe you're the only one she's going to talk to.'

'Do you really think she'll listen to me?'

'I don't know. It just feels like it.'

He nodded, and reached out. Held her hand. He thought of the painting, *Truth Coming Out of Her Well to Shame Mankind*, and fuck his Art History homework, fuck the values of French Academicism and whatever other bullshit Mr. Ruiz wanted him to write, there was something terrifying lurking down that deep hole and it was getting ready to rise. Like with the dreams, Kestrel felt he had little choice.

CHAPTER FIFTEEN

The Violence of Truth

So here he was, showing up at Tala's place without warning, because if she was going to turn him away, she would have to do so at the door. The wind blew through the trees heavy and low, gusting like it could upturn cars in its wake. It felt portentous, the walk down to her house, nestled in that soft corner of the suburban sprawl, it felt as though all the houses here couldn't withstand the might of the wind, too open and comfy and exposed as they all were. The only thing about the weather that gave him a small sliver of confidence was the fact that it differed from his last dream with Elijah. The sun was not shining, and it was not raining. There was only grey, clouded sky.

The music he had playing through his headphones matched it well. Crystal-like guitar that sounded like a promise of rain. Soft bassline with well-rounded notes like pressing his hand down upon a leatherette car seat. He slowed his speed so that the song could finish before he reached Tala's driveway. It was less a matter of satisfaction than it was a ritual, as if it would protect him or prepare him for whatever was coming.

Mr. Ruiz had been right about Tala's mother being busy with work. Her car was not in the driveway.

When he knocked, it took a while for Tala to answer, and when she did, she seemed flustered, as though she had been preparing for his arrival but was still caught off guard when the moment finally came.

'So, uh, I brought the notes. I hope that's okay.' He readjusted his grip on his bag strap, offered a smile.

It took her a moment to let him in. A blip across her face, replaced with something like relief. 'Sure! Come in.' And she led the way, sprightly, towards the kitchen.

She got him a drink. He accepted. He didn't even think about what it was, he just took it politely, then opened his bag, handed over the notes.

'Let me take this to… yeah, lemme just…' She started pottering towards the conservatory. Kestrel followed her, drink in one hand, bag in the other, tugged by the energy of whatever lay at the centre of that room.

'Most of it's just homework,' he said as he trailed behind, 'but one of them's this preferences form that Miss Warren wants everyone to fill out.'

'Huh, interesting,' she said, but she made no effort to look at the sheaves of paper. She put them on the small shelf beneath the coffee table, and turned around to face him. 'Thanks for bringing them over.' She held herself with no small amount of agitation. 'Well, let's go back to the kitchen.' It sounded forced.

'Wait, can we stay in here? I kind of wanted to talk to you about something.'

She stared back at him, frightened, unsure.

'It's all of us. Bethan, Aaron, Bram, me. We all feel it.

There's this...'—he searched the air for the right word, feeling his brow scrunch, feeling his pulse race—'missing punctuation all around us. Like something isn't there that should be. I don't know how else to describe it.'

'You don't remember anything, do you?'

He stared back helplessly, unsure how to answer that question, and in his silence she continued.

'I know Aaron sort of does, that's why he chose the campaign.'

'Okay, Tala, please, tell me what this is all about.'

'Do you remember anything?'

'About what? Belial? The shrine?'

She didn't respond.

'Look, all I know is... I'm struggling. He's there when I fall asleep. When I wake up. He won't fucking leave me alone.'

Somehow, this was the thing that really set her on edge. 'No, no, no,' she started saying, repeating the words softly, barely audible but loud enough to hear the panic. She was thinking about more than just what he had said, it was clear as daylight, but whether he would ever be privy to that was anyone's guess.

'Tala. What's going on?'

'No!'

He watched her sink into one of the sandy rattan chairs and he felt his voice cracking as he said, 'What the hell changed between us? Please, let me in like you used to. You know you can trust me.'

'I should tell you,' she said, then corrected herself. 'No, I have to tell you. You deserve to know.' She bowed her head and keened into her knees. 'Oh God...'

Kestrel was torn between offering her support and showing his mounting frustration. He ended up doing neither—one would have sounded too fake, the other too unnecessary—and instead he simply stood there, leaning against the radiator and staring down at his own shoes. Ignoring her in this manner seemed to give her the space she needed to sort her thoughts out, because at last she raised her head and said 'Okay. Come. Sit.'

The tree branches with their little sprouting buds swayed in the strong breeze outdoors, and much as those buds strained towards the sky, it didn't feel like spring at all.

He perched on the rattan chair next to hers, trying not to let it creak so. Every unnecessary noise felt obnoxious; he was aware enough of his intrusion without that reminder.

She shifted, awkwardly. The rattan complained. Then she looked up and all attention in the world turned his way, bright as a blazing sun and impossible to hide from. 'I was thinking about what you said last time you came over. About the forest, and the deer. I remember that time, like, I remember how I laughed the hardest because I had been so, so scared. And afterwards, I kept thinking, one of these days, it's going to be something really terrible.'

That settled weirdly within him, and for a moment, he didn't want to hear what came next. But when he moved, the chair creaked, and he immediately fell still again. Tala took a breath, then continued.

'I managed to get to you in time. The other week, at the... at his office. I thought I actually might have managed to change something. But it's already righting itself back around. I don't... I don't want to lose you again.'

He swallowed. 'What do you mean? I'm not going anywhere.'

'No, you *did* go somewhere, and you've gone there so many times. You're all acting as though it was me, but really, it all started with you.'

'I don't understand what you mean.'

She hugged her knees, seething out breath in the way that people did when they were trying not to just up and fucking scream. The wind blew the trees about in the garden outside, whipping up a storm, and at the apex of it all Tala drew in to herself, a kernel of truth being born.

Eventually she released her hold, and in a subdued voice, she said, 'You killed yourself.'

'I… I killed myself?'

She nodded.

'How do you know that?' He wanted to add *How does that make sense*, but being belligerent wasn't going to get him anywhere. That, and, there he was standing on the precipice again—that unstable place where anything felt possible.

'I saw it,' she said, 'and I didn't like it. So I remade it, and I locked it away. But—oh God, I'm not very good at it, so I keep trying, but it's hard.'

Hard enough to make you want to die, he thought, and he noticed that as she spoke, she kept glancing over to the windowsill, where her precious sugar sculptures were all lined up like little toy soldiers. Now the dream-memory returned, and he saw Elijah dancing at the edges of his vision, waiting for them to all come crumbling down. Those little sculptures were the key, that was abundantly clear. He still wasn't quite sure *how*, and he didn't like not knowing.

'Let me see.'

'I don't want to show you.'

'Please, Tala!'

He locked eyes with her as he begged, and slowly, he saw her falter. A shiver ran through her and she swallowed, tapped her fingers on the rattan weave, prepared herself.

Her breath was all ragged as she rose and turned her back to him, selecting a sculpture from her sacred shelf. It was the figure of a young man, and it looked like him. She moved slowly, hesitantly, like she knew what she had to do but wanted to delay it for as long as possible.

After laying it on the table, she fidgeted until she once again had composure. One, two, *breathe*.

She moved it to the centre of the table.

And he felt it. The familiar tug at his solar plexus, threatening to drag him out of himself. It was the same thing he felt in dreams. That terrifying swell.

She urged him on with her gaze. The action was implicit. And so, he reached out, touched the figure. He barely had time to notice what the figure was holding—a stick or a rod or a dagger—before the world fell in on itself and he was dragged to the centre of that new and yet horribly familiar nexus. It's cold, everything's so fucking cold all of a sudden, and he blinks wetness away from his eyes.

There's a flash of light like lightning in a storm, and he's aware that his face is streaked wet with rain. He's all alone, and there's a warm feeling in his chest. Triumph.

For a moment, he forgets why he's so happy; he simply relaxes into it, cherishing the relief he feels. Then a sharp pang from lower down hits him. His arm hurts like hell.

Somebody is yelling at him.

He braces against whatever it is that's hard at his back. Concrete, brick, a wall of some sort. Of course—he had wanted to make it out to the car park but he never got that far. Fuck. He raises his head with great effort, because he feels suddenly exhausted, drained of all energy.

Bram is looking down at him, his face a picture of shock.

'Kestrel, what the fuck,' he says, and that tone in his voice makes Kestrel almost regret doing it. Almost, but not quite.

He mumbles something in response, tries to explain what he's attempted to do even though it is clear as can be.

'Shit, shit, shit, we need to get you to the hospital!' Bram crouches down beside him, tries manoeuvring him into a more upright position. He doesn't know what he's doing, else he would have elevated the arm above the level of his heart.

Kestrel looks down at his arm, surveys the damage. He's so fucking happy that he got it right, and he can tell, because the train tracks are thick and wide as a gaping maw even in this deep darkness. Cut down, not across, they always say it's more effective that way. The wound is all torn and ragged at the edges because he had favoured speed and force and fury over precision. His blood is dark as treacle, and this in itself is euphoric. It's all the foul, filthy things that have been living inside him, finally spilled out. Excised like a tumour, and the uglier it looks as it leaves his body, the better he feels.

The price for winning is high, but he will gladly take it.

Bram descends into yelling for help, too scared to lift him to his feet, too panicked to know what to do with the knife. He's yelling for anyone who might be out around campus at this time of night and then he's switching to fussing at Kestrel's increasingly-limp body, telling him he loves him, asking him why, and Kestrel wishes that Bram didn't have to be so terrified.

It's not like he's exempt from fear, himself. Of course he's scared. Saying he isn't would be a goddamn lie. He's terrified as hell because he's made the final cut, it's done, and he has no other choice but to wait for an end to everything amid the euphoric agony.

Bram cradles him in his arms and he is too pained to form the smile he wants to form, too lightheaded from loss of blood to let Bram know that it's the better option and fuck, how he really means that.

His heart is fit to bursting as it fights him every last step of the way.

The roaring in his ears reaches an abrupt halt. The ride has stopped but he's not belted in, he's still moving forward with the inertia. Then the stopping force caught up with him and in a full-body twitch he came out of the chasm and into Tala's conservatory, knuckles white where he gripped the edge of the chair.

The sugar sculpture lay on its side, miraculously unbroken, on the coffee table before him. The loudest sound in the room was his own breathing.

He couldn't make sense of it at first. He was *dead*, he had felt himself die—and God, even thinking about it brought the adrenaline bubbling back up to a peak. It was a disappointment, in a world-breaking sort of way. Death was meant to be the end, so why was he suddenly here?

Then, piece by piece, memories of how he got here slotted themselves into place. The notes from class, the weird conversation, the sculptures.

Tala was sitting stock-still nearby, staring at him with a face he had never seen her wear before. A sad sort of welcome in her eyes. She didn't say anything, she simply nodded. And that brought back another memory. The *you, most of all* echoed in his head and he recalled just how many times, in how many different ways, he had heard that since term began.

It was an attractive idea, to imagine he had just dreamt the whole thing and would be waking up, any moment now, ready to go meet her.

But she looked like she was about to cry.

He tasted salt at the back of his throat, and he moved forward to hug her. He couldn't bear that stricken look any more. She did not move for one lonely second, but after that it came all in a rush, her fingers grabbing his sides, clinging on like she was surfacing from the ocean. Like she needed saving. She buried her face into his chest and her dark, straight hair tickled his chin. He was overcome by the smell of chamomile. Again, like with Samuel in the herb garden, would be nice if time could just stop, keep them safe here forever.

He could feel her heart beating so close to his own.

'I cut along the veins, just like you did,' he said. 'I wanted to feel it, to know it was happening, that it was ending. I wanted that relief.'

She wasn't capable of forming a response, she just clung to his breast, shivering like a baby bird. They stayed like that for a while, both grasping for a hold on their emotions.

'There was a street artist,' she said, and her lips brushed his collarbone as she spoke. 'Back when Dad was alive. We —we went to visit his family in Tianjin…'

Kestrel simply listened. There was no point in ruining the moment by telling her *I know, your mother already explained this to me.* He let her tell him all about the sugar people, the trip, the absolute fascination with the art like magic.

'He said something in Chinese. I didn't understand. Dad laughed. But then…' She sniffed into his shirt, burying her face in it like she was wiping her eyes on the fabric. 'He fixed the little sugar dancer to a stick, and put it in my hand, and put his other hand over mine. Like sealing a pact. I remember the way he looked at me. I knew it was special.'

She did not say it so explicitly, but her meaning was clear. That day, she was blessed.

There wasn't really anything useful he could say in response to something like that. Right now, he was alive, so he supposed he should be thankful. But what a terrible burden to bear on her part, what a terrible power, and besides, there was no assurance that what he saw wouldn't yet come to pass. There were still too many things missing.

Unbidden to his head came a memory of Aaron. *Sometimes I see you die, sometimes it's Samuel.*

His stomach lurched once again. He looked over her shoulder at some of the other sculptures. A diver, complete with suit and balloon-like helmet. An emaciated figure. A bird with a broken wing. A leafless tree. A church steeple. There were so many, so many.

He extricated himself from her grasp, carefully repositioning her hands at her own sides, before settling into his own space again. When she had dabbed the tears out of her eyes, he decided to ask.

'So what are these other ones for?'

'These were the other times.'

'The *other times?* You mean, this has happened more than once?' He already knew what the answer was going to be.

She nodded, and he cursed.

'I have to see.'

'You say that *every* time.' Her voice rose, spitting out enough frustration to match his own, and that only made him angrier.

'Maybe that's because I'm right. This is about me, you

can't keep it from me.'

'How many times do I have to do this?' She was near-on shouting now.

'Well, how many times *have* you done this?'

She winced. And she refused to answer.

In the memory—vision—whatever the fuck that thing was, he had been hell bent on reaching the campus car park before bleeding out completely. He had no idea what that had been about, only that it had been important. Now his eyes were drawn to what looked like the only related sugar sculpture in the room. It did not lie with the others on the windowsill; instead it kept a somewhat lonely vigil off to the side. The toy-like saloon car. He stood up, he walked over to it.

'No, please!'

But Tala's request went ignored. He needed to see, he *had* to see, and she couldn't keep this, the most important thing from him.

'You mustn't! It'll change everything. *Please.*'

He reached out. Touched the golden-white crystal. And at once the clamour in his head reached fever pitch. He heard Tala wail in the background but that didn't matter any more.

The car, it was the fucking car.

Everything around him eclipsed into this one moment, time spun around back to this like it was all it had ever been trying to do. The white noise in his ears and the aching shiver at the back of his head like his nerves had been stuffed, replaced with cotton wool. A thousand well-placed barriers in his mind opened like floodgates and just like Tala's sculptures everything becomes crystal fucking clear.

Night has long since fallen.

Out of the window, the trees and the asphalt race by in a blur. It's a quiet, empty route back to town and the venue finished up so fucking late, but Daran doesn't seem to mind, a contented smile upon his lips as he drives back through the dark and it's because of this that Kestrel doesn't mind either.

The songs Daran has set playing on the stereo are much more mellow than the music at the show had been. Classical pieces, all airy and choral, winding through to indie rock with softly bobbing basslines. It should make him feel contented, drowsy, but he's still buzzing too much from the gig.

There's something in the air that he can't quite place. Excitement. A strange kind of chill.

A car driving in the opposite direction lights everything up for a moment and he sees Daran watching him as he listens to the music. That special gaze.

Daran's eyes shine. His words are calm, commanding, so easy to fall into. He tells Kestrel about the next song as it starts up.

'Requiem in D Minor. Mozart.'

Kestrel nods like he understands. It's different from what he normally listens to by an imperial mile. Music for church. Music for tragedies.

'Can you tell me what's so special about this song?'

The suggestion in Daran's voice is something he responds to so easily. He wants to impress him.

So he listens. Hears the voices rise and fall, some pitching so high, others segueing into a delicate alto. He doesn't know Mozart's Requiem well enough to tell if this is a particularly different arrangement from usual.

Eventually he shakes his head, trying not to feel the failure too harshly.

It must have been the answer Daran was hoping for, because he gives him a wide smile.

'They're all male.'

At that moment, a particularly high soprano peaks, and the note ripples through the car, testing the limits of the stereo. It sends a shiver through Kestrel's entire body, so angelic and euphoric all at once, and he thinks, *that grace is far too brittle to touch.* Like it's a crime to even be hearing it.

'Wow, that's… really cool.'

Daran flashes him this look. *I know,* he seems to say.

The rain has begun to fall. They're about halfway home, as far as Kestrel can tell, although his sense of distance and direction is nothing compared to Daran's. He's only half paying attention to road signs.

Daran flips the switch a couple of times. One wiper arm squeaks against the windshield, judders a bit. He toggles it again, with visible frustration.

'What? The wipers aren't working.'

He pulls over. It's a bright and quiet night and there's barely anybody else on the minor countryside motorway. There's a small lay-by, a clearing lined with pine trees and trash bins, and it's completely empty, with not even the usual lone truck driver making camp for the night. The asphalt glints in the dim glow of roadside lamps that give out light so poor they may as well not exist. Everything is slick and wet with the burgeoning rain.

Expectation hangs in the air.

Daran unbuckles his belt and gets out of the car in one smooth movement, all energy and determination. Long legs and limber strides as he circles round to inspect the front of the vehicle. He pushes the door shut as he does so, to protect Kestrel from the rain, and Kestrel is left sealed from the elements like he's suspended in a vacuum. That brief moment where the wind drove in leaves him cold with the fresh scent of spring rain. The stereo plays on.

Then Daran is tapping on the windscreen for his attention.

He can't hear well enough. He winds down the window.

'Kestrel, we might have to… Here, help me take a look at this.'

He beckons.

Kestrel opens the door, joins Daran by the front of the car, on the side that faces the dark woods. It's cold and wet. He hesitates, considers going back for his hoodie, and that's when everything changes. He feels it before it happens, in the same way he feels eyes upon him in the undergrowth at night.

But there's nothing in the undergrowth here. The only eyes upon him are Daran's, and in this light, they look golden. He's a carnivore on a plastic chair round a campfire in an empty clearing, on a bright, bright night so different from this but only by a few degrees.

Daran murmurs his name, and the way he says it catches at his mind. Kestrel, Kestrel, like it's something far more special than it ever should be, like it's an answer to a question that hasn't been asked. He moves forward, and there's an intention in his movements that feels primal.

Before he knows it he has started plotting the most viable escape route through the bracken. He sees it in his mind's eye for a split second; sloshing through the mud with the demon hot on his trail, scoring his face on stray branches and twisting his ankles in the undergrowth with that animalistic instinct to just fucking get away.

The fact of the matter is, he doesn't have enough time to dart away. He tries, but Daran is faster. One hand on his upper arm, the other clamped down on the soft space between his shoulder and the scruff of his neck. Daran spins him round so he's trapped between him and the car, barely inches to move, and it's frightening how much taller, how much stronger he is.

'Ah-ah, you really don't want to be going anywhere.'

'Daran, no—'

'Shh. Don't worry. How many times do I have to tell you not to worry?'

That tone confuses him for a moment; it's the friendly tone he reserves for when Kestrel amuses him. It seems too kind and too calm when stacked against that intense look he's giving him.

Then he presses his lips to Kestrel's. It's a full and thick kiss, it's too much all at once, and, while his lips are soft enough, stubble prickles at the corners of his mouth, at the velvety space above his upper lip.

Kestrel freezes up before jerking his head away. It's a world apart from when Samuel kissed him. There's no comfort, no soft melt. Only smothering. And now, Daran's looking at him like he doesn't quite believe Kestrel doesn't want it too, like he's surprised that's not the case, and it's hard to tell if he's just doing that in jest. Maybe he's teasing him and this is just part of the fun?

Or had he truly imagined he would reciprocate?

The uncertainty kills him—not knowing if he was putting out signals he hadn't intended to, not knowing if all this time he was leading Daran on.

Not that it matters for too much longer, because Daran's brow is knitted, and emotions are flashing across his face.

Somewhere in there, a decision is being made.

Don't hurt me, he thinks, in the moment before Daran does exactly that. It happens too fast: he knocks his legs out from under him and forces him to the ground, crushing him into the metal regardless of where the fender presses against his spine. His neck throbs. One leg gets trapped at a weird angle on the asphalt, pinioned by the tip of Daran's boot. And now Daran leans down towards him.

'I told you already, not to worry,' he says, hushed and close to his ear. 'You don't get to do this to me.'

Kestrel can feel the next line being crossed, and he pleads and fusses and frets from his lowly position as Daran holds him there and unzips his fly and pulls out his pulsing cock. He says no, he says no, he says stop it, but Daran's so *needy*, his blood vibrates under his skin where he holds Kestrel down. He's restraining himself from simply devouring him whole.

Mud and rainwater is pooling around him where he sits on the ground. There's little bits of moss in the roadside grit and he hyperfixates on their feeling beneath his fingers. Struggles again, until Daran finds his wrists and pulls them up, holding them above his head against the frame of the car. Everything smells earthy. He imagines worms wriggling out of the ground, slugs and snails slithering over his skin, and somewhere in his mind, a nursery rhyme is triggered. *That's what little boys are made of.*

The hot flush throbs through his body like a current, a slow electrocution.

A gentle, coaxing touch on his face, parting his mouth. He averts his eyes. Shouts as his mouth is invaded, tries to bite. This earns him a fistful of hair and a hard slam against the metal frame of the car. Daran tells him, in a voice low with threat, *Don't you dare*, and he holds his throat, makes it clear he can simply take his breath away.

This time, he doesn't bite.

Daran slides himself in to the warm cavity with a shudder, stroking his hair and his face all the while. He starts up a rhythm, slow and restrained, feeling every inch of Kestrel's mouth until his cock hits the back of his throat. Kestrel sucks to keep up, to stop himself choking. The taste is unpleasant, sweetness and salt, and he's terrified of being sick, incurring more wrath. His leg's starting to go numb. He shivers the way he did when that soprano peaked in the car, and now his is the grace that is far too brittle to touch, his is the body suffering under the sun for the sins of the people he tried to befriend. The exposure, the burning, the slow, slow death; it's all his.

It's not like there aren't cars driving by. Any one of them could stop. Any one of them could get curious and intervene, and that, he yearns for and is terrified of in equal measure. One, the fucking justice of it all as he imagines an adult more adult than the one in front of him putting a stop to it, but two, the unbearable shame of being seen. The humiliation has risen so high in his throat that he'll choke if he has to suffer an inch more of it.

He's already choking. Maybe it doesn't matter.

He feels his biceps start to give up. The phrase *sweet surrender* comes to mind, and he's heard his father play that song before. There's never anything sweet about surrender —there's nothing sweet about this position—and the more he thinks about it, the more it makes him angry. He keeps his strength until he can't any more, until his muscles yield in desperation.

Daran takes the opportunity to reassert his grip, slamming his wrists back against the bumper, getting a better hold in the moment of weakness.

No, no, no, no, no.

One last burst. He attempts to push back again, but with

Daran's harsh grip on his wrists, he is left with bucking his legs, trying to angle them in the vain hope he can push Daran off-balance.

'Come on, don't be like that.' Again, the voice, the soft crooning. It makes for such dissonance as Daran grows more forceful, thrusting like this is a punishment. The whole car shakes. Kestrel's head hits the wet metal behind him with a repetitive, rhythmic clang. Bobbing like a rag doll. Daran's grunts of exultation as he abuses his mouth come closer and closer to some kind of religious experience, and he starts thrusting far too violently, no longer willing to restrain himself.

When Kestrel's head hits the bumper too hard he blacks out. It's only for a second, but it's long enough for him to go completely limp, it's long enough for Daran to open the door and drag him inside the car. He's saying something, sounds like *you've got a lot to learn.*

Kestrel winds up on the back seat. His head's throbbing. He's aware he's groaning, he's trying to say 'please'. None of it works. Things are moving around him as he lies there, dizzy, and it's like watching stars streak across the sky and losing all sense of direction in the process. The music's still playing on the stereo, it's shifted again from classical to mellow rock, and he's heard this one with Daran before. *We can't stop what's coming.*

Pressure on his abdomen. The buttons on his jeans are worked apart.

He tries to fight. Daran presses on his chest, presses him down into the seat. He kicks; it doesn't work, he ends up with his jeans pulled half-off one leg and completely off the other, one shoe fallen somewhere on the floor, and something about that state of semi-undress makes everything seem worse: hurried and rushed and disgustingly desperate.

He's still saying please.

Daran sighs in aggravation, and slaps Kestrel across the face. 'I didn't expect you would be this much trouble. For someone so cute—and *otherwise* perfect—you are surprisingly difficult sometimes.'

The slap stuns him into silence.

Now Daran leans on to his chest, pressing in cruelly with his knees, as he reaches over to turn the interior light on.

It's too goddamn bright, it lances so sharply through his head already buzzing with the blunt force trauma.

'Is it too much? Well that's a shame.' He bends down, clasps hands on either side of his face. 'I only want you to see me.'

It's with reluctance that Kestrel looks into the eyes of his captor. They shine so intently, more golden than ever. His blond hair is like a halo around the sun, falling forward in waves, his chin almost regal as he gazes down in triumphant fascination. Kestrel thinks of how this could have been romantic, how it should have been tender. How in another universe he would have considered Daran attractive.

'I see you,' he says, and he says it because he thinks that's what Daran wants him to say. Inside, his mind is still racing through that possible escape route in the undergrowth, calculating, wondering how far it would have been to the nearest town.

'God,' Daran breathes out, and the word is fifteen syllables too long. 'Don't you even realise what a tease you are?'

I didn't intend to be, he thinks. But he says nothing; he's frightened.

Daran keeps his hold either side of his face, and he leans in, kisses him far too tenderly for the position he is in. Kestrel closes his eyes, keeps his lips parted, but tries not to respond.

'Now. I don't want to hurt you. You understand, don't you?'

His grip is a promise. Kestrel agrees.

Daran's looking as satisfied as the cat that got the cream. He lets his hands wander down, cupping the curve of his ass, lingering in the motion so he can enjoy it. The soft breath out, the quickening tone, the need behind it all.

Things have gotten quieter, and less immediately dangerous, perhaps, so he says, 'Please, don't.'

Daran just hushes him. Finger on his lips, trailing down his chest, moving lower and out of sight. There's the popping of a bottle cap, a squirt, a greasy sound, and the finger moves to tease at his asshole, leaving a sticky trail in its wake as it circles and caresses. Daran pauses on the edge, gives Kestrel a moment, a moment in which he panics, worries about needing the bathroom, about embarrassing himself. Then, with a devious look in his eye, Daran presses his finger in, swirls it around, hooks it on the outstroke, drawing a shameful yelp from Kestrel.

It's surprising, in a horrific way; he's jerked off with a finger in the ass before, but he had never known exactly what he was doing. Daran's movements have purpose. There's experience in every stroke, all of Kestrel's disgraceful noises are masterfully manipulated, tugged out of him like he's an automaton, programmed to behave this way.

When he feels something thicker brace against his asshole, he clenches, freezes up. Daran moves a slick finger down his cheek, a mockery of comfort. 'Kestrel,' he says, in that familiar teasing way, 'just relax. Make it hurt less.'

Because he knows what's going to happen, because he knows Daran is right, he tries to obey. But the fear is stronger than he is, and he stays tense—*so fucking tight*, he hears above him—and it hurts as Daran pushes his cock in. It hurts, but it also makes his nerves shiver in a way that isn't entirely terrible.

He wants to fucking die.

Getting it in is enough of an ordeal, but when he starts to move inside him it's worse. He works up to a stronger rhythm, giving Kestrel enough time to adjust, but only barely. It doesn't stop, it isn't stopping any time soon, so somewhere between the push and the pull he gets the idea of bucking in to the action, of sort of... helping Daran along.

'No, don't rush this. I don't want you to rush this. Just take your time... there we go.'

The pressure at his throat returns until he stops trying to take control. He stops the bucking. Shutters his eyes half-closed, tilts his head back so his throat is all the more exposed. Submission is a tactic.

'Ohh,' Daran breathes, so softly. 'You're so beautiful.'

Hearing those words out of Daran's mouth makes him want to rip himself apart. Blot out everything.

There was no reason for it to be me. It shouldn't have to be me.

He's Orpheus, trapped in the underworld, singing to please Lord Hades. And true enough, every noise he makes, every keening cry and shudder, brings such pleasure to Daran. The pleasure is in the claiming, in the raw performance of it all, and it doesn't seem to matter how Kestrel reacts, all of it is exactly what Daran wants.

He can't fucking win.

So it's with complete and total surrender that he goes limp, lets himself be rocked back and forth as Daran drives in so hard he thinks he's going to break. The same repetitive motions, the long drag—it would have almost been boring, if it hadn't been so horrifying. The music plays on, and he sobs on the back seat until Daran has got what he needs. The climax is monstrous—when he comes, it feels like he manages to fill up every empty space inside him. He gets so deep, and worst of all, he doesn't pull out immediately. Instead he holds himself, full to the hilt, and bends down to kiss Kestrel's collarbone, as if they had just made love.

It should make him feel sicker than he does, but it doesn't matter. He's not quite aware of what's going on any more. There's touches, travelling over his body, there's aching and there's fullness, and even in the aftermath he's still held fast, trapped between fake leather seats and the car's low ceiling.

Kestrel slid back into the room with a certain magnetic sharpness, an abrupt snapping into place that might have been satisfying if not for the burning in the pit of his belly. The gravity of the fucking situation.

I don't want that to be real. It wasn't real.

Even as he thought it, he knew he couldn't convince himself it wasn't true.

Something desperate and helpless tried to claw its way up out of his throat. He shuddered out breath. Streaked slick hands down his face.

I don't want to be conscious.

The urge to press harder was so tempting. Hurt himself until that feeling just *stopped*.

He resisted. Turned his eyes to Tala, because *really it's*

okay, you're here, in her conservatory, and your shoes are on your feet—

But what if they weren't and he just didn't know it yet? The wave bubbled up again, threatened to pull him under until it was all he could hear, all he could see.

'Fuck!'

His nerves were still strung high as a kite and he couldn't avoid the rage it brought.

'So you knew. This whole time, you fucking knew.'

'I'm so sorry. I'm so sorry!'

He huffed. It was petulant and shitty and when he did it, it sounded so ridiculous out loud that he wanted to take it back, rage harder against his own weakness. 'I feel like this is some grand cosmic joke.' He dragged his hands down his cheeks, stared up at the conservatory panes and the too-clean wooden beams between them.

Her apologies continued.

Eventually, he glanced at her again through glassy eyes.

'Is there a way to stop it from happening in this reality?'

Tala frowned. '"This reality",' she paraphrased. 'It's not a different reality. It's real, all of this is real. I just… went backwards again.'

He tried to ignore the *all of this is real*, tried not to give it too much room in his mind lest it set up residence there, because fuck, he could not handle that right now. Going backwards again, she was talking about going backwards again so focus on that.

'How? How do you do that?'

'I don't know, exactly. I just, sort of… well, I *drift*, like I showed you. And I try to stop it, I try and fix it but it never works! It never works! And then I make the sculpture and I trap the memory in that.'

'Maybe you don't need to any more. He hasn't got me

yet, this time.' Because he was thinking *well, if I just never get in that car again, everything's okay.*

'It's always the same patterns, emerging time after time.' Her voice trembled. 'Most of the time, he picks you. Sometimes… it's someone else.'

Kestrel thought again of Samuel. He said nothing, only started scanning through the remaining sculptures.

'No, please! This is enough!'

He ignored her, continued looking until his eyes settled on one in particular: a solemn girl, knees drawn in to her chest. It looked remarkably like Tala. He wasted no time.

The real Tala twitched as he touched it. She gave an involuntary yelp, a noise that would have broken his heart had it not been wrenched sideways from his body with the tug of the tide.

He ends up exactly where he started, in the centre of the conservatory, only, his body isn't his any more. He's Tala, and he's bent double over the table, hyperfocussing on the small detail of a sculpture.

This is the first one, and her fingers thrum with energy as she works the sugar into shape. Its caramelised texture threads so easily, catches at her nails. Small pokes with a chopstick to get it into the correct form. His hair, falling to his shoulders. A knife in his hand. When she is finished, the magic starts, and her eyes go wide, she feels like she's falling, she tries to catch her breath.

She's back at the start.

This time she warns him, far in advance, only, he doesn't take it seriously and why would he? She's left watching again, throughout the school term as the divide between her and Kestrel grows, and eventually, Daran slides into his life and gets his way. She doesn't see it happen, but Kestrel holds his arm so curiously in the days that follow, and it gets progressively worse as he tries to write, to work, to paint. It's one lunchtime in the canteen as he's struggling holding a fucking fork when Aaron eventually decides enough is enough, and takes him to the hospital to get it seen to. It's a hairline fracture. Tala sits beside him in triage and watches him struggle for the right words to tell people, just like she's started doing since she rewound time. Eventually he passes it all off like it's nothing, and he stops talking to her at all.

She starts to worry that he blames her, that maybe, somehow, it is all her fault.

This time she sculpts the bird with the broken wing. Reset. Try again.

On the next round, she slashes the car tyres. Daran takes him in the woods instead. Just off campus, down in the undergrowth by the field and the little brook. Weeks pass, and she arrives too late when Kestrel takes matters into his own hands, goes back to the brook with its soft, thick mud, and drowns himself at the bottom of the river. She sculpts the diver. This time she spends a lot of time on the fine detail of the helmet, the little grille at the front; she's remembering back at the start of term, a conversation with Bethan, who had just seen The Graduate, analysing the diving suit scene because it was something to do with her psychology homework but it made Bethan feel uncomfortable and it was almost like she remembered something but not quite.

Then she is gasping for air and she's back again. Telling Kestrel in the college courtyard that no, actually, the youth group thing does sound kind of lame and would he rather go see that band Bram had been talking about? He shrugs, agrees, and she sneaks off to the chapel anyway just to make sure.

There, she watches as Samuel shows up and Daran turns to him, eyes sparkling, says 'Samuel? It's a beautiful name.' Deeper down that route, she follows Daran's footsteps as he walks through the little herb garden to the priory, where Samuel isn't expecting it, where Samuel lets him in.

Every perfect deflection ends in tragedy. And she tries, Lord knows, she tries. She gets creative with it. There's one heart-thumping moment where she turns up at Daran's office, after hours, tries to make herself the victim, but he's not interested, he's not *fucking interested*.

She can't correct it, and with every new sculpture to grace her shelf, after a while, she starts to wonder, *what if it's me, what if I am the problem?*

She takes up the knife, and this time, tries to remove herself from the equation. She remembers exactly how Kestrel tried to do it, she has seen that reality enough times, she's sculpted every last detail of it, and so she repeats it to the letter, reaching for the freedom, the euphoria she knows he felt, but something cold and callous never quite lets her get that far. It's a horrific feeling, as she bleeds out in her own home, thinking that she has failed in every possible way.

When Kestrel came out of it this time, it was with the gracelessness of a fly, buffeted by wind coming from multiple directions. Ringing in his ears that made him wonder, at first, if his eardrums had perforated; such scratchy, fuzzy white noise. Whispers and flashes of scenes persisting through the haze, and that hopelessness, *fuck*, that hopelessness.

'You tried.' He could barely speak, voice all cracked like he had a cold. 'You tried so hard.'

She didn't reply. She was shaking. He recognised that expression: the fear of being seen.

As his mind began to race, as he tried to think about how he could possibly prevent all of it from happening, an unpleasant sensation rushed over him in a wave. He swooned forward. Tala's words became muffled and indistinct, and he's somewhere else now, he's—

—*being offered sheaves of tissue and being gently manoeuvred upright, led back to the front passenger seat. No words are said, and it happens in a blunt, perfunctory manner. The rain makes whorls on the windshield, and somewhere distantly, the engine starts up again—*

He caught himself on the edge of the chair, found his footing.

'I didn't touch anything that time,' he said, and maybe it was the aftereffect of being so close to Daran but he felt like a child trying to avoid being scolded. *Make it hurt less.*

But Tala held no judgement, only sadness, and she said, 'I'm sorry. You slipped in again—that happens sometimes.'

'Fuck. Why?'

'You shouldn't have drifted so much in one day,' she said.

'Drifted?'

'Yeah, like I said before. That's what I call it.'

He tried to wrap his head around it. 'So touching the sculpture makes you drift, and…'

'No. Sometimes the drifting just happens anyway,' she said, and he thought: *Is that what happened with Bram and me, in the canteen?* She continued, 'I'm not really sure what causes it. But the contact with the sculptures makes it easier.'

He was starting to lose his cool. His grasp of reality. Every dream, every nightmare, every uncomfortable thought and imagining—there was no way of knowing if it had all been true.

'You should go home and rest.' She sighed, started to tidy away some things. He noticed now how she took care not to touch her own finished sculptures unnecessarily. 'I understand if you hate me.'

'No, I… you're not the one who did this.'

She didn't seem convinced.

'You're right though, I should go.'

'Don't die,' she said.

He huffed out his breath. It was too blunt but, okay, he got it. His parting words: 'I won't if you won't.'

Out in the driveway, as he passed the empty space where a parked car should have been, a searing white pain took hold of him, lancing through his mind, blinding his eyes. Again, the swooning. He clutched the side of his head, bent double, saw the grain of the tarmac in between flashes of white—

'You understand the position this puts us both in, don't you?'

The road speeds by as the rain falls down. Each strike against the windshield feels too harsh, like it's cutting his skin.

He stares ahead, numbly.

Daran continues after the fact, and it's as though he is convincing himself just as much as he is convincing Kestrel.

'It's suicide for your education. For your future career.'

Kestrel knows what he means. It couldn't be more implicit. *If you tell.*

'Not to mention, what would happen to the group.' Daran glances over; from the corner of Kestrel's eye, that almost-smile, that conversational tilt of the head, as if he's discussing something no more important than the weather. 'Would be a shame to mess things up for dear Samuel.'

He wants to stop him from fucking talking, erase those words clean out of existence. But he continues staring at the windshield. He's so utterly beaten.

It's hard to explain, the feeling of high alert, of being so tense and strained and ready to react, whilst at the same time being completely passive. Heat floods his skin. He's… so aware, but so inert. Everything hurts, he longs for unconsciousness, like —

He imagines it for a second: opening the door on the motorway while the tarmac rushes past at seventy kilometres an hour. Just end it here.

Just end it here.

He doesn't. He stays, strapped in place, dumbly watching the rain streak by. Perhaps his finger twitches by his side, inches from the passenger door, he's not sure. His thoughts converge, and—

It was not what he was expecting, the rough texture beneath his hand. Brick, but at a weird angle. Kestrel became aware that he was bracing himself against the pillars on Tala's driveway. His breathing was all ragged, as if he had just been running. Barely a step away from where he had started to feel strange.

He averted his eyes from the tarmac and its uncomfortable patterns.

Is this what I just have to live with now?

CHAPTER SIXTEEN

Cold Sweat

The night passed in a haze. He missed the first half of the school day entirely, waking up from nightmares far too late in the morning, the taste of tears still in his throat.

As for the second half of the day, even when it was time to go, he didn't want to. Was it Tuesday or Wednesday? He couldn't remember. He didn't want to run into the church group, least of all Daran, and if that was an overreaction at this point, he couldn't tell. All he knew was that, even just thinking about being in close proximity to him brought the images flooding back, and before he knew it, he was cursing and lashing out at the empty room.

For a long while, he agonised as to whether anything Tala had shown him was real or not, and the option that made sense was *probably not*—the logical part of his brain liked this option, told him to trust it and do the adult thing and just get the fuck on with his day—but there was a deeper, more childlike part of himself that was scared and refused to let go of the magic, clinging on to it because it was the only explanation for what had been happening that term.

Avoiding campus entirely was the better idea.

So he stayed indoors. Making a cup of tea like it would calm him down (it didn't). Looking out the window at the gathering fog. As outside, so within.

The problem is, the instant a day is a write-off, you start feeling guilty about it. It would be better to just let yourself have this, just let—

Fuck that thought. Don't turn it into a surrender.

So he tried to be proactive and flipped through his journal, looking for any homework assignments or notes about what he was meant to be studying. He skipped past the page from Art History, the one he had doodled their campaign characters on—

flips back to it, rips out the page on a whim, crunches it in his hand, makes Belial small and insignificant. Feels hands on his waist, the words 'Don't do that,' spoken close to his ear, and he full-body flinches in his chair, hears it squeak pathetically against the floor—

Another blink forward and his hand was unclenched, the sheet of paper still fixed fast to the journal's ring binding. This time, he didn't remove it, although he entertained the idea of throwing the whole damn thing into the paper bin and setting it on fire. The bin was made of metal, surely it would be safe enough.

There was too much to think about, so he left his schoolwork and tried to distract himself with a few rounds of Morningstars battle arena. But even there, the flavour was all sour. He realised the character he usually played had this look in his eye that he didn't like, a few catchphrases that were a bit too close to *you won't be going anywhere* and *I don't want to hurt you (but you leave me no choice)*. And he couldn't avoid doing the unhelpful thing and wonder, did he pick that character because of all this? Did he know before he knew, on some subliminal level?

There came the same hopeless spinning out of control that he had felt in the bathroom at Aaron's. The only difference was, everything had context now. He slumped forward in his chair and pressed his forehead to the desk, scrunching his eyes up and feeling the tightness in his chest, losing track of time while he tried to get a grip on the feeling. By the time he raised his head again, by the time the roaring in his ears had lessened and the prickling on his skin had calmed down, he found that he had been automatically logged out of the game, and his tea had gone cold.

The bathroom mirror was designed to be cost-saving, not flattering, but even still, he didn't usually have much of a problem with it.

Today, he hated everything he saw. Every freckle, every long strand of hair that hung about his neck, every twitch in his muscles that made his eyebrows crease up so searchingly. He wanted to tear the mossy streak out of his hair, as though that would take away the sensation of moss and grit between his fingers.

He spent a long time staring into the mirror.

There was an easy solution to the problem, but getting there was another matter entirely. From one angle, it would be trivial to call her, to say 'Beth, I need the blue dye.' All the same, he couldn't bring himself to do it. The idea of talking to someone, and risking his voice cracking and betraying his mental state was too terrifying. So he sent a text, and flumped on the bed, and waited, staring at the wall until the patterns in the shoddy paint job started to give meaning.

She showed up at the door barely an hour later, armed to the teeth with hair dye supplies and a quizzical expression on her face.

When she spoke, he responded automatically, hiding his grief behind a vacant, blank wall. It was not intentional: it was like his body wasn't even his any more.

'Did you talk to Tala?'

'I did.'

'What did she—'

'I can't really tell you.'

He wanted to. God, he wanted to. He would need to confide at some point, because he would need help, he would need to stop Daran from—

An internal scream rose up, begged him to just stop thinking about it. He said 'Sorry' to Bethan, and waited.

'Oh,' Bethan said, and she proffered the bag. 'I brought the hair dye, anyway. Would you like help applying it again?'

'No, I'm all right on my own. Thanks.'

After she left, face still full of questions he wasn't going to answer, he returned to his post in the bathroom. Laid out the supplies. Turned on the small shaving light. He watched himself in the mirror, cagey as a wild animal, as if at any second his reflection would bolt for cover. This was it: now or never.

He mixed up the dye first: a strong, deep blue like a stormy ocean, all fresh and chaotic and dark. Then, as the dye settled in the tray, he took the hair clippers and, with a lurch in his stomach that bottomed out into a feeling of what must have been euphoria, he started to buzz away at the left side of his head. Praline brown locks filled the sink; the shape in the mirror grew strange and unfamiliar to him, and he was struck by how terrifying and how powerful that was.

Bram meets him by the town's central station, brandishing takeout from the kebab shop nearby. The sky is a bruise, but a soft one; rose pink clouds crossing the darker purple on their way over the buildingtops.

'Thanks for coming. Ugh, what a fucking day.' Bram says it as though the day has personally offended him, and perhaps it has. Why else would he call Kestrel so suddenly? He perches on the low brick wall by the station entrance and Kestrel does the same. While Bram shovels food into his mouth, Kestrel is content in the silence between them, happy to wait for Bram to tell him what's been going on, because listening to him is better than having to explain himself.

'I woulda asked to just meet in the Student Union bar, but I didn't wanna walk there on my own. You can't hear anything in there anyway.'

'That's fine, I needed the walk anyway.'

Bram laughs. 'He says, without an ounce of fat on him!'

That isn't true, but Kestrel does not challenge it.

'So I was meant to be going to a gig with my girlfriend tonight,' Bram begins, and there is an uncharacteristic quiver in his voice, 'but she like—ugh—she only used the gig to break up with me. She gave me a fucking *note* in the queue outside the venue.'

'Oh, shit. The girl from anime club?'

'Yeah, her name's Penny. Sorry I haven't talked much about her.'

'That's okay.'

'I've been trying to figure out my own feelings. I really liked her, though. I thought… maybe…'

Because Bram seems so close to breaking down, Kestrel changes tack, asks something a little more direct.

'Did you still go to the gig?'

'No, that's why I'm back so early.' Bram stabs at a chunk of meat angrily; it leaks oil under the pressure. 'It was this neat local band with a really space rock vibe, too. The Caudal Lure, you heard of 'em?'

The tension rises in Kestrel's chest. 'I… have, yeah.'

An approving nod from Bram. 'I'd been wanting to check 'em out for a while. And I was gutted I missed them at the Boiler Room, so I was like, really excited for this…'

Kestrel pushes down the guilt as fast as it rises. Focusses on the situation at hand, gets angry on Bram's behalf. 'Who the fuck gives someone a breakup note in the queue *before* a gig?'

Bram groans. 'Someone who doesn't care about the music, I guess.' He offers the container to Kestrel and Kestrel takes it out of habit, not really thinking about it. While Bram continues to rant, to get his feelings out in the cold air, Kestrel thumbs the polystyrene, feels how easy it is to break it apart, and hears Daran's voice once again telling him to be careful, lest he get it in his tea.

As for the kebab, he can't bring himself to eat even a small bit. He watches the sauce stick in clumps to the plastic fork. Inches away, but he can feel it between his teeth.

At length, he passes the polystyrene container back to Bram, and gets the note pushed into his hands instead.

'Look. It's a load of bullshit, right? Please tell me she's being unfair.'

He gets as far as *'I can't relax around you when you have*

this much baggage' before letting out a weary sigh. This kind of interpersonal shit tires him out, and if he didn't care so much for Bram he would be tempted to just call it needless drama and be done with it.

They hadn't even been going out that long, so that gives some indication to how deeply Bram had been affected by... not just by the trauma of Tala's suicide attempt, but by everything weird that has been going on this term. He remembers the strange flashback in the canteen. He knows Bram feels it too.

His breath's catching in his throat as he meets his friend's gaze. Bram's face is a picture of anxiety.

'She is being unfair. Being affected by... stuff... isn't having *too much baggage.*'

'Okay.' Bram looks like he's trying to accept this thought, but he isn't quite ready. 'I dunno, mate, I just... I tried so hard to not be too, *depressing*, you know? But recently, with all the bad dreams and the stress and the fucking weird stuff that's going on, it's not something I can just shrug off. I've tried. I don't *like* being a downer. And I feel like I fucked that up, hard.'

'You didn't fuck anything up. She just...' How to phrase it? 'She just wasn't prepared to support you. I mean, it's kind of shitty but at least she was honest.'

'True. Ugh, fuck, man.'

Kestrel pats him on the shoulder, a sort of half-hug that remains a half-hug for fear of making him drop the rest of his food. Bram makes the smallest acquiescent sound, and finishes his takeout wallowing in that mixture of sadness and anger.

The shadowblocks of buildings turn to silhouettes of oak trees and sycamores as they leave the town proper and get closer to campus. There's a field up by the north end but they don't go that way, they skirt the side of it, following a tree-lined path down to a shallow brook.

Bram doesn't turn the focus on him until they reach the brook. By now their walk has slowed to a gentle saunter and the night grows expectant. He doesn't like that feeling.

'So where've you been these last few days anyway? Missed seeing you around.'

Bram sounds so casual when he says it, but there's an urgency beneath that. As there probably should be. They take almost all their classes together, and it's been, what, a few days by now? He hasn't been keeping track.

They stop at a natural point at the highest part of the little bridge.

'Oh, I've just been... I don't know, I still wasn't feeling great, so...'

It's not much of an explanation. When Bram asks him what's really going on, he shies away from the question.

'Please, Kestrel...'

'Don't plead with me like that, I can't stand it.'

'I'm not trying to make you feel bad.'

'I know, I just—'

would rather scratch my eyes out than be in that position above you.

But he says nothing, and this gives Bram the opportunity to say, all quiet and worried, 'Something happened, didn't it?'

Looking down at the water from the vantage point of the little bridge, he is certain he sees glowing eyes in the tufts of juvenile bulrushes. They flash their attention his way, but only for an instant, and he thinks of Samuel's water horse. Of the things in the marsh. Of Poe.

It's over so briefly, but it sticks with him, tugging at his senses, beckoning him down.

He's too open. He has to do something to stop it.

From the corner of his own mind, he sees himself jump into the water. He looks quite graceful in his stupidity, and he probably won't drown, because the water's so shallow and he hasn't been drinking, but he might get hypothermia, or at least a cold.

He says something to Bram, something like 'Let's just go home,' and it's an awkward, unsatisfying moment that leads to them walking away from the reeds and the beckoning stagnant water. Somewhere from the bottom of the brook he's lying on the spongy riverbed, watching himself leave, opening his mouth as if to call out but all that does is let the clumps of mud in between his teeth.

They were in the canteen, all four of them, and the only thing Kestrel was really focussed on was the fact that he hadn't eaten in a while. He kept visualising the kebab from, what was that, last night? Who knows. He had been tired. But he kept seeing the way it stuck together all slimy and sickly. The last thing he wanted to do was eat, but now his mouth felt furry from not having done so in so long, which just made it all the worse. It had reached the point where hunger was gnawing at his stomach and he knew he had to do something about it, and he was sitting with his friends, hoping that he could solve the problem without really having to focus on it.

I want to die, God, I want to die.

'Where've you been lately? Haven't seen you around much.'

Didn't Bram ask him that already?

'I was a bit busy.'

'We can tell. Your hair looks rad as fuck.' Bram turned, as if he was about to high five Bethan, but she shook her head.

'Wasn't me. I just lent him the dye. He did that himself.'

'Wow. Seriously? Dude, I need to up my game.'

Kestrel was confused, but he didn't let it show. He forced a smile, shrugged a little, and turned his attention back to his plate.

Why was everyone being so polite? Why had they not mentioned Tala, or the weirdness from last week? It was possible that they had understood his dramatic hair job as something indicative of a bad mental state, as something requiring tact.

If that was so, they wouldn't exactly be wrong.

But the fact that Bram was only just now noticing Kestrel's hair only added to the strangeness.

Eat your food. They're going to notice otherwise.

'Last week before Easter break,' Bethan was saying. 'Only a few days until we're free.'

This was met with a groan from Aaron. 'You should see the amount of homework I've been given for Philosophy.'

'Same, I have at least one graphics portfolio to finish, and—'

'At least that's creative, though. Not writing essays.'

'Nope. You forgot I'm taking Psychology too.'

'Ugh, kill me now.'

So many jokes he couldn't help but panic that they actually mean it too.

Kestrel's phone was on the table, so when it lit up and started buzzing, everyone could see it. Capital letters on the screen. M U M.

'Are you gonna get that?' Aaron raised his eyebrow.

Kestrel just stared at the phone for the longest time. Then, 'Oh, sorry.' He let it keep ringing but he shoved it into his pocket, careful not to press anything. She would just think he's too busy in class or something, that way she wouldn't feel slighted, and that was important as fuck right now because he really couldn't take anyone else being disappointed in him, he couldn't take anyone else feeling like they were owed something.

He thought about last term, about Aaron buying that rotisserie chicken from the deli further into town, and the four of them dragging it back here and stripping everything off its bones. Arranging the bones in size order, for some reason. How confused the canteen staff must have been.

He looked down at his plate. Right now, he couldn't even handle a fucking chicken wing.

'Student Union's having an Easter party on Friday night,' said Aaron.

'Can't go,' Bram murmured. 'Girlfriend's taking me to a gig.'

'Ooh, get it!' Bethan clapped her hands for Bram.

Aaron whistled.

Kestrel stared. *Girlfriend. Gig. Friday night.* Things were getting too jumbled up, it was all out of order and for a frightening second he thought he saw beyond the veil of whatever tenuous fabric kept everything in motion. It was too much, and all at once.

How nice it would be to have everything just. Stop.

He smiled for Bram, he forced himself to finish his lunch, he lied and swallowed and throughout it all, thought *Shit, I really am not okay.*

Class is about to begin.

There's a knock on the door just as Mr. Ruiz is going through the register. It's unexpected: Daran peeks his head in and the question, when he asks it, is ever so casual.

'Sorry to interrupt. May I talk to Kestrel for a minute?'

Ruiz does not seem to mind. In fact, he's rather offhand about it, waving Kestrel forward, telling him to go on, absolutely, no problem.

It's the worst place for this to happen. He can't say no, and risk explaining himself to Ruiz, his classmates, Bram… He can't let that horrendous thing inside him be *seen*.

His blood feels hot.

Slowly, he pushes up from his desk and goes to Daran. A beckoning hand, and he's pulled aside into the corridor. So close to the rest of his class, but here, shielded by Daran's arm, fenced in by the man's heat, they may as well be in another world. Daran looks down at him with that winning smile. 'You didn't think I'd forget about you, did you?'

He tries to say, 'I don't know what you mean,' and he's stuttering.

'It's okay. I'll see you after school, at the chapel.' He smiles, thin and wry. The threat is there.

Kestrel holds his breath, waiting for it to be over.

'Whyever are you waiting?'

He's as dumbstruck as he was in the car, after the fact. Still impossible to make sense of that feeling. So, he gives no answer, surrendering all power to Daran. And, even though he has said nothing, Daran acts like he has.

'I see,' he says, and the devil grows beneath his face as somewhere, deep inside him, a decision is made. 'Yes, why wait?'

He turns him to face the wall, hands clamped onto wrists until he's placed him where he wants, then he moves down to his belt, unbuckling and exposing him.

And that's when he knows this can't be real. Daran would never fucking risk being seen like this.

Although what if he did, and what if people did nothing?

None of the cars on the motorway bothered to stop.

Fuck—he tries to move, but the pressure between his shoulder blades has him pinned to the wall. He moves his hands, Daran forces them back, then reaches down, strokes him. Slips a finger between his ass cheeks.

The corridor shifts, whitewash and beige becomes tainted with green and blue. He's Quinn, and Belial is shoving him up against the stone in that murky cavern, and nobody, absolutely nobody, is coming to help him. He can feel the demon grip at his haunches. He can feel the pressure as his cock thickens and pushes inside him, the unbelievable girth, the punishing pace; he can hear the roar of blood in his ears—

'You don't look well,' said Bram.

Just hearing that voice was enough to drag Kestrel out of it. The sky was bright with midday sun and both Bram and he were outdoors, walking towards the art block. He checked his phone, well aware that he must look confused as fuck, and discovered that yeah, afternoon classes had yet to start. He wasn't sure what had happened—a drift? A dream?

Not like he would be able to find out. Not without—

visiting Tala again

—fuck that.

He groaned. 'I guess I should've got more sleep.'

Bram watched him with concern.

Walking past the courtyard near the southern entrance was like going through a portal. Things not quite real, limestone blending into the mist. The gravel crunched and it sounded like a texture his hands could feel, and he clenched them in his pockets.

'Obviously I don't mean because you dyed your hair,' Bram continued. 'Like, you know I already said that looks great. It's really drastic! But, great. You look cool.'

You're overselling it, he thought, but he just smiled in response. 'Thanks. Yeah, I needed a change, and it was about time.'

'Time,' said Mr Ruiz, pausing for effect before the projector as he often did, 'is a curious thing. Very important for the artist to consider. Now, we're still thinking about light and shadow, about how to capture that, but consider, *when* you capture it.'

The whole while he was talking, Kestrel had his attention on the door, worrying that his dream-drift-whatever-the-fuck-it-was was going to come true. He didn't notice what Mr Ruiz was saying until it had already cut too deep.

'See, now, the beautiful thing about time, is that it'll never happen again.'

Kestrel saw it happen again. Rain on the windows, pressure on his chest. He tried to hide his wincing. His fingers grew itchy, and he waited impatiently for the main focus of the lesson, for the bit where he could work on something, distract himself, get some of that sickness out of him. *Ruiz, you just don't fucking know.*

'For your main assignment over Easter, I want you to go outside, and take inspiration from the natural environment. Forage for materials that capture a time and a place, and make a final piece based on that. And be warned—I will absolutely shoot you if you all come back from the Easter break with photographs of sunsets.'

Mr Ruiz spread the materials out on the central table. Charcoals, chalks, pastels. All things rough and tactile, bright and beautiful.

'Start mocking up your pieces with these. Think about what I said before, about chiaroscuro. Try and incorporate plans for shadowing into your mockups.'

An idea was being born somewhere in the depths of Kestrel's mind. The thoughts themselves were not good, but the idea was tantalising, might even feel justified.

Working with charcoal was like sticking his hands in the soil. He wasn't sure whether this was a good or a bad thing yet, so he kept at it. Minutes passed like hours, and he didn't talk to Bram much even though they sat side by side, he let the time draw out in his mind like unpicking a thread, unpicking it and laying it down on paper and in that fashion, he almost fooled himself that it—the grand distraction—was working.

He sharpened the blunted end of the stick with a scalpel. Overestimated the resistance of the material. Cut his thumb.

A tiny prick of pain, and blood was beading from the cut. It spilled over, and he didn't care too much that it was mixing with the charcoal on the paper below.

'Mate, you're bleeding.'

Bram, stating the obvious.

'It's probably fine.'

'No… that's actually pretty bad. You should get that sorted, wait, lemme get some tissue.'

Maybe it was deeper than he had first thought. He stared at Bram, then stuck his thumb in his mouth to suck the wound clean. He felt dangerously uncaring about anything. And so it was when Mr. Ruiz came to their table to check out their mockups, when he was asked oh so casually what he was working on, that he said, 'This one is called "Saturn Devours His Son in the Back of a Black

Sedan."'

It was on the nose because it was meant to be, although he was the only one who would realise that. Even if he wasn't, he didn't care how much a point he made of it. He heard the words Mr Ruiz really wanted to say catch in the back of his throat and never surface. It wouldn't have mattered if they did, he felt callous enough to withstand it.

Moments later, Mr Ruiz said instead, 'Good work with the shadows,' and coughed, and moved on.

Bram was looking at him searchingly. He ignored him too.

CHAPTER SEVENTEEN

Kairos tou Poiesai to Kyrio

Seeing Daran again for the first time since the drift was strange.

He hadn't wanted to do this, but it was a thing that needed doing. The practical matter of telling him that Samuel was keen to help with the Easter Mass was weighing heavily on him, and he had decided that the only way to do that successfully was in person. From one extreme and possibly paranoid line of thinking, this was all to stop Daran from having the ball in his court regarding a meeting place and time. If Kestrel sniped him to it, he could at least have some control, and he wouldn't then need to suffer the invitation in his inbox, the uncertainty of waiting for where and when.

At the other extreme, maybe this would serve to recalibrate his mind, to reassure him that Tala's crystalline vision was all imaginary and that he was just searching for meaning where there was none. It was an easy solution that, for all its realism, seemed far too impossible, but he craved it nonetheless.

He had picked the time when everyone else should be there, because he was pretty sure it was the right day (he had checked his phone, for all that that mattered). They would all be in the chapel, the lights would be on, and there would be gentle music playing.

The first thing that happened, when he saw Daran's profile against the stark white wall—the strong cut of his jawline, the wild, wild hair so falsely angelic in the light—was a strong fight-or-flight reaction that had his pulse racing and his muscles tensing like crazy. His brain started running at a million miles an hour, hunting for theories and reasons and excuses to get him out of there.

Much as he knew that was ridiculous. It *was* ridiculous. Everything would be okay.

He pushed down the nausea, the—

oh fuck, what if it was real?

Of course it wasn't. Nothing was ever going to be as dramatic as those ridiculous—

memories

—drifts.

There were people all around them, but at the same time, the room was empty and both Daran and he were the only people that existed. He moved forward through the crowd, murmuring the expected pleasantries to the students who greeted him.

'Everything all right?' Daran asked in that low, soft tone. He had obviously been on his way to sort something out, but he stopped the instant he saw Kestrel. He sounded so concerned; he always did. And it would have been easy to fall into it.

The nausea stopped him. He kept an arm's length between them.

'Yeah, I just… I wanted to tell you that Samuel's on board.'

'Oh? That's fantastic. Thank you, Kestrel.' Again, the focus on his name, the savouring of the word. 'I appreciate you asking.' The look that Daran was giving him, it was like he had just passed some hidden test. No doubt it was imperceptible to everyone else in the room, it probably seemed just like any other moment. But he felt it, God, he felt it.

'I've just finished telling the others about our plans for the holidays,' Daran continued, calm and measured as anything. 'They seem keen. Emily's offered to play guitar.'

'That's… that's good.'

Kestrel had no idea if he still wanted to go through with the whole Easter Mass thing. But he could think about that later. For now—

The stereo buzzed abruptly, then again; harsh feedback that sounded like a bone saw put through layers of fuzz. Michael called for Daran, who sighed and fixed Kestrel with an apologetic gaze.

'Would you mind putting these back in the sacristy?' Daran was proffering the rosary box. 'I was just about to head that way, but—' He jerked his head subtly towards the sound system. Kestrel was stunned for a moment, transfixed by the box and the keys lying atop it, the same fucking keys that caused the problem before, the little frog charm propped unceremoniously atop them. 'It's the smallest key on there, the dark grey.'

'I don't think…'

'Look, I'm sorry about last time.' An anxious upturn of the eyebrow that he wasn't quite sure was genuine or fake. The speakers were still buzzing obnoxiously, and Kestrel was acutely aware that he was the bottleneck of this situation.

'Yeah, I'll… do that right now.' His chest felt tight as he accepted the little plastic box.

Daran thanked him—much as he didn't want to hear it —and the pair of them separated.

Out in the chapel's main hall, every step felt achingly slow. The sound system chaos was muffled through the wall, making everything take on a dreamlike quality. He had that vague sense of fate spinning around again, trying to correct itself, and it had to be, because why the fuck else did he keep ending up in this position of responsibility?

The sacristy, such as it was, was at the end of the corridor. Being a non-denominational space of worship, it was really just a storeroom, but some words seemed to stick. He only had to put the box on a shelf in there, somewhere safe and easy to see, no problem. It would be incredibly hard to fuck this one up, but all the same, the tension was there.

It was as he plucked the keyring off the top of the pile that it happened. His skin made contact with the lumpy figurine, and it felt wrong, it feels… sweaty, almost. It's too close and then he blinks and—

Daran, waving the fucking thing in his face, saying, 'Didn't this mean something?' He's so startled by how close and how angry he is that he stutters a response that goes nowhere and Daran uses that opening to grip with his free hand, forcing him to focus, look at him, while he says, 'Didn't you care?'

He can see the base of the keyring all hazy and far too close to his eye; the scratchy lines in the shape of a familiar initial. His eyes are prickling with tears and he's hit by a strong wave of betrayal. It's unjustified, too, because he's positive he hasn't done anything to deserve this. He wants to say *How dare you use this against me?* because deep down he knows this is just emotional leverage, but Daran's scaring him, and he just ends up responding to the question that's been spat his way.

'I did! I... I didn't spend hours on that thing because I didn't care, I just—'

Daran sighs, pinches the bridge of his nose as though in pain. He lets go of Kestrel's shoulder to do it and Kestrel feels his body sag in response. He's backed against a wall. There's the wrenching in his gut as time twists around the inevitable fact. Then Daran tries to kiss him again.

Kestrel came out of it this time braced against the door of the sacristy, clutching the keyring tightly.

The fuck?

He caught his breath, noticed his surroundings, how convenient it was that the chaos was still going on next door, as far as he could hear. A little bit of space to sort himself out, because fuck, he needed it, he felt ill.

As his pulse righted itself back around, as the shock slowly abated, he realised he was more angry than anything else. Sure, by now he was familiar enough with the drifts, and used to the fact that they could happen so unexpectedly, but this whole thing was fucking weird. It hadn't happened the first time he picked up the keyring. Unless Tala showing him her statues was the catalyst.

And the frog itself—had he made it? The wide, cute little eyes of the creature stared up blankly, offering no clue.

It didn't make sense that objects cross over into other timelines. Wouldn't Daran remember where he got it from? Wouldn't that make him aware of the resetting? The more likely option was that the whole drift had just been a product of his overworked mind, and that felt like the mood for the week. Fuck, this was all too much. Ultimately, he really didn't know how any of this worked.

The modelling clay was velvety-firm under his fingertips. He couldn't stomach turning it over to check out the initials scraped into the base. Again, he saw Daran throwing it back in his face and his skin prickled because that fucking hurt, that felt like such a betrayal.

He clenched his teeth and focussed on the task at hand. Sacristy. Rosary box. Find a decent spot. The frog made no sense, and he just had to settle on that.

In due time he found Daran by the soft drinks, crisis now dealt with. When he returned the keyring, he held it by its outermost key, letting the little anomaly dangle. By some miracle he managed to return it to Daran without letting the figurine touch his skin again. A satisfied gaze, a kind word of thanks, and the whole interaction would be over—

'It's cute,' Kestrel blurted out. 'Where did you get it?'

Daran followed his eyes to the figurine. There was something in his expression, fond and troubled at the same time. 'Oh, that. It's quite special to me.'

'Who gave it to you?'

'I... You know, I can't quite... It was a long time ago.'

Something felt horribly fragile there, reality balancing on a knife edge, so Kestrel left it alone. He was thinking that yeah, a distraction might be necessary, and he was just about to change the subject, but he was beaten to it.

'This is new.'

Daran reached out and touched his hair. Apologised for being so forward, but Kestrel barely heard that, heart thumping in his chest because he had realised what was happening too late and had lost the chance to move away and make it seem natural. *Don't flinch, for the love of God, don't let him see your reaction.*

He didn't know how to feel. What Tala had shown him, what had happened in that vision/flashback/whatever-the-fuck it was, and whatever the fuck he had seen just now, it wasn't *real*.

It would be unfair to treat Daran any differently as a result. Wouldn't it?

'It's such a dramatic change,' Daran said, and he realised he was talking about the hair.

'Oh. I… Yeah. I liked the colour, so…'

Daran smiled, and it was hard to gauge whether it was a warm smile or a smirk that hid some level of dark humour. 'You're still caught up in that storm, aren't you?' He meant the deep electric blue colour, of course he did, but his words had Kestrel's heart racing all the same. Back to the car, to the thunder breaking over the ridge, the colour the light and the windscreen wipers going back forth back forth.

'Hey, I'm sorry to keep asking, but… is everything really all right?' The intensity, those golden eyes, inspecting his body like it was a puzzle to unlock. Fuck, he needed some space.

He was acutely aware that looking so troubled was making Daran reach out more, and that really wasn't helping.

'I just feel a bit ill,' he murmured, and he pulled out the same excuse he had at Aaron's, the one that nobody could really argue with. 'Think something I ate disagreed with me.'

He tried not to give any deeper meaning to those words. It didn't exactly work, and he left a little quicker than was socially appropriate. He knew Daran was watching him go and he hated that fact.

Tala, I wish you'd never shown me. Now everything's weird.

It may have been just a case of serendipitous timing, but by the time Kestrel had returned to his dorm, Tala called him. On the phone.

At first it was confusing. He picked up, and didn't really know what to say. There was the small, nagging idea that this may not be real—because when had she ever called him recently?—but he pushed it down.

They both said 'Hey, are you okay?' at the same time. The absurdity of it made Kestrel laugh shallowly, and then Tala did the same, and that was enough to break the tension, at least for a while.

'I'm, uh… not really,' he said, and that was a phrase that felt strange in his mouth, he wasn't used to it, so he waited for her turn next. Wondered if she would apologise.

She didn't. She said, 'I thought not, but I had to check. What happened at the weekend… it was a lot.'

Again, he felt the weight of everything she had seen and done and tried, and again it was so heavy he thought it would crush him. His heart thumped.

'I…' And he paused, because how should he phrase it? 'I don't even know if this is real or not. I just want to know… how… how does it work? The sculpture thing?'

She was silent, so he filled the space.

'Is it like a bookmark, pointing back to that page in the timeline?'

'Hmm… no, I think it's more than that. I think… once I capture it in the sculpture like this, it can never happen again. In that exact way, at least.'

Wait—that reminded him of something. Mr Ruiz, art

class, and that sickening phrase: *the beautiful thing about time is that it'll never happen again.* There, once more, came the same bristling feeling, the desire to refute it.

What Tala had just said put those words in a different context, and it made him feel slightly better.

But he still hadn't replied, so she sighed in the silence and said, 'That might just be wishful thinking.'

'No, that's… I hope that's true.' It didn't really help him understand how the magic had happened, though. And it didn't clear up any other questions. He thought about the frog. 'Is it only sugar sculptures that can do it? Can it be sculptures that anyone can make? Or is it just you?'

'Why are you asking me? I don't know! I just started doing it because I was sad! I didn't expect—' She broke off, the words turning tight as plucked strings.

'Sorry.'

'No, I'm sorry.'

A stalemate.

He wanted so badly to just tell her about the keyring and what had happened around it. But the memory was still too present, so he cast the focus back on her. He knew it was a shitty thing to do.

'Have you ever tried the sculpture thing before? You know, since that trip with the street vendor?'

He could hear her suck in breath. The reply, when it came, was like acid. 'You're asking me why I didn't do this after Dad died.'

'I—'

'I already said, I didn't know it would have this effect. I was really sad after that. I don't know why I decide to do anything. I just don't want it to hurt.'

He could hear the pain in her voice and he thought about all the times she had tried to make it right, the effort and the agony and everything that entailed and he felt terrible.

Maybe she had tried for her dad. Maybe, after discovering what the sculptures did, she had tried to rewrite that age-old wrong. And maybe she had found that it only worked around the crux of the event. He had died almost a decade ago, so what would it take to rewrite something so very old? Would the sense of constantly living in a state without beginning or end get worse? This week was enough, but what if it was like this for older trauma sufferers? The threat of what the future had in store made his eyes sting.

So he dialled it back.

'Look, I didn't mean to kick up all that stuff. I really appreciate you calling me.'

'You do? Ugh, fuck, this is hard.'

'Yeah. None of this is easy. We're both in hell together.'

He could hear her sob a little on the other end of the line. 'I think we are,' she said softly.

It was getting late and Kestrel was out walking anyway, to clear his head, to give himself some space, when he got the message from Bram. *Mind meeting me at the station?* That faint sense of familiarity shifted like blood beneath his skin. He had not been heading anywhere in particular, but he immediately changed course for the station.

Here it was, the same sky, the same feeling, the same dusky purple backdrop. The way that thin strip of blush-coloured cloud darted over the buildingtops was the final tell that made him know that this, *this* was the walk home with Bram, and he had already seen it before.

'Thanks for coming,' said Bram. 'Ugh, what a fucking day.'

Kestrel let him talk about his girlfriend Penny, he read the breakup note, he declined the offer of food, he felt the guilt over the space rock gig and the car, the car, the *fucking car*, he perched on the crumbling brick wall with him until it was time to amble back to campus slowly.

There, the distant ridge of trees just beyond the field. The blush in the sky, now completely bruised.

He heard down below him the gentle trickle of running water—a little stronger than it usually was, because it had been raining a lot recently—and he felt a thump of foreboding in his chest as Bram slowed to a stop at the crest of the small wooden bridge.

'So where've you been these last few days anyway? Missed seeing you around.'

Bram was worried about him; he knew that much. He felt reality start to bend the same way as it had before—he would offer an excuse that barely covered the issue, and that would make Bram plead with him, which would ensure he never went deeper into sharing this damn issue that was tearing him apart inside.

The gift of insight allowed him to realise something important. He could make a small change, here.

It will feel terrible. You will want to jump. But please don't; you know where that leads.

The water below him gurgled and slapped on the banks, and he couldn't shake the impression that it was hungry.

He was gripping the edges of the wooden handrail. Bram was looking at him.

'I haven't been well,' was what he said at length.

'Damn. Is… is everything all right?'

Kestrel inhaled. Held it. Made his choice.

'What would you do, hypothetically, if someone hurt you—or a friend of yours—like, in a physical way? Like in a really-not-great way.'

'Hypothetically?' Bram's thick eyebrows were doing the questioning thing. Judging him? Maybe.

'Yeah, hypothetically.' He kept eye contact, watched Bram continue to question him without saying anything. The urge to justify himself was overwhelming under that scrutiny.

'Are you… did something happen to you?'

'No, God no.'

Technically it was not a lie. He shouldn't have spoken so quickly though.

'Okay. Is this Tala you're talking about?'

He could see why Bram would think that, and he wasn't far off.

'No, I swear it's not,' he replied. 'This is just… a thought I've been having recently. I feel like something bad's about to happen.'

Bram looked at him curiously.

'I sort of know what you mean.'

The air fell chill around them.

'Well, to answer your question, I think I would… probably be very angry. I guess it depends on who they are and what they'd done but I'd probably want to get back at them.'

'You'd beat them up?'

'Mate, you know my mum's from Colombia. I've suffered the chancla enough to know how to throw down in a tight spot.' Bram puffed his chest.

'Dude, seriously…'

'You know what I mean. And I don't mean it like *that*.'

Kestrel traced the whorls in the wooden handrail.

'What if someone did mean it like that, though? How the hell would we fight that, for real?'

There was a pause, expectant and heavy. Somewhere across the trees a wood pigeon cooed its final lullaby for the night.

'Determination, remember?' Bram playfully shoved his shoulder, offered up a smile. 'I'm here for you, mate. Just don't forget that. If—' His smile faltered. 'If anyone does try to do anything to you, or to Tala, and I know you said it wasn't Tala but all the same, if it happens—or if it's already happened—I really do mean what I said.'

Kestrel looked at him sidelong, watched his bright eyes from under that dark fringe, and felt a glow.

'Now, I need to get obscenely drunk and forget all about Penny. You in?'

Kestrel nodded, grateful he did not push the issue. They walked away from the bridge, and the water went hungry.

Back to the student union bar, to the lights and the heat and the clustering, hungry bodies. Bram wanted to get his mind off the breakup, so they leaned full tilt into a jug of Pimm's that was clearly meant for more than two people. Kestrel thought he had been holding it together rather well, so it surprised him when that tug at his solar plexus returned. It could have just been the drink. He got up from the table, world spinning slightly around him.

That boy with the half-unbuttoned shirt was there again on the dancefloor. He caught Kestrel's eye, smiled.

Something cold and expectant washed over Kestrel and he set aside his drink, moved forward. Why not? He was feeling destructive.

They performed the same moves as before. The boy said something, like 'I was hoping to see you again.'

He wanted to trace a hand down the boy's arm, from shoulder to wrist, so he started reaching out...

And catches himself, reaching out for some inky blackness (the water is calling him again, still demanding tribute). The boy's face transitions seamlessly into Daran's. He pulls Kestrel close, says *oh, I've waited for you for such a long time.* Kestrel knows what is going to happen, beat for beat, his brain flits to different parts of the tracks playing on the stereo, unable to play it chronologically because there is no beginning and there is no end. That purring voice and the way he holds him and the pressure and the heat and, fuck, Daran looks so goddamned delighted as he starts, slowly, to undress him —

Kestrel blinked.

They were in the stairwell, making out without a shred of shame, and the boy was just a normal boy. It was strange: although he was on edge from the vision, he couldn't seem to stop his own hands from reaching out. He moved like he was entranced, and his partner, who, for all his attractiveness was showing his age by moving clumsily, seemed to be spurred on by Kestrel's intoxicated, pliant state.

He told himself everything was fine, and it was, until the guy whispered in Kestrel's ear that he wanted to go outside, take this further. The familiar panic rose up, but again it was stunted behind that inert wall. This was neither fight nor flight, and he couldn't understand it.

Trapped in that state, he did the only thing he could do to take control of the situation. He nodded, wound his fingers round the guy's belt, and gave a half-smile, begging to be led on.

They went outside, round the back of the block, where brick met the cover of trees, and here they resumed their foreplay.

The boy was young and dumb like him, but he didn't really know what he was doing. Everything was rushed, fervent, fumbling, and not in a consuming way like it had been with Daran.

A dark thought: *I bet I'm more experienced than you.*

Then: *Why am I comparing this to Daran instead of Samuel? This is fucked up.*

But the wall told him not to listen. It was too busy thinking about the tenderness that had cropped up amid the violence, the soft touches, the *make it hurt less.*

Fuck that.

He angles his head, baring his face bold and unshielded.

'Hit me hard,' he tells Daran. 'I dare you. I can take it.'

'That's not really my thing,' the blond boy from the Student Union bar was telling him.

A flush of shame kicked his boner down a couple degrees. He huffed out an almost-curse, trying not to ruin the mood, but that was easier said than done.

'Okay, fine, let's do this,' he muttered, and he dropped to his knees, started fussing at his partner's belt. The guy started to protest, perhaps out of courtesy, but by the time his dick was freed and he realised what he was getting, he stopped, shuddering out excited breaths instead as he leaned against the brick wall and let Kestrel drive.

In one smooth motion, Kestrel took in the entire length, choked a little, bobbed his head and curled his tongue and thought *I'm developing a talent for this.*

Above him, his partner his abuser his target moaned and shuddered with ecstasy, twining fingers through his hair.

As he felt the grit shift beneath his knees, as he felt the rain on his face, again there was the panic. But then he turned that panic to rage—he was drunk enough—and he held on to the other boy tighter, hands firm on his waist, pushing up against him harder, inciting him to grab his hair more firmly and drive him onto his cock with urgency.

It's hatesex, that's what this is.

Kestrel drove the other boy into a frenzy, making him lose control with utter abandon. When he came, Kestrel swallowed messily. He was crying, and from more than just the force of the thrust.

'What's all that about?' asked his partner, a little too softly for his liking. He wiped away one of the tears with a gentle hand and Kestrel batted it away.

'It's just… something I do,' he murmured, not quite sure what to say. If the guy thought it was weird, then whatever. He was not going to be sticking around anyway.

'Okay.' A hand ruffled back that wild blond hair. 'I'm into it. I think.'

Kestrel shook off the dirt, the cloying ever-present dirt, and rose again so they were on the same level.

He's not Daran, he hardly looks like him aside from the keen glint in his eye and the blond hair.

For an awful moment, Kestrel saw himself walking up to Daran by the hood of the car, only he was the one initiating the kiss, he was doing everything willingly like he's just done right now and he could see it pleased Daran so fucking much.

He felt like he had lost, out here tonight behind the bar, because in the end it wasn't hard and violent enough to excuse the pretence of *love*.

The blond boy, who had no idea of what was going on, moved to fix a lock of Kestrel's hair out of his face. 'What about you, now?'

He was aware of how pent up he was with the need to get off, but he was not about to ask that the favour be reciprocated. It wasn't shame, it was revulsion. So Kestrel started to leave, and he did not kiss the boy goodbye.

'Wait, where're you going? See you round?'

Maybe in your dreams.

He walked around the other side of the building from the way they had come, because he didn't want the other guy to follow him, he wanted to make it appear as though he was going home. Here, the concrete dipped up and down in a series of steps and ramps, and he idly traced his hand along the metal railing to stop himself swaying too much with the drink.

It was empty out here. Quiet but for the distant throb of the bass.

You were meant to be chilling out tonight, just relax, and as that thought came in it got him bristling, made him stop walking altogether. Prickling under his skin, combined with an intense need to lash out. In the biting cold, the temperature rose a couple of degrees. He looked up above him at the stars and satellites turning, heard a song play out in his head; *the sun is eclipsed by the moon.* All that he felt, and all that he saw, and all he was trying to keep at bay, came crashing down inside.

Why the fuck—why the *fuck!*

He punched the guard rail, once, twice. Something shifted in the bones in his wrist.

Didn't matter.

The music continued as he braced himself against the rail, becoming aware of its presence, its realness. It was hard and solid and unyielding metal beneath his fists but he didn't care: he hit it again, again, again, then dragged his hands down his face. There, the convex shape of his eyes beneath lids stood out when he rubbed, all the tendons drawn tight and tired as if waiting to collapse under the sheer weight of those thoughts heavy like bricks.

It didn't happen.

It didn't even fucking happen, so why is it like this?

It was ridiculous, even acknowledging it.

But then he thought about the diaries. The art. How he had acted and felt, through all these things from the past year, like he had known, like he had *known*. And he thought about the sugar sculptures, how lurid the memory was. It *had* happened, and it had been bad enough for Tala to rewind everything. Enough for her to give up her sanity trying to rewrite it. Perhaps the real question by now was not whether it had happened, but how many times. The one question Tala refused to answer.

A creeping, insistent need began crawling its way around his abdomen. Unfinished business from earlier. Still angry, still unsatisfied, he went back into the building, slipped into the men's room to wank.

Do I look beautiful when I'm doing that?

What the hell does he see in me?

—There's no way to escape.

Back to that one hopeless thought. No way to escape.

Augh, fuck, I'm coming—

It wasn't fair, it wasn't fair.

He thought about stopping time, about going back to that one last beautiful moment in the garden with Samuel. If only he could return there, and never take another step forward again.

The whole encounter seemed unreal immediately after it was over.

Did he really give that guy head outside? Did he really fucking *cry* in front of him?

Either way, he was back at the bar and the other guy

was gone, and the night was still in full swing. He had another drink, and at first that was okay, but then the nausea hit him all at once.

He was dimly aware of Bram urging him to go home, saying *I know you said you'd come with me, but look, you really look like you need to rest.*

He said something then, not sure what.

'I know you care about me, Kes, but you don't have to punish yourself by staying out the whole night.'

Something like that.

Kestrel had a faint memory of hugging him, and then he left.

He didn't know what time it was. Only that it was late at night, and he was standing outside the priory in the mounting drizzle.

Samuel—why else would he be here if not for Samuel?

He checked his phone. No messages. The screen, spattered with rain. He had to rub it against his clothing to clear it enough to select Samuel's number. Incidentally, he discovered it was midnight.

The rain drove harder. There was nobody in the gate-house so he called Sam's number,

Eventually Samuel picked up.

'Kestrel! You okay?'

He chewed his lip. Didn't really know how to answer that.

'I'm outside.'

'Wait, at the house? Or the priory?'

Shit, he hadn't even considered that Samuel might have gone back to his parents' house.

But then again, he didn't really know why he was here, so there were a lot of things he had probably not considered.

'I'm at the... at the priory.' It took him a second to double check.

He heard Samuel exhale, filling the air with what on anyone else would have been a curse. 'I'm on my way down, gimme a sec.'

Moments later Samuel came rushing out of the priory, scattering grit down the garden path, opened the gate with a 'What on earth happened?' and a stricken look on his face. His hair, tousled from sleep and his eyes bleary. His tone, sharp and worried. There must have been an edge to Kestrel's words that he had been unaware of.

Kestrel just stared at him awhile, thinking *Here I am, awaiting grace from an angel, what on earth gives me the right?*

'Can I come in?' he managed to say, and then he started shaking, and Samuel reached out, and he couldn't help but collapse in to him. He let himself be enveloped in a hug in the cold, clammy rain and he stayed there, still as a post, wishing it didn't have to end.

But it had to. It took a while, but it had to.

'I'm sorry. Your shirt's damp.'

'I don't care. But we should—we should get you somewhere better.'

'That's okay, I don't need that.'

Samuel looked out at the garden, arm still wrapped around Kestrel. 'It just feels wrong here. Like we're stuck in a mire.'

Ordinarily, Kestrel would have had some part of his brain tell him that yeah, it was probably just the weather being so miserable. But he was quite ready to believe that there was more to it than that right now. The water-soaked blue grasses seemed to watch them as they went indoors.

The library was empty at this hour, and this was where they went. Samuel had procured a cup of tea seemingly out of nowhere and he accepted it without thinking. The same went for the blanket over his shoulders.

He dried his hair off with it.

'Your hair looks good.'

'Thanks.' He held his breath, waited. 'You're not going to tell me it was a rash decision?'

'That depends,' said Samuel. 'Is it?'

There was no point in lying to Samuel.

'A little. I've been having an odd week. I'm not really sure how I ended up here.'

There was the mildest quirk across Samuel's brow.

'You mean you don't remember, or…?'

'I've been drinking, so it was probably that. Partially that.'

Samuel folded his hands, and looked at him with concern. Under his gaze, Kestrel folded, and it was the care emanating from Samuel that did it. He was so heavy with the weight of the week, and how nice it would be to actually share everything properly with someone. Telling Samuel seemed right.

'I went to see my friend Tala earlier and, well… she showed me something. Fuck, you're going to think it's ridiculous. I… I feel like I'm going insane.'

'Try me.'

'She says she can rewrite time. She showed me some… realities that apparently happened but also sort of not really, and it wasn't great.'

Even as he was saying it, he could feel himself slipping. That magnetic clasp that had him locked in place was so fucking weak, and there, there came the shock as it popped away and sent him sliding sideways from the library and into some place cold and thick with shadow.

He's in the chapel, on campus, and it's long after dark.

Daran's at his back, hand reaching for his shoulder just like the first time they met. His words are a confession in the sanctified hall.

'Don't you understand? I'm powerless in the face of this thing. It's like you with the lightning strikes. Do you remember? You said, *I get… too caught up in it.*'

This is the point where Kestrel wheels round. Confronts him.

'Don't you dare use that against me.'

And when Daran reaches out, he responds by trying to hit him.

'In front of the Lord?'

'God doesn't care. If he did, he would've stopped you.'

They tussle with each other. Daran tries to lay his hands on him. Once again, he's stronger, and Kestrel ends up on his knees, pressed to submit. 'Fine, fine, I don't care.' Because what else can he say? Daran holds him by the back of his neck and forces him down—

The chair confused him. The position of his feet against the table confused him. It wasn't the pew, it had different weighting, and crucially, he wasn't on his knees, there was nothing he needed to push back against.

'Are you okay? What was that?'

He would have admired Samuel's dedication to not blaspheming, had he not been gripping the arms of the chair so damn hard in his attempt to stop reeling.

Breathless, he said, 'I've been getting side effects ever since she showed me. I keep seeing snippets of timelines. Things that happened but not really, or things that happened but not yet. I…' His voice cracked. 'I don't know how to tell the difference between them yet.'

Samuel was staring at his palms.

'You say this is connected to the weird dreams you've been having lately?' he asked slowly.

Kestrel nodded.

Now Samuel swore, a quiet but harsh *Fuck*. 'That gives me the strangest feeling. Like I want to believe you. Like it somehow makes sense.'

The air in the room hung thick and still, and Kestrel got the impression that the ghosts of all the dead realities had come to gather above them in an unmoving cloud, slowing down time to help the revelation come to pass. It had his skin prickling, the idea of vindication, the idea of being *believed*.

But then Samuel shook his head. 'Maybe all this eschatology has been getting to me.' Then he turned to Kestrel, fresh-faced. 'I'm sorry. This was meant to be about you.'

Kestrel decided not to tell him the other thing, the *Sometimes it's you, sometimes it's Samuel*, because the idea of Sam having to confront whatever dark dreams he was having and consider them real was too painful to think about.

'Just promise me something,' Kestrel said, after another sip of tea.

'Of course.'

'Be careful over Easter. I don't want anyone to hurt you. And I mean *anyone*.'

Why don't I just tell him it's Daran? Surely that would be the safer option.

But that would mean two things. First of all, he remembered how badly he had reacted when Tala showed him, and hadn't he just decided that he didn't want Samuel to go through that pain? Second of all, he would have to explain why, and the idea of actually forming the shapes of those words in his mouth had him wanting to tear his skin off.

He hoped Samuel wouldn't dig any deeper.

To his relief, Samuel didn't. He stopped searching for answers in Kestrel's eyes, and said only, 'Don't worry. I'll be okay.'

How could he say that so calmly?

You're never happy, are you?

Kestrel sighed with the weight of that internal voice, and hoped he could pass it off as relief over Samuel's words.

'You'd better be okay,' he said. 'I like you.'

Samuel blushed. 'I like you too.'

Before the wave of guilt overcame Kestrel again, he distracted himself by casting his eyes around the room.

'That's a good idea,' said Samuel, following his movements. 'It's meant to be good for grounding, doing that.'

The room was mostly old varnished oak, in the wall panelling and the bookshelves, and that deep tawny colour was comforting, especially against the amber of the lamps. There were hundreds of books on those shelves that he would want to read, if he had the time, but it wasn't those that caught his attention. It was the small library desk near where they were sitting, only an arm's length away. It was piled high with books, and a laptop that had been unattended just long enough that it was in sleep mode.

'Have you been working late?'

Samuel cast his head behind him, smiled. 'Yeah. Still stuck on John the Revelator. It would be a whole lot quicker if he didn't put so many cross-references into his prophecies, but then again, that's what makes them fun.' He picked up the notebook that was half-dangling off the edge of the desk and flipped through it idly. 'Wow, my notes are a mess.'

Kestrel peered over, and saw a set of words that were so absurd they almost wrenched a laugh out of his weary body.

'Eat the book?'

'Oh! Yeah... this is what I've been studying at the moment. There's this whole bit in Revelation about eating a book. Well, a scroll. The King James version says book, which is weird, because that's an older translation and you'd think it'd use more archaic sounding language.'

Samuel was incredibly cute when he got caught up in his own nerdiness.

'What's the purpose of that? Eating it, I mean.'

'It's meant to give John—or whoever the recipient of the prophecy is—it's meant to give them the sacred message that makes the unbelievers understand how awful their transgressions are. But it's got a major drawback: it's a terrible weight to carry those words in your body.'

Kestrel considered it. It seemed important for some reason.

'Can I read?'

'Sure.'

Samuel passed him the notebook and he scanned down the page, past Sam's notes, finding the scribbled verse.

'Revelation 10, verse 10: "So I took the little scroll from the hand of the angel and ate it; it was sweet as honey in my mouth, but when I had eaten it, my stomach was made bitter." Wow, that's... weirdly vivid.'

'Yep. Revelation's a real trip.'

This was good. Samuel was getting all passionate about his studies again, and it was proving a wonderful distraction for his own anxiety.

He read on.

'"From his mouth issued a sharp two-edged sword, and his face was like the sun shining in full strength."'

'I feel like I've seen that before, somewhere recently,' said Samuel.

Kestrel thought of the way Daran spoke when he had confronted him in the college foyer. The way he had seemed to glow like the sun. The way he often seemed to glow.

He didn't want to linger on the memory. It was far nicer chatting with Samuel; better not to taint that.

Further on in the notebook and Samuel's annotations were still just covering the first few chapters. 'Wow, we're not even past the start yet. They're still blowing the trumpets.'

'Yeah, it's one heck of a build-up.'

'And then you've got all this stuff with... wow, God sure does like making lists. The Church of Philadelphia, the Church of Sardis, the Church of Ephesus... heh, it reads like a phone book.'

'Can you imagine him having to make a denominational list now?' said Samuel, and he started listing modern denominations: 'The Catholic Church, the Syriac Orthodox Church, the Seventh-Day Adventists, the Mormons, the Methodists...' To his own surprise, Kestrel laughed, and how unexpectedly bright that sound was in the quiet, cosy room.

He flipped forward in the notebook, and another passage caught his attention. He read it aloud, hardly thinking. 'Matthew 15, verse 11. *It is not what goes into the mouth that defiles a person, but it is what comes out of the mouth that defiles."'*

Something about that wording tickled the back of Kestrel's throat. By the time he heard the sharp intake of breath from Samuel, by the time he realised that it was coming from a vulnerable place, it was too late to take it back.

'Wait. I only wrote that quote down because I was thinking about the whole eating-the-book thing. It's not part of my coursework. It's not important, you shouldn't... you don't need to read it.'

But Kestrel couldn't avoid it by now: he had already started reading the lines beneath. These were Samuel's footnotes to the quote, and they said: *Sin cannot be planted. It can only come from within. Means that anyone who has been raped is not a sinner.*

He stared at the page. Samuel may as well have slapped him right there and then.

'Why does it say this?'

Rather awkwardly, Samuel replied, 'Well, the Pharisees came to Jesus to tell him off for breaking the rules about eating certain foods and so on. So Jesus said *that*, and they took offence at it. Acknowledging it would have meant a lot of changes in how they handled certain aspects of their society.'

'No, I mean like, why does it say this? Right here?' He pointed at the footnotes and Samuel hastily took the book back. He looked the way Kestrel felt: laid bare.

'I...' Samuel breathed quickly, closed his eyes, folded his hands like this was difficult for him to say. 'I'm sorry. I don't know, I just... got some mileage out of that. It made me feel better. I told you I haven't been sleeping well lately. It's just dreams.'

It's never just dreams.

Kestrel said nothing. His skin was burning, his stomach was flooding with acid, he felt sicker than he could possibly imagine. Again, the world was eclipsing in on itself, again he was slipping.

'Oh! I should get you a bucket, hang on…' The quickest thing Samuel could find was the waste-paper bin. 'That'll do,' he said as he passed it into Kestrel's hands. 'Look, I'm really sorry. I didn't want anyone to read that.'

'It's okay,' Kestrel groaned out as he held the edges of the bin, trying incredibly hard not to let himself actually be sick. He wondered if he was about to drift again, but mercifully, nothing came.

'It's true, though,' Samuel said, insistent on taking the blame. 'It's unfair to fill your head with that stuff. Not when you're so drunk. Hey, we have guest rooms, if you want to stay over until you're feeling better.'

'No!'

He was too loud and too harsh, because Daran sometimes came here, and the idea of running into him during an inopportune visit was terrifying.

Samuel bit back. 'Okay, no worries. I'm calling a taxi, though.'

'No, I'll walk. I want to walk.'

'Are you sure that's okay?' The hanging implication: *You sure don't seem to be.*

'Just let me have this. Please.'

It was with respect and concern that Samuel withdrew.

Kestrel read the quote, turned the pages back, read the other quote too. Consigned it to memory. Then he handed the book back to Samuel, wordlessly. They stared at each other in the gap those pages left. Would have been a good moment to come clean with the details, but Kestrel didn't.

He sighed, let his shoulders drop a little. Felt the blood flow more freely there. As he put down the bin and reached for his jacket, his winding thoughts came swinging back round to worry over Samuel's safety instead, and *fuck*, he couldn't let that potential future come to pass.

'Are you staying with your parents for Easter? You should.'

Samuel opened his mouth to say something, then stopped. 'I will.'

He made to leave then, and when they reached the door, Samuel asked him before hugging. Maintaining a respectful boundary at all times. It felt like a kindness he didn't deserve.

CHAPTER EIGHTEEN

Solar Monstrance

The final session of the campaign was starting, the four of them were gathered in the airy living room again, and Aaron was confronting Kestrel with an unexpected thing.

'You were a real mess the other day.'

'What?'

'You came up and hugged me out of nowhere in the Student Union.'

For a moment Kestrel panicked, hoped Aaron hadn't been the other guy, the blond one. He had not exactly been focussing too hard.

He'd have known if it was Aaron, though, right?

Of course he would. It was utterly ridiculous when he thought about it rationally. This conversation would have been much more awkward if that was the case, for the sake of the dance and all that came after.

'Yeah, I was sympathy-drinking with Bram. I, uh, probably had too much.'

The question was asked—sympathy-drinking?—and

then Bram's news about his girlfriend came out, and that topic stole the spotlight.

'Hell of a way to end the term,' Aaron concluded.

'Yeah, let's just start the game. I don't wanna think about her any more.' Bram frowned, and took a long swig of his drink.

Aaron said: 'Okay, final session then. Or so I hope. We're so close to the end.'

That last line stuck in Kestrel's head, found a deeper meaning. *Close to the end.* He got the feeling his friends were all still studying him, despite the focus having shifted to Bram so outwardly.

Right enough: 'Are you sure you're okay?' Bethan whispered at his side.

'Yeah. Of course I am.'

'I mean, you—'

'I'm fine. Hey, hey Aaron, recap. Where did we leave off?'

'Yeah, set the scene for us,' Bram chimed in, and Bethan had no chance to pry further.

Aaron smiled darkly. 'Okay, so: Last time we left off with Elijah revealing that he is, in fact, the demon Belial. The three of you activated the floor portals, and Belial used them to take Quinn hostage. He's currently off in an unknown chamber, sealed on all four sides, leaving Thorvald and Marcus in the great hall.'

Kestrel whistled low and gave a lopsided grin. 'Well guys, you're gonna have to rescue me. I'm in this mess, now. Get me out of it.'

'We don't have to force it,' Bethan said quietly, and had that not been said in front of the group he might have appreciated it.

'No, we can't just leave it here. That would be... way

worse.'

Aaron clapped his hands together. 'All right, then. We'll start with Thorvald and Marcus. The two of you are alone in the hall, both Quinn and Belial having disappeared after the platforms were activated. The strange ethereal shields around your platforms have dissipated, allowing you to move freely off of them, and the room is pulsing with the aftermath of magic, although you get the sense that any evil presence has left for somewhere much further away.'

'Thorvald turns to Marcus and says, "We need to get Quinn back."'

'"Yer, I reckon the bastard's taken him somewhere as… what do you call it? Collateral."'

'"We won't let him get away with it."' Bram moved his miniature off the tiny platform and looked to Aaron. 'Can we see anything in the room?'

'Roll perception.' This got a fifteen from Bram and an eight from Bethan. 'Right, Thorvald, you notice in the corner of the room, on the wall, there is a stone tile that does not quite match the others; it looks a little out of place. It's heavy, though.'

'I ask Marcus to move it.'

Bethan nodded, and Aaron continued. 'So Marcus readies his muscles and heaves up the stone tile with a massive grunt, revealing a hidden passageway in the wall.'

'I dart into it.'

'You—' Aaron started to say, with a smile on his face, and Bethan immediately interrupted.

'I pull Thorvald back and go "Oi, let's check for traps first."'

A roll of the dice later and 'Yeah, that was a magical ward set into the door. You disarm it, and the poison spell it was connected to, and squeeze through the hidden passageway into a dark corridor beyond.' Aaron fumbled about for a particular sheet of paper, then placed it on the table, laying it over the current map to reveal a new network of tunnels, doodled in soft pencil. 'It twists and turns like a labyrinth, and down here, everything smells brackish and damp. You walk forth, delving deep into the dark… and, let's go see how Quinn's doing.'

Kestrel realised he was fiddling with the cap on his biro. He put it down, ignored the ache in his knuckles—of course, the punching, last night—and focussed on Aaron.

'So, Quinn, you're still standing in the sealed chamber with Belial. You're edged up against one corner of the small cell, watching Belial warily over on the other side of the room. He's pacing, without much care, and he seems to be enjoying the way your muscles tense whenever he moves unexpectedly. But, for now, he's keeping his distance. Now, the last thing he's said to you is he's threatened to hurt you, and it looks like he's waiting for you to say something in response. He does not seem in a particular rush. Quinn, is there anything you want to attempt to do yet?'

'I…'

'You could try to talk to the demon, plead with him, charm him.'

'Can I attack him?'

Everyone glanced at him. Yeah, this might not be wise, but he had had enough of talking. Aaron sucked in his breath, in that way that meant there was probably a caveat, in the way that meant *I won't try and dissuade you*. Then he said, 'Sure. What are you gonna use?'

'I'm going to shoot him. With the crossbow. Please, let me shoot him.'

Aaron nodded. 'Okay. Go for it. Make a dexterity

check.'

He rolled low.

'Fuck!'

'I'm sorry,' said Aaron, and there was that regretful pause before Aaron launched into what happens next. 'You bring up your crossbow and fire a lightning-fast shot at the demon, but the room is too dark and Belial is too quick. The arrow flies off, glancing the stone wall instead. Belial grunts, and the grunt turns into a low cackle. "Bless you, young creature, bless you for trying. But bold moves win you no favours here." And he comes closer, moving ever so slowly. He lifts an oily, bracken-tangled hand and starts tracing the sigils of a demonic spell in the air... Make a saving throw.'

Again, Kestrel rolled well below the check.

Why are my rolls so shit?

'Oh, bad luck. Belial finishes the spell, and a hazy cloud surrounds you, numbing your body. With the twirl of a finger, Belial tests the limits of the spell, and in response to his minute movements, your body moves quite against its will. "You've expended my capacity for amicable conversation," he says. 'Now I think it's time we greet the others." And he turns to the wall, spreads his claws wide, and you watch in fascination as that blackish-blue energy unfurls from his solar plexus, spreading over the wall, which parts into an exit with a terrifying groan. He smirks at you and waves his hand in a careless beckoning motion as he leaves the room. Your body bound to him, you follow.'

Bram was saying 'Whoa, sick, dude,' and Bethan was agreeing. It was a neat little scene, in and of itself, but all Kestrel was thinking was *I'm going to fucking kill him.*

Aaron exhaled. 'Now, back to Thorvald and Marcus.

You're exploring further down the hidden corridor when a distant rumbling noise stops you in your tracks. As you're looking around warily, the walls start to shimmer with a faint blue energy, and a booming voice fills your heads. You hear Belial: "You're going the wrong way, you know. Your dear friend's in the hall, right where you left him."'

'Oh, fuck that fucking douchebag—'

'"That's cute. You should come back. Don't you want to say hello?"'

Bram groaned. 'All right, fine.'

'Wait,' said Bethan. 'That could be a bluff. Maybe we're on the right track here.'

'The shimmering on the wall intensifies and the stone slabs appear to melt and transform into a looking-glass. Through it, you see an image of the main hall, where you've just come from. The massive door stands open now, to reveal a stone altar, and at the foot of the altar, you see Quinn, kneeling like he's about to be sacrificed, arms limp at his sides, head raised to the ceiling. It's quite clear that he's under a binding spell. Behind him, Belial perches languidly on a corner of the stone slab that forms the altar table.'

'Oh, fuck,' said Bram, and his fingers hovered over his miniature.

Bethan stopped him. 'If we go back now, we're playing into his hands. We know where Quinn is. We're gonna be at a disadvantage if we rush back and it's just the two of us fighting him.'

Bram conceded.

'All right,' said Aaron, who had evidently been waiting for this moment. 'Belial can hear every word you say—'

'Damn, this is like some ethereal PA system.'

'—and when you decide this, he starts cackling. It's the

rude, self-gratifying kind of laugh that you only hear used in ridicule. "Well then, let's begin," he says, and he leans over—he doesn't even need to get up from where he's sitting—and sort of, pats Quinn on the head. Then, with a flourish of his hand he produces the lute, the same one he used as Elijah. He starts to pluck the strings and the most otherworldly, disconcerting noises issue from the instrument. It's like listening to the falling of water in a lightless cavern, it's like the rustling of leaves as dead things turn to decay. From all around the altar, dark bracken-like tendrils twine upward and hover, inches from Quinn's body. He strums once on the lute, hard like a flamenco player, and the tendrils whip out, striking Quinn. And now, we've entered battle.'

'What!'

'Oh my God, this is insane.'

Aaron cleared his throat. 'So, this is a sort of unique battle system I've devised. Because Belial is essentially initiating a battle by attacking Quinn, and because he has that sort of, how did you put it… magical PA system going where he can communicate with you from anywhere in the shrine, he's making both of you, Thorvald and Marcus, complicit in the fight, despite the fact you're well out of range. And until you come into range, your battle turns will basically be actions related to exploring. You can't exceed your maximum range of movement per turn, and if you perform any action or spell, even if it's just to examine something in a room, that counts as your move.

'This is Belial's way of saying you're on a timer, and each round he is absolutely going to be attacking Quinn. So you either come back to the hall as fast as you can, or you keep exploring to find something to use against him.'

'God, this is like that old TV show, with the crystals and

the walkie talkies.'

'He's essentially having you play the Crystal Maze, yeah.'

'What about me?' Kestrel asked. 'I'm kind of stuck here, what am I meant to do for my turn?'

'So yours is a special case. You can't move while you're under the binding spell, but you can attempt to talk to Belial on your turn. If you want to get information out of him, you'd be using stats like persuasion, deception or insight. Intimidation isn't going to work.'

'Oh, great.'

'So let's start with the first attack on Quinn. The strange dark tentacles have just lashed out, striking at your skin, and… oof, you lose four hit points.'

'What should we do?' said Bram, and Kestrel hated the tremor in Bram's voice, that wavering quality that advertised just how much of a spectator he had become to Quinn's predicament. How exposed it all was. He would claw his way out, leave there and then, if he didn't so desperately need it to end properly.

Bethan called out, in Marcus's rough voice, '"Oi Quinn, if you can hear me…"' Then, 'Wait, can he hear me?'

'Yeah. The mirror portal goes both ways.'

'Okay. "Try and get some more information!" And then Marcus adds, "Good thing it's not me in there, I'm rubbish at that sort of thing."'

Despite himself, Kestrel smiled. 'All right, fine. I'll give it a shot. Fuck. Okay, I look up at Belial and I—ugh—I plead, "Why are you doing this? What's the point of it all?"'

'Belial just looks at you, eyes narrowed and face full of disdain, like this isn't the question he was hoping for.'

Kestrel huffed, and thought about it for a moment. Then

he started to find his voice.

It was a dangerous game, talking back to a demon. But Quinn did it anyway.

'Are you mad that we uncovered your little cult? You want us to let you continue your killings in peace, is that it? This is punishment for interrupting everything.'

Belial curled his lip, making more of a purring sound than a growl as he said, 'Oh, no, you misunderstand me. I am not concerned about being left in peace. You can hate me, fight me, all you wish—'

'Then why kidnap me?'

'Well, now, there's nothing I like more than a good story. A couple of twists and turns along the way, a terrified protagonist with a bit of fight left in them! You're playing your part wonderfully, on that note.'

'Shut up,' Quinn muttered.

'Shut up? And pause the show? I think not.' Belial cackled, and turned away from Quinn, suddenly more interested in peering at his companions in the mirror. 'Oh, I could watch you scurry about all day.'

They could, of course, hear everything that was being said. Marcus swore loudly. 'Fuck, he doesn't see us as a real threat.'

'We'd better find something we can use, and fast.'

And Quinn watched, helpless, as they moved through rooms filled with trinkets and gold tokens: nothing that could be used against a demon.

Belial interrupted them again when they reached the next room. His voice was a tease, a low and tender growl. 'You know, I've just decided. You can have your sweet rogue back, after all.'

'We can?'

'Yes. Someone must take his place, though. You'll want to go back to the village, continue Reskin Fleetfoot's work for me, naturally.'

'We're not killing anyone.'

Marcus nodded in agreement, slapping his axe where Belial could clearly see it in the mirror. 'Nuh-uh.'

'Oh dear, and time marches on.' Belial cracked a wide grin, and strummed again lackadaisically on the lute. The tendrils took another swipe at Quinn, drawing blood from his chest and an unwilling cry from his lips.

He didn't want to try talking to him again, he didn't, but all the same, there was a frustration building, and there was little other target to take it out on. He flashed an angry glare at Belial, ignoring the pleasure this seemed to give him, and he said, 'Are you honestly finding this fun? You're a demon, right? Why aren't you ruling over some domain of Hell instead of being stuck in this dirty backwater?"'

As he spoke, the aura of menace clustered in around the altar that little bit more. A rustling ran through Belial's entire body, and he shapeshifted instantly back into Elijah's form. The auburn hair fell back behind him in a wave and appeared as a halo in the low light of the ritual hall. Elijah fixed Quinn with that friendly, patronly gaze he usually reserved for his nightmares. 'There, much more personable,' he said, and he held a finger to Quinn's lips ever so softly. 'You continue asking the more interesting questions, my boy.'

Quinn jerked away from his touch as much as he was able to. 'And you're failing to impress me. I get the feeling this isn't the first time you've failed at something.'

Elijah's face twisted into a sour frown. A nerve had been hit, there. He plucked at the palm-muted strings of his lute, barely containing his rising frustration, before looking directly into Quinn's eyes, into his core, and saying, 'Do you have any idea how tiresome it gets? The eternal dance of supervising the souls of the damned, the *middle management* of Hell? Stringing along hapless adventurers like you is one of the few great joys left in life.'

'Sounds like you need new management,' Quinn muttered, and he was honestly surprised when Elijah did not hit him in response. All he got was that steady, lascivious smile.

While Kestrel slipped further and further into his own personal hell, Thorvald and Marcus went on exploring. Every left and right turn was another assault on Quinn's health, another roll of the dice, another moment of intimate awkwardness between Quinn and the shadow behind him.

'Eventually, you reach a dead end,' said Aaron, with performative certainty.

Bram pouted. 'I refuse to believe that. I use Reveal Enchantment.'

'Good move, good move. So: you can tell by the way the wall is shimmering that this dead end is a decoy. There is a door here, but it's hidden, rendered entirely invisible by some powerful illusion magic.'

'All right, I'm going to dispel it.'

'Are you sure you want to do that?' Aaron asked, and his sly smile spelled trouble.

'Yes. Absolutely, yes.'

'I have to warn you, if you fail, it could be quite disastrous for you. Especially because you're not a full party.'

'No, no, this is the right thing to do,' Bram murmured. 'Something's behind here and I get the feeling it's important.'

Aaron nodded. 'Okay. Make your roll.'

He did. 'Wow, that's a perfect twenty.'

'No way.' A smile of utter disbelief spread across Aaron's face. 'You just… You just managed to get past the wards on the door without breaking them. The check was an eighteen.'

'Bloody hell, Bram.'

'It's just like the Labyrinth,' whispered Bethan. '*Things aren't always what they seem in this place.*'

'Well, that's pretty accurate. When you walk in here, it's apparent that this room was not intended for anyone but Belial. As you both pass through, there's a wet sort of bubbling in the air as you fall under the cloaking spell. And, as this happens, Quinn, you lose sight of them in the ethereal mirror. You do not hear Elijah make a sound behind you, but his hand tightens on your shoulder, and you know that your friends have revealed something he had not expected.'

'Oh, neat. We found a secret!' Bram, clearly overjoyed, pushed his miniature into the new room.

'Marcus claps you on the back. "Nice work, Thorvald. So, uh, what do we see in this 'ere room?"'

'This room is a library of sorts, filled with dusty books and strange items, brimming with arcane energy and the promise of dark, illicit knowledge that could probably keep Thorvald fascinated for centuries. But, what draws your attention so completely is the curious statue at the far side of the room. It's ginormous, humanoid, and its features are so piercing and otherworldly that you can't tell if it's meant to be an angel or a demon. It's sort of, set into the wall, and stands legs apart, one foot on a mountain slope, the other in the sea: these two landscapes extend over the wall behind the figure. It holds one hand out, down towards you, and in the hand lies a small book. At least, the book seems small when you take in the statue as a whole, but really, it's about the size of a normal hard-backed spellbook, of the kind you might have in your possession, Thorvald.'

'Oh! Is it written in Demonic?'

'It absolutely is. You can tell just by looking at the cover that it doesn't have any wards on it. It's safe to pick up.'

'How big is this statue? Can I reach it?'

'Yeah, it's like, right up the ceiling, maybe two and a half metres? But the hand is reaching down, so yeah, you're good.'

'I'm gonna do that, then.'

'Okay. You pick it up, feeling its well-aged leather bindings beneath the palms of your hands. You can sense that no magical energy in the shrine has shifted when you do this. Anyway, you open the book, and it falls open at a particular passage, which reads: *When the words are revealed, the heavens shall be ablaze. And once the words are consumed, the demon shall be defeated.*'

'Consumed? What, like…'

'I don't think it means literally. *Heavens shall be ablaze…* it probably means we need to use fire magic.'

Kestrel thought of the sugar sculptures, he felt their stickiness beneath his fingers again, and the texture leapt to his tongue, nestled in the hollows of his cheeks. That passage from Revelation sprung to mind. *Eat the book from the angel's outstretched hand.* He felt a dark tension gather at the base of his neck. An idea was being born.

'No. Make him eat it.'

He spoke with such conviction that the others did not muster the strength to contradict him.

'We need to get back to the hall.'

It took them longer than Quinn would have liked.

'I honestly don't know how you're not unconscious by now,' was the first thing Thorvald said on seeing him.

Is that all you can say?

'I'm hanging on by the skin of my teeth,' Quinn replied. 'Come on and end it.'

Thorvald nodded. So did Marcus. And there, underneath the grim nods: the blush of embarrassment, of uncomfortable rage. They didn't want to be his witnesses as much as he didn't want to be caught here.

'You've run us around too much,' said Thorvald, pointing his words at Elijah. He took a step forward, a very clear grip on the sacred book as he did so. 'But this is as far as it goes. Return our friend to us. Now.'

Elijah looked at the book cagily. 'You could join me,' he said. 'Become my acolytes. You could have anything you wanted.'

'None of us are going to be your bitch!' Thorvald said it so indignantly, and for once, Elijah did not have a snappy retort, still fixated on the book in Thorvald's hand.

Then, everything happened at once. Thorvald stepped forward, brandishing the book, Marcus raised his axe, and Elijah rose up from his perch on the altar slab with a guttural cry, turning back into the demon Belial and gathering unholy strength beneath him. He grew taller, limbs turning black and gnarled and twisted as roots, fingers sharpening into claws once again, teeth elongating, lips curling into a snarl. Back came the horns atop his head and high rose his stance, as he pulled in magic from far below the earth. It was something Quinn could feel in his solar plexus as a deep gravity well, a tug of immense energy.

'Now scatter!' As Belial roared this out, all deep fury and jilted rage, he threw his hand to the side and with the movement, a wave of dark, treelike tentacles began to flow out in a massive arc around him. It was everything pitch bog and black, it was tar and death and decay, the shape of things that lure innocent creatures into the water to drown. Primordial, older than heaven or hell.

Almost every tentacle missed Quinn, and, restrained as he was, he could only attribute this to dumb luck. Thorvald was not so lucky. Halfway to the altar, he was struck down by one of the jet black ribbons, and his grasp on the sacred book started to slip. He caught Quinn's eye, an implicit meaning there as he struggled in the tentacle's hold and readied his arm to throw the book Quinn's way.

Behind him, Marcus was doing a wonderful job of distracting Belial. He had come right up close to the demon in his barbarian rage, swinging wildly but with enough control over the chaos to require Belial's total attention in order to evade each hit. Marcus wasn't immune to getting hit himself: his body was already covered in numerous impact bruises.

On his own, he wouldn't be able to last.

Quinn let his eyes flicker back to Thorvald, watched him draw back, hurl the book, seconds before another tentacle whipped forth, pinning the offending arm to the ground. A sharp yell as bones crunched.

The book landed barely a metre in front of him, falling open neatly on a page as if some magnetic force had designed it so. Quinn struggled against the invisible power holding him down, arms taut at his sides and helpless, and he tried to make sense of the shapes on the page.

'You are worthy to take the scroll, and open its seals, for

you were ransomed with blood. And the devil has come down to you in great wrath, because he knows that his time is short.'

Quinn merely spoke what he read, just under his breath, no louder than a gust of wind through a doorcrack. But once the words were uttered, the world shifted on its axis, and a deep shudder like toothache filled his body. It grew unbearable before it sharply dropped off, and like vision snapping back into focus, he swooned forward. The bonds were broken.

His hands landed either side of the book. For a second he stared at it, frozen in shock.

Then it came to him with a sudden clarity. His hands found the vellum, turned the pages. Landed on the words that meant something, and he knew they were the right words, because when he saw them, he found them impossible to repeat, he found tears springing to his eyes and acid choking up his throat. A crunch of his fist and he balled up the page, tearing it free.

Marcus took another swing at Belial and the demon was on the back foot, one step closer to Quinn. It was the perfect opening.

He leapt forward.

His muscles complained with the ache of what felt like hours kneeling in prayer position, but he pushed past it and shoved the sacred words deep inside Belial's mouth. The reaction: immediate. Belial made a horrific choking sound, and tilted his head back with a massive crack. Quinn was flung to the side in the rebound, and he watched as Belial shifted, from bracken-black silhouette to mewling toothy demon, to wide-eyed human in diminishing states of decay, until finally, he was pulled, sobbing, to the floor, nothing more than a puddle of shivering swamp water.

There was something important waiting there for Quinn beneath the layers of undress. A euphoria he hadn't expected. He turned to his companions.

'Bloody hell, you did it,' said Marcus, staggering to the ground to catch his breath. Thorvald crept forward, sloughing off the dead weight of the tentacles, tears in his eyes from moving the arm that was in all likelihood broken. He echoed Marcus's sentiment in barely intelligible words. Fear and relief and exhaustion, in every twitch of their skin. But for Quinn, there was only pure, unadulterated delight, and as their adventure came to a gentle stop, he felt both closer and further away from them than he ever imagined was possible.

CHAPTER NINETEEN

In Saecula Saeculorum

In the wake of the demon's defeat, the world took on a different hue. The sun rose earlier in the day, giving out more low-angled light beneath blanket clouds that sat on the Earth like they were staking the place out. The rain was persistent, sometimes heavy, sometimes light, and everywhere echoed the yellow-blue-green of the marsh, like it was a parting gift done in poor taste. The campus grew empty as everything came to a standstill for Easter. Dorms all quiet as students returned home to their families, lecture halls locked up as teachers took time off. Through it all, there was a hollowness, as if everyone should have been celebrating, as if it was a crime that something so momentous could occur—Belial was slain!—with so little ceremony.

It should have felt triumphant.

What it did feel like, Kestrel realised, as he watched the dead zone from his dorm window, was a practice run. Everything felt expectant. The air, pregnant with the weight of things unsaid.

It would have been easy to pass it off as newness, because he had gone home for Christmas, and he had gone home for the half-term break, and this was the first time he had stayed on campus the whole holiday. But Easter was different; *this* was different. He couldn't explain it away with excuses and analogies.

A knock came at the door, and this was odd because it was almost midday by now, most people would have left to catch the off-peak travel hours.

His heart leapt into his throat. Somewhere in time, he opens the door and Daran's there on the other side, and it's a continuation of their last conversation, he's still concerned for him, still asking if everything is all right, and the need behind the concern drives him into the room and —*not here, not now*—Kestrel doesn't know what to do.

But in this place in time, there's only a familiar cheery voice joining in with the knocking, and he unfreezes and opens the door to find Bram, smiling but run ragged from what must have been a poor night's sleep.

'Bram, hey. You okay?'

'I was going to ask the same about you.'

He shrugged it off. 'I'm fine.'

Bram didn't ask to come inside. There was a tense moment where he looked at him, wide eyes searching for something in Kestrel's expression, and when he didn't find it, he let his shoulders sag. 'I'm glad. I'm sorry, I was just about to leave for home, and, well... You remember that day in the canteen?'

How could he not? Johnny Cash playing low on the speakers, the pouring rain, the pain in his arm.

'I saw it again,' Bram said. 'You were hurt and I couldn't help you. I had a... I think it was a dream? I'm not sure. But I just wanted to check on you before going back to my parents' place. Just to… put my mind at ease, you know?'

Kestrel's heart felt way too heavy in his chest, and for a moment he wondered if this was what a palpitation felt like. Crushing ache around his breastbone, heart hammering so loud he worried Bram would notice.

'Dreams can be like that. They feel too real, sometimes.'

'It's not real, is it? I mean, we both saw it, right? You…'

Kestrel said nothing, he just stared, hoping the lie by omission would be enough.

'That's dumb. Never mind, that's dumb.' Bram ran a hand through his hair, ruffled his fringe back into position. 'Could just have been fallout from the campaign ending last night.'

Kestrel watched him push down the magic, crushing the possibility that anything else was going on. He could see every part of Bram's instinct rebel against that common sense, he could see the dichotomy of that struggle and it made him sad.

'Hey,' he said, surprising himself with the suddenness, 'if anything does happen, over the holidays… I'll call you, okay?'

There was the smallest tug of some thread hidden in the air as he said this, as he saw Bram's smile return, as he saw relief flood his face. The most minute shift in alignment, and again it felt like a practice run, like he was testing how much he could push the course of fate from within this lane.

When Bram had gone home, Kestrel filled the empty space with the only assignment worth doing. Out came the mockup sketch that Mr. Ruiz had forced himself not to comment on, and out came the scribbles of ideas for *materials that capture a time and a place.*

He needed more time to sort his thoughts out before Mass on Thursday. He needed space and fresh air, and so foraging for materials was the perfect choice.

There were a few people still on campus, as he discovered when he stopped by the cafeteria for some coffee. None of the foundation year folks: these were research students, the ones with thesis defences to write and funding to obtain. Time didn't stop for them just because the Son of God had died.

Rain misted him lightly as he trekked out to the field beyond campus, over the bridge and the brook at the North exit. He sipped at his coffee, squinted at the diffuse light from the cloud cover, avoided the path that led too close to the chapel. He walked past trees and bracken to get to the field, and his eyes were tracking which twigs would be best to pick up and defend himself with, which path through the undergrowth would be best to dart down should he need to escape. He noticed himself laying down these backup plans in a detached way; it was not intentional and it was not desirable, it just *was.*

The wheat in the field near campus was far from gold: it had only recently been planted and the young green shoots were probably destined to be used for silage this early in the year. It didn't matter; he would be taking it anyway.

He stopped at an open patch of ground near the highest point of the field, where he could cast his gaze over the whole area, where he could only be seen by the occasional dog walker. It was quiet out here. Peaceful.

As he sank down to his knees, he felt the soft mud give, yield beneath him to accommodate his form. It was not going to resist as he gathered its fruits; dirt and mud and grass finding their way into used grocery bags and Tupperware containers.

You need to come up with a plan.

Not yet, I'm working. I've got time.

There is too much time and equally there is not enough.

He pushed the thought aside. Maybe there would be clues in the grass.

So he selected a fine, sturdy sheaf, plucking it from its roots with a precise twist—fuck, his hand still ached—and he stared at its symmetry for a moment.

Somewhere, in the distant future, he saw himself with an aged face, crow's feet coming in at the edges of his eyes, pockmarks deepened in the skin. He's hunched by a coffee machine in the early morning, bleary-eyed from a night of bad sleep, ready to force pitch-black liquid down his throat, and begin a day of fielding questions about his mental health, in an office job that sucked, in a city that didn't care for him.

But it was only for a second, and then it was gone: he was back to twiddling the sheaf of grain between fingers all slim and barely wrinkled, he was back to his own young body shivering in the cold field alone.

There was a tug at his solar plexus—that drifting feeling —and he worried that what he had just seen was a flash of his own future. The idea that this would haunt him for so long, the idea that this just wouldn't go away, was more than he could accept.

So he brought the dirt and grasses home, laying them out on his desk, staining the canvas slowly layer by layer like sediment building up over an inland sea. Soil and clay mixed with acrylic paste, grass glued over the top, tactile and fibrous. There was the marsh mallow root still in Quinn's pocket and that joined the mix, too. He noticed the dirt building up beneath his fingernails, but not the sun disappearing behind the treetops, not his own hunger, not the headache building beneath his brow.

When night falls, he goes back there again, to the clearing. Stands beside himself as he steps out of the vehicle, coming round to the leeside, watching his deconstruction again and again and again.

On the thirteenth iteration, he watches himself choke to death on the backseat of the car, and once that last dying gasp has been made, he watches his own face turn his way, with bloodshot eyes and mauve-tinted skin, begging for oxygen five seconds too late. The Kestrel on the back seat seems bent on rising just long enough to utter this; one last horrendous message. His voice is cracked, rasping, fervent. His voice is prophecy. He says:

You'll see yourself murder him multiple times in your dreams. You'll see it happen just beneath your eyelids as you move through the day. Imagine that final thrust into his body as you steal his life from him. You don't care about being the better person, you don't care about not stooping to his level. Justice is a drug, and you crave your fix so badly your veins burn.

Then Hades claims him, and his head lolls to the side, eyes roll up, skin stiffens in the moonlight. Kestrel walks up to his dead self, touches his clammy, translucent forehead. A moment where he finds he cannot speak, for fear of crying and not being able to stop.

Then he takes the dead boy's place, back in the passenger's side, so that they can all continue the ride home.

I hate what you've done to me, he says to the reflection in the window. And the reflection reaches over like he's reaching over from the driver's seat, and squeezes his hand, says, 'I know.'

The next day was much the same. Slow panic in limbo. The executive dysfunction of knowing he had to do something, but lacking the foresight to know what that something even was. The volume on the stereo was something he could get away with, because there was nobody left on his floor to be disturbed by the noise.

There was a break in the clouds and Kestrel used it to trek over to the campus grocery store and pick up instant noodles. He hadn't eaten much. These didn't require any effort.

It was as he was crossing the empty courtyard that his phone buzzed. Another call, and he was tempted to ignore it, but when he saw it was Bram, something pinged in his gut. He picked up.

The first thing Bram said was sorry. 'About being weird earlier, you know? I haven't felt right all term, but, I think it was unfair to bring up all that weird stuff when everyone else was leaving for home around you.'

Kestrel said this was okay, but Bram had more on his mind. His guilt was palpable, and Kestrel had to wonder, was it this easy to notice when he was struck by the same mood?

'I actually considered not going home over the holidays, so I could be like, in solidarity with you. It's your mum, isn't it? The whole Easter thing.'

'Yeah. A little. It's just awkward.'

It wasn't strictly a lie.

And he thought *I both want you to be here and I want you to be as far away as possible, because fuck, I can't let this hideous thing be seen.*

'Is it because you're gay? I know that's a bit blunt, sorry.'

'Oh, no, she actually doesn't know that.' And he imagined how such a conversation with her would go, and it made his skin crawl. 'Nah, this was just... her being her.'

'Shit, mate, I'm sorry. So, if you wanted to hang or something... We could go to the cinema, maybe? It'd just kind of suck to be alone the whole week.'

He said nothing. He was watching a flower unfurl in the crook of the pavement. It moved fast, faster than should have been possible. Time lapsed, cutting through seconds at triple the speed.

The world was off-centre, spinning towards something new and terrifying. He got the sense that it was all happening so fast that he wouldn't know what to do when the important moment came.

'Kestrel? You still there?'

'Yeah, sorry. I'm a bit busy tonight. Oh, and tomorrow, actually. It's a church thing.'

'Your mum's not making you—'

'No, I just want to figure some stuff out for myself. Hey, come by on Saturday if you can. Please. It'll be over by then.'

The flower petals opened up. Strips of corn yellow hiding within their purple bulb heads.

Back to the dorm, where he blasted out music like he was the only person left alive. Time sped by, shedding its leaves, until the shitty whiskey had been worn down to not even an angel's share, until the sun had disappeared below the skyline. And the painting grew, layer by layer.

It wasn't until Indelible came on his heavy rotation that the words finally made sense and the last piece of the puzzle slotted into place.

'Write it in black on the palm of my hand.'

He thought of Revelation, of taking the book from the angel's outstretched hand. And with that, he thought of Belial, of the *find the words, make him eat it.* That dark tension was back. And he knew, with absolute certainty, what he had to do.

CHAPTER TWENTY
Supper's Ready

Time had passed such that, by the time Kestrel came to his realisation, the Last Supper was upon him.

It was the first time he had been to Mass since Christmas, since the awkward, mandatory shuffle towards holiness that his mother was so intent on before allowing the holiday to begin proper. And this place, this situation, held a fraction of the dreariness, because there was an aspect of that in the Catholic Mass that never truly went away, but at least here there was more drive behind it. Nobody here was doing this out of necessity; everyone had a reason, a personal motivation to be here.

Daran looked glad that he had shown up. Grateful, almost.

Samuel was there too. Similar expression, different vibe. Kestrel gravitated towards him, mumbling only a quick hello to Daran as he passed by. There were more people here than he expected, it was enough to warrant the presence of the priory chaplain that Samuel had brought along.

When it started, Kestrel was preparing to distance himself, but Daran was sitting off to the side anyway, where the sound system was set up. He ended up next to Michael, and settled in as comfortably as he could—despite the drumming in his head—as Samuel and his patron from the priory started up with readings and psalms. Everything was as expected until it got to the distribution of the Eucharist.

From the sidelines, Daran drove the music. The procession started up as What Wondrous Love started to play. A chill solemnity fell over the room, and Kestrel felt as if standing on the edge of a precipice. Chords moving through D minor to A minor, choral voices building with *When I was sinking down, sinking down.* It was beautiful, in a monstrous way.

His turn. He slid into the procession line, in full view of everyone. There was something heady about putting himself under that spotlight on purpose, something that conjured up a sense of drunkenness, of being *too open*, and with it he could taste the memory of alcohol on his tongue.

The old priest from the priory was not someone he recognised. His face was wrinkled as cigarette paper, his eyes beetle-black, his hair white and frayed and if Kestrel had to pick a word to describe him, *tepid* would fit the bill.

He was ready, but then there was a glitch in the fabric. The precipice, tipped.

Suddenly it's Daran doing the ministry, beckoning him forward with that shadow of a smile. The deep draw pulls him forward, flotsam in the undertow, and he stands beneath Daran, looks up, folds his hands together and opens his mouth. *The Body of Christ*, Daran says, and Kestrel murmurs *Amen*. Daran places the wafer in his mouth as the music surges, and he touches his lips with gentle fingertips in passing. It's supercharged: it makes his belly burn and his cheeks flush, he's all hot and bothered by the mere fact of the contact, and *in front of everyone too*, that makes it worse. But nobody seems to notice, nor care, so maybe he's overreacting.

Michael prodded him from behind.

'Kestrel! Wake up.'

He blinked. He was still standing in front of the altar, and he had yet to take that final step forward. The old priest from the priory was waiting patiently, without a shred of judgement on his face.

Kestrel murmured an apology, incredibly quiet, and stepped up. The old man gave him the Eucharist and it was, in a word, underwhelming.

Nothing else happened of note. The music died down and any apprehension along with it, and they completed their cannibalistic ritual with every inch of mundane aplomb these things usually carried.

After the Mass, it was time to stop distancing himself. Kestrel sought out his mark, and was unsurprised to find him in a corner, complimenting Samuel. That gentle, measured voice that seemed to seep under his skin and settle there, despite him not being the focus. 'You did great.'

Kestrel interrupted, placed a hand ever so softly on Daran's wrist—enough pressure to quell any resistance, enough contact to captivate—and stepped between them.

'I need to talk to Samuel for a bit. Daran—' and he said his name, breathed it out the way Daran often did with his, '—wait for me, will you?'

Daran met his gaze. The whole room felt like it was

going to collapse in on itself. For a moment Kestrel was not sure if he would have the commanding power to pull it off, but then Daran pulled back—'Of course,'—and it was strange to notice, how such sharp features as his grew suddenly soft with the ceding of power.

Kestrel pulled Samuel into a slow walk around the back of the chapel as smaller conversations split off around them. 'I just wanted to say thank you, you know, for the other day. What you said really helped me. I can't describe how, not exactly, not yet. But I want to, soon.'

'Of course,' said Samuel, only now he stopped the gentle pacing, looked at him. His brow was knitted. 'Whatever happened during the Eucharist, did you feel it too?'

'I... what do you mean?'

'Like a jolt in your chest, like the... like the whole room had dropped away.'

He had to play this carefully.

'Sort of,' he admitted, and he had to play it carefully so as not to get Samuel's interest up. 'It felt kind of eerie; I guess it was the minor key of the hymn.'

Samuel nodded, but there was doubt beneath that concession. Kestrel wanted so badly to ask further, because he desperately wanted to know if Samuel had experienced something like his glitch-out at the altar, something more explicit than just a weird feeling, but it would have to wait. Just a few days, that was all he needed. 'Hey,'—and here he touched Samuel lightly on the shoulder—'I know things have been weird, and it feels like it's not going to get better. But it is.'

That pained expression wrinkled Samuel's smooth skin and he said, 'I wish I could be as confident as you.'

It isn't confidence, Kestrel thought, but what he said was,

'You should go get some rest. Daran was right,'—and fuck, those words made him feel ill, but he had to say it—'you really did do great today.'

'Thanks.'

Samuel beamed at him, and Kestrel wanted nothing more than to keep that glow there, make him happy, banish any worry forever.

Light refreshments in the hall didn't last long. There was only so far a carafe of tea and some biscuits could go, when the majority of the audience were college students, when the mood was this solemn, and although nobody was here out of obligation, everybody now had better places to be.

Daran waited for Kestrel in the vestibule, his silent obedience a thrill tempered only by the knowledge that it had a greedier motivation. Wielding this power was a thin line and Kestrel could not afford to lose his nerve. Easier said than done, when every word, every action, could spiral off into a thousand possibilities: some good, some devastating.

He looked up at Daran.

My tongue slips over the syllable hate and turns it to love.

There must have been an intense look in his eyes, because Daran fixed him with that curious gaze, and claimed some of his power back as he murmured his name, his fucking name again, low and calm and horribly hopeful, 'Ah, Kestrel. You wanted me to wait for you.'

For a moment, those words meant something else and he felt cold; a spoon slicing through jelly. Speak, he had to speak.

It's too thick in my mouth, it's the plump sole of a foot sliding off wet rocks.

He said:

—*Daran, I love you*—

'Daran, I want you to help me with something tomorrow.'

'Are you sure? We could talk now,' he said, in that way that meant he really did not want to talk now. Kestrel could feel that neediness just under the surface, how he longed to drop the goodly-Christian act, to leap at the chance for a private meeting. But appearances, always, were important.

'No, I'd rather… I mean, I'd love to, uh—'

I don't want to love it; I don't want to love him. But my tongue is treacherous. Maybe it thinks it will make it easier on me this way—

'Take your time.'

Fuck.

He leaned in, a brush of his fingers on the cuff of Daran's jacket, claiming back his control. 'Meet me here. Tomorrow evening, around this time.' Then he withdrew, his job done, and Daran did not question it at all.

It was the same night, but darker, by the time Kestrel found himself outside Tala's house. He had the hood of his jacket up, but the rain was still kissing his face as he crept up the driveway, avoiding the rustling plants at the edges. Her mother's car was parked up, but all lights in the house were off.

He was well aware of the lack of motion sensor lights in the garden, and he knew the peculiarities of the latches in the conservatory windows. Nothing here had changed since Tala was a little girl—all work on the house had ceased entirely since her father died—and although this gave him confidence, although he knew he was not going to get caught, it was still hair-raising. He had never done something like this before. In this case, though, it was justified, it absolutely was, it was the only way.

After checking that Tala wasn't doing something unexpected like sitting in the conservatory in the dark waiting for him, he lifted the latch and slipped inside. The wind chime by the door clinked with the sudden onrush of air, and he froze. Seconds passed. Nothing happened. He continued.

Thank you, Aaron, for giving me the key.

He meant it, God, how he meant it, because he wouldn't have considered this quite so vividly had it not been for that campaign, for how it unfolded, for the glorious way it had ended.

Aaron, I wish I could set your mind at ease, I wish I could tell you what an important part you played.

He didn't want to turn any lights on, whether from the mains or a torch or his phone. So, after standing inside for a while, trying to urge his eyes to adjust faster, he began to move, to reach forward, to feel his way through the room.

His hand brushed past something hard but lightweight on what must have been the coffee table. A glint in the shadows, a tug at his solar plexus—he reaches out to steady himself, and he's thinking about how the rain pattering away outside is a nice enough cover for his fumbling movements in that dark conservatory when suddenly the rain is all around him, on his face, on his lips. He's lying down, concrete at his back, sallow street lights overhead, but this time it's not Bram coming to save him, it's Tala. She's too late, though. He's already made the final cut; he's at the end of his story.

'No, don't call anyone,' he's saying to her, his tired arm swatting at her phone. He looks at her and she looks at him and it's clear that she knows it's pointless as well. The phone clatters into the wet and she's crying, *I thought it would be different this time.*

He stares upward. The sky feels limitless, the rain feels like eternity.

'You told me something strange earlier,' he says, and his voice is all choked up, he's spitting out rain as he says it. 'Did you really mean it?'

'Yeah. I'm sorry, I—I tried—' She sniffs and breaks off.

It's getting harder to breathe. 'You said it would be the Caudal Lure. You knew it was going to happen.'

She is silent. There's something terrifying in her expression, and he becomes acutely aware that she was not lying. That rushed revelation in the canteen, he should have believed it sooner. He realises she's trying to correct it, and it scares him for a moment, the idea that what he's going through right now is somehow less real than what he's gone through elsewhere. All of that pain, invalidated. But it's better that way. As he is now, he shouldn't exist.

'Please.' He strains to see her through watery eyes. 'Fix it. Fix it so it never happens!' Then he starts to plead and make the request over and over, running into hysteria as he's running out of time. He's reaching out, palm stretching open like a daisy through concrete.

Tala lies with him and holds his hand. She's sobbing too, but in the manner of one who's close to giving up. There is a serenity to it that makes her seem like an angel, and for a moment everything is beautiful.

Her voice is so sad and soothing when she says, 'Why don't we go together?' But he's already beating her to it.

He slipped back in sharply. A full-body shock. Fingers twitching away from the sculpture, which, by the time his eyes had adjusted, he could see was a pair of figures, lying down by a street lamp. It was the top of the street lamp his fingers had brushed, and he put an extra foot of distance between himself and the table, just to make sure it didn't happen again.

Maybe it was the calmness of those final moments in the scene, but he didn't seem to have made a sound. At least, nothing else in the house could be heard.

He cursed under his breath. The sticky, attractive feeling of wanting to die was still thick on his skin, and, more than that, the guilt of his final, fervent plea for her to just *fix it*. It was upsetting to be confronted with that, knowing what it had turned her into. It was also telling that this sculpture was so separate from the others. Just him and her, together at the end of all things. He was struck by that feeling for a long time.

When he eventually gathered himself together, he found he could see more clearly the array upon the table. In the silence and stillness of the conservatory, Kestrel stood there and faced down the neat row of sugar sculptures like an executioner. They were so small—just sugar and water—so powerless compared to him, and suddenly the idea of doing something to stop Daran seemed ridiculous in the darkness.

Maybe it's not real and I'm just overreacting. Maybe I latched on to some fear that had been in my head all along. I could be paranoid. It would make sense for me to be paranoid because I have no evidence for any of this other than touching a lump of crystallised sugar, for fuck's sake! Nobody would believe me anyway.

Fuck it; he could argue all night with himself and that still was not going to change what he had decided to do.

Finding the right one, now, that was the problem. He

studied the row. Passed over the street lamp, the bird, the diver. Considered destroying the car, when he reached it. But fear made that impossible. Exactly how the magic worked was still unclear to him, there were too many unknowns, and he wasn't about to cast himself into some eternal nightmare loop from making a rash decision. Much as he wanted to crush the thing to dust.

On his way here, he had wondered if he needed to catalogue everything, to go through touching each and every sculpture to make sure he picked the right one. But standing here, now, his eyes fell on the little church steeple, and he knew implicitly that this one was correct; it could be no other. That drift that had happened when he had visited Samuel.

There's a scene, in the chapel, that will try to go down. Time is going to try and swing back round to where it should have been.

You can't let that happen. You have to control it, push it to where you want it to go. But you're going to have to go dangerously close to the edge to break out of this.

He would have the upper hand this time, because he would have the sugar sculpture.

He reached out to lift it from its spot. As his fingers touched the crystallised grains—he had to be prepared for it because it was probably going to hurt like hell—it tugged and pulled at his soul and it showed him…

It showed him Daran, inside and out. It showed him every moment of lust and despair and doubt, every bit of self-hatred, every bit of jilted rage from his youth to the present day. A boy who was not disliked in school, becoming a man who had the capacity for cruelty and the tenacity to mask it. Someone who thought he deserved the world as much as any, coming to terms with the frightening realisation that he might end up alone. The idolisation of youth and the desire to ensure he did not go without. Through it all, one thing became abundantly clear: Daran was aware of everything.

He inspects himself in a bathroom mirror in a single bed apartment. Brushes back his wheat field hair, burnished under the shitty low-lumen shaving light. Looks at his tired, drawn features, feels the weight of the unspeakable thing crushing down on his chest.

He realises: there is no sob story here. Just a man in conflict, who takes the opportunities he finds. He has known it was unforgivable all along, and he's practically rehearsing the lines in his head: *I can't fight this, I'm not strong enough, I had no choice.*

Flash forward, hands gripping further down the base of the steeple now, and Kestrel starts to notice something unexpected. His own point-of-view memories are being worked into the tower's structure alongside Daran's: a sugar brick here and a sugar brick there, forming a hideous patchwork tapestry where the sum of all its parts is the entire deconstruction of Kestrel's body, seen from both sides of the equation. A terrifying moment stretches out into eternity: his head roars with voices, his eyes are blinded by flashes of faces and movements, light and stark shadow, and his skin feels taut, ready to burst with the strain of two people inside of one.

The idea of being trapped in that steeple forever, the idea of that permanence, is utterly terrifying. At its core, it is sheer despair, and it's not easy to come back from that. If he does escape, how the hell would he know? When was the end, *where* was the end?

He wasn't really sure how long it took, but eventually, just as he wondered if his brain was flatlining, he reached the cornerstone of the whole sculpture—*his own suicide, his own slow death*—and the magic chewed him up and spat him out right back where he started.

With an involuntary gasp, he staggered forward, nearly disturbing the rattan coffee table in front of him. He was back, in Tala's conservatory, with nothing for company but a single moth that was panicking against the windowpane. It took a lot of effort to keep clutching the sculpture, because it almost felt like it was pulsing. That gasp had been quiet, but louder than he wanted. Mercifully, it went unnoticed. For another thirty seconds, he waited, but the moth was the only thing that stirred.

Once he had gotten his breath back, Kestrel slipped the sculpture into a paper grocery bag, slowly and quietly to prevent the rustling, then put the whole thing into his rucksack. Without disturbing anything else in the room, he left.

Everything was okay until around noon the following day. He was passing time making instant noodles and putting the finishing touches on his painting. The steeple stood wrapped in its grocery bag on one side of his desk. He had stopped playing music in the background because the songs he wanted had been on loop long enough and nothing else fit the bill, so when his phone rang, he heard it loud and clear, and he could not ignore it, least of all when he saw it was Tala calling.

The first thing she said: 'The sculpture!'

And he said *Tala, wow, aren't you going to say Hi?*, an empty deflection that missed its mark. She snorted, exasperated, and said, 'You need to give it back.'

'I don't know what you mean.'

'Don't even lie to me on this. I know you have it.'

He stalled for an answer.

'Give. It. Back.'

'Okay, fine. You know what?' And once he started, he found he couldn't stop. 'You had your chance to try and I appreciate that you did, but I… I have to get out of this nightmare because it doesn't fucking stop and I can't go on like this any more. I feel it around me, all the time. He's in my veins and I don't want to end up spilling it out like, like we know I'm going to try to.'

'You can't do this!' she said, and he was unsure if she was expressing a lack of faith in him, or just outrage at the situation in general.

'Tala, listen. I've already been in the car with him. Don't panic, no, it was okay. Nothing happened. But that's why, that's part of the reason why I think this is going to work. I think we've shifted things just enough.'

She started to cry.

'No, you can't come in like you know how this works when I've spent—so—many—times trying to fix it!'

'I'm sorry. I'm genuinely sorry. I don't want you to have to experience that, resetting everything, not ever again.'

Because he remembered the *please, fix it*, and he felt guilty for being the cause.

She sniffed, breathed deeply. 'In that case, please, give me the sculpture back and let me solve it. I know my technique's imperfect but I'm so close, I can feel it. You just have to make it through the rest of it and survive.' It was those words that tripped him up, and it was one of those times when everyone coaxing him to just get through it, to make it through the tough bits to the other side, sounded too much like when *he* said it. All this vested interest in keeping him alive and conscious and feeling. Different intentions, sure, but how tempting just to slip, to lose focus, to not have to exist for anyone but himself.

Maybe he should say the awful thing. Maybe he should just fucking say it.

'This is as bad as what he's doing to me! Telling me to just push through it. Survive, suffer. The only difference is you get pleasure out of it once it's over, instead of during. But from my point of view that hardly matters, right, because guess what? I *still* have to go through it. All I'm asking for is a little bit of agency, and nobody, not you, not Daran, seems to want to give me that.'

She bit back; he could hear the hesitance over the line. But he couldn't take back what he had said, so he sat with it, and let her do the same.

'That was really mean,' she said quietly.

He thought about Daran, about how *the cruelty is the point*, and he felt immediate guilt.

'I'm sorry,' he murmured. 'I'm sorry, I know, it was... but I still need the sculpture, and I'm going to stop all of this. You just have to believe me.'

He heard her say *No* before he hung up, but he never heard what followed.

CHAPTER TWENTY-ONE

Epikairekakia

The chapel was quiet after dusk, and that was the first thing Kestrel became aware of after he slipped inside. Not all the lights had been turned off, but enough to make noticeable the dark closing in outside. A blemished hue radiated from the high windows, and it felt like death, those few metres between the waning blue and the waxing orange of the last light left on.

It was normal that the lights would be turned down so low. Of course it was. Daran would have needed to keep the building unlocked for him, but not draw attention to the place.

Speaking of attention, he did not want to consider the possibility that someone other than Daran was already there, perhaps not just someone working late but someone who had gotten wind of his plan. A friend—Aaron, or Tala, or worse, *Samuel*. His blood ran cold. He ended up considering the possibility, of course he did, because your mind betrays you when you're anxious, and—

I can handle Daran on my own. What I can't do is let them know, is let them see these awful, precious things that are only between me and him.

—fuck that thought.

As it happened, he was completely alone.

Each footstep, soft as his shoes were, fell impossibly loud on the wide floor tiles. He walked up the aisle of the sacred space, and as he walked he imagined it lit up in splendour like a Romanesque church, a place of beauty, instead of the utilitarian hollow it was.

He then took his place in the second row, on the left side of the altar, looking the part, feeling the part, waiting for the rain to fall. The paper bag with the sculpture lying inside, placed carefully beneath the pew in front.

When Daran arrived, he could tell it was him from the footfalls, from the expectant pause as he leaned against the doorframe.

'You're here,' Kestrel said, turning around ever so slightly.

'Of course. You wanted to meet me?' A gentle smile dancing across Daran's lips. The air felt sour.

'I did. I really wanted to talk to you, about something.' He stayed where he was, making Daran do the work of coming to him.

The sourness increased with each step Daran took towards the altar. Kestrel stilled his nerves. Every inch of his skin, all it wanted to do was tug away from the man, and the urge to flee was so strong it took all his effort to rein it in.

Don't hunch your back so much. Don't tense your shoulders. He'll notice.

Daran came to a stop beside him, and suddenly the corner of Kestrel's right eye was filled with the texture of his soft and well-worn leather jacket.

Too close, too *close*.

He looked up.

Elijah grass hair, pushed back in waves like it was being moved gently by the wind, and an expression so firm and commanding, so definite, so clean. That amused smile broadcast benevolence and hid danger, and he could see it all now, past, present and future.

'So what is this something, Kestrel?' He talked like he was talking to a child, he hung by his side like he was ready to scoop him up in his jaws. Kestrel ignored the threat, stuck to his plan.

'Revelation 10, Verse 10.'

'What?'

'Revelation 10, Verse 10.' And he shrugged, made clear his disappointment with a pout. '"So I took the little scroll from the hand of the angel and ate it; it was sweet as honey in my mouth."' The speed of his pulse was making his veins fit to burst.

Daran did not understand, but he tried to play it coy. 'Well, that's very evocative, but I'm not really sure what you—'

'Things always are, at first, aren't they?'

'What on earth are you on about?'

The clipped, rumbling notes of his voice made Kestrel twinge with an uncomfortable feeling that had to be humiliation. Because on a primal level, he understood the authority behind that voice, how it eclipsed his own wants and needs, how it made him want to fall in line and please.

Say *you're right, it's nothing.* Bail on the whole effort. Because Daran's voice, his attitude, his *everything*, it felt too great a thing to surpass. And, rising in tandem with that insurmountable fear, came the anger, the *why do I have to go to this effort? I didn't ask for any of this!*

A possible future flashed before his eyes. If he just gave up now, left all this behind, never talked to Daran again and went somewhere far away—

And what? Hope the nightmares wouldn't follow you? You know what Tala said: it always finds a way back around.

He really had no choice.

His nerves chittered away like sparrows, and his heart sped up its pumping.

'"But when I had eaten it, my stomach was made bitter." That's the rest of the quote. That also tracks.'

Something about the way Daran looked at him here made it seem as though he understood what Kestrel was implying. *You knew my intentions?* that look seemed to say.

Kestrel responded as though that had been spoken aloud.

'I'm not an idiot, you know.'

Such a simple phrase, and honestly, it could have been about anything, but it was all Daran needed to start justifying himself.

'Don't you understand? I'm powerless in the face of this thing. It's like you with the lightning strikes. Do you remember? You said, *I get… too caught up in it.*'

'Don't you dare use that against me.'

'Against you?'

And he looked at him in that way, and Kestrel was faced again with that discomfort. *You think I'm so very attractive.*

Such a sad, pathetic, lustful expression. Eliciting pity wasn't going to work, just made him feel sicker.

'There's no sob story for you,' he said. 'I've seen. I know.'

Now that pathetic expression was sharpening.

Something was gathering steam under the surface. A desperate, needy anger.

'How can you claim to know? I've suffered.'

'Even if you had… it doesn't justify *this*.' He gestured between them. 'It doesn't justify what you want, what you're doing.'

'All I wanted…' Daran turned away, huffed out his breath, sharp, pained, 'All I wanted was *communion*.'

For a moment Kestrel saw him as he must have seen himself: a lonely, misunderstood old man. A dark vision of a future danced at the edges of his mind, one where he says yes and gives in, offers up his body to heal that festering wound in Daran's soul. It was a dangerous thing, the risk of sympathy, but he acknowledged the moment, he let it bubble up and pass, and in the end, he found that it didn't change his anger.

Daran went on, in the grand and desperately righteous manner of all apologists.

'Do you have any idea how tiresome it gets? The eternal dance of the bloody nine-to-five, pretending as if it all has meaning when it doesn't? The *middle management* of life?'

Those words had been said before. Kestrel couldn't help but respond, 'You're failing to impress me, and I get the feeling this isn't the first time you've failed at something.'

Now, as expected, Daran's face twisted into a sour frown. A nerve, hit. 'I thought you were worthy of having that connection. I thought you would understand me.'

The burning rose in Kestrel, from his chest up to his throat, darting down to the tips of his fingers. Stronger than it had ever been before. He was fucking *wired*.

He tried to hit Daran.

Although he missed the first strike, this was the turning point, the moment that destroyed all hope of clemency between them. Daran stepped back from the edge of that vulnerable place, and his lips cracked into a teasing smile.

'In front of the Lord?'

'God doesn't care,' Kestrel said hotly. 'If he did, he would've stopped you the first time.'

They tussled with each other. At some point, Daran gave up his pretence and put his hands on him, not just fighting but feeling. And Kestrel was slowly being overpowered, about to give up, about to give in.

I've done this before.

In a minute I'm going to fall to my knees, say 'Fine, fine, I don't care,' and he's going to hold me by the back of my neck and force me down on him.

It was exactly as Tala said. The same patterns, emerging time after time.

Well, he wouldn't let it happen.

'Fine, fine, I don't care,' he said, and he fell slack for a moment, dropping his arms and reaching down in one fluid move to retrieve the sugar sculpture from where it lay beneath the pew.

He felt Daran grip his shoulders. Now he reacted, ducking and headbutting the base of his chin, hard. Bringing a knee up to his groin. Hearing him howl in rage.

No time to focus on the pleasure that noise gave him; he squirrelled his way out of the narrow bench, wriggled and struggled as if trying to get out of Daran's grip, but really, all he needed was for him to come further out, into the open space in front of the pew.

At first he had no idea how he was going to manoeuvre him into position. But when he saw the opening he acted fast, and he was glad he did, because there was no fucking way he would have let himself do this if he'd given any chance to think. Daran tried to pull him closer, expecting him to move away, and he took the chance, pushed into him, and kissed him.

A cluster of thoughts erupted in his brain like fireworks, a million different voices, most of them in shock.

Wasn't this the way it had been in some of his dreams? Taking the initiative like this, as if it would earn him better treatment. Fuck, he wanted to be sick.

Just bear in mind that that's not why we're doing this. Just need him to be off-kilter.

Daran kissed back, and despite the things that had already been said, this was the moment he knew that it was all real, how he felt, what his intentions were.

Kestrel forced himself closer. His kisses grew angry and belligerent as he felt Daran respond, and they continued to tussle, only now he managed to pull Daran down to the ground and subvert their positions, until he was on top of Daran, thighs pinning his torso, one hand gripping the top of his head, fingers entwined in hair. He was fully aware of the contact, of the fact he was pressed so close to him.

Right where Daran had always wanted him to be.

It felt disgusting, it felt gross, it felt triumphant—*though not in the way you imagined*—feeling Daran buck up into his hips just a little; fired-up, excited and horrifyingly aroused.

Kestrel clamped down on that hard, realising with a thrill that, from this position, he had more strength than expected. Daran started to say his name again but he shushed him, his free hand pressing against Daran's lips before grabbing for his wrists, holding him down. At this angle, it was so easy.

And so, by the altar, which was where he felt he should be, he said the words that preceded the fall.

'Do you know what it was that made his stomach bitter?'

He banged Daran's head against the altar when he didn't get an answer immediately, and Daran wailed with the aftershocks of the impact. He didn't buck salaciously any more; perhaps now he was realising the gravity of this situation.

So Kestrel repeated the question. 'Revelation 10. Do you know,'—and he got louder—'what it was,'—and he got angrier—'that made his stomach bitter?'

This time Daran responded quicker; a quiet *no* and a brief shake of the head. And for once he was anxious. For once, yeah, even *scared*. Something bloomed warm in Kestrel's chest. Satisfaction, at the idea that it was finally managing to match up to his fantasies.

He looked down at him, legions of anger in his eyes.

'The truth.'

And he forced Daran down, one knee pressed cruelly on his chest, a final *fuck you*, because that had hurt, he remembered. Now here he was, roles reversed, his right hand gripping Daran's hair, so focussed on its task like it didn't know what the left was doing.

As for the left, the sugar sculpture grew sticky, greasing his palm with a translucent film. Holding it so tight to his skin made his ears ring, made it hurt in his chest like millions of tiny pinpricks underneath the ribs. Echoes of those other places, those other times, flashing in front of him, like camera exposures gone wrong; too bright, too intense, too much to fucking bear.

He just had to get it in, and this would all be over.

There, the confusion on Daran's face when he saw the sculpture. Kestrel let that linger for a split of a second. Then, one swift movement, where he grabbed his jaw and forced the sugar sculpture into his mouth. Pushed it deep inside. Watched his prey with budding elation.

Daran bucked as it hit the back of his throat. It must have hurt. At first, he fought back hard, spluttering and choking and trying to push the sculpture out, but then the magic began to work. Kestrel felt it, drifting away from his own solar plexus like poison sucked from a wound. And he saw it in Daran's eyes, which sparkled like they had never done before. A bitter realisation.

His lower lip started to tremble around the base of the sculpture. A pained cry.

There. He was starting to feel it.

As for Kestrel, he felt euphoria bubbling up inside him.

He never thought that feeling this strongly, that feeling this good was possible. He wanted to crystallise this moment forever, stay inside, watch that pain and suffering play out, and revel in it, all glorious and young and limitless like he was drunk at a house party without a single shred of responsibility.

Daran was shaking. His eyes were dull now—there was no threat, no risk of him overpowering anyone so Kestrel let go, and sank back on his heels to watch as the man, his shadow, his nightmare, rolled on his back and coughed and moaned like a helpless newborn.

He was a newborn, and this was a baptism.

Kestrel sat back on the pew and started to sob.

How can you let this happen to someone else? Even if it's him.

'I feel closer to you than ever before,' he said, watching the man lie trapped in his torment from between the gaps in his fingers. Daran was the one coughing up sugar and spit, and yet Kestrel felt like he was the one going to be sick.

He cried like a child after that; he cried for the longest time.

Tala called. Phone buzzing in his pocket, and at first he took it out and just fucking stared at it, as if that would solve the problem.

Eventually it stopped, but then she called again. And again. It became relentless, and he started to panic that she had figured him out.

He picked up, at last.

'Where are you?'

'Tala, I'm not—'

'You're at the chapel, aren't you!'

Silence.

'I'm coming to meet you, I have to—'

He could hear wind buffeting in the background, clipping the audio as she spoke.

Shit, she was already on her way here.

He forced himself to his feet, and went over to lock the door to the chapel. Just in time, because not five minutes later she arrived. Pressed up against the thin slat of glass, she peered into the space, eyes wide. 'What happened?' Then, more fearful, 'What did you do?'

He followed her gaze. He had not really registered what a mess the chapel was in. The pew at the front was knocked over, the altar askew, the cloth ripped. And the centrepiece, Daran choking in the middle of it all.

'You made him eat it,' she whispered, and she repeated herself, voice growing more tremulous until finally she wailed out, 'I told you not to take it!' And she banged on the door, as if that would be enough to make it yield.

'I had to,' he said, and he moved away from the door.

'Don't kill him!' she said, and that made him stop in his tracks. He hadn't really considered that as an end possibility before, but now that she said it, now that she tried to tell him not to, it bloomed in his mind, more attractive than ever.

'You can just reset everything again if it goes wrong.'

'Please! I don't want to go back again! I'd have to—you'd end up in jail, and we wouldn't be able to explain it, and I'd have to reset, and I just *can't* do that any more! Please don't make me.'

It was that fervent pleading, that fear, which got through to him. The horror of being on the other side of the *please, don't.*

He wouldn't have been able to kill Daran anyway.

With a deep, weary groan, he unlocked the door.

And then everything happened at once, because Bram turned up, and Tala said 'Oh!' and Kestrel said 'What?' and Bram was busy saying 'Oh, thank God I found you here.'

Kestrel turned on Tala. 'Did you call him too? Fuck!'

'No, I didn't. I swear!'

'Uh, what the hell's going on?' Bram was looking beyond them now. 'Oh my God. Oh my God.'

'It's… a little hard to explain.'

'I don't need you to. I think those bloody dreams were right.' Bram faced Kestrel, eyes glistening. 'I came because I couldn't get that vision out of my head. I was worried… so fucking worried…'

He tried to hug Kestrel and immediately Kestrel flinched—nothing to do with Bram, just an automatic response. Bram bit back.

'No, I'm sorry, don't… Come here.' Kestrel pulled him back in. They hugged close for what felt like an age, clinging on to each other in quiet desperation.

Then, eventually, Bram sniffed into Kestrel's hoodie, apologised, and withdrew.

'Tala, you need to get home before you mum finds you gone.'

'Yes,' she said, looking at nothing in the air. 'That's really important, nobody can know what happened here.'

Bram glanced at Daran, still foetal on the floor.

'Is he going to be okay?'

'Fuck him.'

'I mean, we can't just leave him there, can we?'

'He'll come out of it in a while,' said Tala. She appeared calm, untroubled now that she knew Kestrel wasn't about to murder him. 'He's not going to try anything. We're quite safe.'

No sooner had she spoken than Daran spluttered, awakening in fits and starts. Kestrel was on alert instantly, pacing back to the head of the chapel, standing above him and at the ready.

Daran looked up, and it pleased Kestrel that his eyes were like stone.

'Fuck. I didn't think—'

He didn't finish his sentence, because Kestrel said, 'People like you never do.'

'This is just a bad dream, I—I can do this differently! Please...' He tried to get up, but his body was still shaky, and he merely ended up sitting, at the foot of the altar, hugging his shoulders, grasping for whatever shallow comfort he could find.

Kestrel sat on the edge of the pew, the one nearest the front that wasn't upturned, with knees spread casually and hands folded in the gap between, the way Daran might have sat on a better day. He leaned in.

'No, here's what's going to happen. You're going to leave. And if you try this shit with anyone, ever again, I will know. She,'—he jerked his thumb towards Tala—'can make you another prison. She could make it last forever next time.'

Daran's lower lip started to tremble.

'Just think: making more memories together. Isn't that what you wanted?'

He shook his head. He started to form the words *I'm sorry*, but Kestrel raised a hand.

'Stop it. It took you this much to see the light and I don't want to hear it. This is not your fucking Damascus.' He stood up, gestured around at the room. 'You can deal with the rest of this.'

And with that, Kestrel walked away.

CHAPTER TWENTY-TWO

Erase and Rewind

'That was actually really clever,' said Tala. They were sitting in Kestrel's room, recovering after the fact. Bram was busy texting Bethan, who was meant to be coming off her late shift around now.

'I got the idea from Aaron. And Samuel. Hey, should we call them too?'

Bram shook his head. 'They're both at home with their parents. Probably a bit more sus if the pair of them leave the house at this time of night.'

'Oh, true.'

It was probably better to continue keeping Samuel away from campus for now, just for the time being. Everything could be explained to them later.

A knock on the door. Bethan, waiting and painted in anxiety. 'Oh good,' said Tala in an offhanded way. 'Hi, Beth. I'm sorry it's been a while.'

'Hey, you don't need to apologise! I came as soon as I got the message, but like—' Bethan smiled as best she could, but then the armour cracked—something in Tala's gaze must have done it—and she rushed forward and hugged Tala. It was an awkward hug; Tala was sitting cross-legged on the bed, and flinched a little with the motion. The mattress tilted. Bethan, murmuring in a rush, 'Oh my gosh, Tala, please be okay. Please be okay.' Tala, responding by patting her back like she was a frightened animal.

When she recollected herself, she reached into her bag and plonked a bottle of wine down on the desk. Then she sank onto the far end of the bed, looking at the trio.

'Um, so. Is everyone okay?'

'Yeah, sort of,' was all Kestrel could come up with. And nobody knew what to say next.

'I should get back, I don't want to worry my mum,' said Tala, abruptly in the silence. She was eyeing the wine like she knew that was a bad idea, at least for her.

'Are you sure? What... what even happened?'

Tala looked pained at this, and she extricated herself from her cross-legged position, came over to Bethan. A gentle touch on her forehead, pushing the curls out of Bethan's face. 'I don't think I can talk about it much more. I'm sorry. They'll have to fill you in. But... you tried really hard, you know. I saw.'

Bethan just stared up at her, wide-eyed, confused. There was so much care in Tala's gaze as she said those words, and it wrenched at Kestrel's heart. Again, that overwhelming shock of just how much she had seen, of just how many times she had rehashed this story, trying to get to this point. Now, the endpoint finally reached, and she, heading off home with little time to revel in the victory, all run ragged from the journey.

'I'll get you home,' Bram offered.

Tala turned her bright-eyed face to him. 'Thanks.'

She went to get her coat, and at first Kestrel just watched her go, all those big unwieldy emotions still churning in his chest. But he couldn't just leave it at that, not after everything that they had seen together. There was the memory of that one liminal space they had shared together, lying on the concrete in the rain, shallow pools forming around their bodies as he pleaded with her to fix everything. He had to say thank you properly.

He told Bethan he'd be back in a minute. Ran down after them. Bram had already opened the door and Tala was fumbling with her shoes. The rain hissed softly beyond the threshold.

'Hey, wait.'

She looked up.

'I just wanted to… say goodbye, I guess.' He reached forward with one hand, feeling his palm open up the way it had against the rain-spattered ground in that space, and he felt her move towards him in much the same way. A tug within both their bodies, almost drifting, almost casting them both to that time and that place. But somehow, this time, they remained grounded. 'Do you remember? I asked you…'

'To fix everything.' Her eyes were glistening. 'Yeah. I remember.'

'I don't want to put you through so much ever again,' he said. 'I was desperate and I was hurting, but, I had no idea what it would cost you. I—'

She went to hug him, impossibly tight and boundlessly deep. He whispered *Thank you for everything* into her ear, and he wanted to add *If it wasn't for you…* but the words that would have followed were too raw to get out so he left it at that.

'If this works,' she said, 'I'll melt down the rest of the statues. We won't need them any more.'

'Is that safe?'

'I think I can do it. I'll know if it feels wrong. I'm pretty sensitive to that now.'

He nodded. 'Take care of yourself, okay?' You... You deserve the world.'

Once Tala and Bram were back out under the gentle rain, once Kestrel was back nestled in his room, Bethan unscrewed the bottle. The label said *Rough Day*, and that made Kestrel smile. Bethan knew where his glasses were, so she got some without prompting, and filled them liberally.

'It's a discount bottle from our Friday collection.'

'Yeah, I guessed.'

'Still good, though.'

The night was quiet. It still felt dangerous, out there beyond the trees, but he didn't feel alone. He studied his glass.

'What are you thinking about?' asked Bethan.

'Just... little things, like how the oil from your lips gets onto the surface layer of wine—it doesn't take much, just the barest bit of contact—and then you notice how the... slickness and humanness of your body seeps out into everything, how present every bit of fat and flesh is.' He watched the greasy sheen spread out, lipids catching the light, and now Bethan did the same with her own glass, curious, troubled. 'It's just the price of being a part of everything, and I still don't want to accept it.' He breathed in, he breathed out. 'I've been struggling a lot with the idea of surrender.'

'I feel like I was right about the shared trauma thing,' she murmured.

They continued to drink, and they talked around the point until Bram came back. When that happened, he told them everything. He took his time for what he wanted to say, and it was nerve-wracking, being the centre of attention for twenty awful minutes. But they were with him, they were *with* him, not merely bystanders looking at him, and that made all the difference.

It was curious, too, how in a perverse way he felt comforted by the level of shock they put out when he told them about Daran. Made it feel more real, somehow, made him feel vindicated. And then Bethan was crying and Bram was kneading his fist into his thigh, and their pain tempered his euphoria down into something far more dismal, because he had just now realised;

'People expect a happy ending, where justice is served and the bad guy is held accountable for his crimes. But this isn't like that. He gets away with it. *He gets away with it.*' Kestrel put his head to the table and groaned out loud, with more force than usual because he didn't want it to turn into a sob. 'I just have to fucking live with that.'

'I think we're all going to be killing him in our dreams for a long time yet,' said Bethan.

Bram gulped down the rest of his wine and huffed. 'Is there really no way to indict him with any kind of crime?'

'No,' said Kestrel and Bethan at the same time. Kestrel's was more forceful, and he bit back afterwards, tried to curb the frustration. Bethan continued. 'What would we use as evidence? A sugar sculpture with… with allegedly magical properties, made by our friend who tried to kill herself?'

'Right, I get your point,' Bram said miserably.

'There is one way we could do it,' said Kestrel. 'If we got Tala to reset everything, and let it play out as intended. We would have to let it happen, though. Then… get evidence around that.' He felt like he should have been shaking and shuddering as he said it, but all he did was stare blandly into his glass of wine.

'Nope, nope, absolutely not a chance in hell.' Bethan waved her hands wildly, let them slap down on the bed.

'It's okay, I don't think I'd be capable of going through with that sort of plan. I barely held it together over the last few days.'

'Wait, how long did you plan this… this face off thing?'

'Since the last gaming session?' Bram piped up.

'Yeah, actually.'

'I knew it. I knew we all knew *something* on some subconscious level. The stuff with the scroll and the demon and the altar and… and *all* that stuff, it was… we fucking knew, we just didn't have the memory to know properly.' Bram gesticulated as he spoke, trying to give form to the feeling. He was overwhelmed; they all were.

Kestrel went back to his wine. Let the warm buzz calm his nerves.

'So what happens now?' said Bethan, and both she and Bram looked to Kestrel for an answer.

'We continue. We wait and see if anything changes.'

'Go on as normal?'

'I don't really know what else to do.'

A few things were different when the next term started. Under a fresh April sky, between the new module assignments and the first workshop of the term, Kestrel wandered over to the Humanities department, looking for the face of the devil so he could keep it well in check.

What he found was an empty room, and Isabel off to the side, swimming in paperwork.

'Are you looking for the religious counsellor?' She had spotted him, was waving him over with a friendly smile.

'Yeah. I was wondering—'

'I'm afraid he left, hun.'

He left! He actually left!

Kestrel stared, until he realised he was staring, and deflected his gaze. 'Oh. I see.'

'It was all a bit sudden, bit strange if you ask me, but they only just put up the new job ad today, so it'll probably be a while before we get someone new. You didn't need anything from him, did you?'

'What? No! I… I'm okay.' And because that had been too loud, too forceful, he deflected again. 'How's the, uh, internship going?'

'Oh, no, I'm not an intern any more. I got promoted.'

He beamed. 'That's great!'

Fuck the whole mess with the keys, this felt like an extra little victory.

The sense of quiet victory only grew as time went on, and it took on a melancholy flavour. It was one of those days where he wanted the outside world to match what he felt inside, where he wanted the clouds to grow heavy, the storms to break, drowning the cities and towns instead of misting them in this light, uneventful haze of soft spring rain. He wanted crisis, and not because he wanted people to suffer, but because of that desperate sense of wanting to share. He was the custodian of this gargantuan thing that had tried to rip them apart limb from limb, and he could tell so few people that fact.

One of them was Aaron, to whom he spilled the truth in

a secluded corner of the café, because it was only fair, because Aaron needed to stop blaming himself for feeling so, as he put it, *fucking mental*. And, for once in his life, Aaron listened without judgement, without interruption, without challenging even the parts that sounded unbelievable.

'You'll have to talk to Sam, you know.'

'Yeah,' said Kestrel. 'I didn't want him to get too close. I wasn't the only target.'

He had never seen Aaron look so out for blood as he did right then. It terrified him for a second, but then Aaron pushed that down somewhere to deal with later, switched the topic. 'He's considering changing his degree.'

'Fuck.'

'I think it would have happened anyway. He likes you.'

Kestrel stared. 'We… did he tell you?'

'Yeah. Think he needs more time though. I think we all do, because I'm still not really sure what to make of all this.'

'Neither am I.'

Aaron parroted what people older and wiser liked to say—'Things get easier over time'—and Kestrel had his suspicions that this was only true to an extent. The nightmares didn't stop just because the danger had passed, and the time spent out of nightmares felt like an illusion, as if surely the world could not be this kind without wanting something back. He had a vision of himself years from now; better, sure, but still waiting for the other shoe to drop.

He didn't hold back on hugging Aaron this time.

When he finally got the chance to talk to Samuel, in that bright and airy living room on an open-skied day, it felt like coming home, in a way that it had not with anyone or any place else. For a fleeting moment, he was seven and Samuel was nine, and it was unimaginable that anything could ever be wrong with the world.

Aaron had gone out—strategically, he thought—and their parents were busy working in the garden, no assignments to scurry off to for a blessed long while yet. They had been happy to see him. They had offered him ice cream, as if he was still a child. Of course, he had taken it.

Samuel sat at the piano, playing a melody in intervals, and Kestrel perched beside him, not looking at him directly but feeling mercifully close. The gentle melody, punctuated by the occasional clattering outdoors; the sanding of wood, the casual knock of paintbrushes as the patio decking was treated for the summer. The high laugh of Samuel's mother, snatches of conversation. His parents seemed to relish the light.

Eventually Samuel stopped on a high C, a definite press of the finger that was at odds with the gentleness that had come before it.

'I need to stop playing the same tune over and over,' he said.

Before this week, that might have caught at Kestrel's mind like a burr, but as it was, he just nodded in agreement. 'Did Aaron tell you why I came?'

'He said you found out about the dreams. The… weird stuff.'

'We were all feeling it. Some more than others.'

'You and me.'

'Yeah, you and me,' said Kestrel, and he told him the truth. He told him more than he told the others, because he remembered his own reaction, because Samuel deserved to know.

It took a long time.

'I wanted to protect you, just keep it from you forever. Like what Tala tried to do with me. It would have been mercy, but you wouldn't have owned it.'

'I see.' Samuel's lip starting to quiver as he sought the right words, floundering like a fish in shallow water. A few seconds more and it would become too much, he knew that feeling, he couldn't stand witnessing it.

'This can't be real,' said Samuel, and he stopped abruptly after that, as though if he said anything more, he would cry.

'I'm sorry I kept you away, at the end. I didn't want to tell you any of this at all, I was so scared of hurting you. But then I thought it'd be better coming from me, because the truth is violent and it doesn't care, it *can't* care, but I can at least try in its place.' He was scrunching the fabric of his jeans up beneath anxious fingers. Too transparent, too pained.

Samuel put a hand over his, where he rested it on his own knee, and the warmth made him relax his fingers.

'And I'm sorry, for all the trouble I've caused...'

'*You've* caused?' Kestrel laughed, and it was abrupt, too bitter for his liking. 'You haven't...'

'But I have. I've been naive, been an idiot, I should have —'

'Please don't,' said Kestrel, and the urgency in his voice stopped Samuel in his tracks. 'This is the same shit I've been telling myself.'

Samuel made as if to say something, then held back. Outside, the clattering continued. The bucolic spring day, moving forward like it was oblivious to their tension. Or perhaps, despite it. Eventually, Samuel said, 'I don't know. It's just a lot to sift through. I kind of want to cry and scream at the same time.'

'I wouldn't blame you if you did. I've already been doing that a lot.'

Samuel looked at him sadly. 'I thought that those dreams, those *glitches*, were just some fucked-up way to feel guilty about my sexuality. There were a lot of intrusive thoughts about deserving to be hurt. I thought maybe I could just ignore it, focus on the vocation, like it was just some test or challenge to work through.'

'Did you think it was like, a punishment or something?'

'For liking guys?'

Kestrel nodded.

'It's been kind of hard to reconcile that, yeah. So I don't know. Maybe. Anyway. We don't deserve this.'

'No. We don't.'

'There's one more thing,' said Samuel, and those simple words got Kestrel's anxious heart racing. 'I never dreamt about Daran, not directly, not until the… glitch during the Last Supper.'

Kestrel wanted to ask him so badly, *what did you see?*, because he had a strong feeling it was something very different to what he had seen. He swallowed the question, let Samuel continue.

'Before that, it was always a few degrees of separation. Some demon or creature from folklore—like the brook horse, like I said before.' A hard look, now. 'Was it always him? No-one else?'

'Just him, yeah.'

Samuel breathed out heavily. 'In a normal world, I feel like I should be challenging this more. But when you say it out loud, it makes so much sense with what's in my mind, that I… well, I don't think it's a lie.' He paused, considered. 'Does that make me bad, somehow?'

'No. You're not even in the same category as him. I mean, I'll probably keep waking up tomorrow and tomorrow and the tomorrow after that and thinking *yeah, okay, that was fucked-up, that can't possibly be true.* Maybe it's not. I can only trust what I've felt and what I've seen and what he said.' His hands started to tremble. 'He really did mean it. When I kissed him, at the altar, he kissed back, so hard. So *hard.*'

The thought eclipsed his vision. Something burning in his chest. He didn't notice until Samuel was saying 'Kestrel, hey, come back to me, it's okay,' and even then he found he couldn't come out of it fully until Samuel touched his shoulder.

He pushed the thought away; it was too much to deal with.

'Aaron said you were thinking of changing your degree,' he said instead.

'Well… yes, probably. I still enjoy the subject matter, but… maybe I shouldn't go through ordination. I don't know. I just… I like you.'

There it was, that bristling feeling of all attention in the room turned his way. Kestrel supposed there was little he could do to stop the flush of being *seen* from washing over him like that, but at least—at *least*—it was Samuel. At least it was something he wanted to reach out towards too.

He moved closer. Samuel's hand left the piano keys, moved upward, traced the soft skin beneath his ear, running down his jawline in reverence.

Time paused, but in concert with the season—the sun shone down and in the garden the plants struggled up, and Kestrel and Samuel kissed each other with the clemency they had been searching for in dreams, no hard press and no clustering heat; for all the pain relief that would bring, that could come later.

'There will be a later, won't there?'

And Samuel, who got what he meant, said, 'I want there to be.'

The kiss melted into a hug, and the sun continued to soak into the earth.

The last thing Kestrel did to wash his hands of the spectre came during the setup for the Easter term exhibition. He held off until opening day, until not much time remained before the final curtain drew back.

The exhibition hall was alive with the hum of students quietly and frenetically putting their last pieces in place. It wasn't hard to weave his way through, to find a space on the wall that was unoccupied, to unwrap his canvasses, and to start hanging them up without asking for permission. Painting number one, The Great He-Goat Emerges from the Marsh; painting number two, Procession of the Holy Office under the Chestnut Tree; painting number three, Saturn Devours His Son in the Back of a Black Sedan.

It didn't matter that the titles were long. He wrote them down in precise, blocky script on the little description cards, tacked them to the wall like everybody else.

He stepped back to look at them, and like with watching Jesus on the cross there was that urge to immediately take them down, to rescue them, to run far away with them.

This is the sort of spotlight that I have to weather, though.

He let the spotlight shine down. He breathed deeply. And then he walked away.

Mr Ruiz caught him outside the hall.

'Kestrel, I couldn't help but notice—'

'Notice what?'

Mr Ruiz inhaled, like he was about to say something, then stopped. Ran a hand through his thick black curls. 'A lot of things happened over the Easter holidays. We heard that someone broke into the chapel. Some stuff had to be replaced. Anyway. The religious counsellor resigned.'

'I heard.'

Mr Ruiz breathed in, out again, in the way adults did when they were trying, incredibly hard, to say something delicate. Eventually he came out with it.

'He looked a lot like the man in the pictures you painted.'

'Did he?'

Kestrel watched Mr Ruiz try to navigate this territory and come up floundering. 'I... well, many of us in the faculty did notice your Easter, uh, prayers around the arboretum. I know he gave you lifts in his car. And, uh, sometimes things don't seem obvious, or shouldn't be assumed. But sometimes the imagery is hard to ignore.'

'I'm not taking the pictures down,' Kestrel said quickly.

'I won't ask you to. Miss Warren might differ, but...' Mr Ruiz fell silent for a moment as the sentence skittered away. Kestrel waited, for judgement, for scrutiny, for words that were bitter, but what he got instead was:

'Are you okay?'

In that moment, Mr Ruiz was not a teacher, but an ordinary worried man. Kestrel felt something warm and boundless surge in his chest, maybe it was empathy, he wasn't sure. But with that feeling, he discovered that he didn't want the sky to crash down. He could keep painting, keep reaching out, keep telling people the truth without really telling, and somehow, maybe, that would make things better.

'I don't know,' he said. 'I don't think anyone is, not completely. But you don't need to worry about me. Not any more.'

Thank you for reading.

GLOSSARY

Tabletop Role-playing Game / TTRPG – *A game conventionally played around a table, where people role-play characters and engage in quests, taking actions following a formal set of rules, typically involving dice rolls.*

D20 – *A 20-sided die often used in tabletop RPG gaming.*

Perfect 20 / Perfect 1 – *D20 die roll results that confer additional bonuses or penalties. The name of this type of roll varies from system to system.*

Campaign – *A TTRPG adventure that spans multiple sessions.*

Homebrew – *Player-made content for a tabletop adventure that does not use content found in official rulesets.*

Game Master (GM) – *The referee, narrator and organiser of a tabletop game.*

NPC – *Non-player characters, which can only be controlled by the GM.*

LARP – *Live-action role-play, a game that involves players dressing up as their character and physically acting out events.*

Seminary – *Educational institution for trainee clergy members.*

Priory – *A religious building such as a monastery or convent.*

Diocese – *Administrative area of the Catholic Church, similar to a county.*

Vigil – *A contemplative religious service or observance held during the night, often before Sunday or a Feast Day.*

Eucharistic Minister – *Informal term for a layperson who is given authority to assist in distributing (but not consecrating) Holy Communion.*

Transubstantiation – *The act of the Offertory (bread and wine) becoming the Body and Blood of Jesus during Catholic Mass.*

Character Sheet

CHARACTER NAME
Quinn Therion

CLASS
Rogue

RACE
Elf

PLAYER NAME
Kestrel

BIO

PERSONALITY
Quinn is impulsive and excitable, easily scared but very determined.
Absolutely will steal every gem in the dungeon.

BACKGROUND
An elf from the deep forests, Quinn has forsaken his homeland for a life of treasure hunting. He craves excitement and never stays in one place too long.

Character Sheet

CHARACTER NAME
Thorvald

CLASS
Necromancer ☠

RACE
Human

PLAYER NAME
Bram

BIO

PERSONALITY
Curious, stern and very competent
Has a strong sense of morals
Likes history and animals
Actually likes studying??

BACKGROUND
Thorvald comes from a northern city and has studied magic from a young age. He just thinks necromancy is neat, and has no desire for power.

Character Sheet

Leilani
CHARACTER NAME

Druid (Water element)
CLASS

Elf
RACE

Tala
PLAYER NAME

BIO

PERSONALITY

Leilani is kind-hearted and soft-spoken, but very loyal to her friends.
She dislikes things that threaten nature, and will obstinately do whatever it takes to stop innocent creatures from being hurt.

BACKGROUND

Leilani's home town was destroyed by a blight when she was young. Since then she has devoted her life to the druidic path, in the hope of rejuvenating what was lost.

Character Sheet

MARCUS
CHARACTER NAME

BARBARIAN
CLASS

HALF-ORC
RACE

BETHAN
PLAYER NAME

BIO

PERSONALITY

- GRUFF (but a real softie)
- LIKES TO RELAX
- BEER? BEER   :PROTECC:
- HITTING STUFF IS RELAXING

BACKGROUND

LEFT BARBARIAN TRIBE AT YOUNG AGE
WAS BODYGUARD-FOR-HIRE
IS NOW ADVENTURER

Contact the author at **gallant.no**

Download the full tabletop RPG character profiles, and a copy of the Secret of Blackwater Marsh campaign from the website.

www.ingramcontent.com/pod-product-compliance
Lightning Source LLC
LaVergne TN
LVHW030009180726
843489LV00011B/3229